Grace & Favor

Caroline UPCHER

Grace & Favor

WHEELER
PUBLISHING, INC.
ROCKLAND, MA

★ AN AMERICAN COMPANY ★

Published in large print by arrangement with Kensington Publishing Corp. in the United States.

Wheeler Large Print Book Series.

Set in 16 pt Plantin.

Library of Congress Cataloging-in-Publication Data Available

Upcher, Caroline.
    Grace and Favor / Caroline Upcher.
        p. (large print) cm.(Wheeler large print book series)
    ISBN 1-58724-170-6 (hardcover)
    1. Large type books. I. Title. II. Series

2002016700
CIP

For Jessica; and for Frisky; for my first cousin, Annie Shaw, who is more like a sister to me; and for Kate Duffy and everyone at Kensington

And in memory of Donald Cammell

Acknowledgments

I am grateful to the following people for their help during the time I spent writing this book.

Eileen Kling (who as Eileen Campbell is the author of the wonderful novel *The Company of Strangers*) and her husband, Robert, of Highland Locksmith & Security Systems of Inverness.

Max Nichols, Bill Stoecker, Francis Shaw.

Steven, Audrey, Lucy, Benjamin, and Reuben Morgan, and Les Thomas of Upper Pitts Farm.

And a special thank-you to Susan Lamb for being a great paperback publisher.

Favor

I have a sister whom I have never met.
    Until today.
    No, that's not quite true. I didn't actually
meet her today. I merely saw her for the first
time.
    We've had the house in Wales for nearly a
year now. No, that's not true either. I mean,
we've been going there for nearly a year but
we don't actually have it. Not to ourselves. We
have one of those time-share things with two
other families.
    It's not much to look at as houses go. Not
one of those picture postcard country houses.
No thatched roof or oak beams. I don't even
think it's that old. In fact, I know it isn't. About
a hundred years maybe. That's not old, is it?
    I've been telling Gus ever since we were mar-
ried about how I want a place in the country.
In the beginning it was just a dream, out of
financial necessity. We didn't have a bean
and when the kids came along we had even less.
But one of the things I love about Gus is that
he has always understood that I need to have
my dreams. I am without any special talent and
I have no imagination, at least not when it comes

1

to everyday stuff. But in my head I love to go off all over the place, dreaming: I am a successful executive in a fancy corner office one minute and a pampered lady of leisure living in a sun-drenched villa in the South of France the next.

I have never been to the South of France. Maybe I'd hate it. I did go to Puerto Pollensa in Majorca one year. Gus packed me and the kids off for what he called a "bucket and spade holiday with a difference." This was before we went. When we got there we discovered there wasn't much difference. The kids were happy as clams as soon as they found they could have chicken 'n' chips every day just like they could at home. And it rained for almost the entire week we were there, which wasn't entirely surprising since we went off-season in April because it was all Gus could afford.

But there was one day when the sun shone and I left the kids on the beach at Puerto Pollensa with another mother whose children they'd made friends with. I drove the car very slowly around the most terrifying mountain bends I've ever encountered to a place called Formentor. I was so petrified as the car crawled up the hill and other vehicles forced me closer and closer to the edge of the road, affording me glimpses of the hair-raising drop to the sea below. The sea and the rocks. This is how Grace Kelly died, I reminded myself at every bend. This is the first time I have ever rented a car. How do I know the brakes have been serviced? But at the same time I was experiencing a kind of weird thrill I'd never known before, which spurred me on.

It was worth it when I came over the hill and down the other side to the bay at Formentor. I sat on the white sand and sifted it through my hands like sugar. I had the pine trees behind me and the blue sea and sky stretching out before me and suddenly I felt unbelievably calm. On either side of the bay the conical rocks, whose winding roads I had just navigated in terror, jutted into the sky. But now they were objects of beauty—dramatic, exciting.

I wished Gus could have been with me, but he couldn't take time off for holidays in those days. Even now there has to be some excuse connected to work to get him to go away. Gus has a security business. When I met him he was working for a locksmithing company, and a couple of years after we were married he started his own company. It was beans on toast, literally, for the first year. Gus advertised a twenty-four-hour service in the hope of getting enough after-hours work, so if it wasn't a baby waking me up in the night for a feeding, it was Gus leaping out of bed to attend to someone who had locked themselves out.

Our shop was small in the beginning and although it sounds crazy, I think that was the time I liked it best. I was so excited for Gus. Once the children were in nursery school I spent the day typing quotations and invoices, and trying to keep up with the books. I took a bookkeeping course in an effort to save on accountant bills. I'm not sure how much we saved, I was so hopeless. We were exhausted but in the beginning I didn't care. Gus's good-natured, easygoing personality endeared him to people and his reputation soon spread. Between the word-of-mouth referrals and his brilliance at cold-calling, we became so busy that I thought it had to mean we were successful. I even enjoyed working in the shop. We had a small display area with a couple of merchandisers, Yale and Chubb products mostly, and a keycutting area off to the side. I soon got proficient in dealing with our customers, and could even help Gus at the workbench when he needed to pin up a master suite or a quantity of keyed-alike locks. Gus had a desk beside mine in the back, but the paperwork he had to deal with was usually buried beneath a pile of ongoing repairs.

We took Mick on about three years into the business. By then we really needed someone full time in the shop, and Gus was intent on increasing our product range. He had been pursuing a dealership for a range of registered locks which would allow us to write up our own master suites, and, by offering the end-user a restricted key section, we'd also be sure of repeat business. The customer would *have* to come back to us to add on to their suite, or get extra keys cut. All of the major players promoted their own registered systems, but more than one insisted that we carry more stock than we could really afford in order to be granted a dealership.

Around that time I confess I did start to become a little disenchanted. We didn't have any money and we didn't have any time together. Gus was trapped. He was petrified of incurring more overheads, but he also recognized that he needed to expand, to offer newer and more costly technology. It was beginning to dawn on him that locksmithing alone was never going to provide us with the future we had in mind. It wasn't that we were going to send Ned and Mary to private schools or anything like that, but we did want the option of taking a holiday together if possible.

Gus had met Charlie Mackay somewhere along the line. Charlie was an experienced alarm installer who had dropped strong hints about being unhappy where he was. So Gus took him on and suddenly we were in the alarm business. More pricey advertising, another vehicle, and "on call" payments to Charlie...and Gus still had to attend to lockouts. Charlie, like any other alarm engineer, knew nothing about locksmithing. We had an answering machine at the shop which would give the customer our home number after hours, and Gus would either deal with the callout himself or would contact Mick. But it meant we had to be there to take the call or lose the business. Sometimes I unplugged the phone, hired a babysitter, and dragged Gus out to the local Italian, but it wasn't worth it. He just fretted the entire evening, didn't enjoy his food, and woke up with chronic indigestion in the middle of the night.

That's the thing about Gus. He's easygoing on the surface but underneath he's such a worrier. Still, he really isn't doing too badly either. I suppose it's a bit like being married to a doctor who worries about patients—he's called out as much as a doctor. There's also the problem of all the old keys lying around our house in Shepherd's Bush that Gus has deposited over the years. I seem to spend my life pulling them out of the washing machine just in time to prevent mechanical meltdown. And of course once we were in the alarm business we had to have the latest version installed in the house, and the fact that I'm married to Mr. Angus Hardy Security himself seems to make it a given that I can't remember the code.

So I took him up on his offer to send me away for a week's holiday because I realized that at least if he thought I was having a rest it would ease his mind a little.

I stared at my view—*my* view...already I had become proprietary—for over two hours and it was then that I began to think that just maybe, one day, I might be able to turn a fraction of my dreams into reality. One day I would have a view. It didn't have to be sun and sea but it had to give me a break from Shepherd's Bush.

Which is how we came to rent the house in Wales. It happened one miserable November weekend. Gus had been asked by some customers to supervise the installation of an alarm system in a house they'd bought in the country. He had roped in poor Charlie to do the job and he was now suggesting I accompany him as a kind of getaway weekend treat.

As it happened I put up quite a fight about going away for that weekend.

"Why couldn't it be in the summer? Honestly, Gus, Wales in November. It'll be wet. It'll be cold. It'll take five hours to get there. I'll have to find somewhere to farm out the kids as I don't imagine they'll want to come. Give me three good reasons why we should go."

Gus surprised me by coming back straight away. It meant he was really serious.

"One: they've asked me and I don't want to let them down. It's the Robinsons? Don't you remember, right after we first started, they were stitched up by that cowboy and I sorted it out for them. They've never forgotten. And if you're worrying about the cost, don't. They're paying extra to have me do it personally, and I'm letting them, so we can stay in a decent hotel. Two: I can strap my mountain bike on the back of the car and show it some real mountains. Well, hills anyway. And three: you know what they say, a change is as good as a rest, and you need a rest."

"I could rest perfectly well by going to bed for Sunday afternoon and watching an old movie. Those are two good reasons for you to go, Gus. I don't quite see how I fit into the equation."

"True." The thing about Gus is that he's always so reasonable, and not in the passive walk-all-over-me way. He'll always see your point of view as well as his own and if he thinks you're making sense he'll compromise. But he always makes sure he gets something for himself as well. That way he figures everyone's happy. More often than not, he's right.

"So what's in it for me?" I asked.

"Well, by the sound of it, not much as it stands, but I'd like to have you there. Tell you what. You're always at me to look for a place in the country. I'll contact a few estate agents and we'll spend Saturday afternoon looking at a few places. See what they've got in the area."

I'm not a complete fool. I knew he was only indulging me in my fantasies. We didn't have the money to buy a second house, but the estate agents didn't know that. Pretending we were good for it and going and looking at a few houses as if we intended to buy was the first step in the game, and if Gus was prepared to go along, I wasn't going to stop him.

I was right about almost everything. It rained. Not the light, warm, familiar drizzle that doesn't really do any harm, but the constant, heavy waterfall that soaks you the minute you step outside. We hustled Gus's mountain bike into the garage as soon as we arrived and there it stayed the entire weekend. And as for Gus and Charlie, I barely saw them. They came back on Saturday evening wet and dirty, having had to crawl about the loft and under the floorboards to run the required cabling. I'd spent the entire afternoon watching TV waiting for them to return. I might just as well have stayed in London. When the same thing happened on Sunday, Gus knew he had to do something to calm me down.

I didn't entirely understand why the couple needed an alarm system anyway when they lived in an isolated manor house at the end of a dirt track where the only perpetrators of any crime were likely to be a few marauding sheep. But Gus is crafty. He knew what he was doing when he agreed to service the Robinsons. They were the sort of people who never forgot a favor, and it turned out that they had discovered they had moved into an area near a community seriously in need of decent security. There had been a spate of break-ins recently, and the local crime prevention department was beginning to read the Riot Act, not to mention the insurance companies, who often insisted on a range of security locks before renewing policies or issuing new ones.

Charlie disappeared back to London on Sunday night and to my amazement Gus said, "We'll look at those houses tomorrow instead. Fair's fair. Charlie and Mick can take care of business for a day."

He had an incentive. If he spent a bit of time up here, he might be able to step in quick and corner the market on that much-needed perimeter security.

Not to mention keeping his wife happy at the same time.

He drove me to a small market town and

marched me into an estate agent's. I looked around at those tacky postcard-size photographs they have with the particulars typed underneath. They were town houses, probably just around the corner.

"We were actually thinking of something right out in the country. A retreat. Isolated. Few acres of land."

Gus had his back to me but I could see him shaking his head. A few acres of land indeed. And a few hundred thousand pounds we didn't have. Suddenly I saw how futile it all was. It was still raining. What was the point in traipsing around the countryside looking at properties we had no intention of buying? How long would I be able to keep up the pretense?

While I was looking through the books of houses for sale, something niggled at the back of my mind. We were in a place called Knighton. I'd never been to Knighton as far as I knew, so why was the name so familiar? I crossed the room to look at a map on the wall.

"Is this the area around Knighton?" I asked the estate agent, a sturdy man with a florid face and an annoying habit of cracking his knuckles. I could tell he was impatient to get on with something. Either that or he had clocked us for the penniless impostors we really were and was anxious to be rid of us.

"Yes, all around here. Knighton. Stowe. All the farmland."

It was the word *farm* that did it.

"My grandfather was a farmer," I told him.

"Fancy that." I could tell he was beginning to despair. Who was this idiotic woman wasting his time babbling on about her grandparents?

"Yes, he had a farm in Shropshire."

"'Round here, then?" He couldn't have sounded less interested if I'd been reading aloud from the phone book.

"No," I said. "Shropshire."

"We're on the Shropshire borders," Gus butted in quickly.

"I know it was near a place called Knighton. I didn't realize Knighton was in Wales."

Gus and the estate agent exchanged looks. This could go on forever.

"What was your grandfather's name?" asked the estate agent.

"Richard Cammell."

"Upper Stone Farm. Other side of the valley from Stowe."

"Upper Stone Farm, Knighton," I repeated. I'd seen the address written down so many times as a child. My father was a hoarder. He hated throwing anything away. I used to find trunkfuls of plates, linen, clothes all labelled Upper Stone Farm, Knighton.

"The old man left it all to his son when he died—" said the estate agent.

"Lucas Cammell. My father," I confirmed.

The estate agent didn't welcome the interruption. He had something to say, a sales pitch of a sort. If we weren't going to buy one of his ugly houses at least we could hear what else he had to offer.

11

"...and the son sold up pretty soon after that. Wasn't a farmer like his father. Les Bevan bought it, been farming ever since."

"What happened to the house?" I asked. The house where my parents had lived before I was born.

"I was going to tell you." I had really irritated him now. "You wanted somewhere isolated. Well, had you thought about renting? Les rents out the farmhouse. He's had local people living there mostly, but there's no reason why he shouldn't take tenants from London, 'specially as he's looking to up the rent this year."

"No, no, no," said Gus, "we don't want to get into that. We don't want to waste any more of your time. Look, I think we'd better come clean. We're only—"

"Gus, I want to see it," I heard myself say.

"It's pretty run down. I confess I haven't been over there in quite a while. I'm not sure..." Even the estate agent was in the process of making an abrupt U-turn from his earlier spiel.

"It's my grandfather's farm. The place where my parents used to live. It's my family home. I want to see it."

I was aware that I was sounding a little over the top, a child who must be indulged or else it'll throw an almighty tantrum.

"You don't really want to see the place—you know you don't. Not really." I could hear the anxiety in Gus's voice. Don't make a scene, he was pleading silently. Don't embarrass me. Typical Gus. He hated it when I

12

became emotional. He was supportive but he hated it. That's one of the reasons I loved him. My warm, extroverted personality had attracted him in the first place. My exuberance invariably made up for his more reserved nature, but sometimes I was more than he could handle. He always tried, though, bless him.

Still, I knew there was a subtext here. A gentle warning. Did I know what I was getting into? It wouldn't just be a question of going to take a look at the old family home, as I had called it, making it sound like an ancestral pile.

My mother is dead. So is my father, but at least I knew him. I never knew my mother. She died giving birth to me. That sounds a little barbaric given that I was born in the middle of the twentieth century, but there were complications—that all-embracing word—following the birth and they couldn't save her. I grew up without a mother, raised by Dad.

So what Gus was really saying was did I want to take a look at the place where my mother might have died? But hadn't my parents left Upper Stone Farm, sold it like the estate agent said?

"Did you know my parents when they lived there?" I asked him.

"I've only been here for five years. Do you want to see the place or not?"

We drove out to it in a four-wheel drive, turning right about three miles along the main road out of Knighton and climbing higher and higher until we almost reached the top of the hill. For the first time since we had left London I saw that we were in a spectacularly beautiful part of the world. It's amazing how much difference your state of mind can make to your approach to a place. When we had arrived I had programmed myself to resist all possibility that I might have a good time. I get like that sometimes. It had been a soggy Friday night, I was exhausted, it had been pitch black outside and I hadn't been able to see a thing.

Now the weekend was behind me. The skies were clearing. I'd had a good night's sleep and I was embarking on a kind of adventure, a journey into my past or whatever they called it. And suddenly I saw the hills rising up on either side of the valley, covered in forests and warm red bracken and I began to get excited.

The road had disintegrated into a dirt track now overhung by brambles and bushes. Every now and then the estate agent stopped the jeep and got out, grumbling, to kick a fallen branch out of the path. The track climbed and for a minute I thought we were going to go up out of the valley, over the top of the hill and down the other side, but then I saw a group of farm buildings over to the right and beyond them the house.

It was no beauty. Square. Sloping roof. The walls were a sort of sludge brown. There was no garden. No path leading up to the front door. It just stood there in the middle of a field, two steps going down from the entrance, to mud and earth.

The estate agent walked right in, didn't even bother with a key. The place was open.

A horrible musty smell hit me as I followed him. Damp. Gus was still outside, walking around the house, looking in windows.

It struck me after we'd been into a couple of rooms at the front—one of them the kitchen with a huge wood stove—and moved down a stone passage to the back rooms. It wasn't Majorca. No sun, no sea, no fine-sugar sand, but the view from the back of Upper Stone Farm was nothing short of spectacular. It was like a huge double bed covered in a brown and green patchwork quilt spread out before us. The hills made me think there were two people in the bed tossing and turning and causing it to undulate and sag in the middle, but the horizon, the end of the bed, held firm—a high, rolling line punctuated by trees bent by the wind and the odd abandoned tractor. It was bleak—and beautiful.

All the way back to London Gus, perfectly reasonably, tried to point out to me why it would be utter madness for us to rent the house, using, I couldn't help noticing, all the reasons I had given him for not going to Wales in the first place.

"It'll take us forever to get there. It's wet. It's cold. It's miles from anywhere. And where are we going to find an extra seven grand a year or whatever he's asking? Insanity. Although," he couldn't help adding, "if I did get a look-in on that security the Robinsons were talking about it might begin to pay for itself. Eventually." This last was said very firmly and rather gloomily.

I came back with his own arguments about his mountain bike and this security work and what was it he'd said about a change being as good as a rest? And as for the money, why didn't we think about sharing the rental between friends?

There are times when you have a plan and everything goes according to it. You imagine it's going to be like that for the rest of your life and that up to now you've just been practicing until you got it right. Now the hiccoughs are over and it'll all be plain sailing. Then just as you're patting yourself on the back, everything starts going wrong again and you realize nothing's changed. That's life. It was like that with the rental of Upper Stone Farm. We found people to come in with us just like that. No problem at all. We contacted one set of friends, they said yes, they knew another couple who were interested, and suddenly we were all set. We'd never actually met the other couple before, but they seemed perfectly reliable when we all got together with Indian takeout one night in Shepherd's Bush and carved up the weekends between us over the next six months. We didn't even have to like them. It wasn't as if we were ever going to be there together.

Gus moved fast and pretty soon he was working one weekend a month installing locks all around the area. In between he disappeared for hours on his bike while I spent every weekend we were down there painting and scouring antiques sales for bits and pieces, trying to make the place feel homey. It wasn't cozy but slowly it all began to come together, and whenever I felt downhearted, all I had to do was turn around and wallow in my view.

The house was big. Five bedrooms, which meant the kids came down some weekends and brought friends. I felt a bit nervous leaving them in London on their own sometimes but it wasn't as if they were small children any more. Ned was seventeen and Mary just turned sixteen. But when they did come down it wasn't exactly restful, change or no change. Especially when they didn't give us any notice and just descended on us, deciding to come at the last minute, taking the train and calling us from the station at Ludlow when we arrived on Friday, exhausted after a three-hour drive and about to settle in for the night. Poor Gus had to go out into the wet and the cold and fetch them. And the next day I'd have to do battle with the Saturday-morning shoppers, getting in extra food which I would then have to spend the weekend cooking.

But it was worth it just for my view.

I was coming back from one of those unexpected Saturday-morning shopping expeditions, whirring up the dirt road in a hurry to get the lunch going before Gus got back from his bike ride (he'd been gone since seven-thirty, he'd be ravenous). I was going fast. I never assumed there'd be anyone else on the road.

I swerved just in time. It was a dark blue BMW. I ran into the bushes. The BMW braked violently. I was shaken but I was all right.

The driver wound down her window. It was a woman, a beautiful woman, older than I but much better looking. Dark brown hair falling in a long bob to her shoulders, a faint tan (in November!), flawless makeup, pearl earrings.

"Are you all right?" Her voice was strong, autocratic. She might just as well have said, "You'd better be all right or else." In the crisp morning air I could smell her perfume. It was 'Coco' from Chanel. I knew it was 'Coco' not because Gus buys it for me regularly but because I often amuse myself dabbing on those free sachets of perfume they give you nowadays in magazines. Sometimes I dabbed more than one at a time and Gus complained that I smelled like a tart's breakfast.

"Oh yes, I'm fine," I assured the woman, and before I could say anything else she'd taken her foot off the brake and was easing the BMW off down the hill.

"I almost wrote the car off just now," I told Gus over lunch. "Some woman in a BMW was coming down the road like she owned it."

"She probably did once," said Ned through a mouthful of spaghetti bolognese.

"Why do you say that?"

"Because she was here wanting to look around the house. Said she used to live here when she was a little girl. Would we mind?"

"And you let her?"

"Sure. Why not? She didn't take long. Not

18

inside anyway. She did stand around outside for quite a while, though, staring at the view. Nice car. Wonder who she was."

I knew who she was.

If she'd lived here when she was a little girl with my parents when they were alive, and she was just a few years older than me, then she had to be my sister. The sister I had never met.

Grace

I have a sister whom I have never met.

God forbid that I ever should, but I suppose it's inevitable that I should be wondering what became of her, given that I took it into my head to go back to Upper Stone Farm.

What on earth made me do it? I've had nightmares ever since. Whoever lives there now—quite a good-looking boy opened the door to me—has prettied it up quite a bit, but for me there's still a residual feeling of misery about the place.

Of course if I think about it, I know exactly why I went there. It had nothing to do with the past. Not the distant past, at any rate. What I was trying to do was escape my recent past. I imagined that if I drove out of London for

19

the day, I wouldn't call him. If I had sat in my hotel room staring at the phone, the temptation would have been too great. It was a ludicrous excuse. They have phones in Shropshire and all points west. It wasn't as if I even knew he was in London. He might have been in Los Angeles for all I knew. But when it was all over, when I had to accept that he wasn't interested in me any more, I was the one who left.

I suppose it was a bit extreme, moving to America. I could have gone to Cornwall, or the Lake District, or even Wales if I'd wanted somewhere remote, but no, I had to come to Long Island, to a peaceful haven called Barnes Landing. I know back home they all think I'm in the Hamptons, but they're wrong. It's a big deal out here which side of the highway you live. Route 27. The Montauk Highway. Running all the way to the tip of the island. If you're really cool, your house is south of the highway, on the ocean, and your telephone exchange is 324. I have neither. I'm ten minutes north of the highway and my exchange is 267.

I'm not even on the water. I'm in the woods where I'm likely to get bitten to death—literally—by ticks. If a deer tick carrying Lyme disease bites you, it burrows into your skin and sucks your blood and 24 hours later you develop a rash. If you don't get to a doctor soon, that's it. Curtains. I'm probably exaggerating. I usually do, but they're pretty horrible, ticks. They appear as little black dots and they bury their heads inside you and leave their imperceptible bodies on your skin. You have to coat them with Vaseline to smother them to death and then ease them off your body. Then you get Lyme disease and go all floppy.

I can walk to a beach, though. Three miles of sand looking out towards Gardiner's Island. And I can walk to Louse Point, home of the plover, and watch the sun sink into a crimson ball over the osprey nests and an island in the middle of the Accabonac Harbor called—wouldn't you know it?—Wood Tick Island. I avoid Louse Point on weekends because that's when you get the couples. She sits huddled on the beach in one of those collapsible chairs that sink into the sand, pretending she's reading the latest Tama Janowitz, but secretly she's feasting her eyes on her gorgeous hulk as he casts his line into the ocean hoping to come up with their supper. His golden retriever charges into the water each time after the fish and has to be hauled out by his master. I know these guys never catch anything, standing there for hours looking more like a Ralph Lauren Polo ad than the real McCoy.

My caretaker goes fishing for his supper, but he goes out in a little boat, disappearing into the horizon beyond Gardiner's Island, bringing back striped bass and flounder. My caretaker says he hunts deer with a bow and arrow but I don't want to think about that. Bows and arrows in the Hamptons. Bet the real estate guys leave that one out. Pay a million bucks for your home and you get *Deliverance* on your doorstep.

Not that my caretaker is anything like the character Burt Reynolds portrayed in the film. Far from it. Lew is a honey. One of the most gentle men I've ever come across, and to think of him with a bow and arrow in his hands is somehow shocking to me. I suppose it ought to tell me what I've come to realize: that underneath his little-boy-lost demeanor— he really has an amazingly vulnerable look in his eyes sometimes—Lew is pretty tough. Stubborn. Stands his ground. And boy, does he like to talk.

At first I was fascinated. His family are old Long Island stock and have lived around here for over a hundred years. Lew was a mine of information about local history, but he had a habit of repeating himself, and after he'd told me for about the fifth time that he used to walk across my land to school I began to discourage his conversation a little, heading him off at the pass with the odd "Hey, Lew, the new fertilizer you put down last month really seems to be working." Of course then he'd go on for another forty minutes about fertilizer.

I felt sorry for him in many ways. He obviously worked all the hours God sent doing several different jobs at once in order to be able to continue to live in the old family home, paying exorbitant taxes, surrounded by rich New Yorkers who I suspected treated him like dirt. And yet he was the bona fide native, the one who had the most right to the land his family had had to sell off bit by bit until there was barely a quarter of an acre left. He could so easily have become embittered, resentful, but he was too much of a gentleman.

But to get back to the couples. When he's finally realized that he's never going to catch anything and the dog's tired itself out swimming round and round the point, and shaken itself all over her, she leaps up squealing and he runs and puts his arms around her and off they go for a wander down the beach, heads together, and I just can't stand it.

So I go back home and watch the baseball playoffs on TV, or something equally bizarre, to take my mind off him. Because except for the times when my work takes me into New York or, in this case, to London, I can hide away here in Barnes Landing and forget about him.

I'm one of those people who got a fantastic break in the eighties. I'm talking serious money. I was barely thirty. I was a producer's PA and I thought I'd try my hand at writing a blockbuster novel on the side. It was pretty crummy—about a girl who had a pen pal relationship with a boy in America which continued until they were way into their thirties. They poured out their hearts to each other. He was married and divorced. He became a hugely successful rag trade mogul with his own store on Madison Avenue.

And she got cancer, but that was the one thing she never told him in the letters. So of course she died and her sister found the letters, by which point it had gotten to the stage where he'd arranged to come over to England to meet the pen pal he'd fallen in love with via her letters. But the sister managed to head him off at the pass by flying to New York pretending to be his pen pal. (I was amazed that no one asked why she didn't just tell him her sister was dead, but they didn't.) He was duly amazed that the girl he had envisaged as a sweet country mouse straight out of Jane Austen was in fact a great businesswoman whom he wasted no time in hiring to work in his store. (She was conveniently unemployed. No one asked about that either.) By the time the impostor sister confessed her true identity, he'd fallen in love with her and it was clear that it would never have worked with the dead sister anyway.

I called it *Air Male*—you could get away with things like that in the eighties—and sent it to a literary agent. She sent it out to auction and secured me an advance of $750,000. Then the Brits bought it for a quarter million pounds. Even the French were less chintzy than usual. *Par Avion*—they didn't get the pun of the English title—went straight to number one. The Italians bought it, along with the Germans, all the Scandinavians, and people like the Brazilians and the Koreans. Everyone. It was what you might call a global bestseller.

Then came the movie. "*A Touch of Class* with Kleenex," said one review. Suddenly I was so rich I didn't know what to do, so I bought houses like I was shopping for underwear at Saks: a villa in Tuscany, a bolthole cottage in Wiltshire in which to write. And, ironically, a summer house in the Hamptons. That's the only one I still have. I never even moved into the others. I never really felt comfortable with the Chiantishire lot, and once I realized they'd be renting places all around me in Tuscany, I decided I would never go there. The cottage in Wiltshire was just too twee. It drove me mad the way my head kept bumping into the beams the first Friday I went down there for the weekend, so I drove straight back to London and the next day I instructed the agents to sell it. Ditto the villa in Tuscany. The enormity of running so many places suddenly hit me. I don't know what I'd been thinking of, but everyone said "Get into property," so I did. Then I got out of it.

But I kept the one in the Hamptons. I bought it through the Hamptons real estate broker Allan M. Schneider when he was still alive. I'm told he choked to death on a piece of sirloin steak in 1991 while having dinner with the Chief of Police of the town of East Hampton.

"A hundred and twenty-five feet of ocean frontage. New to market. History and beauty abound in this classic East Hampton property complete with gourmet kitchen, seven bedrooms, granite pool, tennis court..." claimed Allan's ad in *Homes & Land of the Hamptons and the East End* before he met his untimely death. It has always amused me that this supposedly ritzy part of Long Island is known as the East End. Nothing could be less like the impoverished East End I used to know in

London. That one had considerably more class.

I like the idea that I own this fabulous property in this pretentious part of the world and don't live in it. Once I'd calmed down, just like with the other two properties, I took one look at it and knew I could never actually live in it. I was persuaded to hang on to it and rent it out in the summer for a fortune, and when the time came, I fell in love with my tree house in Barnes Landing and settled there. Around here in Barnes Landing they have no idea I have another house south of the highway. The brokers who rent it are under strict instructions never to say who owns the property. When I bought my log cabin, a square box of cypress wood and glass built in the late sixties, my neighbors thought this was my first buy.

"Oh, you bought the Hart property," they said when they met me walking on the private Barnes Landing beach. They never revealed whether they thought it was a good thing or a bad thing. Just: "Oh, you bought the Hart house. There's a nor'easter on the way. Better bring in the furniture off the deck."

My closest neighbor elaborated just a little with a piece of advice that left me bewildered for months.

"Gets mighty cold in the winter. Keep a hairdryer plugged in on your deck at all times."

I discovered what she meant when I arrived home late one night in the middle of January and found the lock on the screen door frozen solid. When after a few minutes' wrestling it still wouldn't budge and I was in danger of freezing solid myself, I traipsed through the snow down my drive and up hers and banged on her door.

"I think you might have to have me for the night. My door's frozen. Can't get in."

"I told you to keep a hairdryer outside..." She grabbed hers and marched me back home, plugged it in on the deck where I have an outlet, and set to work defrosting the lock.

"Happened to me in the middle of the night, too. The Millers across the street thought I was out of my mind waking them up at two a.m. and asking for a hairdryer. They must think I'm some kinda closet beauty queen."

I've often wanted to tell Linda about the other house on the ocean. I'd like to take her down there and show it to her. She'd appreciate it. Linda's a great girl but she has just about the worst taste I've ever seen. Her favorite color is pink. And she's partial to purple. The entire contents of her house, with the exception of the fridge, the stove, the dishwasher, and the washer and dryer, are either purple or pink. The house itself is wonderful. It's criminal what she's done. Beautiful hardwood floors hidden by purple shag.

What happened was when she got divorced from Artie (whom she clearly misses desperately), he got the house in Florida and she got the house in Barnes Landing. I don't know for sure—and it's more than my life's worth to check it out with Linda—but I have a feeling Artie probably has pretty good taste precisely because Linda says he doesn't. She made him take all his stuff out of the Long Island house and move it to Florida, and she went down there and brought back her pink and purple world, including her *pièce de résistance:* a mail box in the shape of a pink poodle.

Linda would like my house on the ocean because it's tacky. When I had loads of money I had a decorator go in to fix the place up. I went away and did something else and turned around and the place was full of marble bathrooms and frou-frou chintz in the bedrooms. Downstairs was all faux Spanish hacienda. In America wealth does not necessarily equal taste. In fact it quite often encourages megatackiness.

In the winter, when all the summer rental people have left, I quite often go down the road and sneak a look at my house. Sometimes I let myself in. People leave stuff behind and it can be very telling. My tenants all seem to devour magazines. The people there this year had subscriptions to *Vogue, Travel & Leisure, Harper's Bazaar, Details, Detour, Interiors, Vanity Fair, Town & Country, W, New York,* as well as the local glossies, *Hamptons* and *Hamptons File.* What I do is I look at their names and addresses in Manhattan. If you have a subscription it's pasted on the cover of the magazine. I sit in my hideous, fancy house and speculate on what the people might be like,

28

these wannabe beautiful people from New York who are prepared to spend as much as $100,000 for a summer house where they can "walk to water," cheek by jowl with loads of other fakers. I have their names and addresses from the front of the magazines. Sometimes I'm tempted to go and loiter outside their Manhattan homes to take a peek at them.

There were no magazines in my house at Barnes Landing when I moved in. All I found were twenty-five guides to saltwater fishing, but even so, I do speculate about the family who lived here.

I think there must have been two girls in the family, like we were. Or rather, weren't. I still open cupboards and find old jigsaw puzzles of Cinderella and Prince Charming, or Junior Miss makeup. I detested that kind of stuff as a kid. Books and animals were more my style. I wasn't a tomboy but I was a rebellious child. Independent from an early age, always wanting to be off on my own. The only person whose company I could tolerate was my mother's. I adored her, but then it's easy to think fondly of the dead, to remember only the good things. Not that I remember much. I was only five when she died.

My father spent a great deal of time in London, and my mother and I stayed at Upper Stone Farm. He was a publisher. It was through him that I came to know and love books. I suppose I owe my career as a writer to his insistence that I learn to read and write as early as possible, and my subsequent introduction to his favorite authors—Conrad, Swift, Thackeray—long before I was able to understand them.

Not only was he a publisher, but he had his own small publishing house. In those days it was the norm rather than the exception. There was no HarperCollins, just Collins. Jonathan Cape was not part of the Random House empire, and like my father, many publishers stood alone, known only by their name: André Deutsch, Michael Joseph, Victor Gollancz, John Calder. The offices of Lucas Cammell were situated in a Georgian building in Notting Hill Gate, a far cry from the Bloomsbury crowd scattered around Bedford Square.

Looking back I never understood why my mother did not become more involved in my father's working life. She never went up to London. Never. My parents had a charming apartment above the offices, but to all intents and purposes it was a bachelor pad. My father lived there alone during the week and came down to Wales for the weekend. Les Bevan farmed the land and we lived in the farmhouse. On weekends he came home on the train—Paddington to Newport and change for the branch line to Leominster or Ludlow—exhausted, lugging a pile of manuscripts to be read in two days so that we barely saw him.

I do remember my mother tried to dress me up for my father and I rebelled. She wanted a pretty, frilly daughter and all she got was me. She herself was vain. She dressed immaculately every day in cashmere sweaters and pure wool trousers even though there was no one but the farmhands to see her. She made up her face with the skill of an expert every morning while I sat on a footstool and watched her. Her kidney-shaped dressing table with its chintz frill was such an anachronism in the blunt, serviceable atmosphere of the farmhouse that I have never forgotten it. And her hair was always newly washed and shining. But for whom? Looking back I can only assume it was for herself. Looking closely at the photographs taken just before she died I realize her beauty was beginning to fade. Her hair looked faintly gray even though the photo was black and white. The fine lines a fragile porcelain skin encourages were emerging. And she smoked all the time. Perhaps she died the way she did because she could not face the deterioration of her beauty.

Yet if that was the case why was she so thrilled about Favor? I know I must have been told my sister's real name at some point. It's on the tip of my tongue but I can never quite remember what it is. It's an odd name and to be honest I don't recall who said it in my presence. Certainly not my father. But in my mind I have always called her Favor because even before she was born I knew she was my mother's favorite. It was quite clear to me that Favor was going to be the fluffy little girl my mother had always wanted. As her stomach swelled, distorting her slender profile, she became more and more excited.

31

"I am young again," she said to me over and over. I know I can still remember that. And maybe that's what she really felt. She might be approaching forty but she was still young enough to have a child. To start all over again. She made plans right from the start. "This child will be this...this child will be that..." Every day I had to listen to it. Every day my hatred for the unborn baby increased. If she continued to behave as she did before the birth, by the time it arrived there would be nothing left for me.

I can remember everything that happened the night Favor was born and shortly afterwards, but then everything becomes a blur. I only know what happened because I was told.

The day my mother was driven to Ludlow to have her baby I ran away. I put on my boots, walked out of the ever-open front door up to the lane, scattering bantams as I went, past the stables and barns and down the hill. When I got to the main road I stopped and looked both ways as I had been taught and then marched straight across it.

I walked up the road on the other side of the valley, over the river, climbing higher and higher until I reached Hill House where Mrs. McIntyre lived. I had always liked Mrs. McIntyre. She was a friend of my mother's. When I set out for her house I know I wanted to ask her to help me get my mother to focus her attention on me and stop talking about the baby. I know that was what I was thinking. But somehow when I got there I must have changed my mind because I walked into her house—everybody always left doors open in those days—and sat down in her kitchen and told her I'd come to live with her.

The baby was early. It was the middle of the week. My father was in London and had to be summoned by telephone. It would be at least three hours before he appeared. No one had noticed me leaving. It would be quite some time before anyone at Upper Stone Farm asked where I was.

My father turned up eventually. I'm saying all this now because of what I was told. I don't remember ever seeing him. He brought devastating news: my mother had had a baby, was besotted with her. Legend also has it that I refused point blank to go home with him. I screamed and yelled and embarrassed everyone apparently. My father knew Mrs. McIntyre, of course, and her husband David. I am told that eventually my father gave in and said if they were really prepared to have me until my mother came home, it really would be most awfully convenient.

Most awfully convenient. He'd be indebted to them forever. Polite, empty phrases masking the truth. I wasn't wanted back home.

Why would I want to go home? I was in heaven where I was. Grown-ups hanging on my every word. As much TV as I wanted to watch. Allowed to stay up late. Delicious food. Ice cream with every meal. No brussels sprouts, not if I didn't want them. A light left on all night while I slept. No talk of wasting electricity. I felt safe. I felt wanted. I know I did. I can still remember.

Of course if my mother hadn't killed herself I would never have been allowed to stay on.

Favor

It's official. We're fashionable. Kate Moss has bought a flat in Shepherd's Bush. Not a house. Just a flat. There was a bit in the papers about her having trouble with her builders and I was dumb enough to bring it up at breakfast.

"Mum, everyone knows that. They've known it for ages. Where've you been?"

"Well, I've been right here, same as you. Is it close to us?"

"Yeah. Not far." Ned always ate breakfast in his boxers and what he called a T. I had tried to remonstrate with him, suggested he might be cold, that he'd miss the bus if he didn't get dressed before breakfast, but always in vain. He had a horror of getting dressed. Sometimes, on weekends, he wandered around like that until he went to sleep. Once I'd even seen him wandering half naked out of the house to buy a quart of milk.

"How would you know?" demanded Mary.

"He doesn't know, Mum. He's just pretending he does. Anyway, Creepo, you hate Kate Moss."

"Who says I do? It's common knowledge. You only have to ask the estate agents."

"Who are?"

Ned planted a slice of toast between his teeth and wiggled it at her.

"See, you don't know." Mary was triumphant. "D'you think we'll see her down at the Empire with Johnny Depp?"

"Christ, I hope not. What a wanker."

"He's not. He's gorgeous."

"I thought Liam Gallagher was your favorite." I always tried to keep track of her latest passion although it could change between breakfast and lunch.

"No, he's really sad. Johnny Depp's just a wanker wannabe, but the other geezer's serious rubbish."

"But you fancy that Patsy Kensit though, don't you, Creepo?"

"I do not."

"Oh, yes you do. I've seen you drooling and slobbering over her picture, you and your spotty pals. Picture of Patsy under your bed, fodder for your tumescent fantasies."

"Mary. Please."

Actually I was rather impressed. *Tumescent.* Did I use words like that when I was sixteen? I was going to have to wade in and sort this out, because what I'd gone and done without realizing it was reopen hostilities in World War III, which had been declared over a year ago between Ned and Mary over the Kate Moss versus Patsy Kensit issue. I'd already said it was exciting having Kate Moss in the area. Now I'd better come out for Patsy.

"Patsy's not too bad, Mary. She was really sweet in *The Railway Children.*"

"She wasn't in *The Railway Children,*" said Gus, emerging from behind *Boards. Boards* is a windsurfing magazine. Gus's dream in life is to go windsurfing. He once confided in me very early on in our relationship that he saw himself as a surfer, riding the waves, and the nearest he could get to it was cycling over the crest of a hill. And watching windsurfing videos for hours on end when Ned or Mary wanted to watch something they'd had on order for weeks at Blockbuster.

"Yes, she was—she played Jenny Agutter's sister. The little one with buck teeth."

"You're thinking of Sally Thomsett. Patsy Kensit would have been only a year old when they made *The Railway Children.*"

How did Gus know how old Patsy Kensit was? He had gone a little pink and retired behind *Boards.*

"Ned. Clothes. Teeth. Out the door."

"I don't have to go in today."

He was retaking his exams and cramming. Sweet Ned. My big, lumbering baby. A real dreamer like his mother. Not into football. Not into rock music. I have a suspicion he probably tries to write excruciatingly bad poetry locked away in his room. I can feel him waiting to fall in love. I'm aching to know if he's still a virgin. Sometimes I prod Gus to ask him. Man-to-man talk. Gus just says what's wrong with a woman-to-man talk and why don't I ask him? I wonder if girls fancy Ned. He's so big and clumsy but he has the softest eyes I've ever seen on a male. He looks like a hulk, but a terribly vulnerable one. Probably because he is. He cries, which is something I have not seen Mary do in quite a while. But I do have to be tough with him.

"Go on, Ned. You've got to pass those exams this time."

"What about that *Panorama* hoo-ha?" said Mary.

"What *Panorama* hoo-ha?"

Gus and I had gone to see *101 Dalmations* on Monday night. It sort of says it all. We go out and see a kids' film and our kids stay in and watch *Panorama*.

"There you are, Mum." Mary was in her element. She'd caught me yet again. "You don't keep up with what's what. You've only just found out about Kate Moss buying a flat around here. Bet you don't know Patsy Kensit's supposed to be getting married to Liam Gallagher. And now you don't know about the *Panorama* thing. They claimed working mothers were jeopardizing their children's education, and all the feminists are getting their knickers in a twist because it's what they've always fought for, isn't it? So women could have it all."

I was about to plead guilty and apologize for my ignorance when Mary went too far.

"Although we're all right," she said, "it doesn't apply to us. You can't blame not passing your exams on Mum, Creepo."

"What do you mean?" I asked.

"Well, you're not really a working mother, are you?"

"Gus, did you hear what she just said?"

"Who?"

"Mary. Your daughter. Is there another female in the room?"

"No. And no, I didn't hear."

I knew he'd heard. Gus can be such a coward sometimes. He hates confrontation. Not a trait he appears to have passed on to Mary. But Ned has my dreaminess. He's not exactly get-up-and-go like Gus. The thought of Ned on a mountain bike is sheer fantasy. But he enjoys a good scrap with his sister. Ned's as unlike Mary as it's possible to be, but she's the only person who can elicit a spark of anger out of him. Normally he bumbles along, loaded with charm if people can be bothered to look for it. Hopeless academically. Not in the least competitive.

Whereas Mary is so driven it's terrifying. She's at the top of her class year in, year out, and boy, does she let you know it. I should be proud of her, but instead I'm embarrassed when our friends come to the house. There's Mary telling them how well she's been doing at everything before they've barely said hello. She outshines poor Ned in every way. She's dark and terribly pretty with none of her friends' teenage blemishes and puppy fat. She's petite and vivacious. That awful phrase "cute as a button" comes to mind, probably because Gus never stopped saying it when she was little. She can wind Gus around her proverbial little finger. He's terribly proud of her. Neither he nor I went to university and I think secretly he's a little nervous about the fact that in the not-too-distant future he's going to have a daughter at Oxford or Cambridge or wherever she assumes she'll wind up. Well, she might graduate with honors and she might be the first woman something or other, but meanwhile she's got an awful lot of lip and I'm not about to put up with it.

"Are you suggesting I don't work?"

"Well, you don't exactly have a career, Mum."

She was right, as usual. I had a job. I worked. As a receptionist at an osteopathic practice, but it was only three days a week and I left at four in the afternoon. I wasn't exactly on the fast track for a carefully planned career. But it irritated me the way the young were so obsessed with having a career with a capital C. Mary should have seen what it was like when Gus was first starting up the business. Then she would have seen me working harder than she could possibly imagine, staring at long columns of figures in my nightie at four in the morning trying to balance the books, and, more often than not, feeding her at the same time.

But no, you couldn't call it a career. Yet there was a reason for my not wanting to rush out to an office every day, something the children couldn't be expected to understand because they knew very little about it. We'd talked about me working, Gus and I, when we'd first begun to plan our life together and I'd told him about my mother dying giving birth to me.

"Are you trying to tell me you're scared of having children?" he'd asked me. "Of the pain, that it'll happen to you? Because if you are, it's no problem—we can always adopt."

Nothing was ever a problem for Gus. He always approached everything calmly, convinced there would be some way to overcome whatever obstacles presented themselves. Only I knew how much he worried about things underneath. But I didn't want to adopt. I wanted children and I wanted to be there for them as much as I could, precisely because my mother hadn't been there for me. And if that meant a job where I either worked for my husband in the middle of the night or I came home at four and only worked two or three days a week, then so be it. It wasn't as if the world would be denied a captain of industry or a pioneering biochemist. So when Gus no longer needed me in the shop or fielding the customers' calls at home, I took the job of receptionist at the osteopath's up the road.

I knew Gus was curious about my childhood. Ironically, Dad met him but never knew that I married him. Dad sold Upper Stone Farm after my mother died and he and I moved to London to live in the flat above the publishers. I am told I had a succession of nannies until I went to nursery school, and after that it was made clear to the secretaries downstairs at Lucas Cammell Publishers that part of their duties would include babysitting.

In a way I was brought up in an office, so perhaps it was hardly surprising that I opted to forgo a career in one. I won't deny it was fun, coming home from school and having everyone make a fuss over me. It started in the mail room in the basement with old Fred stuffing manuscripts in Jiffy bags while I made him a cup of tea, at which point he would produce the Oreo cookies, my favorites, which he always kept beside the franking machine. Then it was up to Reception, where Pat would let me work the switchboard if it wasn't too busy, or until I cut someone off. Then I was allowed to escort visitors upstairs to Dad's office on the first floor for their meeting with him. Or with one of the editors.

I wasn't supposed to disturb the editors, who had their own offices and seemed to do nothing but read boxes of paper all day, but I could run riot in Publicity, where the noise was always deafening with people shouting at each other or into the phone.

The art department was my favorite. Ben, the Art Director, always asked my opinion of the visuals for the various jackets. I imagined him passing on my comments to Dad.

"Your daughter went for that one with the sans serif. A little avant-garde for W. H. Smith I would have thought, but perhaps we should listen to the young…the youth market…"

41

Ben was a little pompous and sported a bow tie.

I liked to think my father always replied, "Well, then, that's what we shall go with."

I always did my homework in the accounts department because it was quiet, and then whoever was babysitting that night would take me upstairs for my bath and my supper and allow me to run downstairs again in my pajamas to kiss everyone good night. There were twenty-two people in the entire company including the salesmen and they always worked late.

Of course, once I became a teenager, I marched straight through the building and upstairs to my bedroom in the top floor flat where I would blast out someone ghastly like the Bay City Rollers (not something I'd ever want Mary to know) until the proofreaders in Editorial directly below me went berserk because they couldn't concentrate.

When Dad sold out to Mason House, an American conglomerate, in 1987 it was the beginning of the end. They let him keep the name, Lucas Cammell, and the building and most of his staff (although pompous Ben was replaced pretty smartly by a young buck whose only claim to fame as far as I could make out was that he had "almost got a job on the *Face*"). But they kept interfering, demanding that he drop half his authors, some of whom had been with him for thirty years, and spend more money on marketing.

I was secretly rather taken by some of the new blood being brought in, particularly in the newly formed marketing department which had replaced Editorial below my bedroom. Instead of playing music in my room, I would creep down the stairs to listen to the house music they played non-stop on their boom boxes. Most of them had come from advertising where it was cool to work to music.

Dad published literature. He was a real purist. That's why it hit him so badly when the American-owned conglomerate to whom he'd sold Lucas Cammell started forcing him to publish commerce. I was thrilled. When I heard we were in the auction to bid for the new Judith Krantz or Sidney Sheldon, I couldn't believe it. I began to hang out in Editorial and read manuscripts when they came in, something I'd never done before. I was even beginning to think about asking Dad for a job in the family firm. Cammell and Daughter, purveyors of fine potboilers.

It was when Lucas Cammell was computerized that Dad really began to go into a decline. He just couldn't get the hang of it, mainly because he didn't want to. And it was because of the computers that I met Gus.

They were stolen.

Dad and I were upstairs fast asleep when they broke in and removed $100,000 worth of computers. Dad's proprietors said he had to get better security, which was how Gus came into the picture. He was the one they sent around to talk to us about alarms and security gates.

"You talk to them, sweetheart," Dad told

43

me. Typical. Burglar alarms came under the same umbrella as computers, answering machines, technology—it all made him nervous.

And so I dealt with Gus, although it was another company entirely who actually supervised the installation of the alarm system. Gus just dealt with locksmithing. I took him around the building and the flat and listened to his views on what to put where. I liked his easy manner and the way he laughed when I tried to be funny, and pretended not to notice when Dad's old spaniel, who was on her last legs, let out the most unbearable smell.

I think Dad always hoped I'd marry one of his authors, or at least someone in the literary world, but it just wasn't my scene.

Dad died suddenly that winter after a particularly nasty bout of flu. He was only sixty-eight. He had just given up the will to live. Gus accompanied me to the funeral, which set a few tongues wagging. I don't know if any of them recognized him from the time of the break-in. We'd conducted our courting away from the prying eyes of the office, which was a hotbed of gossip.

We held the wake in the boardroom at Lucas Cammell, and after I'd seen off the last of the mourners, Gus proposed to me by the Xerox photocopier. I took a piece of paper, wrote "Yes, I will, I do" on it, laid it face down on the copier, programmed it to make fifty copies, and pressed Start. Then we both pressed our lips to the screen and made fifty copies of that, too. We only gave each other one copy and I've often wondered what the staff made of our efforts when they came in to work the next morning.

Of course, once Dad had gone everything changed. Lucas Cammell Publishers was swallowed up into a towering modern glass building near Gray's Inn Road with several other imprints and I discovered I had nowhere to live. Dad had sold the building as well as the business.

"But you'll have money," said Gus reasonably, "if your father sold the business. What did he get for it and what did he do with the money?"

"It'll all be explained this afternoon, I expect," I told him. We were due at the lawyers for the reading of Dad's will.

Which was when I had to tell Gus about Grace.

Dad had sold the business for six million dollars, and by the time the overdraft had been paid off and the shareholders had been bought out there was just under two million left. And he'd left it all to Grace.

"Who the fuck's Grace?" exploded Gus, one of the few times I'd seen him lose his temper.

"My sister."

"Your *what?* We've known each other the best part of a year and you suddenly tell me you've got a sister. It's like one of those soap operas where they run out of plot ideas, so they bring back someone who's dead or create a sister for someone. The series has only been running for sixteen years but somehow they forgot to mention it. Where's she been, this sister? Australia?"

I had to tell him the whole story.

"I had a sister. She must have been about five or six when I was born. When my mother died she went away to live with some other people. She never came back."

"That's it? That's the whole story? Don't talk such nonsense. She just ups and runs away and no one ever sees her again? Didn't your father try to trace her?"

"Of course he did. He found her immediately. There's no mystery. She'd gone off on her own. Apparently she was always doing it. We lived on a farm and the farmhands all knew her. No one worried about her going far. But this time she did and no one noticed. Everyone was distracted by my mother being rushed off to the hospital and having me and dying. It became a bit of a legend. Grace walked right across the valley to some friends of Dad's and they just sort of kept her. He went right over but she didn't want to come back."

"But why?"

"She wanted to stay where she was. I don't know why, so don't ask me. And then I understand they wanted to adopt her and my father said they could."

"Just like that."

"Well, not immediately."

"His own daughter. He gave her away."

"I know it sounds incredible but that's

46

what Dad always told me. It wasn't as if he kept her existence a secret. I don't know how I came to know all about it. I just did. At some point it all came out, like when children learn they're adopted. Somehow they accept it. I understood I had a sister and she didn't live with us."

"Did your father see her?"

"He wouldn't. That I do know. She tried to contact him sometimes but he refused to see her. There was a file in the office about her, her progress at school. I found it once but his secretary caught me looking at it and she hid it. I always thought he never forgave her for not wanting to live with him. I only ever saw him get worked up about it one Christmas and that's what he said: that he would never forgive her.

"To me, a romantic teenager, it seemed like a passionate love affair that had gone wrong through misunderstanding, and if only they could meet it would all be all right. I used to dream of making it happen. But when I tackled him about it he used to tell me not to be so utterly stupid, that Grace had a perfectly good father somewhere, someone who had brought her up, and it would only complicate matters if he contacted her. If they never saw each other, neither of them would be hurt. But he was hurt. I know."

"Well, what about you? Didn't you ever wonder about her? Didn't you want to try and find your own sister?"

"It may sound callous, but when I was little

I didn't think about her. Don't forget I had a mother whom I had never seen and she was the one who occupied my thoughts. She was My Mother. I think I probably didn't really believe Grace existed. I'd never seen her. My father wouldn't talk about her. There were no photos hanging about the place. But as I grew older I wanted to see her for one reason: she'd known my mother. Could she remember her? That's what I thought about most."

"But didn't you try to look for her? Didn't you say she was adopted by friends of your father's? Surely it would have been easy to find her."

"It is as if you're a character in an Enid Blyton book. The Famous Five find the Missing Sister. But it's not what little girls do. There are too many other distractions. I knew Dad wouldn't like it, and now I'm scared to. The older I grew, the more I came to see Dad's side of it. What was the point of raking it all up again?"

"The lawyers must know how to contact her. They're going to have to give her all this money. And it's obvious why your father's left it to her: guilt. Guilt that he never forced the issue. Guilt that he made the excuse all these years that he couldn't forgive her, rather than the other way around. Maybe once she understood what he'd done, Grace couldn't forgive him for leaving her to be adopted, for not fighting for her, for not going and looking for her and making it up to her."

Gus was right, of course. It made me unbearably sad to think that Dad died knowing his beloved publishing house was disintegrating before his eyes and that he had never been reunited with Grace. Of course he felt guilty, but would leaving her all that money assuage that guilt even from beyond the grave? Strangely, it didn't bother me not getting much myself. I wasn't interested in money. Two million dollars seemed like Monopoly money to me. I wouldn't have known what to do with it. I was young, terribly young, very green and about to get married. What else did I need?

Now, so many years later, I had all but pushed Grace from my mind. I had never heard a word from her either before or after Dad's death.

Dad's lawyer had been cagey when I'd spoken to him about her legacy. "Of course I know how to contact her, but I'd advise against it. No point now after all this time. Messy business. Best left well alone. Leave it alone."

So I had.

But I often wondered what she was doing with herself.

I found out one morning at work, the very work Mary spurned as not being exactly a career. I made the patients cups of tea or coffee and listened with one ear to them moaning about their sprained muscles and hypermobile joints, then I sent them through to be manipulated back into shape. Sometimes I began to imagine what went on behind the closed doors. I knew they had to strip off down to their undies and then Roger Craig, the osteopath, sort of bent over them and kneaded them and moved them up and down until their bones cracked. I'd had to go in once to give him something and I'd had quite a shock. There was Mrs. Braithwaite, who was sixty if she was a day, lying on the table in a black lace bra and panties which left her Michelin tires of fat exposed, with Roger bending right over her, pulling her towards him. Her nose was about an inch from his groin.

Actually, it was Mrs. Braithwaite who was responsible for my big breakthrough with Grace. Mrs. B. didn't talk to me while she was waiting to see Roger. She always brought a library book to read. Fine by me. I could get on with typing out the invoices. I was in the midst of 'TO PROFESSIONAL SERVICES... For consultation and treatment on January 4th, 1997' when Roger buzzed through and asked me to send in Mrs. B.

"You can go in now, Mrs. Braithwaite."

"Can't I just finish my chapter?"

This was typical Mrs. B. She'd made Roger run late before and now I wasn't having any.

"No. I'm sorry. Please go straight in. He's got a very heavy morning."

She looked around at the empty waiting room (she was the first patient, for heaven's sake) and sighed. Then she moved very slowly in the direction of the consulting room. As she passed my desk, she slapped down her library book and her bag.

"Look after these for me while I'm in there."

Normally I got up to hold the door open for patients but this time I stayed put. Partly because Mrs. Braithwaite was so snotty and partly because she had put the book face down on my desk. I was looking at a photograph of the author.

It was the woman I had seen driving away from Upper Stone Farm.

It was my sister Grace.

Grace

Linda has got it into her head that she wants to see a film called *Ridicule*. I know why she wants to see it and I know she won't like it, but maybe that's me being the patronizing bitch everyone has always said I am. Or at least I imagine that's what they say. No one's ever actually come out and accused me to my face.

I blame it on the *East Hampton Star*. Linda's very much of the opinion that if she reads something in the *Star* it must be true. "A lush and ironic costume drama," said their review back at the time of the film festival last October. "Think *Liaisons Dangereuses* and *The Madness of King George* with a surprisingly contemporary feel." So Linda probably imagines it's going to be a barrel of laughs with John Malkovich and Helen Mirren. I'm convinced she doesn't realize it's about some Frog from the sticks whose peasants are suffering from swamp malaria, and how he braves the court of Louis XVI to try and petition him for permission to dam the river to stop the epidemic—only to find when he gets there that rapier wit at others' expense is the only way to get Louis's ear. Linda never reads to the end of anything. We'll go in, sit down, the movie will start, and she'll scream, "Oh, subtitles! Get me out of here."

I'm growing really fond of Linda, but when it comes to female friends I do miss Margot, no matter how much she used to infuriate me. Margot was my closest friend in London, Before I Met Him. Everything in my mind is divided into Before I Met Him and Since I Left Him. That's being a little economical with the truth. It would be more accurate to say Since He Lost Interest In Me And I Had No Alternative But To Leave. I can't remember much about the people who must have been my friends while we were together. It was as if I was subsumed into his life. His friends became my friends. Except they didn't. I just heard about them. I felt as if I knew them, but he wouldn't let me actually meet them. I suppose he was ashamed of me.

The thing about Margot was that when I first met her she was this positive, proactive woman with a terrific husband, a career, and she was so upbeat all the time it was like a tonic every time I saw her. Some of it always rubbed off on to me. I love people like Margot, people with energy who force me to rise to their standards, who won't let me sink into the depressive, inactive state to which I am prone. People who bring me out of myself. I liked the fact that she was always so impressed by me and my life. She made me feel important. Dear straightforward Margot came from a humble background—she was named for her Canadian grandmother but her father was a cab driver—and had made it into the middle classes. There I go being patronizing again.

I have this horror that one day He'll turn up at the Hamptons International Film Festival, as it's known, although I can't imagine why he should. It's no big deal. Not yet, at any rate. It's not exactly Cannes in terms of star attendance. They rope in local movie celebs like Alan Pakula and Roy Scheider. They do have this session called "A Conversation with..." and it's always a mystery guest. In the past they've had Steven Spielberg, Isabella Rossellini, Martin Scorsese, so who knows, he could turn up one day. But of course he doesn't know I'm here. I've cut off all ties with London and I never go there except when I have to fulfill some kind of contractual obligation to do publicity for one of my books.

I fell out with Margot. It was my fault. I treated her like dirt, I know I did. I lapped it up when she used to sit there wallowing in my stories of life with a celebrity. She let me cry on her shoulder when he began to shy away from my tentative questions about commitment and where were we going, even though she had predicted it from the beginning. And then she ran into problems of her own and she wasn't there for me any more and I couldn't handle it. Her twenty-five-year marriage broke up and she went to pieces. Hardly surprising. She caught him with another woman and that was it. She walked.

Then it all started to come out. The other Margot. It turned out she hadn't had sex with Alan in ten years, that he'd been having affairs all that time and she hadn't cared a bit. In fact, she'd had a fling or two herself. And anyway, there was this new man in her life. He was passionately in love with her, thought she was the greatest thing since sliced bread, called her every day.

What I had never realized about Margot was how much she exaggerated, and always on the positive side of things. She always found the best *crème fraîche,* hairdressers, fish 'n' chips shops, you name it; Margot wouldn't go anywhere else. She always made you feel as if wherever you went was a bit of a mistake, but never mind, she was here to set you straight: "Oh, you must go to so and so, sweet. Absolutely! There's no one else to touch them." She was completely black and white. The only style of dressing was Margot's: simple classic lines, almost masculine. No softness and definitely no fluffiness. And if you didn't have the perfect Margot figure, forget it.

Margot always knew best and I had depended on her for years, so it was a terrible shock to the system when I discovered that underneath it all she was terribly insecure. All the time I'd known her, what she'd actually done was ignore everything that was wrong with her life. Everything was always, "Fine, sweet, we're all hunky-dory. Couldn't be better. What about you?"

The thing that really turned me right off her was when she started seeing a therapist. A bit of the old Margot surfaced for a while: "She's the best, sweet. Honest. Far better than all those Harley Street cowboys. So wise. No one like her."

But after a while every time Margot opened her mouth every sentence she uttered began with the same three words: "My therapist says..."

"My therapist says I should let Alan continue to come and see me whenever he wants...she says I must let him down easy no matter how angry I feel. It'll be for the best in the long run."

"My therapist says I'm doing brilliantly, better than all her other patients...my therapist says I must point out to everyone my incredible qualities and not hide my light under a bushel."

"My therapist says I should sit tight and not push things, wait till I'm ready to re-enter the world." This from someone who claimed she had ruled the world for as long as I could remember.

I suppose one of my own worst traits is that I am often full of resentment. I deeply resented the fact that Margot was getting all this attention focused on her problems, whereas I was getting none. Look what I had endured: my mother had killed herself, opted not to remain alive to take care of me. And my father had never cared enough to come and reclaim me as his daughter. Of course there was nothing to stop me seeing a therapist, too— even if he or she were infinitely inferior to Margot's, as would undoubtedly turn out to be the case—and pouring out the details of my miserable childhood.

But the truth was I hadn't had a particularly miserable childhood. I had grown up in a perfectly comfortable home with two extremely attentive foster parents who never hid the fact that they were exactly that. They went to great lengths to explain to me how enormously lucky they felt to be allowed to bring me up and that it wasn't that my father didn't love me, it was just that it had not been a good time for him and they had been pleased to help him out.

As time went by it began to dawn on me that they expected him to come and get me just as much as I did, but they never came right out and said it. I understood years later that they kept him informed as to my progress and he sent them money, but he hardly ever contacted me directly except to send me the odd book. In the end I think we were all rather relieved, in an odd kind of way that we didn't like to admit, that he left us to ourselves.

Because we were always sort of in limbo, I

never expected anything from them in the way of emotional input. It's absolutely fair to say that they tried their hardest to get through to me, but I remained completely detached. I couldn't let them in, couldn't allow myself to trust anyone. That's why when I met Him and put my trust in Him it was all the more appalling when he turned out not to care a damn. I could have gone to a therapist then, but how did I know a therapist wouldn't let me down, too?

Hardly anyone knows I am Lucas Cammell's daughter except for his lawyers. I read about the American publishers Mason House buying him out. And Favor must know. I imagine he must have told her about me. I write under the name Grace McIntyre, my foster parents' name. I never even told Margot. People know I'm adopted—I haven't hidden that—but they assume I was the result of an unwanted teenage pregnancy. No one knows about my mother.

I know. I remember how I was told. My father didn't tell me. I will never forgive him for that. My future foster parents told me she had died. It was the gentle way they did it that made me know I had to stay with them. And the fact that my father always seemed to come over to the house in Wales when I was in bed. I thought he must be doing it deliberately because he didn't want to see me. I didn't find out till much later that she had killed herself. I couldn't pronounce the words postpartum depression, but I came to understand what they meant and that it was because of Favor that my mother had died.

I suppose he thought he made it up to me by leaving me everything in his will. I took his money because I didn't want Favor to have it. The lawyers tried to talk to me about her when Lucas died but I wouldn't listen.

I wouldn't go to his funeral. I told them if she ever tried to find me they were not to tell her where I was. So far they seem to have respected my wishes.

So I've become a loner, cut off from all my personal contacts in London, relying on the kindness of near strangers here on Long Island to keep me going. I'm in touch with my publishers in London but only via my New York editor, not directly.

I am only forty-two but I am determined not to trust anyone again. One of Margot's more daft announcements was, "My therapist says you can trust people but you can't necessarily rely on them." I've never heard anything so stupid. It's the other way around as far as I'm concerned. I have to rely on people all the time—to come and fix my boiler, to publish my books, to fill my cavities—but I don't trust these people as friends. I don't trust anyone. Much safer all around.

However, "Trust me," I told Linda when she wanted to know just how I knew she wouldn't like *Ridicule*. By way of compensation I said I'd go with her to a yard sale the following Saturday.

Linda lives for yard sales. I loathe them. I

have everything I need. I don't want other people's junk cluttering up my house. I can't remember what we call yard sales in England—jumble sales maybe—but it's not such a big deal. Linda scours the ads in the *Star* avidly every week.

"Early birds welcome. Everything must go. Upscale tag sale including furniture, antique clothes in perfect condition, fine china, old jewelry, leather bound books, beautiful linen. Bargains abound including twin beds, dressers, decorative items. Huge sale. All antiques."

Linda falls for it every time. My experience of yard sales is you follow the complicated directions—"after second set of speed bumps turn left at white pillars and..."—and generally wind up behind someone's barn in a soggy field where either the early birds beat you to it and walked away with all the good stuff, or "antique" just means secondhand junk. Of course, the quality doesn't really matter to Linda because she just takes everything home and paints it purple or pink.

No matter how snooty I am about her wanting to go on these jaunts, I can't help but get a kick out of how excited she gets. She's the eternal optimist looking for a discovery. She's such a good-natured girl, it's the least I can do to go along with her plans once in a while. At least she didn't do a Margot and rush into therapy when she and Artie split up.

She picked me up around nine-fifteen on Saturday and we hit Springs Fireplace Road first because it had the most yard sales advertised. Linda found a pink baseball cap and a set of steak knives for ten bucks. I assumed she would allow the knives to remain untinted but could not bring myself to ask. At the fourth sale, where she knew the people who were selling their house and moving to Florida, trestle tables were littered about the lawn with the most appalling load of rubbish I'd ever seen. Chipped ashtrays, tatty dog-eared paperbacks, bathroom scales clearly broken. They were serving coffee and cookies and I had the impression it was really more of a goodbye party for their neighbors than anything else.

I mooched around wondering how long I would have to stay before I could politely march Linda out of there. I was looking discreetly at my watch when she appeared at my elbow with a man.

Linda does this from time to time. When I first moved to the area she insisted I accompany her to the Barnes Landing Association beach party, where I was forced to wear a sticky label above my left tit that announced: HELLO, MY NAME IS GRACE MCINTYRE. Throughout the hour spent sipping warm white wine and munching on potato chips, Linda appeared every ten minutes with a variety of male senior citizens (most people who live in Barnes Landing seem to be retired) and introduced them. Inaccurately. She was a hopeless hostess. "This is Tommy," she would say, pushing forward a man whose label clearly stated: HELLO, MY NAME IS WALTER BENNETT.

She did it in supermarkets, too. I'd be pushing my cart aimlessly around the A&P in East Hampton and Linda would pop up beside the Diet Coke exclaiming, "There you are, this is Mark, Bill, Fred, whoever..."

"You have to meet someone some time," she protested when I asked her to refrain. "You can't go on hanging out in that house of yours all alone."

"Why not?" I asked perversely.

"Because you're a beauty. You're a love affair waiting to happen."

"At forty-two?"

"You look thirty-two."

I should have known from the start that pink and purple and fluffy spelled incurable romantic.

But I was not going to be introduced to anyone at a yard sale. There were limits.

I turned away. And instantly felt a tug at my sleeve.

"Grace, this is Archie. He's English. And he's a writer just like you."

"Which means he understands the need for privacy, Linda."

"But you're both English."

"I expect we went to school together."

"You did? I don't believe it. Hey, Megan, can you believe this? Grace here just met Archie and she thinks she went to school with him."

"Oh, for Christ's sake, Linda. Why don't you enroll in evening classes in irony?"

"You're being rather mean," said Archie.

Who asked him? "I'm not," I said, knowing I was.

"Listen, I hate this as much as you do. I came here to look for a hall table for my house. I didn't expect to get thrust at some woman as if I were at a pick-up joint."

"I'm not some woman. And if you want a plastic hall table with a flower motif you've come to the right place."

"Oh, look, this is ridiculous. My name's Archie Berkeley. I've just rented a place near here for the summer. I am a writer, but I write music, not books. I'm here to score a film."

He looked at me enquiringly. I was supposed to fill in the corresponding details about myself. I said nothing.

"I'm married with two kids."

"Good for you," I told him.

How much longer was this going to go on?

"Yes, it is good for me except for one thing. She's had to stay in London till the kids finish school. I wish to God she was here now because it'd be nice to introduce you to someone who could teach you a few manners. Goodbye."

I watched him pat his jacket pockets frantically until he found his cigarettes. He lit up with jerky movements without offering me one and walked away to his car. The man was utterly furious. And suddenly, because he was so angry with me, rather interesting. Only when I've managed to turn someone right off me do I begin to find him attractive.

Nothing changes.

Favor

Gus made me go.

The Bambers, one of the families we shared the house in Wales with, the one we hadn't known before, had called a meeting at their house to sort out who would pay which bill and whose turn it was to order the oil for the next six months.

"You were the one who wanted to go into this thing," he pointed out. "The least you can do is show up, take an interest."

It wasn't that I wasn't interested, but I had loathed Amanda Bamber on sight. I hadn't realized it at the first meeting. We were all so full of *joie de vivre* and excitement about the idea of renting the place, that we all acted as if we were going to be friends for life.

But Amanda Bamber had turned out to be a control freak, the kind of woman who always insists you go to her house and sit at her table and tell her how wonderful everything she does is. She had drawn up plans for all the weekends for the next six months and allocated us all occupancy on various dates. She hadn't even consulted us first. She'd just slotted us in where it was most convenient to her.

Our friends, the Latimers, were complete pushovers and said yes, of course, absolutely fine, whatever.

I looked at Gus now and said, "I rather thought we would go at Easter."

"Oh, that's impossible. Jeremy's already asked two friends from Westminster to join us," said Amanda quickly. She had to go and say that, didn't she? She had to go and rub our noses in it, her boy wonder at Westminster. Whereas my old Ned had gone to the local state school. Amanda Bamber didn't like Ned. She had this ludicrous high-minded rule that we shouldn't have television at the house in Wales, that the children should be made to go for long walks all day and play mind-improving games in the evening around the fire. Now that Ned had turned eighteen, Gus and I had decided it was fine for him to go down to Wales on his own with a couple of friends if we weren't able to get away, and there was no way Ned would endure an evening miles away from any action without a television, so he had gone out and bought a cheap secondhand one. Amanda Bamber had been furious when her Jeremy had discovered it and remained glued to it all weekend. The final straw had been when her husband Alec had sneaked into the back room and watched football one afternoon.

"What about the May Bank Holiday weekend?" asked Gus.

"Which one?" asked Amanda. "I'm an executive editor, you know. I have to be there for the Hay-on-Wye Literary Festival—we're practically on the doorstep. Unless of course,

I have to go to the ABA in America. They're desperate for me to go this year."

Oh, shut up, you boring show-off, I seethed. But something had struck me. The awful Amanda was in publishing. She might know Grace McIntyre. She might even publish her.

"Which publisher is it you work for, Amanda? Remind me."

"Mason House. They bought your father out actually, years ago."

Oh, superbitch! Well, I wasn't going to give her the satisfaction of continuing a conversation about publishing.

"I need to be there at the end of May to fit some locks at a house the other side of Knighton. Couple right here in Shepherd's Bush, been looking after their security for several years. They've just bought somewhere in the area down there. Quite a coincidence."

"Should be okay," said Amanda. "Now can we get down to the subject of bulk buying? Where's Donald?" she asked Susie Latimer. "He's always late."

"He's running here," explained Susie. Donald was a fitness fanatic. He mountain biked all over the hills around Upper Stone Farm. Without the mountain bike.

"From Wandsworth?" Even Amanda was thrown for a second. "Well, while he's not here there is just something I do want to say. I was a little put out when I called him the other day to ask him for a check for the phone and he started complaining about the bill. I mean, we agreed that we'd split it three ways. I simply can't bear all this penny-pinching and quibbling and asking for itemized bills. It's so bourgeois."

"But you made all those calls to New York when you were in that book auction that ran over a weekend," Alec Bamber reminded her. "You can be reimbursed. I don't see why the others should subsidize Mason House."

"Well, what about the firelighters?" Amanda was not to be silenced.

"What about them?"

"I bought ten bags of firelighters in Knighton last time we were down there and no one's given me a penny even though I left a note about it on the noticeboard in the hall. Would everybody please look at the noticeboard the minute they arrive to see what they owe."

"I don't understand why we have to buy firelighters when we're in the middle of the country. We step outside and we're knee-deep in kindling waiting to be collected."

"Because we're also knee-deep in yucky mud and my shoes get ruined," whined Amanda.

"But that's what welly boots are for."

"I'm not a welly boot person," said Amanda, implying that anybody who was should be pitied.

I tuned out at this point. I simply could not handle it. It would go on like this for another hour with everyone bitching and moaning about who'd eaten whose Branston Pickle and why didn't anybody ever remember to keep the downstairs bathroom stocked with toilet paper? In any case I wanted to think about Grace and how I was going to find her.

We'd been up in Wales for the weekend that had just passed and I'd been thinking about her all the time. They were in the midst of lambing and the lights were on in the barns through the night. Little lambs, some with long black socks, scampered after their mothers, disappearing underneath them, tails wagging while they fed. The goats were also at it and there were two billys and a nanny born while we were there. There was fencing going on everywhere, and the men huddled under trees during the freak hailstorms that came at us over the hills.

Thank God the shooting season was over so we didn't have to worry about Ned, who had a habit of wandering dreamily into the forests on long, reflective walks, straight into enclosures full of pheasants.

Once the keeper had come to see us in a fury. "Do you want your son to be killed?" he had asked Gus.

"If you hear them shooting, Ned, stand quite still till they move on. Don't move whatever you do," Gus had told Ned.

"What do you mean 'stand still'?" the keeper had shouted. "He shouldn't be in there at all. He should sit still. In here. Don't let him move outside the house—that would be the safest."

"Maybe he could get himself shot and we could eat him for supper. Creepo casserole. Local delicacy," Mary commented last weekend. She was pissed off by the fact that Ned was allowed to go down there on his own and she wasn't.

"Fuck off," said Ned.

"Fuck off yourself. You're so moody. He's got a girlfriend, Mum, did you know? He's in love."

"Have you, darling? Do I know her?"

"No you don't because she doesn't exist. Mary's talking crap, Mum."

"What about that girl I saw you with in the back row of the cinema the other night? Watching *Shine*. You were all over her."

"It was a sad movie. She was crying. I was comforting her."

So there was someone. What a lucky girl, whoever she was, I thought, to be comforted by dear, sweet Ned. I could only assume he was probably crying as much as the girl.

"Oh, so you *were* with a girl, then?" Mary was whooping away.

"Is it a crime? Haven't you got anything better to do than spy on me? Okay, she's a nice girl and I like her. All I did was take her to the movies and take her home. Pretty tame behavior compared to your dirty-stop-out habits."

"That's enough," I snapped. But he had a point. I'd been worrying about Mary for some weeks now. She was never in the house. She went straight from school to do her homework at her friend Shannon's house. Shannon was bad news. She had been raised in Bristol by a hippie mother who ran some kind of community project and was bombed out of her head on drugs most of the time. Shannon's father had rescued her four years earlier and brought her to London to live with him and his new wife. The trouble was, Shannon's stepmother had no interest in her whatsoever, and in any case never came home from her high-powered office job until eight in the evening, by which time Shannon, undoubtedly accompanied by Mary, was out running round London.

You only had to take one look at Shannon to know she had almost certainly lost her virginity the minute she entered her teens. She was multiply pierced in the nasal area, her clothes and hair reeked of cigarette smoke, and if she ever so much as sat down in our house, she was always so out of it she invariably rolled over and went to sleep. Mary wouldn't hear a word said against her and if I ever uttered the remotest hint of criticism I was instantly given a lecture on Shannon's miserable childhood and how we, the privileged middle classes, should make allowances for those less fortunate.

"Well, so long as this making allowances doesn't involve underage drinking, drugs, and smoking..." I made my usual bleat.

"Making allowances at the taxpayers' expense, more likely," grumbled Gus before I could stop him.

"Well, if the Tories get in again..." began

Mary, then stopped. We had an election looming and she was in a quandary about it. It was futile pointing out that she was too young to vote. Mary was violently anti-Tory, but the Spice Girls had come out for John Major. I knew she secretly admired the Spice Girls although she would rather die than admit it to Shannon. Shannon was of the opinion that Tupac Shakur or Snoop Doggy Dog should run for President of Great Britain. The fact that the former had been shot dead six months earlier and the latter had been arrested for murder, both were American, and anyway we didn't have presidents in the UK, didn't seem to enter into the equation.

Needless to say I had no idea who these people were until the kids enlightened me. Ironically I was also indebted to them for filling me in, quite by accident, on a major piece of the Grace puzzle. After seeing her picture on the back of Mrs. Braithwaite's library book I rushed straight to the library and borrowed as many Grace McIntyre books as I could find. I'd heard of Grace McIntyre, of course, but I'd never realized she was also Grace Cammell, my sister.

Her novels were pretty much my sort of thing: romantic weepies, a tad on the light side for my taste—the slurpy artwork on the jackets had always put me off buying or borrowing them in the past—but entertaining enough. Yet as I read my way through them searching for clues I couldn't help sensing an irritation in the author's voice, the feeling that she was writing down to her readers. I don't know what it was, but every now and then, say in about four places in each book, there was a piece of really superior writing which didn't belong, writing that had a darker side, a fierce, passionate quality to it that said, "Here's what I could do if I was allowed to; here's what I'm really like."

Gus was not at all happy about my plan to track down my sister.

"Leave it alone," he mumbled from under his pillow late one night as I was about to turn out the light.

Gus always went to sleep before I did. We rarely had sex anymore. I'm not sure how many married couples do who have been together as long as we have. Maybe I'm just consoling myself because I miss it, but Gus is always so tired and we just seemed to get out of the habit once the business began to take up so much of his time and energy. It's not exactly the perfect aphrodisiac when you're in the midst of tender foreplay and the answering machine by the bed blares a message into the room: "This is Carol McFarlane from 47 Crawley Road and me and George have just got back from the pub to find we've forgotten our keys and I can't remember who we left the spares with. I'm in a phone booth down the road but George is waiting outside the door and it'd be great if you could come over and let us in..." Eleven o'clock at night but all part of the service. The only one who wasn't getting serviced was me.

"Leave what alone?"

71

Gus has an odd way of sleeping with his head under the pillow instead of on it. How he manages never to suffocate himself I can't imagine. "That. Her." I'd been reading one of Grace's books and he nudged it off the bed and onto the floor with his foot through the duvet. "Leave her alone. Don't go raking it all up."

It was what he'd said when my father's will had been read.

"But why not?"

"I don't know. I've got a funny feeling about it, that's all."

He wouldn't say more. It wasn't his style. It must have meant a lot to him that he said anything at all. He usually never interferes—keeps his thoughts to himself unless I pester him. And I often do because he has good instincts. He'll pass up a customer for no logical reason that he can pinpoint, just a "feeling" he has, and then we'll learn that another locksmith who did get their business is still waiting to be paid six months after the job has been done.

There was another bone of contention between us. The business had reached a critical point. Gus either really had to go for it, embrace all the new technology and aim for more business with a higher profit margin by pursuing commercial installations—or he could stay as he was. If he did branch out it would mean we would have to contend with much hungrier and more financially secure competition. He would be up against The Big

Guys. He wanted to do that, he was ready for it, but he was understandably nervous. He wanted me by his side; he wanted me to come back and work for him like in the early days.

I wasn't so sure I liked the idea. Maybe Mary's barbed remarks about my not having a proper career had hit home and it was bad timing on Gus's part that he should suggest I should come back and be his sidekick so soon afterwards. I can't imagine what it is I want to do, if anything, but the kids will be leaving home in a few years and maybe I just don't want to get tied into the security business when there might be something else I could tackle, something, dare I say it—although never within Gus's hearing—a little more exciting? After all, I had a sister who was a successful writer. Who knew what hidden talents had lain buried in my genes?

Predictably, Mary was really scathing about Grace's books when she came across them lying all over the kitchen table waiting to be returned to the library.

"Oh, Mum, how low can you sink? This is utter trash. Formulaic crap, and dated, too."

"How would you know?" I retorted, determined to defend Grace. "Have you read them?"

"As if? Shannon and I rented the video of *Air Male*. It was so schmaltzy Shannon was ill. I just don't get it. Why does she write this junk? It's not as if she's an idiot."

I held my breath. "You know her?"

"Well, I don't actually know her personally, no. But I know of her."

"She is a famous author, of course," I said proudly. Any moment now I could impress Mary for once and tell her Grace McIntyre was her aunt.

"Not because of that. I don't care about her writing—the less said about that the better." This from someone who had never read a word of it. "She was Harry Fox's girlfriend for a while and he wouldn't pick anyone stupid."

Even Ned was shocked that I had never heard of Harry Fox.

"Mum, Harry Fox is seriously cool. Haven't you seen *Craven Image?*"

"No."

"Haven't you even heard of it?"

"Don't think so. What is it? A thriller?"

"It's not a book, Mum, it's a film. *Craven Image* was only the most mega-brilliant film since *Trainspotting* and *Shallow Grave*. Harry Fox is the new Danny Boyle. He's just amazing."

I'd heard of *Trainspotting* and it sounded like something I should steer well clear of. All those needles!

"So this Harry Fox," I ventured, "he's what, quite young?"

"No, not really. He might even be thirty by now." My children believed you were eligible for your pension once you'd reached your thirties.

And Grace had to be in her early forties.

"But Grace McIntyre's older!"

"Well, that was what all the fuss was about, Mum. He turned up at the premiere of *Craven*

Image with this Older Woman in tow, and the press made a big thing of it. And he came out with all that crap about how older women were better value, and how much he was learning from this Grace woman. No one believed him for a second. We all reckoned it was a publicity stunt to pull in an older audience for his movies. Old ladies didn't like *Trainspotting* apparently."

"Old ladies. Oh, great, Ned, thanks. I'm your mother, Ned. Not your grandmother."

"Yeah, maybe, but you're not exactly into today's popular culture, are you, Mum?"

I hate that phrase, popular culture, but I suppose Ned has a point.

"So are they still together, Grace McIntyre and Harry Fox?"

"Dunno." Ned had lost interest.

"No, they're not," said Mary. "He's shagging some Irish actress now. She's going to be in his next film. It's being made in America."

Shagging was a Shannon expression. I had known it was only a matter of time before it became a household word in our home.

So how far had I got? My older sister had had a cult-movie director at least ten years her junior for a lover. Now he'd dumped her she was probably crying her eyes out somewhere. She needed me.

The next day I called her publishers.

"I'd like to talk to someone about Grace McIntyre," I told the girl on the switchboard.

"Is that Sales, Publicity, or Editorial?"

"Editorial," I said, although I hadn't a clue.

"Hello," said a sophisticated voice.

"Hello, I'd like to speak to someone about Grace McIntyre."

"Well, I'm Serena Hay-Miller. I'm Lucy Knight's editorial manager. Lucy's her editor."

And Serena, I guessed, was just her secretary but too grand to say so.

"Well, can I speak to Lucy, please?"

"What is it in connection with?"

"Grace McIntyre." Hadn't I just said that?

"Yes, but what is it you want to ask Lucy about Grace McIntyre?"

"I need to get in touch with her."

"Are you a friend of hers or just a member of the public?" This girl had a real sense of diplomacy.

"No, I'm her—"

I stopped.

What was I supposed to say? *Actually I'm her sister but I have no idea where she is. In fact I've never even met her.*

"Are you still there?"

"Yes, I'm still here. Can you give me her address, please? I'd like to write to her."

"We can't give out authors' addresses, I'm afraid. Why don't you write to her care of us and we'll forward it."

I thanked her and spent the next few days attempting to draft a letter. It was impossible. *Dear Grace, I am your long-lost sister... Dear Grace McIntyre, I'm a great admirer of yours and by the way there's something you ought to know....*

I couldn't do it. I had to meet her face-to-face. I called the publishers again but this time I passed on Serena and asked to be put through to the publicity department, only to be given more of the same but with an additional rather suspicious twist.

"We can't divulge authors' addresses, I'm afraid. Not our policy. Particularly not Grace McIntyre's, anyway."

"Why particularly not hers?"

"It's stamped all over her file. She's had a phobia about keeping her address a secret ever since all that hog-ha with Harry Fox. She's terrified the press will come after her again. Not that the British hacks are likely to waste time trying to track her down in the wilds of New England or wherever she is. Anyway, we never deal with her direct, always through her New York publishers."

"Who are?"

"Who did you say you were?"

Bit late in the day to ask. I had lucked into someone who was naturally indiscreet. Total lack of diplomacy in the editorial department matched by running off at the mouth in Publicity. Grace should change publishers.

"I'm one of her biggest fans. She lives in America, you said?"

"Did I? You're not a journalist, are you?"

"I'm just a housewife. I've read all her books. I want to meet her. I want to tell her how fantastic I think she is. Is that a crime?" I tried to sound peevish.

"Look," said the publicity girl, "I'll let you into a secret. She's coming over next month to do publicity for her latest book. I only know that because it's in her contract. She hates publicity with a passion but there are thousands just like you panting to meet her, so we have it written into her contract that she comes over every other book. She won't do TV but she'll be doing signings. We'll be advertising in the *Standard* if you're in London. Keep an eye out for them. You could come and see her then."

I wrote the dates down in my diary. London. Bath. Bournemouth. Manchester. Edinburgh. Dublin. I asked Roger for a week off from the osteopathic practice and I began to wonder what kind of credible excuse I could cook up for poor Gus to explain why I suddenly had the urge to go gallivanting around the country.

I stared at her face on the back of the library books—dark, soulful, exquisite. Where had I seen that face before, apart from that fleeting glimpse at Upper Stone Farm? It was almost as if I already knew Grace McIntyre.

That night I was slicing tomatoes and onions for a salad when I was struck by the sight of Mary sitting watching television. It was one of those rare evenings when she had decided to grace us with her presence. She was totally absorbed. She was watching *Tomorrow's World*, and an American archaeologist who had spent years studying the mummified bodies of four hundred ancient Africans was expounding on the age-old debate as to whether men were stronger than women. I knew she'd turned on to catch the National Lottery, which had just

78

started to go twice weekly, but her attention had been caught and she was gripped.

Get Mary away from the dreaded Shannon and this was what happened, and not nearly often enough for my liking. I loved this side of her. I winced when she reprimanded me for being so far from the cutting edge all the time, but I admired her often-passionate interest in issues such as the one she was watching now. Her sharp tongue was silent, her features in repose. And suddenly I realized where I had seen Grace's face before. It was right here in my own home.

Mary was very like Grace.

But Mary was nothing like Gus or me. The changeling jokes were now a thing of the past, but there'd been plenty of them at one stage. No one could figure out from which side of the family Mary got her looks.

Well, now I knew.

She didn't look like Dad. So if Mary resembled Grace but not me, then there was only one person whose face she could have: that of the mother I had never known.

Grace

Iam being stalked.

I am in England for my book tour and everyone is in a real tizz about it. Except for me.

It started in London apparently. I had a week of signings there before I went to Manchester and then on to Edinburgh. There was a sighting of the stalker in Waterstones, Deansgate, in Manchester but nothing in Edinburgh.

It's a woman, so I'm told. They say she looks harmless enough. Medium height. Pretty ordinary looking although her hair's supposed to be very pretty, thick and fair with a fringe and falling to her shoulders in a heavy bob. She's in her late thirties. No make-up. Jeans and a High Street jacket. I'm told she looks like your average housewife.

She's been sighted again in Bath. I suppose it was a bit of a long haul to Edinburgh, but if I could make it, why couldn't she? I'm becoming quite proprietorial about my stalker.

They decided she was a stalker when they noticed she never came up and bought a book, never asked for anything to be signed. Yet she's always there, watching me.

I say they, but it's really only the irritating publicity girl who's on the tour with me.

She's the one who's going on about the stalker. It's embarrassing. She's so stupid, I can barely remember her name. She's short and fluffy and talks about herself all the time. It's a form of shyness, I know, and in a macabre kind of way I'm fascinated by her never-ending stream of trivia about her fish in a tank and who's been feeding them while she's away with me and isn't it stupid to have pets when you have a job that takes you out on the road so much? Not once does she ask me if I have a pet. Not once does she inquire about my life on Long Island. Of course I'm relieved beyond belief, and I begin to wonder has she been briefed to steer clear of personal details?

I wonder what it says on my file. Is there a record of the time when I reduced the last girl to tears on the platform of Birmingham New Street by shouting at her to mind her own business when she asked me if it was true about me and Harry Fox? It was precisely because I had no idea whether Harry and I were an item that I was in such a state of agony, so wired I was shouting at anybody about the slightest thing.

I will never forget that book tour and the way I raced back to the hotel after each stupid TV talk show or radio phone-in to see if Harry had called. We had kissed. Once. But I didn't know if he meant it. If it was going to go further.

Now here I am being stalked by a woman. They'd love it in America. Publicity-wise it'd be a real story. This woman is probably in love with me. Overnight I could become Patricia Cornwell, Martina Navratilova and Ellen DeGeneres all rolled into one. I should do something with this, exploit it, get a photo opportunity with my stalker.

She doesn't make it to Dublin but she's back again in Bournemouth. By now I'm crazy to see her for myself but I'm too busy signing, sitting at those ridiculously exposed tables in spaces cleared in bookshops, surrounded by posters of me grinning away—why ever did I allow that photo to be used?—and politely asking each purchaser of my book for their name, how do you spell that? With a "y" or an "ie"? Oh, it's your sister and this one's for your mother, and she's read all my books, oh, how nice. After two hundred signatures they all merge into a sea of middleclass housewives.

I made an executive decision. If my stalker turns up at Harrods then I'll confront her.

The night before the Harrods signing they called up to my room from the front desk and said they had a Miss Harris to see me.

I didn't know a Miss Harris and I certainly wasn't expecting one. I was about to ask them to send her away when I remembered.

Margot.

Harris was her maiden name and she must have resumed using it.

"A Miss Margot Harris?"

There was a pause.

"Yes."

"Please send her up."

I was on the seventh floor. In the time it took Margot to come up in the elevator I went into panic alert. Our last meeting had been confrontational. Harsh words had been exchanged. I hadn't spoken to her since.

We'd had a row about Harry. Naturally. All the bad moments in the last eighteen months could be blamed on Harry, whether he was responsible for them or not.

Harry entered my life when I walked into a hotel suite for a meeting with a producer called Irwin Heller who wanted to buy the film rights to one of my books. Following the massive success of *Air Male*, producers and money men always came sniffing around my books no matter how trashy they were.

I had always had a bit of a tussle with myself about the kind of books I wrote. In the beginning, of course, when I was writing *Air Male*, I was on cloud nine. I had everything before me. It was all a bit of a dream, and then when it came true and I made so much money I was seduced into continuing with more of the same. I think it began to hit me around the third or fourth book that what I was writing was meaningless trash, but when I tentatively broached the notion with my editor of trying something different for the next book she threw a monumental fit and predicted a drastic drop in sales. I was young. My life was relatively easy. Why change it?

I didn't. But from then on I did begin to feel

uneasy each time I started a new book, each one worse than the last because my heart was no longer in it.

So when Irwin Heller came on the scene I wasn't quite sure what to do. I knew for a fact that he was one of the prime exponents of some of the more dreadful TV miniseries that had tainted our screens in the eighties, and for this reason alone I wasn't about to let him get his hands on anything of mine, although on the surface my books would appear to be perfect fodder for him. Yet I was intrigued by the thought of meeting a Hollywood producer, even if he was a television producer. It might lead to something, not necessarily with him. I could have just said no, go away, but it was at a time when I was bored, both personally and professionally, to the extent that I was more or less prepared to meet anyone.

He was American, short, balding, a red-haired Jew with pale skin and freckles. He had the customary Rodeo Drive made-over wife with coiffed hair and red nails and far too smartly dressed for the middle of the afternoon. She kept wandering into the sitting room of his suite from the bedroom, wafting Giorgio, a scent I particularly disliked.

Harry Fox was the writer Irwin Heller was thinking of hiring to script my book for him. He was sitting on the sofa in front of the coffee table when I arrived. Irwin was in the midst of pitching my book to him and I couldn't help noticing that Harry was looking rather bored. He stood up to meet me and he was tall. He whipped off a pair of chunky black square glasses before shaking my hand as if it were a kid glove and I saw he had soft, gentle eyes. He smiled and said, "How do you do?" like a well-brought-up little boy. There is a small elastic band of resistance somewhere inside of me that protects my feelings from men like him, and I felt it snap and disintegrate.

It was his manners. He must have thought my book was a load of tripe. God knows, I did. But he never referred to it in anything but the politest of terms. He was a diplomat to the end. Halfway through the meeting I think we both knew we were wasting our time. He caught my eye and he didn't wink or anything crass like that but he looked at me. We had an opportunity to extricate ourselves, but then Mrs. Heller reappeared and it was the way he treated her that made me begin to ache for him.

He stood up. He poured her a cup of tea. He turned towards her. He lit her cigarette. And he listened to her prattle on about Harvey Nichols. He knew all about the collections, and not just the young, hip designers. She even took him into the bedroom to show him her new Ungaro. It wasn't as if he was even smartly dressed himself. He was wearing a pale pink shirt with a button-down collar hanging loose over a pair of not entirely pristine beige jeans and sneakers. Yet the panther-like grace with which he moved made him appear to be wearing a beautifully cut suit. Mrs. Heller was putty in his hands.

I left with him, of course. We shared a taxi and when we drew up outside the flat where I was living I found I couldn't bear to let him go and I asked him upstairs for a drink. I noticed that, tactfully, he avoided talking about the fact that we were both writers. Instead we exchanged opinions of recent films we had both seen—he dismissed the Coen brothers as "wannabe auteurs" and praised *The Fisher King,* which I had loathed, but I kept quiet about that.

I asked him if he had dinner plans. I asked him. I had no shame. Of course he had dinner plans. Undoubtedly with a twenty-one-year-old whose arse had twenty years to go before it dropped. When he left I told myself I had escaped from potential indignity and went to bed with a mug of cocoa laced with whisky.

I saw him two days later in Harvey Nichols. I was about to go off on a book tour and hadn't been able to lay hands on a single pair of tights without a run in them. He was with Mrs. Heller. I would learn later that she had called and invited him to lunch and caught him on the hop so he couldn't think of an excuse. He mouthed the word "Help!" at me across a stand piled high with DKNY hosiery. I rushed over and we did a fair amount of "Hello" and "Fancy seeing you" until Mrs. Heller was obliged to ask me to join them.

Over the coffee Harry pleaded a meeting at three and asked if he could drop me somewhere. Once in the cab he said he didn't have a meeting, and as we went around a corner he was thrown against me. He took the opportunity to clasp my chin, turn my face towards his, and place his mouth on mine. He was what I call a bruiser. No gentle exploration with the tip of his tongue, but forceful kissing, mauling my lips. It excited me so much I was literally shaking.

And I had to push him away and tell him I had to go home and pack for five days out of town on a book tour, the same tour during which I crushed that publicity girl at New Street Station.

He had the upper hand from the beginning even though he was twelve years younger. He treated me rather as if I were a friend of his mother's. His manners were impeccable at all times and he had complete control of me because of this. He'd booked a table at such and such, was that all right with me, would nine-thirty be too late, was I tired, could he be of any help with any of my errands during the day? And then, in bed, he behaved like an animal, ferocious, thrusting me this way and that with no regard for my comfort or dignity. But I loved it. He was a coarse lover, pulverizing me with his body and never apologizing for the bruises he left on my skin.

Then, when the sex was over, he would revert once again to the well-brought-up schoolboy, politely complimenting me on my new haircut, shoes, scent.

He always came to my place for sex. He claimed to live alone, but when I called him at home, young raucous voices answered the phone and shouted for him over loud music. They never asked who was calling, almost as if they didn't care. I tried not to think about the other calls he received, from younger, fresher women. He assured me there were none. I was special. It wasn't his style to spread himself around. He was lucky to have met me when he did. So many of his friends were being taken for a ride by callous—and callow—young women who competed with them professionally, emasculated them, put them down sexually. He was fortunate, he felt, to have someone who was secure in herself, someone who was relaxed about her femininity, someone who had nothing to prove.

I fell for it. Why wouldn't I? I waited patiently for the day when he would suggest we look for a place together. I cooked him extravagant suppers, never noticing that he was taking me out less and less. I listened as he described the progress on the screenplay he was writing, taking care never to mention my own writing for fear of boring him.

No one had heard of Harry Fox back then. And while *Craven Image* was being filmed I sat in London and waited for his phone calls from location. When it became an instant box office success and he an overnight cult sensation, I was thrilled for him, recalling my own euphoria when *Air Male* was published— although the two works could hardly be mentioned in the same sentence. *Craven Image* was art. Of course. I understood that. The reviews confirmed it.

I was so proud of him at the premiere, walking into the Odeon Haymarket holding his hand, ignoring the incredulous looks from the public, smiling at the photographers. I laughed when someone called out, "Is that your mother or your older sister?" Now we were a couple. Now we would live together.

The woman I lunched with the following week was the kind of woman I despise more than any other: a gossipy, indiscreet, stupid woman who had no idea of the kind of harm and pain she inflicted on those of us who were by nature private people. To give her her due she had been out of the country for two months and she did not know that I had been the woman who had accompanied Harry Fox to the premiere of his movie. She missed the massive press coverage in the papers the next day speculating on his affair with an older woman, and nobody had told her about it. It was just one of those things.

I barely knew her. I had met her at a friend's and she had suggested getting together for lunch and I'd agreed. She was a fashion person of some description and the lunch was supposed to be about how she could get me a discount with one of my favorite designers. I didn't need a discount. I had money. It was that pointless, our lunch.

And what I will never know is whether I would eventually have been even more hurt had we not met for lunch, or whether I would still be with Harry.

She chattered on about this and that and then,

I suppose inevitably, she asked, "Have you seen *Craven Image?*"

It was a perfectly natural question. Everyone was talking about it. She didn't wait for my answer but ploughed on in between forkloads of *tonno e fagioli*. She spoke with her mouth full. I was disgusted just watching her.

"Isn't it amazing? The guy's a genius and I hear he's only a kid. And that's not all I hear. Cute as hell, they say. Fucks like a rabbit. A friend of mine had him for lunch yesterday."

My gazpacho was spicy anyway but suddenly it began to erupt in sharp darts of fire in my throat and stomach. All I had to do was change the subject. But I couldn't. I said nothing. I waited. Not for long.

"She met him at the party after the premiere and he took her number. Called her the next day. He's seen her three times already. She says he likes it pretty rough, throws her about a bit in bed, but she's always liked that. He's got this mole in the middle of his chest apparently, makes him look as if he has three nipples. And he coughs when he comes, almost chokes. Very strange sound. She couldn't stop going on about it."

She was leaning forward, whispering across the table, a piece of tuna stuck between her teeth.

I don't know how I managed to listen to her inanities for the rest of lunch, but I did. I was in shock. I recognized everything she'd said about him. That strange choking sound he made, it was unique.

I had been living in a cocoon, imagining that he was mine and mine alone. I stepped out of it the very next day and began to put out tentative feelers for information about him. Suddenly everyone seemed to know someone who had slept with Harry Fox. No one really knew about our affair because we hadn't made it public until the premiere, and then they just assumed I was a new item on his agenda. But the most hurtful moment of all was when I went crying to Margot.

"What do you expect, you silly cow? He's a man—they deposit it everywhere," she told me crudely.

"But I never knew."

"Well, now you do."

"But can't you understand what I'm going through?"

"What you're going through? What do you think I'm going through? Twenty-five years of marriage down the tube. You get back what you give out." This was one of Margot's favorite expressions, handed down, I suspect, by her therapist, although quite how she applied it to herself and her marriage I never quite managed to work out.

"Obviously you were such a doormat with Mr. Harry Fox that he felt he could go and wipe his feet wherever he liked. You've only yourself to blame."

She was as harsh and aggressive as only somebody in great pain could be, but I couldn't appreciate that. I lashed out at her.

"Why do you have to be such an unfeeling

bitch, Margot? I thought you'd be the one person who would understand. You were the one who walked out on Alan because he fucked around. You've become so self-obsessed. Only you have problems. The rest of us couldn't begin to understand what you're going through. Over and over again you tell us, you've got the monopoly on hurting. Go on, say it: I've never been married so I wouldn't have a clue what you've been through. Betrayal is betrayal, Margot, married or unmarried. I feel you're betraying me by not supporting me when I'm hurt like this. Okay, so you've been through the mill, but at least have the grace to acknowledge you're not the only one. Pain's not something you can be competitive about—my pain's greater than yours, so shut up and listen to me. It doesn't work like that."

"Oh, stop whining," said Margot. "You're always whining."

I couldn't believe this. For months I'd listened to Margot complaining, and now when I'd had the biggest shock of my recent existence she accused me of whining. And she wasn't finished.

"You're pathetic, Gracie. You let a guy walk all over you and then you start moaning about it. You're so naive."

"And you're fucking Pollyanna," I screamed at her. "You think just because you've been seeing this wretched therapist you're okay now, but you're not. You're ten times more fucked up than I am and always will be because you just won't face up to it."

I was being horribly cruel and knew I would feel really bad about it afterwards. The trouble was, I knew she was right about me being naive. I was one of those people who float along in a bit of a dream and then I get a hard knock and wise up. But how many more hard knocks would hit me?

"Now who's getting competitive?" yelled Margot. "This conversation is going nowhere. I'm leaving."

And that was the last time I saw her. Shortly after that I left London, ran away from the pain of Harry's infidelities.

Now Margot was on her way up to see me.

Margot's very sexy. She looks like a monkey: small, lithe, and olive-skinned. She came running along the hotel corridor from the elevator and hugged me as if nothing had happened between us.

I'd forgotten this side of Margot. She'd made so many U-turns during our friendship, I was surprised her head still faced the same way as her toes.

"Hi, sweet, I heard you on the radio and realized you must be in town. Your publishers told me where to find you. Anyone would think you were the Pope, they were guarding your whereabouts so closely, but I managed to persuade them I was your best friend."

I'd only done one radio interview (signs of my waning popularity?) and if she'd caught it she must have heard my reaction when the presenter asked me—right out of the blue—if I was going to see Harry Fox while I was in town.

"Whatever for?" I'd shot back at him before I could stop myself. Sounding bitter. On air. Live. He'd left it alone after that.

"So how are you, Margot? Better?"

"Absolutely fine, sweet. Nothing wrong with me. It's you I'm worried about. How are you?"

Oh no, she wasn't going to get away with that, not after our last encounter.

"I'm fabulous," I said. "Are you still seeing your therapist?"

"Was I seeing a therapist? Oh, her. That was ages ago. Didn't really need her. Just a phase I went through before I discovered aromatherapy."

Next minute she'd be telling me she'd never had a problem with her marriage.

"And Alan?"

"He's fine, sweet. See him all the time. We get on really well. Better than we ever did when we were married. So tell me what you've been up to."

She might just as well have not seen me for a couple of weeks instead of going on two years. As I described my new life to her I couldn't help noticing a rather bored expression emerging on her face.

"So you're there all by yourself? No men? No action?" She was looking a bit incredulous. "Poor sweet, you really are having a miserable time, aren't you? Come here, let me give you a hug."

Suddenly it was my turn to be incredulous. When we'd last met she hadn't wanted

94

to know about my unhappiness. Now here she was more or less telling me what a sad person I was. And when she put her arms around me, to my horror I began weeping on her shoulder.

"Poor old sausage," she said, stroking my hair, "what a mess you're in. If only I'd known." I hadn't actually known myself until she told me. "I'd better come and sort you out over there on Long Island."

"Oh yes, come and stay," I heard myself say, "whenever you like."

Once she'd gone I sat in front of the television in my hotel room, too stressed out even to undress. We were friends again. I should have been pleased, but all I felt was a sense of unease. Somehow Margot had regained the upper hand, yet why should I care? I'd loved her energy in the past, but now it seemed to be channelled in a different, somehow rather threatening, direction. Why did I always feel this competitive element to our friendship?

I was still worrying about it as I sat at the little table in the book department of Harrods. It was all rather ludicrous. There was a cordoned-off bit and the public had to file past me and present their copies of my book for signature. There was something of the factory conveyor belt about the whole affair. A Harrods official summoned the next person forward as the publisher's publicity girl took a book from the large pile on the table and opened it in front of me at the title page. I looked up, smiled, if I remembered, then signed my name.

"It's her," hissed the publicity girl suddenly.

My stalker. She was finally breaking cover and bringing a book up to be signed. Would she whip out a knife and stab me?

"Hello, what's your name?"

I looked up at the woman. She had a nice face. Open. Warm. Nothing special about the features, although attractive enough. But they'd been right about her hair. It was extraordinary. Thick. Fair. A veritable crowning glory. If Robert Redford had hair down to his shoulders it would look like this.

And it was strangely familiar.

"Could you sign it to Ned. My son. Please."

To Ned with best wishes, Grace McIntyre, I wrote.

"Your son reads my books?" I smiled up at her. I'd definitely seen her somewhere before. "How old is he?"

"Well, no. He's eighteen. But he ought to. He will." She seemed confident.

"An eighteen-year-old boy who likes my books. That'll be a first," I told her. She was staring at me. She seemed about to say something, then she moved on.

It was as I was riding out to Heathrow to fly back to America, brooding over the bad reviews I'd received—all part and parcel of being a popular author—that I remembered where I'd seen her before. In Wales, coming out of Upper Stone Farm.

She'd seen me there. She'd been stalking me ever since. For a second I was quite scared.

She wouldn't follow me to America, would she?

Favor

None of my family was speaking to me. This was not something that had ever happened to me before, so I was a bit thrown. Not that I could really blame them.

Gus had shown a rare flash of anger when I announced my plan to follow my sister to her book signings. His anger manifests itself in a kind of quiet rage. He doesn't yell or shout. He just goes very quiet and glares at me. I think he imagines he looks threatening—which he couldn't in a million years—but I'm always so miserable to see him angry at all that it generally has a pretty devastating effect on me.

"Gus," I pleaded with him, "if you suddenly discovered you had a long-lost brother wouldn't you want to go and find him?"

"Yes."

"Well, then?"

"I'd want to. It's only natural to be curious, but I'm not so sure it'd be such a good idea. It's not as if you haven't always known about your sister's existence. I can't understand why you suddenly want to hook up with her. If you'd been supposed to meet, it would have happened by now."

Halfway through the week I came back from Bath to find a note saying he'd gone to Wales to attend to some work there and wouldn't be back for the family reunion. Underneath the note was a folder about the Associated Locksmiths of America convention in New York later that year. America leads the way in both locksmithing and alarm technology. Was Gus planning to attend? By leaving the literature where I was bound to see it, was he trying to tell me something? I'd heard him talk about ALOA, as it was known, which made the children laugh and sing it out like an Indian love call.

I picked up the phone to call him in Wales and then replaced it. I wanted to talk to him face to face, make him understand about Grace. It could wait.

Now I was back but Gus wasn't. He'd told the children to tell me he'd be back in a day or two. This wasn't like him at all. He never spoke to me via the children.

Mary was so disgusted that I'd gone traipsing around the country after such a trashy writer that she would barely even say hello. At Gus's request, I had not yet revealed Grace's identity so I suppose it did look a bit odd for me suddenly to turn into an ardent romantic-fiction fan.

As for Ned, his main beef was that I hadn't managed to elicit a single piece of gossip for him about Harry Fox.

But there was another reason I wanted Gus home so I could talk to him; something that had upset me so much that I buried it for most of the day, only allowing it to surface when I felt strong enough to face it.

It was odd. I had expected to be in a state of shock seeing my sister close up for the first time. For the first couple of signing sessions I just stood at the back and observed. Her startling resemblance to Mary somehow brought me closer to her. Otherwise I think I might have been scared away on the first day. She was so urbane. So poised. So charming to her readers, smiling like a real celebrity. Yet as I watched I sensed an irritation that surfaced every now and then on her face. Then back came the smile. She was easily bored. She hid it well, but then no one else was watching her the way I was. She didn't like the publicity girl, I could see that.

I was dispassionate about her at this stage. I felt a bizarre sense of power over her. I knew who she was but she didn't know about me. And then, after I'd been to three signings, I noticed something else. Once she was "off duty," a sadness crept over her face when she thought no one was looking at her anymore. That's when I resolved to follow her to Bath, to check into the same hotel, to watch her.

I felt completely stupid sitting alone at the hotel bar like a hooker waiting to be picked up. I'd seen her stride through the lobby and disappear into the elevator barely able to speak a civil word to the wretched publicity girl. What would happen about dinner? Would they be stuck with each other at a table for two in the dining room? Or would they go out? In fact, it was a third option I hadn't thought of: the publicity girl went out about an hour later looking suspiciously as if she might have been crying. And Grace must have ordered room service. At any rate she never came into the dining room. I sat there like a lemon at a table for one nibbling pâté and Dover sole. And by the time I realized she wasn't going to appear, and that if I wanted to have a sisterly reunion that night I was going to have to pry her room number out of Reception and go upstairs and confront her, I'd also realized I'd lost my nerve. On a whim I decided to chicken out altogether and catch the last train back to London.

Which was how I came to let myself in for the shock. Admittedly I was a bit upset when I arrived home to a house of near total darkness to find Gus's note saying he'd gone. And there was one from Ned saying he was staying with his friend Stuart down the road. The house was quiet. Mary was presumably out raving with the awful Shannon, but just in case some miracle had come to pass, I tiptoed upstairs and soundlessly opened her bedroom door. Just as I thought. Chaos unlimited, clothes all over the floor, bed unmade but no Mary.

I kicked off my shoes, undressed, wrapped my dressing gown around me, and padded barefoot downstairs again. Suddenly I wanted a drink. I went into the living room and turned on the light.

There were four bodies lying on the floor. Shannon had nothing on below the waist and the boy whose limbs were entwined with hers had the fly of his jeans undone.

Mary still had her skirt on but her upper body was naked and another boy's hand was frozen on her left breast. I walked out and went into the kitchen, squeals of "Shit! You said she was away" following in my wake.

Several reactions vied for priority. Shannon had been having sex. Mary wasn't but she was in the same room. They were under age. If I hadn't come home would Mary have been fucking by now? Had she done this before? Who were the boys? Had they been wearing condoms?

When they left, Mary didn't come and find me in the kitchen. She just went upstairs to her room and closed the door.

And I did nothing. I was in total shock, and in any case I am such a coward where Mary is concerned. Little by little I am beginning to acknowledge this. I have great difficulty challenging her about anything and she knows it. If I had what I imagine is a healthy mother-daughter relationship, I'd have charged upstairs after her and confronted her, but she would have turned on me and accused me of being a prudish old crone. This was the exact expression she'd used once before when I'd tried to remonstrate with her about going to a particularly wild-sounding party with Shannon.

"It's too far away and I don't want you coming home at all hours like that."

"What are you afraid of, Mum?" she'd taunted me. "Think I might have my eyes opened to a little sexy action? Do you want me to stay a virgin the rest of my life? Is that it?

The trouble with you, Mum, is I don't think sex plays too big a part in your life these days. You have all the makings of a prudish old crone."

Of course at the time what I'd focused on was, "Do you want me to stay a virgin the rest of my life?" which implied she still was one. It was only later that the words "prudish old crone" struck home.

Were all teenage daughters as despicably rude to their mothers as Mary was? Was it a phase? Would she grow out of it? Soon? I was too ashamed of her to discuss it with my friends. Their daughters all seemed like little angels when I came across them. Maybe that was how Mary seemed to them.

The real trouble stemmed from the fact that Mary had a knack of hitting the nail on the head, and the truth invariably hurts. I wasn't exactly a prudish old crone. That was unfair. But I was a bit of a prude where sex was concerned. I hadn't had more than two lovers before Gus. It's not that I don't enjoy sex but I'm not very experimental. I only know there are positions other than horizontal from reading trashy novels, and I have to say I find much of the sex I come across in popular fiction rather shocking. All that talk about fingers and orifices and sexual organs—it's exciting in a rather unfamiliar way but totally alien to me. Gus and I make love about once every six weeks these days and even then it seems to be rather by accident. Our toes touch as we roll over in the middle of the night and he runs the soles of his feet up my calves and I sort of roll towards him. He pulls me to him and we kiss and I feel his erection prodding me so I wriggle around until my nightgown is rolled up to my waist. He climbs on top of me and feels to see if I'm wet and even if I'm not he comes into me.

It's sort of furtive and tender at the same time and I like it but in the morning we never mention it. My trouble is I don't know what other women my age experience. Do they still fuck like rabbits every night with their husbands? Surely not. I'm too shy and private to ask. And as a result the last person I can talk to about sex is my own daughter.

Ned, however, is another matter. The girl he took to *Shine*—and I've yet to meet her—is his first real girlfriend. He's been out on dates but he's so appallingly shy he never seems to get anywhere. I know I should be pleased that he comes and tells me everything, and I am, but I can't help feeling most boys his age don't confide in their mothers as much as Ned. I suppose it's precisely because he's got nothing to hide that he's so open about it all.

We have these long, agonizing conversations which usually start with him saying something like: "Mum, you know that girl I took to the pub the other night?"

"Which one?"

"She's got long blond hair, sort of like yours but not as nice."

Bless him.

"Well, did you bring her here?"

"No."

"So how am I supposed to know her? Are you going to see her again?"

"That's just it. I don't know what to do."

"Do you like her?"

"Quite. She's a bit stupid."

"Doesn't sound like there's much point seeing her again, then."

"But she's..."

"She's what?"

"She's great looking. Not her face, her..."

And then, after a good deal of prevaricating, it will eventually become clear that the girl has extremely large breasts and not much else going for her.

"You fancy her, Ned, why don't you just say so?"

"Yeah, I do, but isn't it awful just to want to touch her and hope she keeps her mouth shut all evening?"

"Absolutely dreadful. But perfectly normal."

"Seriously? Is that what you wanted from boys when you went out with them?"

"Well, no, but what girls want and what they can expect to get from boys are two entirely different things. Besides, what makes you think boys wanted me to keep my mouth shut? Am I that stupid?"

"Don't be daft. But, Mum, how do you know if a girl wants to, you know, like, do it?"

I was shocked. He didn't have a clue.

"Ned, do you kiss girls? Don't answer that if you think it's too personal a question."

"No, it's OK. Yes, of course I kiss girls."

"And then what happens?"

"Well, we go on kissing. Sometimes. Sometimes they don't seem to want to." He cupped his hands in front of his mouth and breathed into them. "Sometimes I worry my breath smells or something. I don't know if I've got the kind of body girls like. I don't have hair on my chest and I'm a bit on the thin side. And I still have the odd pimple that I can't get rid of. I'm tall and they're supposed to like that, but Matthew Williams is only five seven and he's shagged loads of girls."

"And do you like any of these girls Matthew's supposed to have...shagged?" I hated saying the word but couldn't think of a substitute other than fucked, and that didn't sound suitable either for a mother-son heart-to-heart. Matthew Williams was a cocky little guy. I could see exactly how he could talk a girl into bed with him in twenty seconds. A stupid girl, at any rate.

"No, they're really tarty. The girl I was just talking about, Diane, she was one of them. Matthew said I could get my way with her, no problem, but when I kissed her she seemed sort of surprised."

"Tell me something, Ned. What had you and she talked about while you were having a drink in the pub?"

"I asked her how she was getting on in school. She said she wasn't too bothered with it. She said she was trying to get a job as a receptionist or something and then I asked her what she was reading and she said *Bella*. I tried to tell her about the goats having kids in Wales but she wasn't very interested."

"Did you make her laugh at all?"

"Not that I remember. Why?"

"In my day if a boy could make you laugh you were always supposed to be more inclined to go to bed with him."

"That's not very romantic."

"Romance comes later, Ned." This was crazy. He was more like a lovesick girl than a sex-crazed teenage boy. He was so transparently vulnerable I wanted to rush out and round up all the eligible girls in the area and give them a pep talk about not hurting him.

"It's just when I overhear Mary and her friends talking I want to curl up and die in panic."

"Why?"

"They're so awful about us boys. They laugh about us and make fun of us. It's disgusting."

"How is it disgusting?"

I knew I was being unusually nosy but I couldn't pass up this opportunity to get an insight into Mary's secret life.

"They talk about who has a big dick and who has a little one and how pathetic the little ones are."

"Mary says things like that? How does she know?"

"Well, I've never actually heard Mary say that, but Shannon is always going on about how long we last and how excited they become how quickly and how much she can get away with in a cinema."

"Ned, stop!"

"Well, you asked, Mum."

He was right. I had asked. And I don't know why I was so shocked when I discovered Mary about to have sex on our living-room floor. I wondered whether to tell Ned what I'd seen, ask him if he'd known Mary had planned to take advantage of Gus and me being away. But after thinking about it for a minute I decided it might seem threatening to him, knowing his sister was bringing sex into his home and flaunting it in his face.

Instead, I asked him: "Tell me about this girl you took to see *Shine,* the one who was crying on your shoulder. She sounds nice and romantic."

"Sophie."

"Pretty name. She's not stupid, is she?"

"No, not at all. She's musical. She wants to be a concert pianist. That's why we went to see *Shine.* She's really beautiful, Mum, she's..."

"Special?"

"Yeah. Special."

It was wondrous to behold. My great big hulking boy, with his floppy light brown hair and his soft, sensitive face that always reminded me of a rabbit's, was in love. And what he needed to be was in lust.

"And do you talk to her about books and music and stuff like that?"

"All the time."

"And have you kissed her?"

He went red. He was embarrassed and clumsy talking about girls, but he'd never actually blushed before.

"Yeah. We've kissed. But there's never anywhere to go. If I brought her here Mary would ruin every second, and she comes from a huge family, little brothers and sisters yapping about all over the place."

Suddenly I had an idea.

"Why don't you take her to Wales? It's our turn this weekend. You could take her for long walks through the forest and then have supper in front of the fire."

"But Dad's there."

"Yes, I know, but he'll be leaving on Sunday. He has to be back, he's got a big installation starting on Monday. And it'd be good if he's there to begin with. She won't feel she's being set up."

I was beginning to get the feeling that this girl was as sensitive as Ned. Someone like Shannon would make sure there was going to be no parental supervision before agreeing to go, but Sophie sounded as if she wouldn't feel comfortable if she was put under any pressure to have sex with Ned.

"It's the Easter hols. You could stay on after Dad leaves—once you've broken the ice."

I could see he liked the idea. He was looking all dreamy.

"Go and give her a ring. It's a bit short notice as it is."

"What about you, Mum? Aren't you coming?"

"I'm going to stay in London this weekend." I didn't say why.

I didn't mention Grace McIntyre's Harrods signing.

And once I was there, standing at the back of the room watching my sister smile up at people while she signed their books, I found all I could think of was how like Mary she looked. Dark, whereas I was fair. Brooding, sultry almost, whereas I was light and airy.

I realized as I watched Grace I was looking at her like she was just another person, a stranger in the street, someone I didn't know. I wasn't reacting to her like she was my own flesh and blood. She was just a woman whose appearance had caught my interest—that's exactly what she was. I didn't know this woman. She didn't feel like family. Mary was family and Mary was the one I was concerned about. Not Grace. Grace I was just curious about.

But I couldn't help thinking as I stood there, anonymous, how nice it would be to be able to go up to her and say something like: "When you've finished with all this, can we take off somewhere for a bite to eat? I'd really like to ask you what you think I should do about Mary."

And if Grace had played the role of a normal aunt I could have done it. It dawned on me that she might not even know Mary existed. Or Ned.

This was all nuts. I had to get out of there. I'd somehow got myself into the line and it was moving forward and I couldn't get out without drawing attention to myself. Suddenly I found myself propelled forward and standing right in front of my sister. Everyone was looking at me—rather nervously, I thought. Did they know, somehow, that she was my sister?

She looked up at me with that professional smile and I looked back into her eyes and saw how sad she was. She had one of those smiles that doesn't reach the eyes because it's been so long since she really had anything to smile about, the eyes have forgotten what to do.

I asked for the book to be signed to Ned and we had some kind of daft conversation about eighteen-year-old boys liking romantic fiction. Well, she'd never met Ned.

I opened my mouth to say what I really wanted to say. It would be my last chance. She must be leaving soon. And I lost my nerve. It wasn't the right time. I'd achieved something. I'd seen her. I'd spoken to her. The rest could wait.

First I had to sort out Mary—who turned out to be the least of my worries. When I got home there was Ned sitting in the kitchen making a cup of tea for one of the prettiest girls I'd ever seen. Long, tapering legs and a sweet smile.

"Mrs. Hardy? I'm Sophie, Ned's girlfriend."

I felt, rather than saw, Ned gulp and almost choke in surprise. The idiot. He had her home and dry and he hadn't even known it. And what on earth was he doing here anyway? He was supposed to be in Wales.

"Sophie, it's lovely to meet you at last." Pretty good that—it implied Ned had been talking about her, something she probably needed to hear. "But I thought you'd be hiking through the forests in Powys…"

Ned put his arm around me.

"We drove down last night. Got there about eleven. But we left again this morning. The thing is, Mum, I don't know whether or not I should tell you this but I'm bloody well going to. Dad was there with Amanda Bamber."

Grace

"Okay," said Linda, "headlines. Here's what happened while you were away. Kids have been vandalizing the mailboxes, driving by and bashing them with a hammer. Indiscriminately. They didn't touch yours, but my pink poodle's like that Yorkshire terrier that was squashed in the middle of the road by Michael Palin in *A Fish Called Wanda,* a total mess. Thank Christ I bought two. Then the couple who own those hardware stores here and in East Hampton got divorced and she got the East Hampton store and he got ours. I went in there last week and bought a hundred and twenty-five bucks' worth of stuff I don't need because he's so cute. Now he's a free man, how else am I going to get his attention? And you keep your hands off. You're younger than I am."

I promised that if I needed anything at the hardware store I'd send her to get it; that way she'd get to see him more often.

"What else? They came to spray against the ticks so I had them do yours as well. You owe me ninety bucks."

We'd been through this before.

"Linda, my caretaker does it for nothing. I just buy the stuff and he sprays."

"Oh well, you weren't here. By the way, fillet steak is on special at the A&P. The weekend crowd is starting to open up their houses for the summer. The real estate brokers are having a fit because it's such a slow season for renting. They have nonstop calls from people saying "Why haven't you rented my house yet?" I blame the husbands. Those Manhattan workaholics, they've been renting places every summer and packing the wife and kids off from Memorial Day to Labor Day while they drive out on weekends, and it's suddenly hit them what a nightmare drive it is out of the city every Friday. Four to six hours on the highway for a two-hour journey. They don't want to do it any more. Suddenly they all want to rent in Connecticut for the summer. Anyway, I'm thinking of getting a hot tub for my back yard. Want to come in with me?"

"What, and come running through the

woods in my birthday suit? Why don't we put it in my back yard?"

She ignored me.

"And I'm having the landscapers in. I'm upgrading my lawn."

"How?"

"Gee, I don't know. Up. Hey, and you missed the comet. You could go to Louse Point and see it clear as anything. Only when I sat down to go 'Wow!' I found a whole load of condoms in the sand."

"I think we had the comet in England too, Linda."

"Yes, but not clear on the end of the land like here. So, how'd you go over in England? Big success?"

"I was stalked."

"No shit. Who by?"

"I've no idea, but she saw me first the last time I went, that time when I went to Wales. Did I tell you?"

"No, why'd you go to Wales?"

Of course I hadn't told Linda about Wales. What was I thinking about? Linda didn't know anything about Upper Stone Farm and my mother dying and my father fucking off. No one did. But I didn't have to worry about Linda. While she had a never-ending curiosity about my love life—even though I'd told her over and over again it was nonexistent and I wasn't interested in being fixed up, thank you—she only ever made polite, perfunctory inquiries about my professional and family life, and if she did ask a question, she rarely waited for the answer. So by the time I opened my mouth to say, "Actually I had family in Wales once..." she had already pitched in.

"Here, they wrote a piece about your boyfriend in the *Star*. Look, I gotta run. I just stopped by to check on you. I thought you were kind of down before you left. I was worried about you."

"Well, don't be," I said, rather more harshly than I meant to. This was typical of my behavior. It was a wonder I had any friends at all. Time and time again I ask myself, why am I so ungracious, and I never come up with a satisfactory explanation. Somebody tells me they like my dress and I immediately tell them I've had it for ten years. Someone else tells me they like my hair longer and I blurt out that I'm having it all cut off any day now, it looks terrible. Deep down, I was touched by Linda's concern, so touched that I was embarrassed and had to go and push her away.

Plus I couldn't wait to get to the *Star*. Had I let slip about Harry in an unguarded moment? Who else could they be writing about?

It was on page one of the arts section, where they do big profiles of artists, writers, photographers, sculptors, and the like. And it wasn't Harry.

For a moment I had a hard time figuring out who the hell it was. I stared at the black-and-white photograph dominating the page and tried to think where I had seen the rather dishevelled yet attractive man before. The eyes were familiar. Suspicious. Slightly anxious. He obviously wasn't comfortable being photographed. But they were intelligent eyes, staring right at the camera. No bullshit. I liked them. And I knew them.

ARCHIE BERKELEY. A COMPOSER WITHIN OUR MIDST, read the headline. Why did I know the name? I knew zip about composers.

The yard sale. It was the angry man in a tweed jacket I'd met at the yard sale Linda had dragged me to.

"This is the biggest challenge of my career..." Archie told us.

What career? I asked myself. Why are we always expected to know immediately who these people are? I read the piece and from it learned that he was in America to score the music for a new film called *Rapture,* which was about a love affair between an older woman and a gangsta rapper. Mr. Berkeley, it would appear, was a classical composer with whose film music I was indeed familiar. He had written the music for a number of lavish costume dramas of the kind Linda imagines she wants to see and then screams with boredom when she actually gets there. The aforementioned challenge would manifest itself in the juxtapositioning of a fully orchestrated romantic score for the "older woman" element of the film, with the rap theme for the gangsta lover.

"Mr. Berkeley has rented a house on Atlantic Avenue beach and will be joined by his wife Sonia Shulman, the writer, and their two children later in the year. *Rapture* will be filmed on location in New York and in Connecticut, but Mr. Berkeley, who says he has always wanted to work by the sea and has long been attracted to the East End, will work here throughout the summer."

Well, bully for him, I thought. And bully for the wife, too. I'd heard of her all right. She was rather highly regarded as a literary writer in England, although as far as I was concerned she wrote rather depressing little novels set in Islington featuring bleak, angst-ridden characters who worked in the City and thought about killing themselves. I knew someone who knew her who had told me she took herself desperately seriously.

I ought to take myself more seriously, I thought, not for the first time. I ought to sit down and write an angst-ridden documentary about my traumatic childhood and my awful father. I could throw in a bit of fashionable child abuse. My father was dead. How was anyone to know he'd never come near me? I'd probably make a fortune.

But then I had already made a modest fortune so what was the point? And in any case all I could write was fiction because I had never known my father.

Of course, there were the books he had sent me. Twice a year, at Christmas and on my birthday, I received a large package of books from Lucas Cammell Publishers. They were not all published by my father. He made a separate selection from other publishers' lists.

With the first package, which arrived when I was about nine, came a letter to Biddy, my foster mother, asking her to elicit my opinions of the books and write back to him. Within a year I was writing my own "critiques" and mailing them back to him. And then he began to include a terse note written in a small staccato hand in black ink on gray postcards with his name printed at the top.

"Perhaps the new John Fowles will be of interest," he wrote when he sent me *The French Lieutenant's Woman* for my thirteenth birthday. "More of a woman's book for you." He'd sent me *The Magus* and *The Collector*, neither of which I'd been able to make head or tail of, since I was barely ten years old at the time, but he never seemed to take my age into account.

And so began my interest in fiction. The postcards were always signed Lucas Cammell. He never ever indicated that he was my father. Perhaps he didn't know I knew. My schoolfriends had pen pals. I had my father, only there wasn't much pen and absolutely no pal to our relationship. Yet I have to admit that it was because of this early introduction to books that I became a writer.

In my teens I began to send him my scribblings and this was when I learned that I could overstep the mark. There was only so far I could go with him. My material always came back with a polite letter from his secretary saying Mr. Cammell was unable to consider unsolicited material, and informing me that

I could find a list of literary agents in the *Writers' & Artists' Yearbook.*

I knew what he looked like. Occasionally he was in the papers and I would clip his photograph and hide it in my diary or the book I was reading. But I had a kind of built-in self-preservation instinct that told me to keep my distance. I liked and respected Biddy and David. Right from the start they had, deliberately it seemed, maintained near silence on the subject of my father, almost as if they knew he would never take much interest in me. And they were right. Only through books did he communicate. If I confronted him surely I would be rejected, and I didn't need that.

When I turned fifteen I was at my most vulnerable. Suddenly my life changed overnight, as it does for most adolescents. All the things that had interested me no longer did. Biddy and David seemed boring. My father seemed exciting. From the confines of my teenage bedroom, the walls of which were plastered with pictures of Jim Morrison, I imagined what would happen when eventually we met, but I was too nervous to do anything about bringing about such a meeting. Until finally something happened with Biddy that put a stop to all my dreams of reunion with my father.

Shortly thereafter I left home, went to London and found a job, and from then on I seemed to hear nothing but bad things about Lucas Cammell. I don't know why it doesn't happen more often. Perhaps it does. People have no idea that you know someone, let alone might be related to them, and they trash that person right in front of you before you can stop them.

I was at a dinner party. We were a group of smart young wannabes. We all had jobs in television or movies or books as assistants to names people read about in the newspapers. This was long before *Air Male*. Somebody had brought along their new girlfriend and it turned out she worked as an editorial assistant at Lucas Cammell Publishers. Of course I couldn't resist it.

"What's he like, Lucas Cammell? Is he brilliant?"

"Brilliant?" She seemed totally nonplussed. "What? As a publisher? I suppose he is in an old-fashioned kind of way. Publishing's so market-driven these days, poor old Lucas invariably misses the point. He still believes in talent. Goes on about the author's actual writing even though their profile is nonexistent. No promo potential. Zip. But every now and then he still pulls something out of the bag and it wins the bloody Booker and we have to start tugging our forelocks again. If he wasn't such a monster, I don't suppose we'd mind so much."

"He's a monster?"

"The worst. He's the coldest man I've ever come across. Yet it's not as if he's without charm. When he wants something he's the most seductive creature alive. Talk about sexual harassment in the workplace. He's got to be, what? Fifties? But he has women drooling

119

when he wants to. The younger the better. He comes up behind you while you're sitting at your desk and he puts his hands on your shoulders and grips you. Hard. Then he asks you if you want to read the new, I don't know, Martin Amis for him. Overnight. He says he really wants to know what you think. What are you going to say? No, thanks? And kiss goodbye to your promotion to senior editor? But it's the kid I feel sorry for."

"The kid? What kid?" I was as devious as my father.

"He's got this daughter. She's in her teens. The mother's dead. The daughter lives with him in this apartment above the offices, the one where he invites those young women editors upstairs to have a drink and discuss a manuscript. And sometimes they sort of don't come down again, you know? She goes to bed early, I suppose. She's really sweet. Pretty. Fair. But a bit stupid. She used to hang out in the office when she was a kid. It's clear she didn't get his brains. She worships him. Dad this, Dad that. And he totally ignores her. I'd hate to be his daughter."

And then someone asked her about something else and the conversation drifted off in a different direction. A month or so later I heard she'd left Lucas Cammell Publishers and I never saw her again.

It was alarming, the insight she'd given me into my father's personality, but not half so horrifying as the information I was to receive a couple of years later.

It was at another dinner party. It's astonishing I went to so many when I was younger, given that I never leave the house now if I can help it. The man who leaned over to speak directly into my left ear was what they call over here a real piece of work. He was a good twenty to thirty years older than I was but he still seemed to think it was a cinch that a woman my age would find him fascinating. He was attractive in an old roué kind of way, I can still remember that, but there was something overtly sadistic about him that warned me off him. That's basically my problem. I'm only alerted to the ones who advertise that they're out-and-out shits right from the start. The seductive charmers who seem oh so kind and gentle have me eating out of their palms in an instant and then I'm blind to their bad behavior in the future. Until it's too late.

I was expecting him to say something like, "What are you doing later? Want to leave early and go and have a drink?" A euphemism for "How quickly can I get you into bed?"

But I was in for a shock.

"You look a hell of a lot like your mother," he told me.

"My mother's dead," I said without thinking.

"Yes, I know. But you're not. You're very much alive and as beautiful as she was."

Well, at least I was right about one aspect of him. What a line. What girl is going to be turned on by being told she looks like her mother?

"You knew her, I take it."

He nodded. "And your father. How is he, by the way?"

"I wouldn't know," I answered truthfully.

"Like that, is it? Don't blame you. Wouldn't want to go the same way as your mother."

I didn't like the sound of this, but I knew I had a live one. I couldn't let him go. He could tell me all sorts of things.

"How do you mean?"

"You are Lucas Cammell's daughter, aren't you?"

It was then that I realized I had no idea how he knew. I was introduced as Grace McIntyre. No one knew I was Lucas's daughter. There was only one explanation. I really must look like my mother. I had pictures of her, of course, but I hadn't realized the resemblance was so strong.

"I nearly had a bit of a turn when I walked in and saw you. I wanted to marry her myself. Asked her. She wouldn't have me. Besotted by your father, beast that he was."

"Beast," I echoed.

"It's the worst kind of violence, the non-aggressive kind. I used to think it would have been better if he'd actually hit her, knocked her about, left his mark, so to speak. Those silences of his made just as much impact. He dragged her away from London, which she loved, I might add, and God knows we missed her, and took her to this miserable pile of stones halfway up a freezing Welsh mountain and then he fucking left her there. He was in London all week. She was so lonely she used to call me every night and tell me what a mistake she'd made and I'd say, "I'll come and get you, I'll drive down now," but she always stopped me. She was terrified of him. And then you came along. There was another one, wasn't there? But you're the oldest, yes?"

I looked at him. If he knew about Favor, how come he didn't know that I had never lived with my father? But he was completely drunk in any case so who could say what he knew?

"I ought to hit you," he said suddenly with a violence that made me realize that however cruel my father had been, my mother had had a lucky escape from this man. "You took her away from me forever. She adored you. You were a bond between her and him. She stopped calling me after you were born."

But what happened then? I wanted to ask and knew that I couldn't.

"There's nothing so awful as someone who freezes you out," he continued, very maudlin by now. "I ought to know. I married someone just like Lucas Cammell. No dialogue whatsoever. Except she froze me out of her bed, too, frigid bitch. By all accounts Lucas went on fucking your mother every weekend. It was how he got her in the first place. Pure sexual chemistry. She couldn't resist him. He was like a big magnet, drawing her to him. And once he had her she was his prisoner. If it hadn't been for you I think she might have escaped, but you became the center of her universe up there. And Lucas hated that. We heard about it as far away as London. To begin with, your existence created a bond between them but then Lucas became jealous. He hated you. Because if you took her away from me, you also took her away from him."

I excused myself at that point, went to the bathroom. Went upstairs. Went to the kitchen. I don't remember where I went. But I had to get away from him.

Lucas hated you.

For years those words have haunted me. I never even found out the man's name. It would have been so easy.

I could have asked my hostess, got in touch with him, found out more. But *Lucas hated you* was pretty final. What was the point of seeking further pain? Although, to be honest, it's not quite as devastating as you might think when you hear that someone you don't even know hates you. It hurts a bit like a bad review but you turn the other cheek and get on with it.

The seagulls were making a hell of a noise. There must be a storm coming. They always kicked up a fuss before a storm and then they had a whale of a time bobbing up and down on the rough sea.

I swept out the ashes from my grate and spent twenty minutes laying a new fire. It was one of those rituals that I always found deeply therapeutic. I started with balls of newspaper and I took a certain amount of pleasure in scrunching up Mr. Archie "This is the biggest challenge of my career" Berkeley's profile and piling kindling and logs on top of it and lighting a match.

And yet I don't know why I was so dismissive of his talk of the biggest challenge of his career. The truth of the matter was that I was facing one of my own. Shortly after I had arrived to live out here in the woods I had begun a new book. In secret. No one knew anything about it, least of all my boring editor in New York. It was what was generally known in the trade as "dark." Indeed, compared with the frothy romance I'd written in the past it was positively satanic. It wasn't about a love affair, it wasn't a woman's book as such, it didn't even have a heroine as its central character.

It was about a man. I called him Luther. He was a manipulator. He got a kick out of ruining people's lives. He didn't need to kill them. Nor was it enough for him just to have power over them. He got off on seeing their lives in tatters and knowing it was all due to him. He picked his people at random. I would have him standing on the sidewalk at, say, Wooster and West Broadway, or 62nd Street and Park Avenue and he would tell himself that the next person to go past him would be the person whose life he would have to ruin. He would have to engineer a meeting and infiltrate himself into their lives.

Luther was a jack of all trades. If his victim was a rich person he became their financial adviser. If it was a beautiful but susceptible woman he became an interior decorator who ruined her apartment once she had placed its restyling in his hands; or he became a chef who claimed he was cooking calorie-free food while watching her balloon up to gross proportions as a result of eating his delicious concoctions. And if they were poor he merely concentrated on winning their trust in some way before he betrayed them.

And then he discovered that his latest victim, a young girl who trusted him implicitly, was none other than his own daughter whose mother he had abandoned. The girl was a herbalist and Luther had persuaded her to hand over everything to him in return for being set up with her own store on Madison Avenue.

But the girl knew exactly who Luther was. He had ruined a friend of hers, not to mention her mother. She had set him up. Never mind the fact that he was her father. She wanted revenge. He was a patronizing bastard, claiming to believe in the potions she mixed for him each day for his headaches, his sinus trouble, his hair loss. Even the elixir she claimed would iron out the wrinkles on his forehead.

She was careful with the amount of poison she slipped into each potion. She reckoned it would take about three or four months to kill him.

Lucas hated you.

I know I didn't begin to sit down and write the book until I came out here but I suppose I began it in my head the day I heard those words.

The morning after the storm was calm and bright. It was the perfect day for walking at Louse Point, but it was the weekend and I hated going to Louse Point at the weekend. The couples were there, walking hand in hand along the water's edge, sitting huddled on the sand, whispering, sharing.

But I was too restless wandering around the house. I couldn't work. After about an hour's frustration I gave up and set off up the path through my woods to the road, across and down the steep wooden flight of steps that led from the top of the bluff to the beach. I walked along what were essentially people's private beaches, climbing over the breakwaters that divided them, peering up as always through the trees to see if I could see the fancy houses at the top of the bluff, but they were well hidden from prying eyes. This was where I should have spent my money, in this private backwater, not on the modern monstrosity perched precariously on the dunes south of the highway.

When I finally reached Louse Point, nodding to the osprey nest en route, I found that of course I was too early for the couples. It was the middle of the morning and the activity centered around dogs. Most people had retrievers or Labradors or German shepherds. There were a few Westies, but golden retrievers were definitely the dog of choice. They loved the beach. They charged in and out of the water, chasing each other, shaking themselves dry when they came out and then plunging straight back in again. I threw a stick for one, just to see it rush to retrieve it, swimming strongly out to sea.

"She's yours now," yelled her owner. "I ain't done that in years. Be here all day if I did."

He was typical of the male dog walker who came in his Chevy or Dodge pickup during his lunch hour. I loved the way all the men working in the area—carpenters, contractors, chimney sweeps, electricians—all rode around with their dogs sitting up in front beside them and how they often drove out to the beach just to sit in their trucks and gaze out to sea. I wondered if their wives knew they did this. Because they were mostly ugly brutes, the kind that when they bend over, if you're standing behind them you find their jeans have slipped halfway down their fat buttocks and you can see the top of the crease. They looked like the kind of slobs who would yell "Hey, honey, what's for dinner?" the minute they walked in the door and then lie in front of the television scratching their bellies until she brought it to them. And if she didn't they'd probably beat her up.

But walking along the beach with their dogs they were kind of cute, and the thing about these dogs was that they were obedient. They came when they were called—just like the little lady. So I noticed immediately that one dog was completely out of control. It wasn't any particular breed, although if anything it came closest to a standard poodle. It obviously thought it was a water spaniel and kept rushing into the sea. No matter how fiercely its owner shouted at it, it just went on swimming, looking like it was trying to make it to Ireland. It failed to notice any sticks thrown for it. It just wasn't interested in any of that.

Finally it came out of the water and rushed towards me, barking. It shook itself all over me, soaking me, and then growled. I dropped to one knee and held out my hand, low, palm upward. The growls continued but softened a little. I began to talk to this wayward animal. I love dogs. Dogs love me. Dogs and children like nice people, or so they say. I hadn't ever experimented with children, but then I'd never pretended to be nice.

The dog finally approached. They always do, eventually. I tickled it under the chin—it's all you ever have to do if you can get that close— and it was mine for life. It made as if to go into the water again.

"Stay," I said with considerable menace in my voice.

It stayed.

"I don't fucking believe it. I've had that dog for three weeks now and he doesn't even so much as look at me when I open my mouth. Now you come along and it's like he's had six months' training with Barbara Woodhouse. Maybe you *are* Barbara Woodhouse?"

It was Archie Berkeley. Naturally. Who else did I want to run into on the beach?

"No, I'm not Barbara Woodhouse. We're

in America, remember, and if this is an American dog it wouldn't understand Barbara Woodhouse anyway. Look, I'll say 'Walkies' and let's see what happens."

I said "Walkies" with meaning and threw a stick into the sea. The poodle rushed after it and brought it straight back to me.

"We've met before, haven't we?"

"Yes," I said. Nothing more. I'd trained his dog for him in five minutes. I wasn't about to give him any lift.

"Ah, I remember. You're the rude, monosyllabic Englishwoman who was at that yard sale."

"Where you were looking for an antique hall table. At a yard sale."

"Well, for Christ's sake, I'd never been to a yard sale before. I mean, I didn't think it would be a Christie's auction, but then again I didn't know what to expect. The good thing about it was that it was in this neck of the woods and I drove around afterwards and discovered Louse Point. It's stunning here on the Accabonac Harbor."

"Has your family arrived yet?" I remembered his barbed remark about his wife teaching me a few manners.

He didn't answer straight away, and that slight pause turned my question into more than the polite inquiry I had intended. It turned it into: "Are you available?"

Oh shit!

"No, no, they don't come out for quite a while. It's just me and the dogs at the moment."

130

"Dogs? Plural?"

"Yes. Leo and Theo. Not mine, I hasten to add. I'm writing the music for a film. That's why I'm out here. The film's being shot in and around New York. I could have sat at home in London and done it there, but I decided to pretend I needed to be out here. It'll be great for my sons to spend the summer out here. Anyway, the studio rented me this house—hideous modern pile but it's right on the beach and I can sit at the piano and look out at the ocean. Highly inspirational although not really good for the piano having it so exposed to the elements. And the costume designer, who's English but works out here and lives in New York, said would I like to have her dogs for company for the duration of the movie. She's running around like a blue-arsed fly and if I had them they could be at the beach and so of course I said yes, I'd love to. I like dogs. I just didn't bargain for these two."

And I didn't bargain for the story of his life.

"Which one's this? Leo or Theo?"

"That's Leo. He's the extrovert. Loves the beach. Loves the water. Won't do a bloody thing I tell him. Completely out of control."

"And Theo?"

"Your basic agoraphobic dog. Won't leave the house. I have to push him outside to pee. He sits in a closet all day and shivers in misery."

"What breed?"

"Whippet variety. All bony and skinny. I don't know what to do with this animal. I'm worried sick. I can't work."

He studied me for a second. I backed away. "Oh, no…"

"Listen, please. Look at Leo. He's crazy about you. Just come to the house and see if you can work your magic with Theo. Judging by Leo it'll only take a few seconds. If you could just get this fucking dog out of the cupboard I can't tell you how relieved I'd be. Come for a drink tonight, why don't you."

He was terribly seductive standing there on the beach in his jeans and sweatshirt with his hair all tousled. He needed me. When was the last time someone needed me?

"Okay. What time?"

"About six? Got a pen? No? Wait a second, I've got one."

He fumbled in his pockets and produced a scrap of paper with a shopping list scrawled on it. He turned it over and scribbled hurriedly.

"Here's the address. See you later."

He was off pretty quick once he'd got my okay, I noticed. Leo looked at me inquiringly.

"Go on, Leo," I urged. "Go with Master. See you later."

I didn't look at the piece of paper until five to six when I was about to set out, and then I nearly fainted. I rummaged around in my desk drawer until I found the lease I'd signed a few months earlier. I'd just gone into my lawyer's office in East Hampton one morning and scrawled my name and when he'd sent me a copy I'd thrown it in a drawer. Sure enough it was with a major studio and I'd never even noticed.

I'd rented my house on the dunes to Archie
Berkeley.

Favor

Gus denied everything.
In fact, he was completely devastated
when I confronted him. I've never seen him
look so shocked.

We were in the bathroom. He'd been called
out after supper to an exceptionally neurotic
client, a woman living on her own in a gloomy,
five-bedroom Victorian house and who per-
petually locked herself out. And immediately
called Gus to come and break in and change
her lock. In fact, if I hadn't seen the woman
and witnessed for myself how deeply sexless
she was, I might have suspected Gus of having
an affair with her, so often did he visit her at
night. She had confessed to him that she
thought she locked herself out on purpose, subconsciously, in order to have an excuse to
change the locks on her door, so paranoid was
she that someone could get hold of her keys
and break in and attack her.

"I've told her this is absolutely the last
time," Gus called out while flossing his teeth.

"I know about you and Amanda Bamber,"

I said, coming into the bathroom and standing behind him so I could see our reflection in the mirror of the bathroom cabinet. He turned around and looked at me as if he wanted to be sure he wasn't seeing things in the mirror.

"You've been up in Wales with her. I know all about it. Ned found you up there together," I blurted out miserably, aware of how shrewish and accusing I sounded.

"Yes, what of it?"

I couldn't believe this. Did he expect me to condone their relationship? Was I supposed to know he'd been having an affair with her?

"Well, you and her. While our son was in the house."

He stared at me in total amazement and then put out his hand to grip my shoulder as if to steady himself. Then suddenly he was shaking me.

"You think I was there with her like...like that?"

"Well, weren't you?"

"Have you gone totally mad? Do you seriously think I would let Ned see me with Amanda at the farm if there was something between us, and then let him come back here and see you before phoning you myself before he got home? Do you?"

"Well, he did get back and you didn't phone and he told me he'd found you with her. Are you trying to tell me he was fibbing, that she wasn't there?"

"No, she was there."

"But you never told me she was going to be there." I had begun to raise my voice.

"Will you let me finish? I didn't know she would turn up. Tell me something, did Ned actually say he saw us in bed together?"

"No, of course not, he..."

"Because you know he arrived with this girl, out of the blue, no warning to me. They raided the fridge, made themselves something to eat, disappeared upstairs to bed. Amanda followed soon after and I stayed up for another couple of hours. When I got up the next morning Ned and the girl had left. I thought they must be on their way somewhere. Frankly, I thought it was a bit rude just turning up like that. You might have phoned to say he was coming."

"So you could get Amanda out in time?"

"Oh please! Amanda slept in her room. I slept in ours."

"But why was she there?"

"Why on earth shouldn't she be there? They have a share in the place, after all. She'd been at some book festival and she was too tired to drive back to London, so she called and said would I mind if she came for one night and drove back on Saturday. I didn't know I had to get your permission. Call Alec if you don't believe me. She called him and told him that was what she was doing, and he didn't have a problem as far as we could make out. I don't know what's got into you. I honestly don't."

And I had to be content with that. Had

Ned got it wrong? Were they in the same room or did they sleep separately? The children's rooms were at the other end of the house from ours and the Bambers'. Ned wouldn't necessarily have heard anything unless he'd gone to listen deliberately, and I couldn't bring myself to discuss it with him any further.

Not that we'd seen much of him. He'd disappeared with Sophie, and when he did materialize, usually with a pile of laundry under his arm, he never mentioned it. There was probably a good reason for this. He and Sophie were now obviously an item. Whether or not Gus and Amanda had slept together, I couldn't be sure, but Ned and Sophie certainly had. He was like a different creature. The confidence suddenly oozed out of him. He almost pranced about the place, so that even Mary was forced to comment: "You know, Creepo, you might be quite attractive when you grow up."

I had listened to women in the past who had suspected their husbands of having an affair and I had always felt rather high-minded about it. It's all about trust, had been my line. I know I'd said that on more than one occasion. Because up to now it had never entered my head for a second that Gus might be unfaithful. Well, now the joke was on me. Maybe. Maybe not. It was the tiny niggle of doubt that kept worming its way back into my mind that worried me the most. I'd picture them together when I'd least expect to. Standing in line at Tesco's I'd see not the checkout girl but Amanda sitting there stuffing groceries into plastic bags with Gus leaning over and whispering sweet nothings in her ear. When I came to I saw it was her supervisor come to tell her to take her lunch break. Gus and Amanda were on every giant roadside billboard I passed, cavorting in place of couples advertising designer underwear. I recalled all the times at parties when I'd thought Gus was just being friendly and polite with the other women guests, and how proud I'd been of him because he was so considerate with women. Maybe it was all just a prelude to something else. Maybe I'd been blind and naive and stupid all these years.

Things came to a head about two weeks later in the middle of the night. I woke up and found he wasn't beside me. He'd been called out to a job earlier in the evening and I was more or less convinced I'd heard him come in again as I was dropping off to sleep.

But maybe not. Maybe he was still with her, whoever she was. By this time I was in a state of serious confusion because I'd been forced to think twice about the possibility of an affair between Gus and Amanda Bamber.

I had run into Amanda with a man. He might have been someone's husband but he certainly wasn't either mine or hers. And he was a good fifteen years younger than she was.

They were walking through the lobby of the Kensington Hilton. I'd nipped in there on my way back from Sainsbury's on my lunch hour—makes a change from Tesco's every now and then—to tell Roger that his two-thirty had cancelled. He was having lunch at the Japanese restaurant at the Hilton. He'd become obsessed with all things Japanese. In the waiting room at the osteopathic practice I was now hidden from view by a shoji screen, and Roger wore some kind of weird Japanese belted jacket that made him look like a sumo wrestler and sent Mrs. Braithwaite into a state of panic. He tried to persuade me to wear a kimono but he didn't get very far. It was bad enough having to shout around the shoji screen, "You can go in now, Mrs. Braithwaite," while she yelled back, "What?" and then I had to repeat myself or get up and go around it.

Roger was like that, always getting caught up in different fads and completely changing his lifestyle to suit them. Then he'd discover something new and it was as if the last obsession had never happened. Mrs. Braithwaite said it was because he was a Gemini, they were all like that. I never could work that one out. Roger's birthday is on 12 December unless he's lied to the passport office.

He'd been off guzzling sushi for the last two weeks so I thought maybe he'd like an extra half-hour to relax over some green tea ice cream or whatever they give you for dessert. So I popped in to tell him. I should have telephoned instead. I don't think he was terribly pleased to see me. It might have had something to do with the very pretty, and extremely young-looking, Japanese girl who was lunching with him. He does like to keep his private life to himself, does our Roger. I'd always assumed he was gay.

And then, on the way out, I ran into Amanda walking through the reception area. She looked terribly shifty when she saw me. Because of Gus, I thought immediately. But then I saw her step quickly away from a man walking beside her. He'd been holding her elbow.

She saw me and she called out to me. She didn't have to do that. She could have pretended not to see me. But she didn't introduce me to the young man and he stood there awkwardly beside her. Finally he said, "I'm Martin."

"He's my editorial assistant," said Amanda, far too quickly. Martin looked surprised. "We've been at a sales conference here at the hotel. We're just leaving. How's Gus? It was so nice to see him in Wales. And Ned's girlfriend is so pretty. What a dark horse he is."

"Were you in Wales, too?" I asked Martin, beginning to put two and two together.

"I was, actually," said Martin before Amanda could shut him up.

"At the book festival?" I inquired, smiling.

"At the book festival," he confirmed. And winked. Amanda didn't see that.

"We have to be back at the office at three. 'Bye, darling."

'Bye, darling. She'd never called me *darling* before. Why was she being so nice to me all

of a sudden? And when I asked Roger if there was a publishers' conference going on at the hotel, he said he hadn't been aware of one. And it was the sort of boring detail Roger would know.

So either Gus had competition or I'd got everything wrong about Wales.

Well, then, where was he at four in the morning?

I found him in the kitchen.

I had never seen him looking so unhappy.

"I'm just not like that," he said when I walked in. He didn't look at me. I sat down opposite him at the kitchen table. He was naked from the waist up and I longed to reach across the table and stroke his bare arms. He was in terrific shape and he looked so young and vulnerable, not much changed from the man who proposed to me beside the photo-copier in Dad's office.

But he wasn't looking at me and I didn't dare touch him.

"I've been thinking about it a lot," he went on. "It's probably incredibly boring of me but I have never even flirted with anyone since I married you, let alone slept with them. Yet I have to admit you're right to suspect me of being unfaithful. I don't take enough notice of you. I take you for granted. I don't tell you I love you, but I do, I do. I just find it so hard to come out and say it. Some guys can go on about all that stuff all the time but I can't. I'm awkward. It makes me embarrassed talking about it—but it doesn't mean I don't feel it.

And I know I'm weird, but I only love you. I've never loved anyone else, not even before you came along. Some blokes need masses of women. I hear them going on about them. Makes me exhausted just listening to them. I don't. Way it is. I just need you. All right?"

He was looking at me now. Fiercely. Like a little boy spoiling for a fight. Ned and he were so alike, my heart ached for them both. I don't know if I had realized it before, but Ned got his clumsiness from Gus. They were both big, soft hulks, bumbling along in their cheerful, good-natured ways, until they felt passionately about something and then they turned into intense and highly sensitive men.

I stood up and went to stand behind Gus, leaning over him with my arms around him, burying my face in his neck. He reached round and pulled me down to sit in his lap.

"I love you and I'm unbelievably lucky to have you," I told him. "I don't know why I doubted you for a second. Please, please forgive me."

We kissed each other and giggled and whispered in the semidarkness like teenagers fearful of waking their parents, rather than the other way round.

"Will you do something for me?" he asked. "Will you come back to work with me? I need you."

It wasn't the first time he'd asked. He saw me hesitate.

"At least come with me to this." He pulled the brochure for the International Security Conference Exposition in America across the table.

"Did you leave it out on purpose? I looked at it while you were in Wales. Where is it?"

"New York. End of August. There's so much new technology I'd like to take a look at. I've heard that quite a few of the big guys are going from the UK. We could take the kids. Make a holiday of it, go over there a bit before. I could book us into a family suite— it'd probably be all that's available I've left it so late. Accommodation's at a premium during the convention, so I've heard. Ned could come with me to the convention if you didn't want to. Who knows, he might get really into it, lots of gadgets, giveaways."

The truth was I could see the pair of them already, father and son wandering around like a couple of schoolkids. It'd be good for them.

"And you and I could get some ideas to inspire us to expand the business together."

He had it all worked out, didn't he? I thought of Roger and his obsessions and wondered what he'd be caught up in next. It wasn't much of a career working as his receptionist, but that had always been my problem. I just wasn't particularly ambitious. I don't know why I hesitated about going back to work for Gus. I just sensed that we shouldn't always be in each other's pocket. We should be able to give each other space, to coin a bit of psychobabble.

I didn't want to get snowed under with

running the business again. I wanted time to think and read and explore. Explore what, I hadn't a clue. This was not something I could discuss with Gus, but the fact that I had a sister who was a writer had stirred up feelings of unfulfillment in me, not ambition for power but a yearning to find a similar creative instinct lurking within me, too.

And then I slapped myself mentally on the wrist. Creative instinct? In my dreams. I was just an ordinary wife and mother with an adorable husband and for that I should be grateful.

And then something occurred to me. I hugged Gus.

"I don't know about coming back into the business. Don't press me, not just yet, okay? But it's a wonderful idea for us all to go to New York with you. Get on to booking those tickets first thing tomorrow."

Of course it was a great idea. I'd just remembered. Grace lived on Long Island, and that was in New York State. If I went with Gus, I could go and look for my sister.

Grace

"**I**'m sorry this is all so awful," Archie Berkeley told me as he opened the door and let me into my own house. And I warmed to him considerably. Only a European with a certain amount of taste could recognize a pretentious nouveau New York decorating job when they saw one. "My broker and I did not have the same what they call in America 'sensibilities' when it came to interior design. To be honest I don't think I'd have chosen anything this modern and ostentatious if it had been left to me, but the studio sent someone to pick out a house in advance of my arrival and this is what I got. They're paying. I can't complain but I would rather be in that nice secluded wooded area near where we were today."

I looked around. It had been a while since I'd been there. From the outside it didn't look too bad. After all, I was the one who bought it in the first place, seduced by the attractive gray shingle, the dramatic proportions, the wonderful position right on the beach. But when I walked in, I shuddered. It was like some kind of Mexican health club. There was a vast open space in front of a huge picture window—looking out on to the beach—where his Steinway had pride of place. In the middle of one wall was an oblong, split-level modern fire-place built into the brick with a smoked-glass screen. Around it was a ghastly semicircular sunken seating area resembling a Roman arena. Turquoise lounging cushions were arranged on three levels of steps. The walls were white. Huge terracotta urns were placed where you were most likely to walk straight into them. A guitar hung on one wall. A row of Spanish hats on another. A big, white, circular table that would have looked better in a space-ship stood in the dining area. Spanish tiles adorned the floor.

"Where exactly were you going to put the hall table had you found it at the yard sale? I mean, there isn't a hall as such as far as I can see."

"I suppose what I really meant was that I was looking for a dining table to replace that monstrosity. At the moment, I eat on this. The painters left it behind and I snuck out on the deck and stole it. Hid it and feigned ignorance as to its whereabouts until they'd finished and left."

He had led me into my kitchen, and there in the middle was a beat-up trestle table with a tall glass vase of cheerful yellow tulips in the middle. It was laid for dinner with some really quite attractive Italian pottery—I dimly remembered providing it in desperation when I'd seen how the decorator had ruined every-thing else—and two tall candlesticks with the candles waiting to be lit. It really did look quite cozy.

"Oh my God, you're expecting a guest for dinner. Introduce me to Theo and I'll be out of here in twenty minutes."

He looked a little crestfallen. "Oh, will you really? I went into East Hampton this afternoon and bought some fresh pasta at Villa, you know? The Italian shop by the railway station. I thought you might join me."

Of course I knew Villa. It was the best food shop in town as far as I was concerned. Their sweet sausage was to die for and at lunchtime you could hardly get in the door because the locals were lining up around the block for their giant Italian hero sandwiches.

"I'd have thought you would have frequented the Barefoot Contessa." A very pricey deli. "On a studio expense account."

"If I went in there with the star of the movie, they might begin to take notice of me. It's that kind of place."

I wondered if his profile in the *Star* would change things on that score.

"Wait till the season. The place'll be a nightmare," I told him. "You'd be better off just doing your shopping up the road at the Farmer's Market. You can practically walk there."

"I plan on it," he said, "but I can't speak for Sonia. She might get a kick out of the Barefoot Contessa, especially if we have to entertain. But listen, will you stay for pasta?"

I was very tempted. I had become such a hermit since I'd moved here that a movie and a burger with Linda followed by her in-depth dissection of my horoscope was about the height of my outside intellectual stimulation.

"What about Theo?" I stalled.

"Step this way." He led me through my kitchen in this house where I had never lived but whose every nook and cranny I knew intimately, to what the broker had always insisted on referring to as "the family room."

"But I don't have a family," I had protested when I had first looked at the house. And here the broker had been stumped. She had her spiel down pat. Deviations from the norm were not allowed.

Archie had really made the room rather homey with TV and cushions on the sofa and books scattered about the place. Sliding doors opened on to the deck where he'd strung up a hammock. Along one wall were bookshelves above waist level. I had had them built specially, intending to convert the "family room" into a library if I ever moved in. Which I wouldn't. Below was a line of cupboards. The door of the one on the far right was slightly ajar.

"He's in there."

I dislike whippets. It's because they're such miserable-looking creatures, so fragile. They make you feel guilty. Theo was shivering in his basket, big, sad, almond-shaped eyes looking reproachfully at me. I reached in and pulled the basket towards me. Theo looked petrified.

"It's all right," I said over and over again in my most soothing voice. "It's all right,

Theo, no one's going to hurt you. Put the water on for the pasta and bring me in a glass of wine," I told Archie, surprising myself by my brisk commanding tone, "and when you come back I'll have him out of here and in my lap."

In my dreams! After two glasses of Sagaponack chardonnay, Theo hadn't budged an inch.

"I think this is going to take a little longer than I thought. Didn't the owner warn you he was like this?"

"No. In a word. And you can see why. Who'd ever take on a dog like this? She was a bit naughty actually, only introduced me to Leo in New York. Probably because Theo was hiding under the bed and wouldn't come out. And Leo is so engaging—if a little uncontrollable. How could I resist?"

"What about...where does Theo crap?" I looked about as if I expected to see a giant cat litter tray lurking in a corner of my family room.

"I leave the slider open. He scuttles out of the cupboard, across the deck and on to the beach like a crab when he thinks I'm not looking. So how long do you think you'd need to train him?"

"I think we might be talking about a week at least, for him to be really used to me." This, I assumed, would let me safely off the hook.

Wrong.

"The thing is...here, have some *parmigiano*, fresh from Villa... I've got to go into the city next week. I can't take the dogs."

148

"What on earth are you going to do with them?"

I fell right into it. Was that why he'd asked me for a drink in the first place? He'd seen I liked dogs. He needed someone to look after them. My face must have given away my thoughts.

"Would you?" he asked. "I mean, I don't even know where you live, how big your house is—do you have room for them?"

"I live in the woods. They'll probably get ticks, but no more than they would from frolicking in the grass in the dunes out there." I realized as I spoke I'd already agreed to take them. "When do you leave?"

"I'm taking the one o'clock Jitney tomorrow. This is sensational of you. The terrible thing is, and I meant to say this the minute I opened the door, I don't even know your name. I think we were introduced at that yard sale, but it's completely slipped out of my mind and I was too embarrassed to admit it on the beach."

"I'm Grace Cammell," I said, using that name for the first time in my life. I hadn't said Grace McIntyre because at some point he'd realize it was my name on the lease of his house. And then, far too late, I remembered I'd signed the lease with the studio. He'd probably never even seen it.

"Cammell? Cammell Laird? Are you part of the shipbuilding family?"

"No. My father was a publisher." Another stupid mistake. What was wrong with me? I never mentioned my father.

"Oh, of course, Lucas Cammell."

"You knew my father?"

"No, I didn't know him but I've heard of the publishing house. They published quite a few of my favorite authors." He rattled off a few of my father's discoveries.

The pasta was delicious. I don't know whether he'd made the mushroom sauce himself or bought it at Villa but I was lapping it up. And gulping down the wine. He'd opened a bottle of cabernet sauvignon from the North Fork which wasn't at all bad. Leo was sitting beside me with his head on my lap, no doubt waiting to be fed titbits.

"So tell me about your father. What was he like? Quite a brilliant man by all accounts."

"He was a monster."

I was drunk, of course, otherwise I would never have said it. He looked a little startled.

"You didn't get on, I take it? What about your mother?"

"She died when I was five."

"Good God, how awful. I'm so sorry. And you had to be raised by your father and you didn't like him?"

"No, he abandoned me."

I should have got up and left or at least excused myself and gone to the bathroom and splashed cold water on my face to sober up.

Instead I let him fill my glass and push a plate of delicious-looking cheese towards me. I swallowed half a glass and proceeded to tell him the whole story: my adoration of my mother, her pregnancy, Favor's birth, my mother's suicide, Biddy McIntyre's intervention, my father's total lack of interest in my future, how I came to remain with Biddy and David, my attempts to reach my father through my writing, the awful things the man at the dinner party had told me about him and how he treated my mother. Not only did I let it all come flooding out but I failed to make any attempt to tell the story in any kind of rational chronological order.

"...and then I met this man at this dinner and he told me how much I looked like my mother, oh, and I forgot to say that when she died she killed herself and it was because my father had been so cold, at least that's what this man said and..."

Archie Berkeley was a brilliant listener. He sat on the other side of the trestle table with his legs crossed and his hands on his knees and he didn't move the entire time I was rambling on. He just sat and watched me and listened and when I finally came to a juddering halt, he said, "Why have you told me all this?"

"Oh, God, I'm so sorry. I've sat here and bored you to death. I've never done this before, I swear. I think it's like those people you hear about who pour out their troubles to complete strangers on airplanes and it's only because it's a complete stranger that they can do it."

"I'm the complete stranger," he smiled. "I

151

endure your rudeness at the yard sale, I cook you pasta, I offer you wine, I entrust these two dogs to you and you still look upon me as a complete stranger."

"Oh, no, I'm sorry. But actually…" A stray thought occurred to me. "I am a complete stranger to Theo and Leo's owner. Won't she mind?"

"She won't know. Who's going to tell her? She's off with the unit on location. If she calls to inquire after their welfare—which, I might add, she hasn't done since I've had them, not once—she'll get the machine and when I return from New York I'll call her back and pretend I forgot before. Let's get back to you. Your father dumped you, I can't think of any other way to put it. Has that made you wary of relationships with men? You're not married?"

"No."

"Have you ever been?"

"No, I don't want to get married."

"Do you really mean that?"

"I absolutely do," I protested. "I'm a writer. I value my solitude."

"Well, I write music and I need my space but it hasn't stopped me wanting a wife and family. Didn't you ever want kids? Look how wonderful you are with animals. Don't tell me you wouldn't be the same with children."

I didn't say anything. He was getting a bit close to the mark.

"Why do you live out here?" he persisted. "Are you here year round?"

"Pretty much."

"Have I read your books? Are they published in England? Grace Cammell. I don't know that name. Do you write under a pseudonym?"

I nodded.

"And you're not going to tell me what it is? Go on, don't be a spoilsport. I won't tell."

"Danielle Steel."

"Very funny. I've seen her picture. She doesn't look anything like you. She's years younger."

I threw a cushion at him. Leo raced around the table and retrieved it, brought it back to me.

"Let's go and sit on the sofa." He waited for me to join him. "Now, why are you so unhappy?"

"I'm not," I said, shocked.

"Don't get angry. I shouldn't be asking you such direct questions, I know, and you can tell me to take a running jump if you want, but your sadness is palpable. I sensed it at the yard sale."

"And then you stamped off in a huff."

"Well, do you blame me? As I drove off I found myself thinking someone who is that disagreeable has to be utterly miserable. I wonder why. Of course, your childhood explains part of it."

"Do you enjoy being some kind of amateur shrink? Do they hire you for parties?"

He laughed. "If you really want to know, when I'm not working I'm bored out of my skull here. I took the dogs on for a bit of amusement."

"And you found me."

"It's not quite as bare-faced as that. You're attractive, for God's sake. And however irritating it might be, your prickliness is interesting. I guessed you'd have a story to tell and I was right."

I am a complete sucker for being told what I'm like. It's blindingly obvious why: it means someone's taking an interest in me.

"Well, you might be lonely but I'm not," I told him. "I love being out here on my own, and it's time I went home before I make an even bigger fool of myself. Do you want to drop off Leo and Theo on your way to the Jitney or shall I come and pick them up?"

"You know what would be really terrific? Could I bring them over and then you drive me to the Jitney in your car and meet me off it on Friday?"

"Tell me something. If I hadn't been willing to take the dogs how would you have found someone in twenty-four hours?"

"I wouldn't have bothered, and you were. Give me your address and I'll see you at noon tomorrow."

He walked me to my car in the moonlight. When his lips pecked my cheek as I was about to get in the car, they were red hot on my skin.

They burned me all the way home.

"What in the hell is that?" shrieked Linda, pointing at Leo lying on the rug in front of the fire. May was setting new records for coldness.

"What does it look like? If you go upstairs

and open the closet in my bedroom you'll find another one."

I had been wondering how Archie would get Theo out of the house. He did it lock, stock, and barrel, transporting him in his basket, dragging it out of the cupboard in the family room, into his car, driving it over to my house, and carrying it upstairs into my bedroom closet when he arrived. It was the only closet big enough to take the basket. I'd driven him to the Jitney in Amagansett. No burning goodbye kiss this time, just a request that I meet the five-forty Jitney on Friday.

"You can't get a man so you get yourself a dog. It figures, I guess."

"Who says I can't get a man?" Sometimes Linda could be a complete pain.

"Aha!" She wagged a finger at me. Linda did things normal people did not do. She copied things she saw people do in movies, mostly movies made pre-1950, and never noticed that people in real life did not behave in that cartoon-character fashion any more.

"I'm dog-sitting for a friend," I said truthfully. If Archie Berkeley cooked me dinner and gave me a peck on the cheek that required me to squeeze out the last drop from last year's suntan lotion to cool it down, then he could be described as a friend. If I omitted to mention he was male what harm could it do?

"No one around here has a dog like this." Linda was instantly alert.

"The owner lives in the city," I said. Again truthfully.

"How long you got 'em for?"

"Till Friday."

"Well, I just came over to invite you to dinner Friday. I've got my friends Hal and Sallie staying for the weekend and they know a couple of guys who live over at Montauk and they wanted to take me to Gosman's but I thought hey, wait a second, I'll cook—then I can invite Gracie over and who knows?"

"They're probably gay, Linda."

"And maybe they're not. Think about it. Let me know. And you know what? I just caught the news story at the top of the hour. You got a new person in power over there. Anthony Blair. Looks kinda cute."

She said Anthony in such a way that she managed to make Tony Blair sound like someone in the mob.

"My jury's out," I told her.

"Well, I wouldn't kick him out of bed."

"Linda, I'm talking about his ability to be our next prime minister, for Christ's sake. He's sat on the fence throughout the entire campaign, he's just another politician. Most people over here think he's just like Bill Clinton. All I mean is I want to wait and see what he does before I pass judgment."

"All righty. No need to get aggressive. Anyway, he's got little Cherie right by his side. No room for me."

Of course, she made Cherie sound like a country singer.

"Shall I make you a cup of coffee?" she

asked. It was my house and my coffee but Linda never saw it like that.

"Go right ahead," I said. At least she hadn't arrived brandishing a bottle of rosé, insisting I drink it with her. Linda adored rosé. It was pink, of course.

She yanked the filter out of the machine with such force that it fell apart.

"Well, that's not very well made, is it?"

Typical Linda. She was never wrong. She reminded me of Margot. I would ask Margot something like: "Can I put this in the washing machine?" showing her a sweater I particularly loved and she would say: "Oh, of course, sweet, I always put sweaters in the machine. Foolish not to. Why waste money on dry cleaning?"

And then the damn thing would shrink beyond recognition and Margot would walk away from any responsibility just like Linda was doing now. "Of course it'd shrink," she would say, after the event. "Cheap clothing always does."

There was a knock on the glass slider. It was my caretaker, Lew.

"C'min, Lew," invited Linda, "I'm just making coffee. Gracie here's dog-sitting. Imagine that."

"I saw your mail box got vandalized," said Lew cheerfully. "Kids. I see 'em go by on their bikes."

And of course he did nothing at all to stop them. This was typical Lew. He and Linda were

157

a pair. Lew would wait until I'd spent a fortune having a chimney sweep come by and put a stainless steel cap on my chimney and then he'd tell me he could have got me one for fifty bucks. But whenever I actually asked Lew to get something for me, it was always: "Oh no, couldn't do that. You have to ask somebody else."

Yet everyone wanted him as their caretaker.

"You've got Lew, you're all set," I was told all the time.

"New couple moved in over on Highwood. I said they ought to hire you, Lew," Linda told him.

"You did? That's terrific." Lew looked as proud as if she'd asked him to play center field for the New York Yankees. He positively glowed with happiness, a silly smile spreading across his face.

I'd never been able to understand why Linda didn't see it. Lew was in love with her. It stood out a mile every time he was within fifty paces of her yet she never noticed. Or if she did, she kept mighty quiet about it and he was clearly too shy to come right out and tell her.

Meanwhile he talked to me about her all the time.

"Linda about?" he'd ask whenever he came by the house.

"No idea, Lew. Haven't seen her today. Why don't you take a look next door."

"Nah. Just askin'. Wouldn't want to bother her."

Why not? I always wondered. Bothering me when I was trying to work seemed to be one of Lew's favorite occupations.

"Well, I'm off to Maine next week with my girlfriend," he would announce from time to time. "You'd better tell Linda in case she needs me while I'm gone."

"You could tell her yourself, Lew."

"Nah. You tell her. Maine. With my girl-friend."

I knew what this was all about, but did he seriously imagine that the thought of him off with another woman would bring Linda to heel?

"How's the arthritis, Lew?" I asked, if for no other reason than I couldn't bear another minute of the sight of him standing there beside Linda, looking all goofy. That was the other thing. Lew could never do anything physical for me because of his arthritis. Or so he said.

"Same old, same old. Getting pretty bad. So these dogs. Saw a fella drop 'em off this morning." Lew missed nothing.

Linda turned on me. "What fella?"

"Oh, he was just delivering them for my friend in the city." Why was I lying?

"Nice car," Lew commented. "Mercedes?"

Linda's ears were twitching.

"So, Linda, did you report your mail box to the police?"

"No way," she said.

"How come?"

"I don't want my name in the *Star.*"

"But you love the *Star,* Linda, you read it

every week. Anyway, why would your name go in it?"

"The *Star* has access to police records. So if I reported my mail box they might print it and then whoever it was would come and vandalize me."

"Nah, Linda, they'd be looking for someone way younger," Lew said.

I knelt down to pet Leo. I couldn't trust myself to look at Linda's face. How could Lew think he could get away with saying something like that and imagine he still had a chance with Linda?

"Why don't you go the whole nine yards, Lew? Say I'm a silly old has-been whose husband left her for a younger woman?"

"He did?" This was the first I'd heard that Artie had done something like that.

Lew suddenly realized he'd overstepped the mark.

"Hey, sorry, no coffee for me. Just came by to say I'm over at your place putting down some fertilizer on your lawn. You have your coffee and then you'll be over. See you in a few."

He was gone, leaving me with the dejected Linda.

"Artie and a younger woman?" I prompted.

"Way younger and I don't want to talk about it. I'd better skip coffee and go make sure Lew doesn't ruin all my planting." The pink and purple color scheme of Linda's herbaceous borders had to be seen to be believed. Lew would be doing everyone a favor if he eradicated them at birth. "So I'll see you Friday.

160

About seven-thirty. Maybe I'll get some lobster. Okay? I don't hear you. I'll take that as a yes."

But it wasn't an automatic yes because Friday was the day I was due to pick up Archie and I realized I was nurturing some kind of teenage girlish hope that he would ask me to stay longer with him than the time it took to drive him home.

Theo had become worse, not better, during his stay with me. Whatever magic I had worked on Leo and other dogs made no impression on Theo. He refused to come out of the closet in my bedroom, and as it was upstairs I had to call Lew to come and help me carry him in his basket downstairs. We eventually installed him in the tool shed on the back porch and left the door open so he could sneak out to pee on the lawn.

So when I went to meet Archie off the Jitney, I went in my own car, not his, and I was minus the dogs. The Jitney was on time. I parked behind it and watched the taxi driver in front of me searching for the party boxes he was supposed to pick up. It always happened. People giving parties on the weekend in the Hamptons ordered crates of glasses and food to be delivered from New York on the Jitney. They bought a ticket and told the caterers to put it on a particular bus and then call the cab company and describe the pickup. But the connection was rarely made. The caterers either missed the bus and put it on a later one and neglected to tell the cab company, or they described the delivery so vaguely that the poor taxi driver couldn't possibly identify it.

"I'm looking for a gray box," he told me, a note of despair in his voice, "that's it. A gray box. No indication of size or what's in it. Do you see a gray box?"

I peered into the vast hold in the bottom half of the giant bus where the luggage was stashed. It was hard to see anything clearly.

"Those two suitcases are mine," said an English voice. I hadn't noticed Archie coming up behind us. "I was looking for my car. I don't see it."

I explained. I detected a small hint of irritation crossing his face. I opened the trunk of my station wagon and he tossed in his bags.

Sitting beside me as I drove up the Old Stone Highway, he asked, "So how've they been?"

"You really want to know?"

"That bad?"

"A nightmare. Leo was okay but Theo's spent the entire week in the tool shed."

"I'm so sorry. Listen, I'll take them off your hands as quick as I can. Leave you in peace."

I felt suddenly bitterly disappointed. He wasn't going to ask me over to his house, he wasn't going to spend any time with me. Of course he wasn't—he was tired and he wanted to get home and take a shower or whatever.

But I couldn't let him go that easily.

"Why don't you come in and have a drink? I've got a big pot of homemade tomato soup and I could scramble some eggs, repay you for the other night in an extremely humble way."

In fact what I had was a container of Italian tomato soup from Villa in the freezer which I would surreptitiously decant into a saucepan and defrost when he wasn't looking.

"I'm supposed to go to a party. I think that taxi driver was probably looking for the caterers' deliveries in the Jitney."

I waited for him to ask me to go with him but he didn't, which made me want him to stay with me all the more. He still hadn't responded properly to my invitation by the time we were turning into my drive.

"Is that Theo?" he shouted, pointing to something disappearing around the side of the house.

"No, that's a very brazen fox that runs around the house when he thinks no one's looking and sniffs my garbage cans. Theo's terrified of it."

"You have foxes in your back yard?"

"Foxes. Squirrels. A big, black pig once. And raccoons.

The chimney sweep found raccoon pups in my chimney. I'd burned them to death with my fire without realizing it."

"Raccoon holocaust."

"For Christ's sake, I didn't mean to."

"Don't be so prickly. You're like a porcupine. I'm going to call you Porcy. Hey, Leo, pleased to see me?"

163

Leo had escaped as soon as I opened the kitchen door. I don't think he was pleased to see Archie as much as pleased to be let out of the house.

"What'll you drink?" I asked Archie.

Two vodka tonics and a bottle and a half of some disgusting bilge from the local vineyards later he was in the middle of telling me about his experiences in a hip-hop club, doing research for the movie, when the phone rang.

It was Linda wanting to know if I'd be joining her next door for dinner. I'd forgotten all about Linda, and after one vodka tonic I'd forgotten all about pretending the Villa tomato soup was homemade. I'd tipped it out of its container in full view of Archie.

"Who was that?" he asked when I'd gotten rid of Linda. "You were dead cagey. 'I might come over later.' Where are you going? Can I come?"

"You didn't ask me to go to your party with you."

"Oh God, I forgot all about it. It's nice being here with you in your funny tree house."

"This tree house, as you call it, made of cypress wood and glass, was architect designed and made the cover of *House Beautiful* in 1968."

"I'll bet. It's much nicer than the pile of crap I've rented. What do you do with yourself out here? Oh shit, I forgot, you're a writer, aren't you? You must be successful."

"If you like mindless, middle-market women's rubbish."

"Oh, Porcy, Porcy, why are you always putting yourself down? It's probably extremely commercial and lucrative and what's wrong with that? This film I'm scoring at the moment, the script is pure drivel in parts but it works."

"What's it about?" I knew it had said in the *Star* that it was about an older woman's affair with a gangsta rapper but I didn't want him to know I'd been reading about him.

"It's about a love affair between an older woman and a younger man. I say older, I mean..."

"My age," I prompted.

"I have no idea how old you are. Let's say she's in her mid-forties." He knew he was on the mark.

"And the younger man?"

"In his twenties. Maybe twenty-four."

"Is it sad?"

"Why do you ask that? It is, as a matter of fact. It's terribly sad. He treats her like shit and she's at that terribly vulnerable age where she imagines her looks have gone and no one wants her any more and suddenly he comes along and she's completely knocked for a loop."

"Tell me about it."

"Sounds like you've had a run-in with a younger man yourself?"

He didn't miss a trick. Before I knew it I was telling him the whole sad story about Harry Fox (without actually mentioning him by name) and about how stupid and hurt and betrayed I felt about the whole thing.

"Is that why you came here, to be alone? To get away from him?"

"You've got it in one."

"Life's a real bitch sometimes, isn't it? Tell me something, and this is going to sound pretty heartless after what you've just told me—by the way I think you're incredibly brave to let it all out like that—"

"I'm really sorry. Must have bored you to tears. Very self-indulgent of me. And anyway, who are you going to tell?"

"Precisely. Listen, what I wanted to know was, in your really vulnerable state, just like you are now, what kind of music really tips you over the edge, what songs really get to you?"

I felt rather flattered to be asked.

"It's an age thing, I'm afraid," I told him. "Sinatra. Singing 'All the Way'—it's no good unless he needs you all the way. And there's some awful Barbra Streisand song in *A Star is Born*. 'Evergreen'? Gets me every time. Ditto Bette Midler with 'The Rose.' There's hundreds of them. Why?"

"It's the sort of note I need to hit when I'm doing the music for this film. For the older woman. What'll make her cry. It's a crossover market."

I remembered all the crap about it being the biggest challenge of his life.

"So what influences are you going to use for the youthful lover?"

"Well, talk about you feeling middle-aged and out of touch, they've only gone and made the lover a rap singer..." I hadn't said a word

166

about feeling middle-aged and out of touch but maybe that's how he'd read my running away from Harry Fox and burying myself in the woods of Long Island. "I know absolutely zip about rap. I've had to take a kind of crash course in it, self-taught, starting with Africa Bambata and Public Enemy, Run DMC, NWA..."

"NWA?"

"Niggers With Attitude. And I've been playing around with turntables in real old Grandmaster Flash style, twisting them by hand to get short bursts of a record repeated over and over again. Did you notice the turntables at the house in the room where Theo hides?"

I hadn't. In fact I didn't have a clue what he was going on about, but his enthusiasm was engaging.

"Of course it all started with Cassius Clay."

"What did?"

"Hip-hop. Rapping. Remember those poems he used to come out with? Float like a butterfly, sting like a bee? That was rapping of a kind. But what I really like is the De La Soul influence: they started using electronics to take a snatch of a song, had to be careful they didn't get sued for copyright. It's amazing what you can do with music on a computer now."

"So you have to compose this hip-hop, do you?"

"Actually, I don't. They've got a music supervisor at the studio who'll pick certain rap songs for the movie and clear copyright. I'll listen to them and they'll help me with the rest of the music. You're not into rap, I take it? No kids?"

I shook my head.

"It's my sons who've got me going on it. They've been a great help. You've never been married?"

He kept slipping in these questions.

"No. I never have."

"No one special?"

"No, not really. I told you about..."

"Not ever? Before him?"

He was getting near my danger point where I start feeling really sorry for myself. I'd never been what you called spoiled by a man—flowers, romantic holidays, walks on the beach, expensive presents, jewelry. I'd had flings, plenty of them, candlelit dinners in expensive restaurants, then a night or two of drunken passion before I started getting clingy and put them off, but apart from Harry and a couple of people before him who were keen on me but who didn't really interest me, there'd been no one serious.

I changed the subject.

"What about you? Has your wife been the only one?"

"More or less. Obviously she wasn't the first but we've been married nearly twenty years."

"No extramarital flings?"

"Not my style. I never have affairs. I know a lot of men who do, especially in the film industry, but I'm just not the type."

Of course not—he was decent, honorable.

There were men like him around. I'd always been convinced of it and I was determined that one day I'd find one for myself.

I made coffee, lurching around the kitchen in a drunken stupor. I wondered if I ought to offer him a liqueur. Did I have any to offer him? In any case he'd probably drive straight into a tree. He was thinking along the same lines.

"I don't think I'd better have any more to drink if I've got to drive these animals home. I know there's no more wine left but I'm saying that as a precaution because I know if you offer me anything else I'll accept. So please don't."

I didn't.

"We'd better start trying to entice Theo out of the tool shed. It could take all night," he said.

We abandoned it after half an hour, by which time Theo had nipped Archie on the thumb, and I noticed after this he was a real nervous nellie about going back into the tool shed. Theo also savaged me on both hands and forearms. I'd never had it happen before. I'd always been able to reach out to a dog with my hand, nonthreatening, lower than its head, and coax it towards me.

But Theo was a neurotic bundle of quivering bones. He was the most suspicious dog I'd ever encountered. Matters were not helped by Leo prancing around on the back porch in the background, barking.

"Shut him up, for God's sake," I told Archie, "I'm bleeding, I'm calling it quits. Theo's

169

not coming out of that tool shed for anyone. We'll call a vet to come give him a tranquillizer in the morning. That dog's dangerous."

Archie looked startled. "Whatever you say. I'll just grab Leo and be off."

"Oh God, Archie, it's three-thirty in the morning. Crash on the sofa if you want. I'm going to bed."

I was fast asleep upstairs in my bed. Leo had spent the week lying on the covers beside me, so when there was movement on the mattress I assumed it was the dog and muttered, "Fuck off, Leo," and rolled over.

I rolled right into Archie's arms.

He was still wearing a T-shirt but he was naked from the waist down.

"I thought you said you didn't have affairs."

"I know I did but I've decided something."

"What's that?"

"You're special."

"Why am I special?" I had to ask, of course. I couldn't just leave it alone, let the affair proceed at its natural pace. Because that's what it had turned into pretty quickly. I was having an affair with Archie Berkeley, the kind where you sleep together almost every night and, when work doesn't interfere, you spend the days together. Everything you do, you imagine yourself telling the other person about it. And you look forward to hearing about everything they've done since they last saw you, no matter how mundane. He calls when he says he's going to and you always know when you're going to see him next. There's no sitting by the phone chewing your nails, no calling him in desperation pretending you've been out for hours and maybe he was trying to reach you? I was experiencing something with Archie that I hadn't experienced with anyone—least of all Harry Fox—in years: a feeling of security.

We became a foursome—Archie, me, Leo, and Theo. The day I persuaded Theo to come out of the tool shed on my back porch we celebrated with champagne. The day I got him into the car, Archie produced a jar of beluga caviar in a picnic basket and we drove to Louse Point. At last I was one of the couples, sitting on the sand, huddled inside one of his sweaters, leaning into his side with my head on his shoulder.

I felt eighteen again, on the brink of an adventure but not quite sure where I was going, so I asked him: "Why am I special?"

"Because you're you."

"No, really..."

"Because..." He hesitated, looked at me, realized I was serious. "Because you're brave and independent and you don't seem to need a man like all the other women I've come across. If only I'd met you fifteen years ago. And then of course..."

"What ?"

"Theo and Leo like you. What better recommendation is there?"

He first told me he loved me on a Sunday

morning. We were at his place. We'd made coffee and brought it back to bed to read *The New York Times* but we were naked and I could feel him becoming excited. Leo and Theo were draped across the end of the bed, lying heavy on our feet. We began to make love and I moved on top of him, arching my back and moving my hips to bring him into me. Afterwards I collapsed on top of him and that's when he said it. Very quietly.

"I think I love you."

I raised myself on both elbows and looked into his eyes. He looked apprehensive. Wondering how I'd react or nervous that he'd made such a committed declaration so early in our relationship?

"I think I love you, too," I said. Why were we being so tentative? I was absolutely crazy about him. I couldn't believe he had come along just like that, just when I needed someone like him so badly. He was so romantic. He was considerate. He was the right age. He was successful. He was fantastic looking. And he loved me.

It was probably just as well the letter came the following week. I needed an out. I needed space, time to breathe, to take stock and calm down before I did something really foolish.

Biddy's letter, forwarded by my father's lawyers, saddened me not just because it contained the news that her husband David, my foster father, was dying of prostate cancer but because it brought home to me the fact that I had neglected Biddy and David for so long.

They were perhaps the only two people in my entire life who had never demanded anything from me, yet at the same time they had given me unconditional love and respect. And I had departed their home under something of a cloud, gone out into the world and left them behind.

I didn't feel guilty, exactly, about losing touch with them apart from the annual Christmas and birthday cards. There had always been the feeling that they had fostered me as a job, a job they had carried out to the best of their ability. But they had never pretended to be my real parents; they had given me a certain kind of freedom, and since I had ceased to be in their care I had thought about them less than I should have.

"You'd better go to her right away," said Archie when I told him about Biddy's letter.

"You want me out of the way? Am I crowding you?"

It was extraordinary how my old insecurities could return so easily.

"Of course not, Porcy. Don't get all prickly on me. It's the last thing I want. But from what you tell me the man is dying. And didn't you say she had to find you via the lawyers? How long have you had this house out here? A year or so at least, right? And you haven't been in touch to give her the address. She had to get it from your lawyer? She's gone out of her way to find you and she needs you by the sound of it. You were fond of her, weren't you?"

He made me feel terrible. Because the truth

was I didn't want to go. I wanted to stay and bask in his love rather than go and comfort Biddy. But Archie had helped me decide what to do. He expected me to go, therefore I would.

"What will you do while I'm gone?" I asked him. "It may take a week or so. If he dies while I'm there I'll have to stay for the funeral."

"I'll work like crazy," he told me. "That way when you return I'll be able to spend more time with you. I'll have cleared a lot of stuff out of the way."

"Oh my God, I'm keeping you from your work. You should have said."

"There you go again. Overreacting. Defensive. Stop it! If anything I've been interfering in your work."

There he was quite wrong. I needed distraction more than anything. I'd finished *Luther* and sent it off to a couple of top literary agents in New York under the name Grace Cammell. I think if I hadn't had Archie to keep my mind off it I would have gone quietly mad waiting for a reaction.

"I feel bad. I know so little about your work," I told him. "What stage have you reached?"

"I've been struggling with the main theme, the love theme. The director's screaming for it. He told me what he wanted before he started shooting but I just couldn't come up with it. I saw dailies when I was in New York but even that didn't help. Then you came along and suddenly writing a romantic theme was the easiest thing in the world. Corny but true. I can't wait to play it to you. I'm going to play it to the director early next week—he's coming out here for the day. You'll be gone. I have to get his approval on it and then when you come back you can come over and I'll play it for you on the piano. Maybe I'll go right over the top and call it 'Grace's Song' like 'Lara's Theme' from *Dr. Zhivago*. But you know, seriously, there is something I've been meaning to ask you: would you read the script for me? You're a writer—I'd welcome your thoughts on it. You might come up with some suggestions, some insights into the characters. You could read it on the plane maybe?"

I wouldn't let him drive me to JFK, citing Leo and Theo as an excuse. I had a terrible feeling that if he was beside me I wouldn't leave. I called him from the gate but there was no reply. Probably out walking them.

I began the script before take-off, as soon as I was settled in my seat. I was on an overnight flight but I didn't sleep the entire six hours. I stayed awake, reading. It was a strong story. And a familiar one.

Too familiar.

I think subconsciously I knew the truth long before I came across the letter that had been slipped inside the script as a marker a few pages before the end. I think I knew when I read in the *Star* that the film was about an affair between an older woman and a younger man.

The letter was a short note to Archie from the director of the film saying he'd be coming out to the Hamptons the following week to hear the main theme, just as Archie had said.

It was signed "Harry."

Harry Fox.

Favor

How was I going to find Grace? My initial euphoria about having the perfect excuse to go and look for her in America was evaporating in the face of a problem I had not anticipated. I had thought it would be so simple to get her address. I had written to the lawyers for my father's estate, with whom I dealt on a fairly regular basis; it wasn't as if I was unknown to them, and they had written back and told me quite firmly that they had strict instructions not to give out Grace's address without her prior approval. It was a delicate affair. They were probably the only people with official knowledge that Grace and I were sisters, yet they were forbidden to put us in touch.

Although maybe Grace knew exactly where she could find me but had never wanted to. These instructions to Dad's lawyers sounded pretty final. And I already knew her publishers weren't going to help me. I could write to her care of them and they would undoubtedly forward it, but somehow I did not want to forewarn her of my arrival in America. I did not want her to have the chance to put me off going.

But then, as I was beginning to work myself up into a serious fret, domestic distraction manifested itself in the form of Frisky giving birth to four kittens.

As far as we could make out, she had them while Pete Sampras was beating Petr Korda in the men's quarter finals at Wimbledon. Sampras had won the first two sets but was having a bit of a problem in the third and had obviously decided to do something about it.

Ned and Sophie were sitting on the floor in front of the television, their arms around each other and their eyes glued to the set. Sophie had revealed herself to be a tennis nut, and Ned, who had never been known to show any interest in it before, appeared to have become addicted overnight. Suddenly his entire conversation was peppered with references to lobs and passing shots and half volleys, which resulted in snide asides from Mary about ground strokes and Sophie.

Mary wandered in and out, driving everybody crazy, predictably pronouncing Tim Henman to be "really sad and boring." She declared she was mourning the absence of Agassi. I said since he wasn't going to be around this year why didn't she go off and get on with her homework.

Frisky wandered in and settled herself on Sophie's lap where she began to purr.

Frisky was what the vet called a black-and-white long hair, although officially she was known as Frisky Hardy, a name I was particularly embarrassed by when it was called out in the waiting room to summon me in to see him. It always looked as if it was my name when I stood up, clutching the cat basket. Anyone who clapped eyes on Frisky with her turquoise eyes and fluffy black-and-white hair, always announced she was the prettiest cat they'd ever seen. Plus she was a Class A trollop. She flirted with everyone—dog, cat, human—rolled over on her back and flashed her fluffy petticoats in the air.

She was, in short, a loose female who seduced The Enemy, as we called him, a filthy great tom who drove us all mad by spraying everywhere and stinking the place up. Inevitably Frisky became a teenage mother.

While still not much more than a kitten, she had appropriated one of my better sweaters, a gray lamb's-wool number long enough to cover my bulges, that had cost more than I usually paid for an item of clothing. She used to drag it from room to room and lay it out like a picnic blanket to sleep on. In the last stages of her pregnancy she had draped it across the end of our bed and Gus and I went to sleep each night after carefully positioning our feet so as not to disturb her, convinced we would awaken to witness her swallowing the afterbirth or whatever it is they're supposed to do.

In the event she elected, rather thoughtfully, to give birth in our next-door neighbor's living room. He was on the phone at the time. Frisky apparently roamed about the place for half an hour, annoying him, and finally jumped into an empty box that had recently housed a newly acquired vacuum cleaner. Five minutes later he was staring down at four kittens and nearly dropped the phone. He claimed he tried to get our attention by shouting at us from the communal garden we shared, but, presumably because we were engrossed in Wimbledon, we didn't respond. So he put the vacuum cleaner box, complete with Frisky and kittens, in the bicycle shed.

And forgot all about them.

Frisky walked in considerably thinner, and looking very pleased with herself, the next day while the Frenchman, Cedric Pioline, was knocking out a British hopeful, Greg Rusedski, and we all embarked on a frantic search for her offspring.

The biggest surprise was Mary's intense interest in Frisky's new state of motherhood. I would come upon her kneeling on the floor beside the vacuum cleaner box, which we had brought into the house and lined with an old bolster covered in a sheet, staring down at the squirming creatures, helping them to locate Frisky's teats.

Frisky proved to be an unexpectedly conscientious mother, given her early tacky behavior. She cleaned them regularly, eating their little droppings and licking their bottoms. As they grew older and started charging about the place, chasing each other and climbing up curtains, she followed them, keeping a close eye on them, picking them up by the scruff of the neck if she thought they were liable to harm themselves, and dumping them unceremoniously back in the basket Mary had now provided for them. And she talked to them. When Frisky entered a room she gave a kind of high-pitched squawk and the kittens squeaked back from under the bed or wherever they were and Frisky would go to them.

And Mary, if she was home, never left them alone. I couldn't get over it. Gone was the tough-talking rebel. It was as if she was following Frisky's example and revoking her dirty habits, too, in favor of nurturing and caring for the young. But it was when I came upon her weeping, cradling the Little Black One as it was known, that I felt I had to say something.

"Mary, what's all this? What's the matter with you?"

"Oh, Mum, do we really have to give them away? How will Frisky be able to bear it?"

"Cats don't care. She'll be fine. In any case, by the time they're ready to leave she'll be worn out feeding them. You'll see, after three months she'll have lost interest in them."

"*No!* They're her babies. How can she possibly... I don't believe it. I can't." She broke into a fresh bout of weeping.

"Darling, don't." For the first time in ages she let me take her in my arms and hug her.

"Are you premenstrual? What's the matter? Tell me?"

"I never realized babies could be so small and helpless."

"But they're growing every day. They'll be great big cats soon. They're fine."

She wouldn't be comforted, however, and after a while I began to yearn for the old Mary, the one with life and backtalk and spirit, the one who smiled. She wouldn't even come to Wales when it was our turn. She insisted on staying in London with Frisky and "the babies" as she always called them.

Walking into Upper Stone Farm for the first time since I'd accused Gus of infidelity made me rather nervous. It's sort of typical of Gus that he acted as if all that had never happened. I suspect that it does cross his mind from time to time but he'd never bring it up unless I did.

I decided not to mention it. What was the point? He'd looked startled enough when I'd told him how I'd run into Amanda in the Kensington Hilton and he'd changed the subject pretty fast. That was Gus all over. You couldn't really call it brushing things under the carpet, but he did like to move forward all the time. Once a problem had been dealt with he didn't like to bring it up again.

We had Ned and Sophie with us and I found myself watching them rather more closely than I might have. If I'd bothered to get to know Sophie a little better perhaps I would have raised it with her, but while I warmed to this beautiful, talented young girl—who wouldn't?—at the same time I backed away from the idea of becoming really close to her. I knew why. It didn't take a genius to work it out. She'd come between me and my beloved hulk of a son. Not in a hostile way. It was breathtaking to see the change in Ned and the way she'd built up his confidence in himself. She ought to get a medal and I ought to be down on my hands and knees thanking her instead of feeling all this silly resentment. But he didn't come to me for confidential chats any more and I missed that.

So all in all, while I went through the motions of playing the good wife and mother— standing at the stove stirring delicious-smelling pasta sauces, making up the beds, shopping in Knighton— I was actually feeling a little sorry for myself.

We did have an extra guest. Totally unexpected. The Latimers had been down the weekend before and when it was time for them to leave on Sunday night and begin the long drive back to London they discovered their dog, Marcus, was missing. No amount of calling and whistling could raise him, so Les, the farmer, promised to look out for him and, when he found him, keep him safe and sound and deliver him to us the following weekend to take back to London.

Marcus had turned up only a couple of hours later, soaking wet, and Les had kept him all week. Now he'd been handed over to us for the weekend and someone had to take him for walks. Gus was out checking on the progress of various security jobs—maintaining PR goodwill he called it. I don't know why Ned and Sophie bothered coming to the country. They had turned into near professional couch potatoes since Wimbledon and it was a bit of a rarity seeing them vertical.

So on top of everything else I had to take Marcus for long walks. That was the frame of mind I was in: why was it always down to me? sort of thing. In truth, however, I rather welcomed the opportunity to get out on my own and think things through.

Think what through?

By the end of my first walk my thoughts were decidedly morbid. There was such a lot of death in the country. It took Marcus to show me what I had never noticed before. He tore apart a rabbit before my eyes, then a pheasant. And then I came upon a sheep lying on its back, stupid eyes gawping at me, petrified. It had a gash down its side where it had caught itself on the barbed wire, nothing serious but ugly all the same. I knew what I was supposed to do. The farmer had told me. It was stuck on its back and couldn't get up because its fleece was too thick on either side for it to roll over on to its feet. If I gave it a kick it could right itself. But I couldn't bring myself to go near it. Which meant it would probably die.

Death. It was everywhere.

When we were next down, about a month later, even though we no longer had Marcus (or any of the children, for that matter), I still went for walks on my own. I would be out for at least two hours, striding through the fields in my Wellingtons as protection from the ubiquitous mud. I was always a bit stiff for the first half-hour and then my muscles would begin to loosen up, especially if I began by climbing to the top of the hill and walking over into the next valley.

The next morning I was so stiff I woke up thinking about Roger and whether I would require his healing hands. At least I always imagined he had healing hands. I'd never actually experienced them, and on the odd times I'd had to go in and interrupt one of his treatment sessions, I'd heard the ominous cracking of bones and squeaks of pain and shock from the patient. Still, they came back for more so he must be doing something right.

I was particularly sore and exhausted the day I limped back and saw a car parked in the lane outside the second set of gates that led to Upper Stone Farm. Visitors. The last thing I wanted. But then I saw there were two people still sitting in the car, making no move to get out. If I hadn't been so tired I would have gone over and asked them if they were lost, but the imminent pleasure of soaking in a hot bath proved infinitely more tempting.

Gus met me in the hall.

"Did you see them?" he asked.

"That couple in the car? Did they come to the house? Who are they?"

"No idea. They didn't get out of the car, just

184

sat there staring at the house. Did you get a look at them? Were they having a picnic or something?"

"I didn't get close enough to see."

"Weird," said Gus and went back to the box.

Half an hour later when I came down from my bath they were still there. I didn't say anything to Gus and went outside. As I walked up to the car I saw to my surprise that they were quite old, in their seventies at least. As I approached, the woman, who was in the driving seat, wound down the window.

"Hello," I said, "have you broken down? We couldn't help noticing you've been out here quite a while."

"I'm awfully sorry," said the woman, a little flustered. "You must think us a little odd. I used to know this place rather well. We didn't want to intrude as we didn't know the new owners."

"You mean you knew the previous owners? The farm belongs to Les Bevan now and we rent it from him, but maybe you knew my father, Lucas Cammell, or even my grandfather, Richard Cammell? My father sold Upper Stone Farm to Les. I was born here. Maybe you'd like to come in and look around?"

There was a rather odd look on her face now. I couldn't quite figure it out.

"You're Lucas Cammell's daughter?"

She was looking at me very intently. Her face might be lined and her skin and hair parched with age but her eyes were still sharp.

I nodded.

185

"I'll talk to you later," she said abruptly. "I'll telephone you this evening if I may?"

Before I could say anything more than yes, of course, we'll be there, let alone ask why she wanted to phone me, she had started the car and propelled it into a lurching bounce down the hill. Only as I turned to go back to the house did I realize that the old man sitting beside her had not uttered a word, had not even looked at me, just sat there staring out over the valley as if he were deaf to the world.

I walked over to Les's that evening to collect some eggs and help myself to a little parsley from his garden. Les poked his head out of the door.

"Just had Biddy on the phone asking me for your number. Gave it to her. Hope that was all right?"

"Who's she?" The name rang a bell.

"She's an old lady. She and her husband have a house over on Stowe Hill, used to come down on weekends like yourselves but they haven't been here in years. Not since I've had the farm. When your mother was around. Her husband's got cancer, see, and her's brought him down here to die. He asked her to do that. Her's driving him around to see all the places for the last time. He's always loved it around here. But they never came back down here when they had the girl, you see?"

What girl? The name Biddy did ring a distant bell. And she'd known Dad.

"Some woman's just called," said Gus when I got back.

"An old woman?"

"Well, yes, she didn't exactly sound in the first flush of youth. Can you call her back? Here's the number. Local. Stowe."

She answered straight away, as if she'd been sitting by the phone. Her voice was a little quavery, nervous.

"I had a message from my husband to call you," was all I said but she recognized my voice immediately.

"Thank you. It's Biddy McIntyre."

Biddy McIntyre. Grace McIntyre. It couldn't be....

"Yes. I saw Les Bevan. He told me about..."

"...about David. Yes, I didn't want to talk about him to you with him sitting in the car, even though I'm never sure whether he's taking anything in. He hasn't got long. He isn't very good at communicating any more but I know he likes sitting and looking at the views around here. It's so peaceful. I picked that part of the hill outside Upper Stone Farm because, well, I remember it so well. I hope you don't mind?"

"Not at all. I'm sorry about your husband."

"He's asleep now. We should talk, really. I can leave him for a bit. Would it be... I mean, could I possibly come over now?"

I was completely taken aback. Why did this strange older woman feel we should talk? There was a real sense of urgency in her voice. Then I remembered. She had known Dad. Maybe she wanted news of him.

"You knew my father?"

"Yes. Of course."

"Well, I don't know whether you heard, or when you last saw him, but he died quite some time ago, I'm afraid."

"Oh yes, I know."

Well then, what did she want? Was it to do with Grace?

There was a silence on the line, then she said, "You don't know who I am, do you?"

"When Les said your name I knew I'd heard it somewhere before but I don't think we've actually met, have we?"

"Not since you were a tiny baby."

"Then you knew my mother too?"

"Of course." She sounded quite impatient. "I was your mother's best friend. I was the one who adopted your sister, Grace. Not officially, but David and I fostered her until she left home. Now do you understand why I want to come and see you?"

"I'll come to you if I may?" I said quickly, congratulating myself on my presence of mind. If she came over here then Gus would be around and I didn't want to talk about Grace in front of him.

I called out to him as I left, "There's a woman across the valley who has some books on the area I'd be interested to see. That was her on the phone. Les suggested she call me. I'm just going over there to pick them up. Won't be long."

Why all the unnecessary explanation? Why the lies? Recently I had suspected Gus of lying to me. Now here I was deceiving him. Just a little. And why had I mentioned Les? If Gus spoke to him about it Les might explain to him exactly who Biddy McIntyre was. Maybe Les had mentioned her in passing to me before. He probably assumed I knew all about her.

I knew a few estate agents who would love to get Biddy McIntyre's house on their books, I thought as I drove up to it. Directly across the valley from Upper Stone Farm, Hill House was appropriately named. It was the highest building as you climbed Stowe Hill and the view back across the valley was commanding. However, the attractive classic stone exterior of the house belied a gloomy atmosphere inside. I wondered how many other houses up and down the country were in this situation, lying empty for twenty, thirty years waiting for someone to take them over. It was a waste, but people with money often never thought to sell such houses that they owned but didn't live in, especially if they came with acres of land as this one obviously did, land that was presumably farmed successfully for the McIntyres.

Biddy let me into the house. I glimpsed rooms off the hall with furniture covered in sheets.

"David's upstairs, tired out. I've only opened up two rooms upstairs for us to sleep in so come into the kitchen, will you? What'll you drink?"

She moved relatively quickly for someone her age. I noticed a glass of whisky on the kitchen table.

"I don't know what to do, whether to open up the rest of the house or what. I just don't know how long we'll be here."

How long it would take for her husband to die, she meant.

"You wouldn't think of moving back here for good?" I asked, accepting a glass of whisky.

She looked a little surprised at the thought of it. "Never." She was quite firm. "Since your mother's death I've never felt the same about the area. David is the one who loves it. He used to come down here on his own. He liked the country. He wasn't really cut out for London. He was born around here, you know."

And he'll die here.

"His family must have known mine. Maybe he grew up with my father?"

"Possibly." She didn't seem interested. "They knew each other certainly, that's how I came to meet your mother, but that was in London and my husband isn't—wasn't—a bit like your father. Well, now, here we are. Take a pew. I expect you're looking at me and thinking if my mother had lived she'd be like this old bag by now."

I was thinking no such thing. Indeed I was rather shocked by the casual way in which she introduced my mother's memory into the conversation. She was direct, this Biddy McIntyre. No nonsense. No mucking about.

"I don't look like her, do I?"

"Not a bit. You've seen pictures, I imagine. She was a real beauty. Probably why she took me as a friend. Beauties often choose plain girl-friends. Know they won't be upstaged."

"Oh, I'm sure it was nothing like that."

"So you think I'm plain too, do you? How on earth could you know it was nothing like that?"

She had a point. Her unswerving candor was beginning to get to me.

"My daughter looks just like her."

This caught her attention.

"You have a daughter? There's a grand-daughter? Is she with you?"

"No."

She looked suddenly bored again. I wasn't enough to interest her.

"And a grandson," I blundered on, "Ned and Mary."

"And do they ask after their grandmother?"

"I'm afraid not. They never knew Dad either, really. They just know my mother died giving birth to me and that's that. I mean, I didn't know her so it's not as if I can even tell them about her."

"It's as if she never existed," Biddy whispered. "But why did you tell them she died in child-birth? Best to tell them the truth, isn't it?"

"That is the truth."

"And who told you that?"

"My father."

"I see." Two words. Clipped. Abrupt. And, for some reason, angry.

I sensed this woman didn't like me much. But she'd only just met me. Why had she asked me here? Why had I come?

"I'm so sorry about your husband," I said

for the second time, trying to soften her attitude towards me. "Do you have children?" Even as I said the words I realized how stupid they were. "I mean any other children?"

"No. That's why we took Grace."

Another cold silence. I gulped some whisky. I never drank whisky. It was making me drunk. And bolder.

"I've never met her."

"Extraordinary. Your own sister. Of course you had your father. You didn't need her. Weren't you even curious?"

"Of course I was. Often. But Dad always made it seem as if we'd be getting together some day. That it was just a temporary thing, our being apart, her living with you."

"So he told you about me?"

"Well, no, not really, but I knew Grace had to be with someone. And it was sort of like my kids and my mother, like me and my mother. I'd never seen her, I'd never seen Grace. I was a kid. It was hard to picture her in my life. She was like some fictitious character in one of my children's books. I mean, I knew Jo in *Little Women* better than I knew my own sister."

Biddy smiled at this. She clearly liked honesty.

"So, yes, I didn't really begin to think seriously about her until I grew up and realized Dad was dead and he'd left her everything and I was never going to meet her. By that time I had Gus. And Ned and Mary. My husband. My family."

"And you didn't need Grace."

"No. Not then. But I do now. That's why I'm here," I said, answering my own earlier question. "Why did you adopt her? Why didn't she grow up with us?"

"Isn't that something you ought to have asked your father?"

She was cruel, this old woman, sitting here immaculately turned out in her cashmere sweater and amber necklace, nursing her whisky while her husband's life ebbed away upstairs somewhere in this forsaken house.

"Grace grew up here?" I asked, trying to picture a child running about this clinical kitchen devoid of the clutter I was used to. No pots and pans piled up in the sink, no half-loaded dishwasher left open for everyone to trip over, no bottles of ketchup with the tops off, no remains of breakfast or tea with half-eaten crusts of toast and congealing butter. I imagined if I opened the fridge, I'd find it empty save for a dried-up lemon wedge and a carton of milk. Mary's favorite adjective suited this place: sad.

"No, Grace grew up in London. We took her there about six months after you were born, when it was quite clear your father wasn't going to come and get her."

"Have you read her books?"

"Every one. I think they're a load of rubbish. Not worthy of her."

"What do you mean?"

"She could do better. She had a fine mind."

"So what happened?"

"I've no idea. She left home—I mean David

and me—far too young. No university. She insisted on working straight away. We were living outside London by then and she hated the suburbs. So did I. I never blamed her for leaving. David and I always agreed we wouldn't interfere."

"But she came to see you often since then?"

"No."

It was chilling the way she said it. No. There was a lifetime's resentment in that sentence. *David and I agreed we wouldn't interfere.* But this woman had interfered. She'd got her hands on Grace for some reason. And she'd had to let go.

"I've barely seen her since."

"Do you miss her?"

"It's been over twenty years since she left for good. I have no idea what I'm missing. She must have changed from the child I brought up."

"But you've kept in touch?"

"On and off. That's why I wanted to talk to you when I found out who you were, if you really want to know. I wanted to see if you'd discovered her, if you were in touch with her."

"But I've just told you. I've never met her. Nothing. No contact."

I didn't mention the signing sessions. Something told me that if this woman knew Grace had been in London and hadn't contacted her it would hurt her. Although she could have heard her on the radio and figured it out for herself.

Biddy McIntyre slumped. "I'm sorry. I've

been hard on you. It's not your fault Grace was turned out of her own home. Well, it was, but you were too young to be any part of it. Did you love your father?" she asked suddenly.

"Very much," I answered without hesitation.

"Well then, there's nothing more to be said. Thank you for coming." The interview—for that, I now understood, was what it had turned out to be—was at an end.

"But I want to know about Grace. That's why I came to see you."

"Bit late now," said the old woman bitterly. "Please close the door quietly on the way out. David gets little enough sleep these days as it is."

"Well, thank you for the drink," I said, getting up. "If there's anything I can do to help...with your husband, I mean."

"I know what you mean. You're very polite. Lucas always did have good manners—on the surface. I will say that for him. You've turned out well."

She let the word *considering* dangle between us. *You've turned out well.* She made me feel like a cake she'd baked in the oven.

I grilled Gus's lamb chops in a daze when I got home. Biddy McIntyre didn't like me. Or maybe it wasn't that personal: she didn't seem to like what I represented. I felt that in some way I had disappointed her and I could not understand why. It had something to do with Dad. She obviously hadn't liked my father. Yet, apart from Dad, she was my biggest link to my sister and I'd blown it.

195

She had asked me over there, yet as soon as I arrived I felt as if she wanted me to leave. And we hadn't talked about my mother.

I couldn't go back to Hill House, though. I represented something unpleasant to Biddy McIntyre, and whatever it was I didn't want to remind her of it again.

So I was amazed when on Sunday I returned from my walk and Gus came rushing to meet me in the hall.

"They were here again. Can you believe it?"

Of course Gus had no idea that I had been to see Biddy in the interim. Once again I felt a stab of remorse at deceiving him.

"And I found this on the doormat."

He handed me an envelope with my name on it.

I thought you ought to know that I wrote to Grace about David nearly three weeks ago but I have had no reply. I have not been in touch with her for some time but I know your father's lawyers have been instructed by her to give me her address whenever I ask for it. I've collected several addresses over the years. I don't know whether I should do this, but I am passing it on to you. I could have given it to you yesterday but I wanted time to think it over. It could be that she will not contact me again, and in the event that the two of you ever do meet, please tell her David was ill and near death when we met. I have things to reveal about your parents but

*I feel I should talk to her first. I hope you will
understand.*

I stared at the address in East Hampton on Long
Island. My initial feeling was one of resentment that Grace should allow her address to
be given out to Biddy and not to me, but
then Grace didn't know me.

And that would change now that I had her
address.

Everything was set for our trip to America,
at least as far as Gus and I were concerned.
Mary was still obsessed with Frisky's "babies"
and didn't want to leave them and Ned was
beginning to go into a deep funk at the thought
of being parted from Sophie.

The family holiday of a lifetime was only
weeks away but our children were refusing to
go.

Grace

"You're too late. He's dead," said Biddy
with the tactless, direct manner I'd
forgotten was part of her. I called her from
Heathrow on arrival. I didn't tell her, but
the scenario was exactly what I'd hoped for.
I had not wanted to sit with Biddy while

197

David died, keeping a tense vigil that would undoubtedly force us to talk intimately, opening up old memories and sadnesses I was too cowardly to face.

"Where are you?" I asked. I didn't even have to go into the 'Oh Biddy, I'm so sorry, poor David, it must have been awful' routine. She wasn't one for that sort of thing. But when I'd called the house in Berkshire I'd been redirected by her voice on the answering machine giving me another number.

"Wales. Hill House."

"Oh shit!" We would have to go down memory lane.

"Well, you said it. He wanted to come back here and see it all one last time. Wasn't my idea. You'd better get a car to bring you here from Heathrow, if that's where you are. Unless you don't want to bother now that he's actually died. You could turn right around and fly straight back to New York."

"No, I'll come to Wales. Have you buried him yet?"

"Yup. Day before yesterday."

"Well, I'll come and put some flowers on his grave at least."

"Freesias," said Biddy, "he always did like the smell. Soft old bugger."

Seeing her again was extraordinary because for the first time I was seeing her as another woman instead of a mother figure. There'd been enough of a gap in time for me to become objective about her. Away from her, I remembered a reserved woman, always immaculately dressed and always there for me. She was firm but never, except for one nightmare occasion, angry, at least not with me. I did sense a certain irritation from time to time with David, for whom she "kept house," as she put it.

"I produce meals for him, I entertain his boring work colleagues and their even more boring wives, I supervise his laundry being sent out, and I see the silver is cleaned regularly. And what does he do for me in return? Play golf all weekend and take me to Cornwall on holiday instead of Tuscany or the South of France."

Now, looking at her from my perspective of a woman in her forties, one woman sizing up another, I could see with not a little shock that despite being plain she must have been very attractive. All those barbed remarks thrown at David's back were about sex. Biddy was still sexy at seventy-six and, I now realized, the problem must have been that David, the "soft old bugger," had never given her enough.

I opened my mouth and shut it quickly. What would I say? Oh Biddy, I never realized you were so sexy. It wasn't the sort of thing you said to a woman in her seventies. But why not? Biddy wouldn't have minded a bit. I could see that now. But I was, after all, still mildly inhibited by the foster mother-daughter history. However much Biddy might have welcomed being told she was sexy, it wasn't the sort of thing you said to your mother.

And maybe there was something else. Maybe

I was wary of unleashing the suppressed fury I had encountered so many years earlier, shortly after my eighteenth birthday. For it was this bewildering flash of sheer hatred and bitterness that I had felt emanating from Biddy that had made me keep my distance for so many years. I had seen her and David frequently, of course, since I had left home. I had spent Christmases with them, weekends, my birthday, all the normal parent-child get-togethers. But our reunions had been distant, almost frigid. Biddy and I were excruciatingly polite to each other at all times, but underneath I was screaming silently, "You hurt me so terribly and I have no idea why but I know I have to be grown up about it and pretend it never happened so we can avoid confrontation at all costs. Everything's fine between foster mother and foster daughter."

But it wasn't.

The problem arose following a minor breakthrough with my father on my eighteenth birthday. I received a first edition of *Vanity Fair*. The postcard read: "This was your grandfather's." Of course I recognized Lucas Cammell's black, spiky hand. No indication as to who my grandfather was. I wrote to say thank you and asked, "Which grandfather?" No reply.

I showed Biddy. She glanced at the book, shrugged, made no comment.

"I think he's trying to reach out to me," I said.

"Rubbish," said Biddy curtly, "just a present. You're eighteen. Obligatory."

"No, I really think he must want to communicate. It's time I met him. He's my father."

"Really? So who's David?" she said. Very cold.

"Oh, I didn't mean David wasn't my father."

"I'm exceedingly glad to hear it."

"Can't you understand I'm curious?"

She didn't answer. Just walked out of the room.

I was furious. So furious I did something I had never done before. When Biddy was upstairs I sneaked her little pocket address book from her handbag and looked up Lucas Cammell's telephone number. Not the office. Not Lucas Cammell Publishers but his private number.

It took me two weeks before I could summon up the courage to call.

I got the answering machine and perhaps it was just as well. I left a stammering, emotional message saying who I was, how pleased I had been with all the books he'd sent me, and how much I wanted to meet him. I went on and on and on. I must have taken up the whole tape. And then I went to my room and wept.

Afterwards, however, I felt an enormous relief.

Two days later I picked up the phone when it rang in the kitchen and listened to one of the sexiest voices I'd ever heard ask to speak to Biddy.

Not me. Biddy.

I knew immediately who it was.

"This is Grace," I said.

There was a short silence. Then he said, "I know. I want to speak to Biddy."

Well, okay, fair enough, I thought. He wanted to meet me but he wanted to discuss it with Biddy first.

I waited for Biddy to tell me what he said, to fill me in on the arrangements. Where I would meet him for lunch or when he was coming down for the weekend.

She said nothing.

I answered the phone to that voice again. Two or three times.

"It's him, isn't it?" I tackled Biddy after the fourth time.

"Oh, don't be ridiculous," she told me. "Why on earth would he suddenly start calling now?"

Well, as far as she was concerned, why would he? She didn't know about the message I'd left for him. So I told her. I went on and on about it day after day. When could I meet him, what had he said, should I phone him again? Until finally she turned on me and I never felt the same about her again.

"Yes, Grace. Yes," she shouted in a voice I didn't recognize. "Yes, it was Lucas. But if you want to claim him as your father you're a stupid, stupid girl. He doesn't want to see you. Ever. He does not want to see you. Do you understand? How can you go on pretending there can ever be a relationship between you? Why don't you face facts? The man isn't interested. He gave you away. David and I brought you up and now it's as if we don't exist."

"That's not true," I protested, "that's not what I meant."

"You're a cruel, heartless child. You think you can just use me and then throw me away and run back to Lucas when it suits you. Well, go ahead if that's what you really want, but he doesn't want you."

"I don't believe that. I'm his daughter."

"You don't want to believe that. There's a difference. But if you've any sense, you will. You're eighteen. You're almost grown up. Face it, Grace. You're stuck with me and David and you're bloody lucky you've got us."

She was cruel. Cruel to be kind, she implied, but I always wondered.

Now, as she began to describe David's funeral, I couldn't help noticing what a dramatic person she was, how much she used her hands to emphasize a point, how expressive she was, how alive. But I had never forgotten the force of her cruelty the day she told me my father didn't want me. I went to London shortly after that, and now, I realized, we were about to have our first proper conversation since then.

"It rained, naturally. Poured down even though it's July. The mud! My dear, you should have seen it. There was quite a turnout even though we hadn't lived here properly for years. I think they were just curious to see what had become of me. They had to park a bit of a way down the hill and walk up to the church, ruining their best shoes in the mud. Made me laugh. Boring service. Usual hymns. Day thou gayest. Dreadful woman vicar, kept talking about David having passed away. Shame you missed it in a way. I'd have liked to have had someone to giggle with."

"Will you miss him? Oh sorry, I suppose that's not the sort of thing you ask at a time like this."

"Don't be ridiculous. Whyever not? At a time like this. At a time like what? Another stupid expression that always pops up when someone dies. And yes, I shall miss him a bit to begin with. I was very fond of the old boy. We had a good marriage and—and we had you. David was very proud of you, you know."

"Was he? Weren't you?"

"Not like him. It was tricky for us. We weren't your parents. We never could be. We never knew if your wretched father was suddenly going to demand to have you back. I don't know why I say have you back. He never had you in the first place."

We were sitting in the gate at the entrance to the churchyard. We had set out on a walk up Stowe Hill but Biddy grew tired almost immediately. Clearly she was more stressed than she was letting on. We sat down to rest and stayed put. And began a conversation that I knew would, inevitably, deepen the more we talked. There was a notice pinned up that read: "The grass has been allowed to grow in order that over a period of time an abundance of wildflowers can flourish in this churchyard."

I want to be buried here, I thought suddenly.

I wanted to be laid to rest in this place of peace alongside David and, in due course, Biddy.

"Why didn't he have me? Why didn't he want me?"

I had never asked these kinds of questions about my father before but we were talking woman to woman. I had grown up enough that she could no longer treat me as a girl.

And then Biddy suddenly looked ashamed and I was astounded. I had been fishing, I had expected her to tell me that of course he'd wanted me but it just hadn't been convenient for him, he was too distraught when my mother died, something like that, some kind of platitude.

But she didn't fob me off. She said nothing of the kind.

"It was all my fault. I held on to you. I wouldn't let him have you.

"Lucas was like one of those middle-European immigrants who came to London during the war, only he wasn't Jewish and he was born here. Yet he never seemed English. He was always exotic. I was smitten by him from the moment I first saw him. I had never been so attracted to a man."

My heart started hammering inside my chest when I heard this. This wasn't what I had expected. Biddy was certainly coming out with a few surprises.

"But I had a problem."

I looked at her.

"I was with your mother, and while I was smitten by him, he was smitten by her. We were best friends, your mother and I. In London. We met in the country at somebody's weekend party. Can't remember where. Except it was funny because we discovered we both loathed the country. That's what brought us together. She came upstairs when everyone else was out for one of those interminable walks in the pouring rain. I thought she'd gone with them, and she found me hiding in my bedroom, smoking furtively, sending puffs out the window like smoke signals. She joined me."

"Was she very pretty? As pretty as I remember her?"

"Prettier. You're not unlike her, you know, Grace. A little heavier perhaps, a little stronger looking, although that wouldn't be hard. She was so fragile. I felt protective towards her from the start. She was sensitive and—I hate to say it but it was true—she was a little bit stupid, which was odd because sensitive people are usually highly intelligent. I had the feeling she'd been spoiled as a child, smothered by over-protecting parents. She was used to being cosseted, to having people take care of everything for her. And that's where your father scored. I watched her fall under his spell. I could do nothing about it. He promised her everything and then he brought her down here and made her his prisoner."

"That's what the man at the dinner party said."

"Who?"

I told her about him.

"That would be Monty. Miserable creature. Just as well he never got his hands on her. Used to beat up the woman he did marry, so we heard."

"My father—was he violent?"

"Oh no, he was seductive. Soft talking. A crooner in your ear. All charm when he wanted to be. Then he could ignore you for days. And he could also destroy you with words. I've never known a man so articulate. Vicious. He left you gabbling, searching in your mind for the right phrases to hurl back at him while he walked calmly out of the room or picked up the telephone and started talking to someone else, seducing them with sweet talk right in front of you when he'd just finished annihilating you."

"But you loved him?"

"I never said that, Grace. I was attracted to him, physically. To his magnetism. I wanted him, in a way I know your mother never did. But he chose her and that was that. Then he did something for which I could never forgive him."

"What?"

"Once he had her he started to betray her. Indiscriminately. He was so duplicitous. I married David and we were mostly in London. David knew I hated the country. He was a kind man. The total opposite of Lucas. And we witnessed Lucas's affairs in London. He was quite blatant about them. He knew no one would tell your mother, parked safely down here with you. He knew no one would be able to bear seeing her hurt. And he was right."

"But she found out. Is that why she...?"

"Killed herself? Who knows? She was beginning to despair long before. She was like a young plant that needed constant watering and light and people talking to it or whatever it is they need. And down here she was so isolated and hidden from admirers."

"If you didn't love my father, it sounds as if you hated him. The other side of the coin."

"Not at first. Only when he did the unthinkable."

"What did he do?" I was riveted by the story that was unfolding. I knew that later I would wake up and realize it was my own father who was at the center of this horror story, but for the moment I didn't care. I just wanted to hear everything.

"He tried to seduce me. Five years too late. He was married to your mother. They had you and finally he came after me. Maybe I was the only woman left in London he hadn't had, I don't know. But he came after his wife's best friend."

"You had an affair with my father?"

"*No!*" Biddy turned to face me. She was furious. Once again I sensed the fierce passion that must have consumed this woman who had brought me up.

"No, I never slept with your father. I turned him down. We were in that apartment he had above his office. I'd gone to collect some stuff for your mother. She was pregnant, about to have your sister. I was driving down to Wales the next morning. He gave me a drink, we were in the kitchen. It was small, narrow, like a galley. He reached past me to open the fridge and get some ice and when he put the ice tray down on the counter he grabbed me by the waist and drew me against him. I had my back to him. I could feel him pressing into me. He bit my earlobe. He kissed the back of my neck. My skin was on fire. He said, 'Oh Bid, I've wanted you for so long.'"

I noticed she remembered every detail. She must have been tormenting herself for years. "And I raised my knee and kicked him as hard as I could. I was wearing heels. It must have hurt like hell. He probably had a scar till the day he died. I hope he did. I bloody well hope he did. I screamed at him, told him he didn't deserve your mother, or you, that I wouldn't touch him if he were the last man alive. He told me not to be such a shrew. I remember the word: *shrew*. I ran out of the apartment and down the stairs through the empty offices where every surface creaked under piles of man-uscripts."

"What did you mean when you said you held on to me?"

"When your mother had her second baby, you know what you did, don't you? You left the house and walked across the valley. Of course that sounds more dramatic than it actually is. You knew the way across the fields and that only takes about ten, fifteen minutes. Still, it must have been pretty brave of you. You came here and we put you to bed. David called your father and told him where you were. Shouldn't tell you this but I'm not sure he'd even noticed you'd gone."

"And he never bothered to come and get me," I said triumphantly, "and I lived as happily as could be expected forever after."

"Oh yes, he did." Again Biddy caught me by surprise. "Admittedly he let a few days go by before he came over, and that's understandable. His wife had just killed herself, and despite his philandering I know he did love your mother. And there was the newborn baby to deal with. He telephoned every day. David spoke to him. And then one night he came over to get you. If I tell you what happened will you promise to forgive me?"

"Yes, of course," I said, knowing it was the sort of thing you agreed to to get someone to reveal something as fast as possible.

"I held on to you. I told him you were sick, although you were just upstairs asleep. And he went away. And then he came back again. I said you were not there, and each time he came I made an excuse until he had to go back to London to his office. He took the baby with him and hired a nanny in London. I just went on making excuses. He hated me. Ever since I'd rejected him he had avoided me. Now he only spoke to me through David.

"Poor David. He couldn't understand what was going on. But the thing was, David wanted children and I never did. It was a problem between us. I'm afraid, Grace, you were the solution to our problem. You were an adorable little girl, spirited, loads of character even at that age, and David was enchanted by you. I knew one thing: I would rather die than let you be raised in the house of Lucas Cammell. I suggested to David that if Lucas agreed, we would keep you. We could give you a good home. It would be easier for Lucas. I was awful. I really worked on David, pointed out over and over again how much it would complicate Lucas's life if he had two children to cope with on his own. It wasn't like now. You didn't have all these New Men and single fathers. And, of course, I had another reason for keeping you."

I looked at her.

"As long as I had you with me it meant that Lucas would have to keep in contact, that I would see him regularly when he came to visit you, until the day when he took you altogether. And, as I said, I didn't want children, so knowing I would not have you forever suited me fine."

I didn't like what I was hearing. Biddy had never wanted me. Was this what I had to forgive her for?

"But I was completely wrong about two things," she went on. "First, Lucas knew exactly what I was doing and he called my bluff. He never came to see you because he didn't want to see me. You lost your father because of me. I'm afraid he was that callous. I don't think he could have cared for you very much because he was able to leave you behind so easily. Or maybe he cared too much because

211

you reminded him so much of your mother, made him feel guilty, who knows? Anyway, even though he tormented poor David by intimating every now and then that he was thinking of having you live with him, he never did anything about it."

"What was the second thing you were wrong about?"

"I discovered I did want children. Or rather I wanted you. Once I had you, I knew that if I ever had to I would fight very hard to keep you. I used to wonder if I should ever try to get your sister, but I had no access to her and now, having finally met her, I'm glad I didn't force the issue."

I held up my hand. "Stop. Wait a second. When did you meet her? How could you let me sit here beside you for so long and not tell me you'd met Favor?"

Biddy smiled. "Favor. You always called her that. Not that we ever referred to her if we could help it. That subject was taboo. You were wrong there; you called her Favor because for some cockeyed reason you convinced yourself she was your mother's favorite even before she was born, but she turned out to be your father's favorite instead. I only met her the other day, actually. She rents Upper Stone Farm as a weekend getaway. Don't ask me how that came about. I didn't bother to find out."

"Well, did you at least find out her real name?"

"Pat. Pat Hardy. Very ordinary."

I was puzzled. That wasn't the name I'd associated with my sister.

"Short for Patricia?"

"Presumably."

"It doesn't sound right. She wasn't called Patricia."

"No, she wasn't."

I turned on Biddy. "You knew what she was called. You just never told me."

"Of course I knew but you never wanted to know. Lucas never talked about her. And it wasn't Patricia. It was Pat. Pure and simple."

I felt uneasy, as if there was something missing, some vital link I couldn't put my finger on. Pat didn't fit but I couldn't say why.

"So what was she like?"

"Medium height. Ordinary looking. Thick, fair hair. Not a bit like you. Adored your father. Married to a nice-looking man, name of Hardy. It's a bit of a cliché, but you got your mother's looks and your father's brains. She got your mother's slight stupidity—maybe I'm being unfair but she didn't make much of an impression on me—and I suppose she does look a bit like Lucas. Same thickish nose and wide mouth."

"And she's married? Children?"

"Two, so she said. Girl and a boy. She's a good mother, I expect. I sort of recognized her type immediately, probably because I'd seen it in your mother. She doesn't look for complications. She's a bit naive and accepts everything quite happily and trustingly and never sees beyond, never questions anything. Just like her mother. So if she's with a nice husband, she has no problems unless he starts behaving like a shit."

"But my father, Lucas, was a shit," I pointed out. "Why did she adore him?"

"Because she was his daughter, a nice, trusting little girl who didn't give him any trouble, so he was as nice as pie to her. If he'd been unkind to her like he was to her mother she'd have been miserable. I doubt he really cared about her; I don't imagine she interested him enough, but he tolerated her and she was dim enough to settle for that. But your mother had bad luck. She needed a kind husband as opposed to a kind father, and he wasn't that. He needed a quick-witted, strong-willed wife who'd keep him in line, and she wasn't that. He got what he wanted in a daughter but not in a wife. So I suspect his daughter never got to see the monster, but your poor mother saw it and she couldn't cope. Who knows what you would have made of him. You'd probably have stood up to him and he'd have loved you and then poor Favor's eyes would have been opened. She'd have realized that he didn't care for her. She owes you a lot for not being there."

"And her husband? Nice?"

"Didn't meet him properly. Only saw him briefly but enough to know he's a David type. Kind. Boring. Oh, poor David..."

I didn't think I could remember having seen Biddy cry before. She listed towards me and I caught her as she began to heave with sobs into my chest.

"You'll get over him, Biddy. You have your memories of him."

Stupid, empty words, the sort of thing you said "at a time like this."

"Oh, you idiot," she growled, suddenly sitting up again, "I'm not crying because I miss David. I'm crying for what might have been, don't you see? If I had to live my life over again I wouldn't choose David in a million years. I'd have succumbed to your father and become his mistress no matter how much he hurt me. I'm that kind of woman. I know that now and it's too late. And he never married again. I don't know what your situation is, Grace, but for God's sake work out what kind of woman you are. Beware of men like your father. They're everywhere. But at the end of the day you have to decide whether or not you're someone like me, someone who would be happier with a grand passion that leaves you devastated than none at all and a calm and peaceful life. Don't settle for humdrum; if it's not for you you'll regret it for the rest of your life."

When I left, I wondered if this would be the last time I'd ever see Biddy. As the driver took me down Stowe Hill I recalled the last time I'd been to this part of the world, the time I'd visited Upper Stone Farm. The woman I'd passed who had been driving into Upper Stone Farm, the woman I had thought of as my stalker—now I knew, she wasn't my stalker.

She was my sister.

Favor

" **I** think," said Gus very calmly and deliberately, "that if that's the reason you
came to America you'd better leave now."

He had his back to me. He was silhouetted
in front of the window, with nothing but rows
and rows of other windows behind him in
the offices of the skyscraper across the street.
He looked as if he was in an old-fashioned black-
and-white movie, except King Kong should
have been climbing up the building. He
couldn't be looking at the view. He just didn't
want to face me.

We were in a vast, anonymous midtown
hotel whose lobby resembled the main con-
course of a train station, on occasion a Japanese
train station. I allowed myself a fleeting wave
of nostalgia for Roger and his passion for all
things Japanese, although who knew what he
might be obsessed with by now. In our hotel,
in order to get to the front desk you had to fight
your way through hordes of businessmen
scurrying towards the bar or herded together
in massive groups, clutching their passports,
waiting to check in. They all seemed to wear
short-sleeved white shirts, like airline pilots,
whose breast pocket bore their name tag. To
pass the time, I used to test my eyesight by

seeing how many names I could read from a certain distance.

The fact that we had been allocated a family suite was a joke. We were fast disintegrating as a family. Ned had stayed in London to be with Sophie, and his point-blank refusal to accompany his father to the convention had been the beginning of the end for Gus.

Mary had no option. We insisted she come, and her resentment towards us for the fact that we had allowed Ned to stay behind had manifested itself in near total silence. We had flown Virgin. For some reason I associated Virgin's bright red symbols and Richard Branson's cheesy smile with trendiness. I had thought Mary would be pleased.

She didn't appear to notice. There had been no sign of her looking forward to the trip at all. She could only look back and pour scorn on Sophie, whom she loathed.

"I mean, Mum, she is the most uncool girl in the world. Do you know where I just saw her?" Mary asked me, sauntering around my bedroom as I was packing, never offering to help.

"No, where?" Had Sophie been caught helping an old lady across a road or going to bed before midnight?

"There was a picture of her in *Bratler*. At one of those upscale parties. And she wasn't with you, was she, Creepo?" Ned had just wandered into the room. "Girlfriend's playing away already."

"What you talking about?"

"Downstairs on the dining room table. *Bratler.* Kiddies' *Tatler.* Go take a look. Sorry I had to be the one to tell you."

"Oh, I've seen that ages ago," said Ned cheerfully. "Great picture of her, don't you think, Mare? She's with her cousin. It was his eighteenth in Gloucestershire. Great bash."

"You went to Gloucestershire?" Mary looked utterly disgusted.

"You make it sound like I spent the weekend in Soweto."

"Well, you'd probably meet more interesting people there."

"What have you got against Sophie? She's pretty. She's smart. She's going to be a successful musician one day. Oh, I get it. You're jealous."

"Of that prissy straitlaced prune? You must be off your head."

"Mary, that's enough. Why don't you ask Shannon around before we leave?"

It was a stupid thing to say—as if she were still a little girl who had friends around to play. If Mary wanted to see Shannon she would spend an hour in the bathroom making up her face and then walk out the door, presumably to some club where she would pretend to be eighteen, and she wouldn't come home till the early hours of the morning.

As if on cue, Mary flounced out of the room.

"Is there something wrong between those two?" I asked Ned. "I haven't seen Shannon around here since I found—"

I stopped in a hurry. I hadn't told Ned about Mary and Shannon's orgy in our front room.

"Since you walked in and found them shagging on the carpet."

"Ned, I didn't think you knew."

"Of course I knew, Mum. I just didn't want to get involved. It was bad enough having my sister lose her cherry before I did. I didn't exactly want it to be up for grabs at a family conference."

"Mary lost her virginity that night?"

"Well, I don't know if it was that night specifically. Might have been before then. Anyway, she's not getting any at the moment. Shannon went off with that guy Mary had sex with. I think in Shannon's big plan they were supposed to swap but Mary didn't go for Shannon's boy. Complained about his zits. Although I did sit her down and read her the Riot Act about safe sex and HIV and stuff so maybe that had something to do with it."

"Did she listen?"

"She said it was 'a bit rich coming from someone who wouldn't know what to do with his dick if he could find it'. I think those were the words she used. But yes, I could see she was listening. She's not bad, Mum. She's just in with a bad crowd at school and she's been with them for quite a while. They were all at primary school together, remember, and that school just got closed down because a girl was raped there in the lavatories by four boys aged ten. Think about it."

"You're saying Mary's been raped?"

"Oh, no, Mum. Calm down."

"Are you saying she's on drugs?"

"I'm saying she's probably been offered them."

"Have you?"

"Loads of times. Been offered, I mean. But I haven't touched them. Nor has Sophie. And maybe Mary hasn't either."

I put it out of my mind. If only Ned was coming with us. I know I embarrassed him when I kissed him goodbye over and over again, clinging to him in front of Sophie and entreating her to take good care of him. Was it a sin to care for one child more than the other? To have a favorite? But Mary didn't really make it very easy for me. As I watched the woman sitting on the plane trying to make conversation with her—"Where do you go to school? I expect you'll be running the country soon. I've got a girl about your age, we should get you two together"—stupid, banal airline talk with no more depth than the stewardess's "Coffee for you at all?" I wished Mary would at least smile and play along with it as Ned, or even Sophie, would have done, laughing, albeit feebly, trying to think of something to ask back, making some kind of effort. But Mary just glowered and barely looked up from her magazine.

She was travelling light, carry-on baggage only. Just a few skimpy, rose-print Top Shop dresses (just like the ones all the girls in *Bratler* were wearing!), a sponge bag, a Walkman and her Baby Face tapes, and a copy of *Junk* crammed into a Sainsbury's bag. And she had insisted on travelling in a pair of frayed, cut-off denim shorts.

I could see it now, the same Sainsbury's bag, propped up by her bed in our family suite. Handy for the quick getaway Gus was proposing.

He had found out about my proposed visit to Grace.

Earlier that day I had contacted the Goose Neck Inn in Montauk, recommended by the East Hampton Chamber of Commerce, to check on the availability of rooms for Mary and myself. I planned to go out there once Gus was ensconced at the convention.

I had also planned to tell him in due course what I was doing but the Goose Neck Inn had beat me to it, in a manner of speaking.

"What on earth," Gus had demanded when I returned from one of my quick forays in Manhattan, "is the Goose Neck Inn and why are they calling you?"

I had been in a state of utter frustration ever since we had arrived in New York. I had envisaged taking Mary around the city and showing her the sights. I might be just a Shepherd's Bush housewife, but astonishingly enough I did know my way around New York. I had been there enough times with my father when he had come over on business trips to see New York publishers and agents. But Mary refused to step outside the hotel. She certainly wouldn't go near the convention, and because I was so shaken by what Ned had told me, I was not about to leave Mary roaming around Times Square on her own—because that was where the hotel turned out to be.

It was in a pretty seedy part of Manhattan. If you looked up it was fine: all neon lights and giant billboards of gorgeous young men in their underpants and the tips of dramatic skyscrapers disappearing into the atmosphere. But down on the ground were the dregs of the earth. Dirty sidewalks, crowds of miserable-looking people, dirty old men, dirty old women, too, for that matter, bag ladies huddled in doorways. Hard-faced women, hookers intermingling with women in business suits with too-short skirts and clumpy high-heeled shoes in fake patent leather, and not much difference between them. Everyone waited impatiently at the curb for the WALK sign and shouted into their mobile phones. Everyone else I assumed was an addict of some kind. Horns blared. And absolutely everything stank of the fried onions on the hot dogs on sale at the fast-food wagons at every corner, wagons that added more heat to the blistering August humidity.

And yet I had no difficulty restraining Mary. She sat in the family suite all day glumly watching MTV. I suggested shopping—there was a Gap right across the street—but she had no interest whatsoever.

In the evenings Gus returned exhausted with bags of baseball caps, T-shirts, and badges for Ned, all gathered from the enormous variety of exhibitors' stands, and sank into a chair asking with genuine interest the standard American question we had all heard in TV movies: "So how was your day?"

And we had nothing to tell him. He could not believe that he had brought us all this way so that we could sit in the hotel watching TV. Inevitably it came down to money.

"I thought you said you could write this off against tax?" I shot back, feeling guilty and neurotic.

"Looks like I might as well write it off period the way you two are behaving. I don't know why you don't come to the convention if New York's not good enough for you. There's so much I could show you. They've got all these new systems, electronic locks, digital entry, coded access, you name it, and it's only a matter of time before they're imported back home. I'd like you to see them, hear what you think. They've got loads of sideshows Mary could go to."

"Not really her thing, is it?"

"Well, why doesn't she go out and buy up Tower Records or something?"

Why indeed?

It was Mary's attitude—or rather lack of it—that was bothering me the most. I'd never seen her so lethargic. And it was the reason I made myself do something about moving on to Long Island.

Pretty soon I found out there was something I simply had not taken into account. It was August. High season. There wasn't a hotel room to be had in the area where Grace lived. In the end I went back down to the front desk of our horrible Times Square hotel and explained my predicament. They looked at me as if I was mad.

"You wanted these brochures for this season? We thought you were talking about next year. Why don't you just call the Chamber of Commerce? They'll have listings. But you won't get very far."

I have always responded well to a challenge. If someone assumes it's a cinch I won't be able to do something, it always riles me. Which begs the question: why am I living in a rather run-down, end-of-terrace, three-bedroom house in one of the less salubrious parts of Shepherd's Bush and dividing my time between Sainsbury's and Roger's reception area instead of running the world? There was a simple answer to that. Nobody had ever challenged me to do otherwise.

Except maybe they had.

Hadn't Mary dismissed my job with Roger as not being a proper career? And hadn't Gus repeatedly asked me to come back into the business with him? Yes, to both questions, so why hadn't I responded to the challenge? Because deep down I knew that neither option would satisfy me. I had a more important goal forming in the back of my mind. Granted, originally this had been to bring Grace back into the fold, make her one of us. A romantic fantasy that I hadn't really thought through properly—indeed I hadn't really been aware that this was my primary aim until the rest of the family began to crumble around me. Suddenly, far from being the center of my family as I had always been, I was on the outside. Ned had Sophie, Mary wasn't speaking to any of us and had become this forlorn creature I didn't even recognize.

As for Gus... I was about to find out.

The East Hampton Chamber of Commerce put me on to the Goose Neck Inn and I didn't stop to wonder why they alone might have rooms when no one else did. I went ahead and called them. And of course they were full, too, but they took my number in case they had a cancellation. Which they did, so they called back.

And Gus took the call.

"Well?" he asked when I didn't answer straight away.

"I thought as Mary didn't seem to be responding to New York very well I'd take her out to the seaside for a bit."

"Bucket and spade?" said Gus with uncharacteristic sarcasm in his tone. "You're looking forward to building sandcastles with her? We could have gone to the beach at home. She's sixteen, not six. I'd have thought she'd find a lot more stimulation if she bothered to step outside the hotel right here in Manhattan."

"Gus, there's something wrong. I think she's going through some kind of breakdown."

"Oh, don't be so dramatic."

"I am not being dramatic. She's never been like this, sitting around moping. I know she hasn't got Ned to snipe at but you'd think she'd

225

be moaning and griping about something. This sitting around all day close to tears is just not her."

"Boyfriend trouble. Has to be. Moping about some pimply youth who kissed her once on the top of a Number 49 bus on the way home from the movies."

If only! Where had Gus been? But then how could he know? I had never got around to discussing Mary with him. When we'd had our run-in about Amanda Bamber it had been Ned who had been part of the equation. Ned and Sophie. I had never even mentioned finding Mary on the point of having sex on our living-room floor. Here I was having dreams of uniting the family and I didn't even talk to my husband about our children.

"Well, Ned did say there was someone who went off with Shannon."

"What did I tell you?" Gus was triumphant. "But why drag her off to the Goose Neck Inn? They said you only wanted a twin-bedded room. You weren't planning on inviting me on your little jaunt. So what is there at the Goose Neck Inn, wherever the hell it is, that could possibly interest Mary and not me?"

"Her aunt."

I had envisaged how it would be when I eventually told him and of course I had romanticized the whole thing. He would support me, praise me for my courage in coming all this way to find Grace. But while I had witnessed Ned succumbing to Sophie, and Mary disappearing into a world of her own, I had, at the same time, been oblivious to growing changes in my husband. His outburst when I finally revealed my plan to seek out Grace and get to know her now I knew where to find her came as a complete shock.

Ironically Mary had been the one who had first noticed a change in her father and I hadn't listened to her.

"I think Dad's going through...what do they call it? The male menopause? His clothes are unbelievable. He's started shopping at Paul Smith and suddenly there's Ferrari shower gel in the bathroom."

"It's probably Ned's."

"It's not. I asked him. I thought the girl wonder had bought it for him but he said no, it was Dad's."

The trouble was I'd got so used to Gus looking like an ageing hippie with his thick hair worn rather long—at least he wasn't going bald—and his perennial T-shirt-and-jeans look that I barely noticed what he wore. I was aware that he'd brought a suit to New York for the convention. Was it a new suit?

"And his hair, Mum. If it wasn't my dad I'd say it was pretty cool. Wonder where he went."

Again I thought Gus had merely had his hair cut for the trip and had it cut considerably shorter than usual in order to be prepared for the hot weather. In fact I had deliberately not commented on it because I thought perhaps his barber had gone too far and he'd be touchy about it. It had never occurred to me he'd adopted a new hair style deliberately.

"Her what?" His closely shaved head made him look like a skinhead and rather frightening.

"Her aunt," I repeated.

"I don't have a sister. What are you talking about? Oh, no, don't tell me. No. Not her. You haven't gone and found her?"

"Not yet but that's what I'm planning. I have her address. She lives on Long Island. I want to go and see her."

"So she doesn't even know you're here?"

"Not yet."

"But you've known all along she was here. You found out when you went traipsing around after her at those book signings. I never did understand why you didn't introduce yourself there and then and bond with her, get it all out of your system. Although I'm bloody glad you didn't. But I thought it was all over and done with. Really fooled me, haven't you? Pretending you wanted to come to the convention. You're a deceitful bitch. If that's the reason you've come to America you'd better leave now."

He had never spoken to me like this. Never. Not once in our entire marriage.

"I know I should have spoken to her in England but I was just plain scared. She's never tried to get in touch with me. Maybe she wouldn't like me."

"Well, what makes you think she'd like you any better here in America, suddenly turning up on her doorstep? And anyway, you never tried to get in touch with her until this year. Hardly even mentioned her. I can't understand why you're suddenly so het up about it."

"Because I saw her. Coming out of the farm in Wales. I told you."

"You didn't know it was her."

"No. But then I found out and I couldn't get her out of my mind. Gus, aren't you just a tiny bit curious to see her for yourself?"

"Not in the slightest."

"But why not? She's my blood relation. She's part of me, she's part of our family."

"She bloody well isn't. She's just a damn nuisance. Anyway, what family? If we get any more dysfunctional, or whatever the word is now, we'll be invited on *Oprah.*"

I was shocked. "What do you mean?"

"Well, for starters my children barely speak to me any more. Ned wouldn't even come with me to the convention. Have you any idea how long I've been looking forward to showing him all about what I do for a living? It's not as if I expect him to join me in the business. I just want to share my work with him. But he just isn't interested. And of course you don't give a damn any more."

"I do care. It's just that I've been..."

"...taken up with your bloody sister. You thought I didn't notice what was happening? Mary's off the rails, snapping at me all the time, and you don't seem to be able to do anything with her. Can't you see I don't know where I am any more? I don't know where the business is going. I can't make love to you like I used to be able to. I'm always so bloody tired."

Even as he said it I was already thinking it. Not that we'd tried much over the past couple of years, but the last time we'd come close—after we'd kissed and made up over Amanda Bamber in the middle of the night in the kitchen—we'd failed. Or rather, Gus had. We'd gone upstairs, clinging to each other and going "Shhhh!" and toppled back into bed, tearing off our nightclothes in the process.

Half an hour later and still no sign of an erection, we gave up and went to sleep—in each other's arms, true, and I'd been emphatic in my assurance that it didn't matter and I was too tired anyway—but it had obviously rankled with Gus.

"I'm tired. We're all tired. This bloody jet lag isn't something you shake off in five minutes no matter what they tell you about flying west. I've been waking at five or six every morning, and to tell you the truth by lunchtime at the convention I'm exhausted. I've been wandering around aimlessly in the afternoons, didn't want to come back too early and admit the trip was a total failure. The stuff I'm seeing there is great, it's just I'm not seeing it with you. I'm a mess. Look at me. Can't you see, can't you help? Can't you do something? I've had this vision for so long that we'd both build up the business together and make money and go travelling once the kids had left home. Now I just think: what's the point?

How have I missed out? Where did I go wrong?"

And I had always thought I was the one with the dreams.

"I had no idea, Gus. I really didn't. I'm completely appalled."

"So you won't go rushing off? You'll stay and sort me out? We've got another week. We can still make this holiday work. We can still make our..."

What had he been going to say? "We can still make our marriage work?" He was asking me to choose between him and my sister. Well, that was childish of him. I wasn't going to get so close to the chance of getting to know my sister to let it slip through my fingers again. I might not have another opportunity.

Gus was going through some kind of midlife crisis. He was seven years older than I, after all. It was just a male ego thing. We hadn't been paying him enough attention. I'd read about all this countless times in the magazines Mrs. Braithwaite left behind in Roger's waiting room. He'd get over it. I'd sort him out when I got back. No worries, to use one of Roger's favorite expressions.

But as I sat on the swanky Jitney bus the next morning, with Mary beside me plugged defiantly into her Walkman, and looked out of the window at the surprisingly uninspiring landscape either side of the Long Island Expressway, I was worried my solid, reliable Gus had flipped just when I needed him to support me in bringing the family together.

And speaking of pulling the family together, I still hadn't told Mary the real reason I was taking her out of Manhattan.

Grace

"Don't settle for humdrum if it's not what you really want. You'll regret it for the rest of your life."

Biddy's words reverberated around my head throughout most of the flight back to JFK. Going through Arrivals I was so caught up in my own thoughts I walked straight past the driver from East Hampton Limousines holding up his piece of white card with my name on it. When we finally connected, mainly because he recognized me, having picked me up several times before, and were cruising smoothly along the Long Island Expressway, I returned to my agonizing.

My instinct said I didn't want humdrum. Who in their right mind would opt for it out of choice? But I was smart enough to know that humdrum probably made you happier in the long run. Words like security, solid, calm, peaceful flitted through my brain with tantalizing seduction. I yearned for equilibrium yet how did you establish it without being bored?

After all, hadn't I moved to Barnes Landing with that in mind, only to walk straight into Archie Berkeley, a married man with a connection to my last disastrous relationship. Was Archie at this very minute sitting in my house on the dunes in a meeting, or whatever those pretentious film people did, with Harry Fox?

There were no messages from Archie on my machine and after the initial stab of disappointment I decided this compounded everything I'd been dreading. Harry had met with Archie. Archie had told him all about me. Harry had told Archie all about me and him. And then they'd both sat back and had a good laugh at my expense and I'd never hear from Archie again. Neither of them wanted anything more to do with me. I was destined for humdrum whether I wanted it or not.

On that note, too tired even to make it upstairs, I stretched out on one of my seven-foot sofas and fell asleep.

Next morning Lew turned up with my mail. Ever since the mail box vandalizing he'd become paranoid that it would be stolen, and when I went away, even if it was just into New York for the day, he collected it for safe-keeping.

Bills, bills, and more bills and two envelopes with the names of the literary agents to whom I had sent *Luther*. In my anxiety to hear Archie's voice on my machine I had overlooked messages from two female voices whose names were unfamiliar to me. The

233

praise from the literary agents was nothing short of ecstatic about *Luther,* but both complained that they had left messages for me and I had not returned them so they had followed up with a letter. Would I please get in touch with them immediately.

I replayed my messages and identified the two mystery calls as the names of the assistants of the two agents. Assistants were now often so self-important that they thought you ought to know them by name as well as their employers. Both agents wanted to meet me, but the last thing I wanted to do was to trail into Manhattan. I wanted Archie, and the sooner the better.

I chose the agent who made the most intelligent comments about *Luther* and told him he could do what he liked with it providing he sold it to someone who would take me seriously. Was it a first novel? Well, no, not exactly, but a first novel under my own name, I told him truthfully. Hearing his excitement about *Luther* was one of the best things that had happened to me recently, a close second to meeting Archie. Suddenly I was no longer a dumb romance writer. This agent didn't know he was talking to Grace McIntyre. He thought he had discovered Grace Cammell, a new fantasy/suspense author of "a dark tale of good and evil." He was pitching my book in just as corny a fashion as my last editor had pitched my romances but I didn't care. I was reinventing myself and it felt good.

"I'm sending it out to the Coast," my new

agent told me grandly. "It has hit movie written all over it. A movie sale first will really help with the book sale in New York."

"Fine, fine, whatever," I told him and stepped into the shower to savor my new-found status.

"Shall I put up the water for your coffee?" shouted Lew from the kitchen. What he really meant was "Shall I make myself some coffee?" Linda had taught him bad habits, coming into my house and helping himself. I just wanted him to go so I could call Archie.

"So," he said, making himself comfortable on the telephone stool almost as if he were guarding it to prevent me from making my call, "you didn't tell me you were planning on renting your house out this summer."

Lew was caretaker to at least fifty people in the area and he was rushed off his feet during the summer rental season. No matter how insistent he was that his various employers should not give out his number it always managed to find its way into the hands of the renters from hell who called him daily to come fix deck planks, shower doors, screen doors that wouldn't close, anything that needed mending. It had sometimes crossed my mind to rent my house to extremely demanding people as a way of getting everything in the house fixed once and for all by Lew, since if I asked him myself it was always: "Nope, no way. Couldn't do that."

"I haven't rented my house, Lew. Why on earth would I do that? I live here."

"Well, see, there's this lady been coming by past couple days to take a look at it. I saw her day two. I said, 'Ms. McIntyre's away over in England. Anything I can do for you?

"'Oh no,'" she says, "'I'm just here to look at the house. Estate agent in East Hampton sent me.

"So I ask her: 'You want to go inside, take a look?' but she never does. 'Course, she can take a look through the windows and she can see everything, can't she? She had her daughter with her. Nice-looking girl. But they spoke funny, all I can say."

"Funny? How?"

I was slightly appalled that Lew might have let a total stranger into my house without instruction from me.

"Like you," Lew said cheerfully.

"You mean they were English?"

"Yup, s'pose so."

I might have interrogated him further but the phone rang. He answered it. Naturally. He was sitting right by it. It had to be Archie. I reached out to take the receiver. Two minutes later I was still waiting.

"Oh, hi, how are ya? Yeah, she's back. I think she got in last night. I brought over her mail. No, she's not renting the place out, so she says. I made coffee. You coming over? Oh, you are? Yeah, I know, it's been on special all week. I'd hurry if I was you. At the A&P, a buck forty. What? Hold on, I'll ask her. It's Linda, she says maybe you're too tired to go out. D'you want her to pick up anything from the store?"

"Tell her I'll go with her. I'll go over to her place in half an hour."

That would give me time to call Archie if Lew ever decided to leave.

But it was another hour before I was able to leave the house. Lew had something on his mind. He poured himself another cup of coffee and settled himself for a chat.

"Linda ever talk about me?" he asked, not looking at me, trying to make it sound like a casual inquiry and failing miserably.

"All the time."

"She does?" Nothing casual about the way his head shot up with excitement.

"Yes. You know, Lew's the best, we're lucky to have him, that sort of thing."

"Oh." Not exactly what he wanted to hear. Then he took the plunge for the first time since I'd known him and said, "Think she'd go out with me if I asked her?"

"Can but try." How much longer would this take? Playing agony aunt really wasn't my style. I didn't have the patience.

"Think she'd say yes?"

"Why wouldn't she? Great big hunk like you."

He looked very surprised, then giggled. "Aw. You're teasing me. Thing is, I'm crazy about her. Always have been. Strawberry blondes, they get me every time."

Only problem seems to be you don't get them, I thought.

"She likes the movies," I told him.

"She does? There's an idea."

"Yes. Especially those French ones with subtitles." I was feeling a little wicked.

"What do you mean? Subtitles?" Lew made them sound like some kind of perversion in a porn movie.

"Never mind. So should I say anything to her? Prepare her?"

"Well, you might ask her how she feels about me before I go and make a fool of myself. Wouldn't want to do that."

"It might take you asking her out for her to realize just how she feels about you. Had you ever thought of that, Lew? Never mind. I'll test the water and let you know."

"Gee, thanks."

He had a third cup of coffee and only left when I asked him if he could have a look at the coat rack that had plunged to the ground the second I had hung my raincoat on it the night before.

"Nope. Don't think I can right now."

And he was out the door in a flash. At least I knew how to get rid of him.

My forefinger stabbed out Archie's number. Was it too early? Would I wake him? Had he been working the night before?

There was no reply. It rang and rang. Strange. No answering machine. I waited half an hour, using the time to unpack, sort through my mail, dump a pile of wash in the machine. I tried again. This time he answered.

"Archie. It's me. I'm back."

"Who's this?" He didn't recognize my voice. After only a week?

"It's Grace."

"Oh, yes." His voice had dropped right down. It was barely audible. I waited for him to tell me how pleased he was I was back, how he couldn't wait to see me, when could I come over?

He didn't say a word.

"Archie?"

"Yes, look, it's a bit inconvenient at the moment. I'm rather caught up in something. Can I call you back?"

"Yes, of course you can. But soon, Archie. Please make it soon. I'm about to go shopping. If you miss me I'll call you when I get back. I have so much to tell you. I really want to see you and—"

He cut in: "Sure, sure. Talk soon. 'Bye."

On the ride out to the Island the night before, I'd told myself over and over again how lucky I was to have found a man like Archie who loved me and could give me support just when I needed a sympathetic listener, someone to whom I could pour out all I had learned about my father. For once I had someone who was there for me.

Of course, I did have Linda, but the idea of telling dippy Linda, with her pink-and-purple poodle lifestyle, what I'd been through in Wales was so ludicrous. I made a quick shopping list and fought my way through the shrubs (probably getting ticked to death in the process) to her back porch instead of going down my drive and up hers. I didn't want to waste any time. I wanted to be back for Archie's call.

As I rang her doorbell it occurred to me that Archie had not once said my name. I was right: Harry had been there and Archie had not wanted him to know he was speaking to me.

Linda's door was open so I let myself in to find her spread-eagled on the floor stark naked. Her arms were stretched out on either side of her and she was tossing something across her body. After a while I realized it was a tape measure.

"Linda," I said cautiously. I knew Linda was nuts but this was going a little too far. The door was open. I could have been anybody.

"I'm trying to measure my wingspan," she announced. "I read somewhere that you're as tall as your wingspan."

"Linda, if you just want to find out how tall you are, why don't you stand against the wall like everybody else and make a pencil mark and measure from there to the ground?"

"Oh, I've done all that. I'm five-five exactly. I just wanted to see if this other way with the wingspan was true. Help me out here, could you?"

I took the tape measure and ran it from one of her hands to the other.

"Five-five exactly," I told her, although I never actually looked, "but why are you naked? Lew could have walked in."

"Oh, Lew's seen me in the buff plenty of times over the years. I just thought I ought to take my clothes off for it to be dead right, you know, like when you weigh yourself on the scales, so you don't have to take away the weight of your clothes to be accurate."

I couldn't quite work out how this applied to measuring your height but I wasn't about to go into it with Linda.

"Well, just so long as you're not planning on going shopping in the raw."

A flicker of consideration crossed her face before she went to get dressed.

"Good trip?" She made the obligatory casual inquiry as we drove into town. "Guess where I'm at since you left?" As usual she didn't wait for an answer to either question. "I've met someone. He's a meteorologist."

Only Linda could do it. She'd liked the sound of the guy's voice on the radio so she'd written in to him to tell him so. And he'd responded. They'd had one date. She was seeing him again tomorrow. What would I tell poor Lew?

"What do you talk about? His conversation must be riveting. Does he pour you a drink and then tell you the marine forecast for the coastal area? Does he advise you to exercise caution in your relationship, visibility five miles, body temperatures in the upper forties? What's going to happen tomorrow night? Will showers move east and skies become partially clear, do you anticipate variable clouds with lows in the mid-fifties or what?"

She ignored me. Linda is a scream but she's the last person to realize that. She takes herself quite seriously to the extent that it's possible to tease her a lot and she'll never notice.

"Stanley and I discuss a variety of topics," she informed me primly. "Stanley is an educated man."

Stanley! Not the most romantic of names. And in any case, Stanley might be educated but unfortunately Linda wasn't. However, I would hold my tongue. I had this tendency to be a patronizing bitch and I knew how it could hurt people. I was genuinely fond of Linda. I didn't want to hurt her. I'd shut up.

In East Hampton Linda left the car in the A&P parking lot and I set off purposefully for Villa. Half an hour later I had everything I needed for a quick Italian dinner for two and none of the basics I needed for just me and the house. Tiramisu, prosciutto, and buffalo mozzarella won hands down over Comet and paper towels. After all, I wouldn't be alone for long—I'd be entertaining Archie within hours.

There'd been a space beside us in the lot when we arrived but now a car had pulled in and there was barely any room to squeeze past to the trunk, let alone open the back door. Something stirred in the car beside me and I glanced in to see Theo cowering on the back seat. Of course, it could have been any whippet but suddenly I realized that this was Archie's Mercedes, and besides, no dog cowered in such a cringe-making, guilt-inducing style as Theo. He did at least look pleased to see me. The thing about whippets is that they are dogs who really can appear to smile. Maybe he was just shivering with pleasure.

I put my bags in Linda's car and wondered

what to do. If Archie appeared I wasn't sure I could be responsible for my actions and Linda would inevitably return and witness everything. Before I could come to any sort of conclusion there was a frantic scrabbling at the door and there was Leo, tongue and tail wagging themselves stupid in his anxiety to get at me. He was straining at his lead but it wasn't Archie who was trying to pull him away.

"Our dog seems to know you," said a bird-like Englishwoman as I got out of the car and immediately succumbed to a full frontal assault from Leo, leaping in the air, paws on my breasts, licking my face. I couldn't exactly deny it.

"He's a lovely dog," I blurted to cover my shock. "How long have you had him? He seems almost a puppy but for his size."

"Oh, he's not ours. My husband in his own typically foolhardy way agreed to look after them for someone—there's another one in the car. Not a word to me back in England. Can you imagine? Our two boys are bad enough, let alone two strange dogs."

"How are you coping with Theo?" Too late I realized I'd given the game away.

"Oh, so you do know them. I thought you must, given the way Leo greeted you."

"I met..."—I paused as the penny dropped and finally sank in—"...your husband walking along the beach one day and I offered to take them for a run—or rather Leo—while he went back and did some work." In a way, that was nothing but the truth, with a few crucial details omitted.

"And you're English too. Here on holiday?"

I was about to say I lived here but thought better of it. It wouldn't hurt for her to think I was just a casual tourist. I nodded.

"Well, I'd better get back and give Archie and the boys some lunch. Very nice to meet you. Maybe I'll bump into you on the beach."

Of course she meant Atlantic Avenue beach where I had my house, the one her husband was renting. She had no idea she was talking to her landlady. I was rather pleased with myself for not revealing that Archie had met me at Louse Point.

"Hello, hello," said Linda very brightly behind me, and I was relieved to see her. Sonia Shulman in shorts, a pocket T, baseball cap, and sunglasses was very different from the earnest-author photo—black-and-white head shot, over made up, black sweater, pearls, chin resting on her hand—I'd seen in the press, which was why I hadn't recognized her at first. And, of course, standing here in faded jeans and my hair up in a knot, I hardly resembled the epitome of power dressing synonymous with blockbuster writers of the eighties that my publishers had deemed appropriate for the look of my own author photo. Yet if she heard my name she might well recognize it just as I'd recognized hers.

"This is my friend, Linda. Good to have met you," I said and ducked into the car.

"Sonia Shulman. So sorry. Got to rush."

"Sure." Linda was clearly disappointed but at least we hadn't got into a situation where I had to reveal my name. "Those dogs..." said Linda.

"I told you I was looking after them for a friend."

"And that was her. Oh. Only I thought she was in New York."

"And now she's here." I would have to keep some kind of record of my fabrications now Linda was on my case.

"And she's English. You should have said. Poor creatures."

"Why does her being English make them poor creatures?" Linda's reasoning was invariably beyond me.

"Well, it's a pretty selfish thing to do, bring them all the way out here on vacation and then take them home and leave them for six months in quarantine or whatever it is you do over there."

"Yes, Linda," I agreed meekly. It was the only thing to do.

There were two messages on my answering machine when I got home. The first was from Archie—a completely different-sounding Archie from the nervous voice I'd heard when I called him earlier. And now I knew why.

"It's me." No name but I recognized his voice right away. If anyone else was listening to the tape and he said his name they'd hear it. So he was being careful already now the Little Lady was around. "Sorry about this morning. I was a bit tied up. I long to see you. Please

245

meet me on the beach at Louse Point at four o'clock this afternoon. I'll be taking the dogs for a walk."

It was perfect. I couldn't go to his—correction, my—house any more because of her. And he could use Theo and Leo as an excuse to get away.

The other message was a real surprise.

"Hi, sweet, it's Margot. I'm in New York. When can I come out and stay? Where are you? Why aren't you there? Call me. I'm at the Gramercy Park."

I called her and got an earful of pure, unadulterated Margot.

"Grace, how are you? Are you okay? You sound a bit down."

I'd only said "Hello, it's Grace," but immediately she had to start putting me down.

"I couldn't be better. Why are you in New York?"

"I just got the greatest offer. I couldn't say no. A friend of mine was coming on a trip with his wife, all expenses paid, and then they discovered she had to go to Zurich at the last minute, so I came with him instead. Nothing going on between us. We were booked into this crummy little hotel in Chelsea and I took one look and said no way, we're going to the Gramercy Park, it's the best and in such a great part of town. So here we are. Separate rooms, of course. She's one of my best friends."

"Of course," I said. "How much is your room, by the way?"

"Oh God, I don't think I even know.

Graham's dealing with all that. Anyway, he's leaving tomorrow and going on to Phoenix on business and I have a few days before the date of my return ticket so I was wondering..."

I got it immediately. If she stayed on she'd have to pay for herself. Margot was one of the great freeloaders of our time. I knew what she was after.

But Margot. Here. For a week. And if I wanted to see Archie I'd have to have him here.

"Margot, you might as well know. There's a man."

"So you finally found some action. Only don't tell me it's Mr. Harry Fox. I heard he was making a picture in your neck of the woods."

"No. It's someone else."

"Okay. I hear what you're saying. How many rooms you got?"

"Three bedrooms."

"Bathrooms?"

"Two."

"So what's the problem? You and lover boy in one. Me in another. And one to spare. I'll check out the buses and be in touch. Do I get out at East Hampton or Amagansett?"

"Amagansett," I said wearily. "I'll come and meet you."

Margot. And Archie. And Linda right next door. I couldn't handle it. Of course in the couple of hours I had to wait until I could go and meet Archie my mind began to dwell on Sonia Shulman.

She was pretty. And the total opposite of me. Small where I was big. She hadn't appeared neurotic like her heroines—one critic had dubbed her the Islington Anita Brookner—but she was small and nervous. I hadn't immediately warmed to her but I hadn't disliked her on sight as I had thought I would. I had assumed I would dislike her on principle because she was Archie Berkeley's wife.

I wondered if Archie would still turn up. When she got home Sonia would undoubtedly say something like: "I ran into a woman in the parking lot who met you on the beach and took the dogs for a walk. I never got her name. She was English. Who is she? We should have her over."

What shook me the most was that I never once considered not going to Louse Point now I had concrete evidence that Archie was married—and to a perfectly nice woman. All I worried about was whether he would show up and what I would do if he didn't.

Not only did he show up but he was there before me. As usual, he was having problems with the dogs. I had walked to Louse Point and now I crept up behind him through the dunes. It was incredibly hot. There was a haze over the sea and every now and then the water sparkled with little glints of sunlight and almost blinded you. Theo, sensibly, had dug himself a deep hole in the sand and was lying in it to keep cool. Leo, too stupid to think of digging his own hole, was trying to climb into Theo's, but Theo wasn't having any. He kept snarling and snapping at Leo. Archie was trying to keep the peace and getting his hand nipped by Theo for his troubles.

"Can I help you? You seem to be in some difficulty and I am rather good with dogs."

Archie flung himself at me and hugged me around the knees in mock desperation as I stood, patting his head and going, "There, there." I slumped down on to the sand beside him and we melted immediately into a long and increasingly urgent kiss. Mercifully, the beach was totally deserted.

He started to run his hand up under my loose shorts, poked his finger through my swimsuit, felt my wetness, and sighed. He guided my hand to the front of his boxer swimming trunks and through the slit I felt his erect penis poking through. Before I knew what was happening he had pulled down my shorts and swimsuit and was lying on top of me, pushing himself inside me. After a second he pulled out and wiggled deftly out of his swimming trunks and plunged back inside me. The sudden renewed thrust of his penis aroused me and I arched myself up to him.

"I've missed you so much," I heard him whisper.

"I've missed you, too," I whispered back.

He seemed to be swelling inside me, gently swaying from side to side and sliding around in my wetness, touching me everywhere inside. Then he brought his legs together so that his hard penis was a straight shaft piercing me. As he began to pull it in and out, it rubbed against my clitoris and then returned deep inside me. My climax when it came was a cacophony of moaning and crying out while he just groaned, "Oh God" over and over again.

"Stay in me. Don't pull out," I begged him.

"I might fall asleep," he warned me, "that was pretty energetic."

But Leo and Theo, who had been watching with interest, began to bark furiously.

"I think they enjoyed that. I think they want us to do it again," I said.

"Well, who knows, we might."

We swam. Or at least we went into the water but we could not stop touching each other and kissing and feeling each other. Under water, away from prying eyes, although there was no one on the beach, I could not stop touching his penis and bringing the tip to rub my clitoris. He entered me several times as we stood in the water and when a wave came it knocked him out of me and each time I almost came.

We had no towels so we ran up and down the beach until our clothes dried on us in the hot sun, much to the delight of the dogs, who chased us, even Theo. We slowed to a walk, holding hands, with Leo prancing about beside us and Theo, who had returned to his hole, occasionally popping his quivering head above the parapet to make sure we hadn't left him behind.

"I have to get back soon," he said suddenly, looking at his watch.

"Your place or mine?" I asked with not a little cunning.

"Neither. I have to get back. To work."

"How's it going? Did the director like your stuff? Who is the director, by the way? You never said."

"Harry Fox." He said it quite openly, in such a way that I knew he didn't know about the connection between me and Harry. And I was beginning to think Sonia couldn't have said anything about our meeting in East Hampton.

"The guy who did *Craven Image?*" I asked as innocently as I could.

"Yeah. Big hit, that film."

"What's he like?"

"He's okay. Pretty young and pleased with himself but smart. He liked my theme. There's a bit of a romantic in him somewhere although you'd never know it judging by how he behaves."

"What do you mean?"

"He fucks like a rabbit. Every chance he gets. Bottle-blond bimbos mostly. He's had half the unit already. We all thought he was just a young, sex-mad nerd and we couldn't understand how he came to write such a wonderfully perceptive script about an older woman. So someone asked him about it. You'll never believe what he said."

I looked away. I knew what the answer would be. What had Harry said about our affair? Should I stop Archie before I heard things I didn't want to know?

Of course I didn't stop him. But it was even worse than I expected.

"He researched it," said Archie. "He had the idea and he deliberately went out and found an older woman—in fact he said it was the first older woman he came across who wasn't a complete dog. He's a pretty calculating young

251

man. He had the idea before he'd even started shooting *Craven Image*. Apparently he was so convinced *Craven Image* would be a success that he knew he had to have something else lined up to go straight after. So he contrived to have the affair with this woman, took notes, and began the script of *Rapture* as soon as *Craven Image* was in the can."

"Then he dumped her."

"Ironically, no. She left the country, apparently. He thinks she must have wised up to him."

"Who was she?"

"I knew you'd ask me that. No one can remember. She went to the premiere of *Craven Image* with him because he wanted to plant a gossip item in the tabloids and then use it for publicity to get backing for *Rapture*. But the woman split and he got the backing anyway."

I was suddenly so furious I needed to release my anger. Harry Fox had used me more than I could possibly have imagined. And the fact that nobody even seemed to remember who I was—in a way it was a blessing but my pride was still in tatters.

And here was Archie, who was apparently not even going to mention that his family had arrived. Nor had he asked me how it had gone in Wales with the funeral. I decided to give him the benefit of the doubt. Maybe he was desperately trying to think of a way to tell me Sonia was there.

"So when does your family arrive?"

"Oh, not for a while yet. Sonia has to finish a book and the boys are in some sort of camp."

So now I had it. I'd caught him out in a blatant lie.

"So shall I come over later when you're through working?" I could be devious, too.

"No, I think I'm going to work through the night. Why don't I come over to you tomorrow lunchtime? You can make me a snack and we can find something to do in the afternoon." He put his hand inside my shirt and rubbed his palm in a circular movement over my nipple until it became hard and I shifted unconsciously as my juices started flowing again and mixing in the sand between my legs.

"You'll have to bring Leo and Theo for a walk anyway, won't you?"

He glanced at me hard for a moment. Of course, Leo and Theo would be his excuse to Sonia to get away.

"You're all sandy," he said, changing the subject, feeling between my legs, "let's go back in the water."

The beach was still completely deserted. We lay like Burt Lancaster and Deborah Kerr in *From Here to Eternity* and kissed and fondled each other in the shallows. Out of the corner of my eye I saw a figure approach from the far end of the beach by the rocks.

"Girl at three fifteen," I murmured in his ear. He had already lied to me and here I was back in his arms two seconds later.

"Pretty?" he whispered back and I gave his

bare buttocks a playful slap under the water. "If you lie on top of me she won't see my dick."

"I think she's seen enough already. She's getting pretty close. Actually," I said, pausing and lifting my head to get a better look at her, "there's something wrong with her. She's crying her eyes out. She's staggering a bit. It looks as if she's not at all well."

I rolled off him and pulled up my swimsuit. Looking decidedly pissed off, he did the same and got to his feet just as the girl collapsed in a heap on the sand.

"She's fainted," I said, running out of the water. Archie followed. We were standing over her, preparing to kneel down and examine her when she opened her eyes.

"Fuck!" said Archie. ·

I could see what he meant.

"I mean...do you know her? Is she a relation? Is she..."

I knew what he had been going to say: Is she your daughter? The girl, whoever she was, was my double. It was like looking down at a younger version of myself.

"I'm sorry..." the girl began.

"Don't worry. You'll be fine," I said quickly, "take your time. You fainted, probably the heat. Who are you? You're English."

"So are you," commented the girl. "I'm Mary. I'm here on holiday."

"Where are you staying?"

"Goose Neck Inn. We've been staying there. But Mum's up the road at a house. She gave me the address when I said I wanted to come for a walk on the beach. Here it is." She fished out a piece of paper from the pocket of her frayed denim shorts.

"Fine. Give it to me. We'll drop you off. You're obviously not in too good shape."

I looked at the address and nearly had a fit. It was my own house. We only had Archie's car and by the time we had persuaded Theo to come out of his hole and had bundled both him and an overexcited Leo into the back of the car, Mary had recovered somewhat. She was young, just a teenager, so like I had been at that age. I decided not to ask her why her mother was at my house. It made sense just to get there as soon as possible in case she left when she found I wasn't there.

We arrived home to find a welcome committee. Linda was there. Lew was there. And a woman I had seen before.

"There you are." Linda came running out on to the deck. "Thank God you came home. Lew got me over here. You know that woman who kept coming around here to view your house? Well, she's come back. She's here now."

"It's all right, Linda. I know who she is."

"You do? Oh God, there are those dogs again."

Leo and, surprisingly, Theo had escaped and were running into the house, with which they were of course entirely familiar.

"Is that their master? Hi, how are you?" She greeted Archie, who was helping Mary up the steps. "We met your wife in East Hampton."

"We?" said Archie.

"Me and Gracie here. Your wife, if it was your wife, had the dogs in the car. I'd recognize them anywhere. Gracie looked after them for you, didn't she? You told me the owners had a Mercedes, didn't you, Lew? Well, we had a very nice talk with your wife, at least Gracie did. I just caught up with them at the end. What a nice lady."

Well, at least that cat was out of its bag. I'd deal with Archie later. Now, I noticed, he couldn't wait to get away, rounding up Leo and Theo and disappearing down the drive in the car.

"So who's this? Here, honey, let me give you a hand. Are you sick or something?" Linda took Mary by the arm and helped her to one of the deck chairs. "God, you're so like Gracie. You must be related."

I looked at the woman with the thick, fair hair who had followed me around my book signings and whom I'd first seen driving out of Upper Stone Farm.

"I think we're related," I confirmed. "I think this is my sister and I'm guessing but I suspect Mary here is..."

"Your niece."

Linda was silenced for once.

"We found her on the beach," I told the woman. "She fainted, just like that."

"Mary, what's wrong? Are you ill? Why didn't you say?"

The girl in the deck chair suddenly burst into tears—great, heaving sobs so that her whole body shook. Slowly gulping for breath, she recovered.

"Mum, I think I'd better tell you. I don't suppose I can delay it any longer. I haven't had my period in nearly two months. Mum, I think I'm pregnant."

Favor

Grace didn't live up to her name. Gracious she most certainly was not in handling what was admittedly an extraordinary introduction to her sister and niece. But even in my shock at hearing Mary's announcement, I couldn't help noticing that Grace lost her cool far more than I did. And it was my predicament. I was the one who was going to have to deal with this.

"Well, you can't stay here. I've got a guest coming."

Those were Grace's first words to us.

"I'm not going back to that filthy Goose Neck whatsit. Not for one more night. Not ever." Mary was adamant. I didn't blame her. I was proud of the way I'd set about renting a car, a Subaru, navigating the American highways for the first time in my life, driving on the right side of the road, but I had made a serious mis-

257

take with our accommodation. I'd booked us into the nearest thing to a retirement home I'd ever seen. There was not a single other guest under seventy. They tottered about, grinning at us with their ill-fitting dentures, little old men and women with spreading girths and spindly legs sporting garish, baggy tartan shorts and sun visors. We ate breakfast in a ghastly communal dining room done up like a fake wood cabin but with very harsh lighting, where a man who clearly fancied himself as a comedian served coffee.

"Hey, you little cuties," he greeted us our first morning, "whatcha doin' in a place like this?"

"You may well ask," Mary told him.

Somehow he seemed to take this as some kind of encouragement and sat down beside her on the banquette, draping his arm along the back so it lay half across her shoulders.

"C'mon, sweetheart, it's not so bad. You're close to the ocean. Want to take a walk with me later? And you, too, of course." He looked across at me.

Mary hit him. She lashed back with her arm and slapped him in the face. Now, in retrospect, I knew why. In fact, at the time it was pretty disgusting—a man in his forties leering at a teenager and letting her mother know she'd be welcome in a threesome.

Even if she hadn't been pregnant it would have been out of order.

"We won't go back there, angel." I was glad to have something to say to her other than:

"What do you mean, pregnant? Where? Why? Who?" That would come later.

"You guys can come to me," said Linda suddenly, "I'd love to have you. Gracie's sister. I never knew she had one. Didn't you know she was going to show up today, Gracie? Got your dates confused?"

"In a word: no. And I've got Margot arriving any minute."

"Who's Margot?" asked Linda.

"My best friend," replied Grace curtly.

"Oh, alrighty." Linda was clearly thrown. Maybe she thought she had some claim to the best friend position. I liked Linda instinctively. I had been alarmed when I saw her charging across the space that divided her house from Grace's, knowing she'd caught me snooping, assuming she was going to have a go at me for trespassing. But she'd been warm and friendly.

"Hi, how are you? I'm Linda. Grace's neighbor. She is back from England but she went out. But hey, she didn't take her car so she can't have gone far. Probably to Louse Point. I saw your daughter walking up that way. She is your daughter, isn't she?"

Bit of a concierge we had here, I realized. Kept an eye out for every little thing. I had been about to embark upon some long, fabricated explanation as to how I was a friend of Grace's, when she turned up.

"Well, if you're sure," I said to Linda. "I mean it's a hell of an imposition but if we could just stay with you for one night while we look

259

for somewhere else. It'd be nice to be close to Grace," I added lamely, "until we go back."

Grace looked at me as if I was quite mad. "When are you going back?"

"I have to ring my husband on that one."

"Where is he?"

"In New York. He didn't join us. He has business there."

"Well, I think this house is cool. I want to stay here," announced Mary suddenly.

"Mary, we haven't been invited," I told her.

"Oh, it's okay. She can stay a night. I guess if Linda can have you I can find room for Mary. I have three rooms and I've only got one guest coming." Grace was actually smiling at Mary now. "You can have what I call the kids' room."

"Do you have kids?" Mary asked her.

"No," said Grace curtly.

"Are you married?"

"What is this? The Spanish Inquisition? Now, where's your stuff?"

"We'd better go and get it from the Goose Neck Inn. Mary, come with me."

"But I want to stay here with Grace and—"

"*Mary, come with me.*"

I knew what she was doing. By clinging to Grace she thought she could put off the inevitable discussion about the pregnancy. If indeed it existed.

"I'm right next door. Just go and get your stuff and come right over," said Linda. "I'll go and make up a bed for you."

"I'll be back soon," Mary told Grace with more enthusiasm than she'd shown in quite a while.

We were almost down the road all the way to the Montauk Highway and she still hadn't said a word to me so I pulled over and cut the engine.

"Okay, Mary, what was that all about? How can you be pregnant?"

"God, Mum, if you don't know by now..." The old Mary was definitely back.

"Cut the crap," I snapped, and my uncharacteristic use of the word crap was enough to chasten her.

"I only did it once. My first time and look what happens. Just my filthy luck!"

"Who was he? A friend of Shannon's?"

"He was a friend of mine," she said with some indignation.

"And then he became a friend of Shannon's?"

"How on earth do you know that?"

"Never mind. So he's not even your boyfriend any more. Does he know you're pregnant? How do you know, by the way? Have you tried anything, one of those tests? Or are you just worried because your period's late?"

"All of the above. I did one of those tests in that creepy hotel in New York. You sure know how to pick a crummy accommodation, Mum."

"Your father booked us into that one."

"Well, whatever. The test was positive. And no, Jason doesn't know. There didn't seem any point in telling him."

"Jason?"

"Yeah. You don't know him."

"I don't want to know him. He gets you pregnant and then moves on to Shannon." I was aware I was being unfair even as I said it.

"He doesn't know I'm pregnant."

"And you're not going to tell him."

"No."

"So have you thought about what you're going to do next?"

"No."

We were neither of us going to say the word, the phrase. Abortion. Termination. Getting rid of it.

"Mary, you're only sixteen."

"Just don't start telling me I have my whole life ahead of me and I've gone and fucked it up. Just don't, Mum."

"Why did you let him...you know..."

"Fuck me? What's the matter, Mum? Can't you say the word *fuck?* Is that a problem for you?"

"Yes, I fucking can if I fucking want to but I don't fucking choose to every single fucking sentence I speak." Suddenly I was quite angry. "So why did you let him fuck you?"

"Because I was turned on by him. I wanted him. I still would if..."

"If Shannon hadn't taken him away from you!"

"Oh, go right ahead, rub it in, why don't you?"

It was terrible. She sounded so old and jaded, and yet as she sat there beside me in her denim shorts and T-shirt she seemed so young for her age. I remembered that conversation I'd had with her when she was about thirteen, about sex, about contraception. Even then she'd been sassy.

"Oh, Mum, we don't have to go through all that. I know all about it. We get taught it at school."

Like hell!

We still hadn't resolved anything when we arrived at the Goose Neck Inn to pick up our things, and on the way back as we sat side by side in stony silence I realized what else I had to do.

I had to tell Gus.

Mary grabbed her Sainsbury's carrier bag from the back of the car and disappeared up Grace's drive without even waiting for me to park the car. I drove up Linda's drive past a mail box in the shape of a prancing pink poodle. I suppose it should have told me everything, but even so when I stepped into Linda's house it was a shock to the system.

The walls were pale violet. The carpet was a deeper shade of violet, wall-to-wall. The sofas were upholstered in a pink-and-purple floral design, very pretty actually but it would help if pink and purple were your colors of choice. They weren't mine. The woodwork—bookshelves, cupboards, baseboards—were all painted a pale lilac. Fuchsia scatter pillows monopolized the sofas. Linda herself was wearing a purple tracksuit and her strawberry-blond hair was tied back with pink ribbon. As for the bedroom—well, I'd never seen purple sheets before.

"You must be feeling awful," she said, "I can see the stress in your face. Want to take a nap?"

I shook my head.

"I'm much too wired to sleep. This is very good of you, Linda. I'd better start looking for a place for us to stay. Do you know anywhere around here? Oh, what am I saying? Who knows if we'll even stay here longer than a night? I have a pregnant teenager on my hands and the clock's ticking."

"You know what? You need a massage. I have really healing hands. Let me give you a massage."

Linda was advancing. I backed away. I couldn't help recalling the sight of Roger sinking his healing hands into Mrs. Braithwaite's pulpy flesh, kneading her muscles, when I'd walked in on them once.

"Don't be afraid to let yourself be pampered," said Linda firmly, "you should take time to relax. Now I want you to undress—keep your bra and panties on if you'll feel better that way. Then lie down on your stomach. Here's a towel. I'm going to use a blend of oils on you. Mostly lavender and rose."

Naturally. The right colors.

"And while I work we can talk. You know your sister Gracie has never mentioned you. I'm serious. I never knew she had a sister."

"We haven't seen much of each other in a long while." Well, that was the truth.

"So you're not close?"

"No, not really." At this rate I wouldn't have to tell a single lie. And Linda was right. She did have healing hands. She had started with my legs, her thumbs pressing into my aching calves. Then she slapped me up and down with ultra-light karate chops. I felt as if I were being swished with a fine broom. And when she started on my back, running her thumbs up and down the length of my spine, I could smell the rose and lavender rising off my skin. Against all odds I began to relax for the first time since we had arrived in America. I might not be with my sister but I was close by, and maybe here I could find out a thing or two about her.

"You've lived here long, Linda?"

"Eleven years. My husband left me for a younger woman. He went to Florida. I didn't. It's been eleven years and I've only just met someone. Stanley. He's a meteorologist. I wrote to him. You have to be pro-active to find a man, I'm here to tell you. Look at Gracie. She needs a man but she makes zero effort to find one, buried out here. Has she ever been married?"

I stiffened and she felt it.

"What's the matter? You're tensing up again. Did she have a bad marriage?"

How could I tell her I didn't even know if my own sister had ever been married?

"Don't ask," I muttered into the towel.

"That bad?"

"She never told you?" Now I was really getting the hang of it.

"She never even talks about you. Your sister is so secretive. Has she always been like that?"

"She's never told me a thing." Wasn't that the truth?

"Imagine. Her own sister. Turn over, honey, and turn around so your head's at the end of the bed. There you go."

She sat down on a chair behind my head and began to stroke with the tips of her fingers, lightly tracing my eyebrows, cheekbones, down to my chin and up again.

"Open your mouth, sweetheart, it slackens the jaw. You never realize how clenched up you are until you try and open your mouth. Only way to relax the face."

"Are you and Grace close?" I asked her.

"You know what, I ask myself the same question sometimes. We live next door to each other, we do stuff together, but I know I drive her nuts. We don't have much in common. That so-called English reserve. She's got it in spades. She winces every time she comes over here. She thinks I don't notice but I do. I don't mind. She hates my taste but she's too goddamn British and polite to say so. She thinks I'm vulgar. Well, maybe I am. Who cares? But I like her. We get along."

"Why do you like her?"

"Because she's real. Okay, so she's reserved and secretive, but in other ways she's so honest and direct and open I can see her hurting and I want to reach out to her, but I know she wouldn't let me in. She just arrived here one day, bought the house, and moved in. She goes for long walks by herself on the beach, she sits there all alone in that house. I mean, I know she's writing her books and I know I'm here all alone in my house, but with me it's different. I'm out there in the world every day looking for life, while Gracie's hiding from it. She just sits there and lets life pass her by. So what's he like?"

I didn't answer for a beat or two. I was too busy thinking about Grace and what a sad picture she presented.

Linda nudged me, her fingers probing my muscles, causing me to recoil as she hit tension.

"What's who like?"

"Your man. Your husband. Mary's father. Beautiful girl. So like Gracie, now I think about it. Did Gracie look like that at Mary's age?"

"Gus is wonderful," I replied, neatly evading the question about Mary, "I'm very, very lucky. He's thoughtful. He's kind. He's a great father. We're each other's best friend."

Even as I rattled off this litany of virtues I realized how boring I was making him sound.

"And he's great in bed, this paragon?" Linda laughed.

I laughed, too, and that way I didn't have to answer. Poor Gus. At the moment a stud he most certainly was not.

"Stanley's like a puppy in bed. He's all licks and tail wags and eager to please. He's a widower. He hadn't had sex in quite a while before he met me, or so he says, and now he's making up for it. We behave like kids. We have picnics in bed, that kind of stuff. And he says he loves me. I told you he was a meteorologist, didn't I? He says my breasts remind him of the sea in a hurricane, swells from four to six feet. He's a darling. So what are you going to do about your little girl?"

Not my "little girl" any more.

"Mary and her pregnancy? What would you do, Linda?"

I was grateful to her for not making me feel guilty, for not asking, "How could you let your little girl get pregnant?"

"If I were a mother? That's a tough one. I guess I'd have to listen to my daughter first, see what her state of mind was. How far gone is she?"

I realized I had no idea, although I now vaguely recalled Mary saying she had missed two periods.

"You don't know? What will her father say?"

Again I was silent.

Linda was beginning to sound a little critical. "Don't you think you ought to tell him? Phone's right over there. Be my guest. We'll be through in a second. I'd like you to lie quietly for about fifteen minutes and I'll bring you a robe. Okay?"

She came back with a pale pink terry cloth robe with the name of a hotel on the breast pocket and a label saying "Do not remove" inside.

"Here. Put this on. It'll keep you warm while you relax. I have to go down the road for a second to drop something off to my neighbor. I'll be back in a minute."

I lay there and thought how kind she was and what a shame she didn't have children. Maybe she and Stanley...but then, how old was Linda? It was hard to tell.

I was quite warm enough. I didn't need the robe. In any case I found the pink fluffiness of it rather offputting. Or was it more that I didn't fancy wearing what was obviously stolen goods? I'd always been a bit of a goody-goody, scared to bend the law in any direction. Somehow I had it programmed into me that rules were rules and not to be broken. So I lay there feeling rather sinful in my birthday suit.

The door opened.

I waited to hear Linda's voice telling me she was back, to relax, take my time. When I heard nothing I turned my head.

A big bear of a man, not unlike Walter Matthau with a beard, stood there looking horrified. He was so embarrassed he literally could not move. His cheeks were going red.

I grabbed the robe and covered myself but he must have seen me.

He found his voice.

"I'm just so sorry. I thought...Linda. I came to... I'm awful sorry. I didn't mean, I..."

Why didn't he just stop babbling on and back out through the door? He was only making things worse.

"Linda's gone out for a second," I told him. "She'll be back any minute."

"She'll be back any minute," he repeated stupidly. "I'll go wait for her. You know I didn't mean... I'm just so sorry."

"I know you are," I told him, "you said."

"Yeah. Well."

He left. Finally. I tried hard not to giggle. It never occurred to me to be scared. Somehow the man had not been threatening in any way. He was an old sweetheart, you could tell.

I heard Linda's voice crying, "Stanley!" and I wondered whether Stanley would tell her what he had just seen.

Before I tried to reach Gus I called Mary. Grace answered the phone.

"Who? Oh, you want to speak to her? Yes, she's fine. Mary, it's your mother."

"Mary, are you okay? Shall I come over there? Or do you want to come around to Linda's? We could go out and get something to eat later."

"No thanks, Mum. I'm completely fine. I love being here with my aunt."

My aunt! She hadn't even known she had an aunt until a few hours ago. Suddenly Grace was flavor of the month.

"Well, I'll come over in the morning. Put Grace on. Grace? Is it all right with you if I leave her there? You're sure? Send her to bed early. Don't feel you have to entertain her."

"I'll do exactly what I'd normally do," said Grace without revealing what that was.

"Thank you," I said meekly. She was my big

270

sister. She was the boss. "Oh, and please could you tell Mary I'm about to ring her father. Is there any message?"

I heard Grace relaying what I'd said to Mary. Suddenly Mary was back on the line.

"Mum? Promise me something."

"Of course." This was rash but I was so pleased she was asking me for something.

"Promise me you won't say anything to Dad about the baby. I want to tell him myself."

"But I have to tell him. He must be told."

"You promised, Mum."

"Well, come over here and you can tell him yourself."

"No, I want to tell him face-to-face, I want to see his reaction, hear what he thinks I should do. It's important to me. Make him come out here, Mum. And then he can meet Grace."

Oh great, I thought, just exactly what Gus wants to do. Meet Grace and hear he's going to be a grandfather all at the same time. Great cure for the male menopause. And, I noted, it was his reaction that was important to Mary. Not mine.

"But if I don't tell him about the baby, how am I going to get him to come out here? He's really busy with his work. You know that."

"Just tell him I really really want to see him. Will you, please, Mum? Yes? Thanks. You're a star."

She didn't wait for my reply before she hung up.

Tell him Mary really wanted to see him. Now

that would really make Gus's day. And if he did come out and if he could be persuaded to meet Grace—and suddenly I was thinking I could use his support in confronting my complicated sister—then I would have achieved my aim. I would have reunited my family.

So why did I feel so nervous as I dialed him in New York? But nothing could have prepared me for the operator's words when I asked to speak to Mr. Angus Hardy.

"How are you spelling that?"

"Hardy. H-a-r-d-y."

"We have no Mr. Hardy listed at this time."

"But you do. He's my husband. Room 1471. I was with him there at the beginning of this week."

"One moment, please."

When she came back I was pleased Linda had her back to me so she didn't see my horrified reaction.

"You're right, ma'am. We had a Mr. Hardy in one of our family suites but he checked out. He's no longer with us. For your information my associate says your husband went back to London yesterday."

"And he didn't leave any message for me?"

"No, ma'am. No message at all."

Grace

She was one hell of a chatterbox, my niece. From the minute she came back from picking up her stuff she never stopped talking.

"I think your house is really cool. Mum would never think to live in a house like this. Can I watch MTV? Do you watch MTV? Are you really Mum's sister? Why didn't anyone tell me I had an aunt? Are you really my aunt?"

"Are you really pregnant?"

"Of course I am. At least according to the test I took. Don't you believe me?"

"It crossed my mind you might just be pulling some stunt to get attention."

"You think Mum doesn't pay me enough attention?"

"I have no idea. I haven't exactly been around the pair of you long enough to find out, but I know when I was your age—how old are you? Fifteen?"

"I'm sixteen," she said indignantly.

"Well anyway, when I was sixteen I know I behaved badly. I showed off. I said things to get a reaction, and looking back I can see how stupid I must have sounded."

"You think I sound stupid?"

"What difference does it make what I think?"

"It makes a lot of difference. I want to be

like you. I look like you and that's a start, but I want to be like you, too."

"You don't even know me."

"I know you went out with Harry Fox and he's seriously cool."

She had no idea how close I came to throwing her out there and then. I suppose I had always known it would happen, that Favor would seek me out, that I'd have to face up to my family history, but I hadn't bargained for being made to face up to my recent murky past as well.

"How do you know I knew Harry Fox?"

"Mum had this library book, one of yours, and there was a picture of you on the back and I knew you were the woman who was with Harry Fox at his premiere. But I thought you looked familiar in another way and I didn't know why and now I realize it's because you look like me. But Mum never said a word about you being her sister. She just went off running around the country after you when you were on your book tour without saying why and we thought she was mad. Why do you write such crap books?"

This was right out of left field and for a second I was stunned into silence. "You've read my books?"

"Me and my friend Shannon watched the video of *Air Male* and I flicked through the books Mum had. They're downmarket romantic crap. Nobody who lives in a house as cool as this and who goes out with Harry Fox can be stupid. And those books are stupid."

"They pay the rent, though." I was hurt because the truth always hurts. It took a sixteen-year-old girl to have the honesty and courage to tell me what my stupid fucking editors didn't have the guts to admit to me. If I hadn't had the positive reaction to *Luther* to bolster my confidence I would have felt dreadful. Which reminded me: with the arrival of my sister and Mary I'd barely thought about *Luther*. Wasn't it about time I heard something?

"Why did you ask me to stay?" she asked suddenly.

"Because you wanted to move out of the Goose Neck Inn, whatever that is."

"You could have let me go with Mum, to your neighbor's."

"Yes, I could."

"So why didn't you? Was it because I looked like you?"

I laughed. "Mirror image?"

"Do you have any children yourself?"

"You know I don't." Where was this leading, as if I couldn't guess.

"So you looked at me and you thought I'd like to play mother and daughter for a night or two. I could be your daughter, couldn't I? I look far more like you than like Mum."

Was that really what I'd thought subconsciously? Maybe, although the more immediate reason was (a) I wanted her to be here when Margot arrived so I didn't have to face Margot on my own and (b) I wanted the opportunity to quiz her about her mother.

Only I didn't know how to go about it. I was somewhat appalled that Favor hadn't told her daughter I existed. If I had had children would I have told them the truth, that I'd elected to leave home at the age of five and my father had never bothered to seek me out? It was so humiliating that I might well have kept quiet about the whole thing once he was dead. But how should I deal with Mary? I decided to tell at least part of the story in order to elicit more information in return.

"The truth is, Mary, I haven't seen your mother in ages, and fair enough, she didn't tell you about me, but then she didn't tell me about you."

"No shit!"

"Does your mother like you talking like that?"

"No, she hates it. But you don't care, do you?"

She had me all figured out.

"Are there more of you?"

"You mean brothers and sisters? There's Creepo."

"Is that a human?"

"Barely. It's my brother, Ned. Two years older. Soppy and slobbery. He's just fallen in "lurve." And he's finally had sex for the first time."

"Whereas you..."

"Well, me too, as it happens. I finally let a guy put it all the way in and bingo I'm pregnant."

She was a crude little creature. I could tell

she didn't really understand how pathetic she came across. She said things for effect, but instead of making her appear tough, she came across all the more vulnerable. And I had been exactly the same. In a way I still was. I shot off caustic remarks, hid behind self-deprecating witticisms, and yearned for love and affection while pushing people away at the same time.

"So what's my brother-in-law like?"

"Dad? You don't know him either? I can't believe all this. Well, Dad, he's, you know, sweet."

"Sweet!?"

"Yeah. I really like Dad. He sort of keeps himself to himself. But he's kind. And he puts up with Mum."

"What do you mean, puts up with? She's his wife."

"But she's so boring."

So Mary thought Favor was boring and Biddy had indicated that she wasn't exactly a live wire. I found I was rather pleased to hear this and felt a little guilty. But not much.

"And they hardly do it at all."

"Do what?"

"Have sex. Fuck."

There she went again. Little Madam trying to shock. But she amused me. I had to admit it.

"How on earth do you know a thing like that?"

"Well, it shows when they have. Stands out a mile. Mum's all pink and giggly in the morning and you hear them going 'Shhh' to each other in the bedroom."

"So your house in London is quite small?"

"It's just an ordinary London house, two rooms on each floor, front and back. It's not like this house. This is so cool."

"So you keep saying."

"How long can I stay?"

"For the moment till tomorrow. We'll take it day by day. Have you any idea what your mother's plans are?"

"Well, whatever they were they're fucked now, with me being pregnant. I'm supposed to go back to school at the beginning of September."

"What's to stop you? Some women work right up to the week they have the baby. Why can't you keep going to school, at least until you start showing, then I concede it might be a bit embarrassing."

"So you think I should have it."

"I didn't say that."

"Have you ever been pregnant?"

What should I tell her? She was sitting across the room on the other side of the fireplace, curled up in a ball on the sofa, staring at me with those dark, penetrating eyes. My eyes. My mother's eyes. She defied me to lie to her. Besides, she deserved the truth, this kid.

"Yes, I've been pregnant once. It was right after I left home and went to London. I wasn't much older than you are now."

"Were you, like, a rebel when you were a kid?

278

Were you the one who ran away from home and stuff?"

"You could say that." Years ago, when I was barely five years old.

"And Mum was the goody-goody. I knew it."

"I wouldn't know."

"So you were pregnant. What happened?"

"I had an abortion."

She hadn't been expecting that, I could tell. She flinched. She had thought I would tell her about the boy who made me pregnant, not what happened to the baby.

"And have you regretted it ever since?"

"Not at all."

She didn't like that either.

"So you think I should have an abortion?"

"That's not for me to decide. You must talk it over with your parents." She made a face. "Listen, Mary, running wild and being a rebel might sound all romantic and fun but it doesn't necessarily get you anywhere. If you want to spend your life living on the edge, fine, but it gets pretty wearing after a while. Men, boys, are cruel. They don't mean to be, they just are. And they go on being cruel even when they realize what they're doing. They don't change. You always think they will but they don't. It's better you know this now at the outset rather than expect a lot from men. You'll only be disappointed."

"That man you were with on the beach, has he disappointed you? What was it Linda was saying? You'd just been talking to his wife. No wonder he ran away so fast."

"So where's the father of your baby?"

"He went off with my best friend."

And suddenly she was crying, burying her face in the blanket hanging over the edge of the sofa. She looked about eleven.

"I'm not crying because I loved him or anything stupid. I didn't even like him very much. I'm crying because what you say is true and it's so sad. Jason was cruel. And he doesn't even know about the baby, about how he's fucked up my life. I won't be able to go to a university, all the stuff I was aiming for. You had an abortion. I guess that's the only thing to do but I'm so scared."

I went over and put my arms around her and hugged her to me. It was a strange sensation, not at all unpleasant. Suddenly I had someone who needed me, someone I could help, someone I could love—who wasn't a man.

Favor came over the next morning at the ungodly hour of eight-thirty. Mary was fast asleep and although my eyes were open I wasn't vertical.

I made coffee in silence. I just could not think of a single thing to say to my sister, and judging by the way she kept calling out "Mary, time to get up" in a highly irritating way, she wasn't finding it any easier talking to me.

"Look," I said awkwardly, "what do I call you?"

It was insane asking my own sister what

her name was but I could hardly explain why I called her Favor.

"Pat, of course. What else would you call me?"

"Is that really your name?"

She looked a little nervous. As well she might. Why would anyone think she didn't know her own name?

"I mean what is it short for?" I persisted.

"Nothing. I've never been a Patricia."

"No, you've got another name. What is it?"

"Yes," she said slowly, as if talking to a complete idiot, "I do have another name. It's my married name. Hardy. I used to have the name Cammell. Just like you. But I dropped it when I married. I'm Pat. Pat Hardy. All right?"

I let it go.

But I knew I would never be able to call her anything other than Favor even if I never said it to her face.

Mary finally staggered out of her room to the bathroom mumbling, "Hi, Grace," and glaring at her mother. She joined us at the table without getting dressed, her T-shirt barely covering her behind. I couldn't help glancing automatically at her stomach. She caught me and grinned, pulling up her T-shirt and unabashedly displaying her bare, flat stomach. And her bush of black pubic hair. Just like mine.

"Mary, please. Not at the breakfast table."

I winced on Mary's behalf. Favor was just so prim. How could this plain, boring-looking woman with her neat white blouse buttoned up to the neck and her super-clean jeans and sneakers be my sister? She was wearing pale blue eyeshadow at nine o'clock in the morning and she smelled of Pears soap. And if she really was my sister how come she had fabulous thick hair instead of strands of limp spaghetti like me?

"So when's Dad coming?" asked Mary.

"I don't know. I haven't reached him yet."

"Why not?"

"I just haven't, that's all. He's working very hard at the moment."

"No, he's not, Mum. The convention's about to pack up."

"Yes, well, be that as it may, I haven't spoken to him and that's that."

Be that as it may. I had never heard anyone actually say that phrase out loud. I looked to see if she was pursing her lips. It certainly sounded as if she was. Something was up. I could sense tension at five hundred paces and right now I was smothered by it.

"So, Mary, why not take a little stroll down to the beach?" suggested Favor.

"I was there yesterday." Mary looked at me and smirked. Oh God, Archie. What on earth was I going to do about him?

"Wasn't that Louse Point? There's another beach just down the road here. I've been there. I've been awake since five."

"Don't be so pedantic, Mum. A point. A beach. It's all sea and I saw it yesterday."

I could see what Favor was getting at. She

wanted to talk to me but she didn't want Mary sitting there taking notes. And Mary knew exactly what was going on. Why didn't Favor just come right out with it? Couldn't she see that Mary needed to be told, not asked, that Mary needed force and discipline as a sign that someone really cared enough? Favor's passive, nervous approach was all wrong.

"Mary, why don't you just take the hint and leave us alone for an hour or so? Take your Walkman down to the beach. We'll join you later. Go on."

"I'll put my bikini on and then I'll be off."

Favor's pursed lips were now falling open. "That's truly amazing. She went like a lamb. What kind of wonder did you work on her last night?"

"No kind. I'm just direct with her, and firm. That's all. That way she knows exactly where she is."

"You're like Biddy. She was direct, wasn't she?"

"Still is, as far as I can tell. I imagine that must be how you found me. Biddy told me you'd met."

"You saw her? You were there, in Wales? You went to say goodbye to your...to..."

"To David. My father. I'm rather lucky, aren't I? I have two fathers, yours and mine. No, in fact, I missed him. He'd already croaked by the time I got there. Bit of a relief, to tell you the truth. But I was pleased to see Biddy again, especially as I have a hunch it might be the last time. She must have known that.

Probably why she had the goddamn nerve to give you my address."

I could see Favor was a bit thrown by me. Had she really expected us to fall into each other's arms like two sisters separated at Auschwitz? Someone ought to tell her to get a grip, and sooner or later that someone would probably be me if I didn't watch my tongue.

"You must have known we'd meet one day," she wheedled.

"Actually, since we'd got this far without coming across each other I'd sort of assumed it wasn't going to happen."

"But didn't you want to see Dad even if you didn't want to meet me?"

"Dad, as you call him, was actually the last person I wanted to see," I lied. "Why would you want to see someone who had thrown you away?"

"He didn't throw you away. You left. You ran away."

"Is that what he told you? And if I did run away haven't you ever asked yourself why?"

"I don't know. I never understood why."

"Shall I tell you?"

"Only if you want to."

"I don't want to. I don't want to tell you anything. In fact I don't give a flying fuck what happened in the past, but you came schlepping all the way out here to find me, so presumably you're going to force it all out of me whether I want to or not." I was beginning to get seriously angry. "Well, here's the first thing you ought to know. I walked out of that house because of you, because all my mother talked about was you and what would happen when you were born."

"You can't possibly remember that."

"No, I don't suppose I can. I've probably embellished the whole shitty episode in my mind out of all proportion, but one thing I do know: our father was a complete bastard. I was better off without him."

"That's not true," she protested, going pink, "he was a wonderful man. He was kind. And brilliant. And generous. Loads of fun, too."

"And rich," I added. "How can you say he was generous? He left all his money to me. Didn't you feel pretty bitter about that?"

"Not in the slightest. It was his money. He could leave it to whoever he wanted. Gus and I don't have a lot but we're fine. We're not on the breadline."

To my intense irritation I could see she meant it. She honestly didn't begrudge me a cent.

"What about Gus? Surely he must have been a bit disappointed?"

"Why? He didn't marry me for my money." She said this without a shred of irony. She was completely without guile, this one. "But I suppose he could have used a little help in his business."

Aha!

"His business?"

"He runs a security business."

"And that brings him to New York?"

285

"To an annual convention. Yes."

"And he's joining you here?"

"I don't think so."

"Why not? Surely he ought to come and see Mary."

"I think that's between him and me."

"Or him and Mary?" Something had her rattled. I sensed all was not well between her and the hubby.

"What did he say when you told him about the pregnancy?"

"I think that's—"

"Between you and him. Something tells me you haven't told him yet. You told Mary you hadn't reached him. Let me guess. You don't know where he is."

Her obvious discomfort told me I'd struck home. I recalled Biddy's theory that if Favor had a nice, kind husband she'd be okay. Oh God, don't say she was about to experience what our mother had been through.

"He went back to London without telling me," she said quietly. "Mary doesn't know."

"Well, I never married, as you know, and it's when I hear things like this that I realize how lucky I am. You can't trust them an inch."

"How can you be so smug?" she lashed out at me. "You have no idea what my marriage is like. I have a wonderful marriage. I'm very lucky with Gus. He's kind and considerate."

"Like our father."

"Exactly."

"Oh, pull the other one. Our father was a shocking husband."

"He wasn't. He was devastated when our mother died. I don't think he ever got over it."

"Told you that, did he? Played the poor, grieving widower to the hilt?"

"Listen," she attempted an idiotic placatory smile, "you can't imagine the guilt I feel having had him to myself all these years. I can understand why you have such a negative attitude towards him, but you never knew him, did you? He was a good man. I never had an argument with him."

"Did you discuss things with him? Did you talk?"

"Well, no, not really. He was always pretty busy and..."

I remembered how Biddy had said she was a little stupid. Biddy was cruel and sharp and this well-meaning woman must have been anathema to her. I felt a little sorry for Favor. Obviously our brilliant father hadn't felt inclined to shoot the breeze with her, hadn't been much interested in her opinions. She probably hadn't stimulated him enough for him ever to become angry with her.

"He was a cruel man."

"He wasn't. You think he didn't care because he let Biddy and David raise you but I'm sure he did."

"Our father was a shit. Let's face it."

"Your father might have been a shit. In your mind. My father was wonderful."

My anger was rising fast as it always did. She wasn't quite as stupid as Biddy had thought. She understood that Lucas had represented different things to each of us, but it still irritated me that she was so pious, so magnanimous, so bloody understanding. I hated her so much at that moment that all my resentment at my father manifested itself in the desire to hurt not him but her, my sister. I couldn't help it. I had to do something to get back at her.

"If he was so wonderful, why did our mother kill herself?"

"She didn't kill herself. She died giving birth to me." She looked at me. I shook my head. "She killed herself?"

I told her everything Biddy had told me, culminating in her graphic description of our father's attempts to seduce her in the kitchen, the kitchen Favor must have known so well. And as I watched her confidence in her father—not mine—disintegrate in one look of horror after another I tried to feel triumphant.

But I couldn't. I was destroying her childhood in horrible, flamboyant brushstrokes and I couldn't paint over them. The damage was done.

She didn't say a word for several minutes. Then she asked, "Could I have a drink? A real drink."

"It's ten-thirty in the morning."

"I need a drink."

"Vodka? Gin? Wine?"

"Brandy if you've got it."

I fetched a bottle.

So when Mary finally came back from the beach an hour later she found her mother

288

and her aunt sitting sloshed over the breakfast table.

We'd crossed some kind of divide but we
weren't sisters yet. Not really. I found it hard
to believe I would ever accept this woman as
my own flesh and blood. I'd never been able
to accept anyone as my own flesh and blood.

Except maybe this complicated teenager
who already reminded me so much of myself.

"Why are you drunk?" she asked us, as
direct as I would be in her place.

But before either of us could attempt to pour
out the whole sorry story we heard a car
coming up the drive and staggered out onto
the deck to see who it was.

If I felt bad about what I had done to Favor,
all I can say is I was about to be punished for
my sins.

The car was a taxi, full of people. The passenger door beside the driver opened and out
stepped Margot.

"Hi there! These great people were on the
bus with me and said I could share their taxi."

"These great people" didn't bother to get
out and help the driver as he staggered up to
the deck with Margot's bags. Then he turned
the cab around for departure and as it disappeared down the drive one of the passen-
gers turned to look out the back window.

It was Harry Fox.

Favor

Icould understand how Linda felt with Grace. My sister obviously thought I was an unsophisticated halfwit, the crusading, long-lost relative come to atone for the loss of the father. She had a mean streak in her that I had often observed in unfulfilled people. Yet as much as she pushed me away, at the same time she reined me back in. She didn't have to have Mary stay. She didn't have to let us into her house at all. Then again she didn't have to destroy totally my memory of my father in quite such a devastating way. But it was almost as if she wanted us to have the same father, the monster who had destroyed our mother. By revealing him to me she had somehow brought us closer together than I had been able to with my Pollyanna vision of the man I had thought was my father.

But was her portrait an accurate one? It was, after all, based on hearsay. She had never experienced him as I had, yet they had something in common, she and Dad. They both managed to make me feel a little stupid. I'd never thought about it before. I'd never had to. Dad had never lost his temper with me, never let me down, but then I had never made any demands on him other than the need for a roof over my head and to be fed and clothed.

When I'd encountered the odd moment of turbulence during my adolescence, it had never occurred to me to talk to Dad. He was distant, always busy, always downstairs in the office. I accepted him without question. But now that I thought about it we'd never really talked.

I'd been lucky. I'd met Gus at exactly the right time. I could talk to Gus. I had never felt stupid with him.

Until now.

Now I realized what an absolute fool I'd been. I'd been cocooned in my little family nest, oblivious to Gus's middle-aged angst. And now when I needed him to help me cope with Mary, I'd lost him.

I knew I ought to pick up the phone and book us on the first flight back to London, back to Gus. But over the breakfast brandy I'd achieved a tentative bonding with my sister, an unspoken acknowledgement that we were who we were, even if we weren't particularly happy with the relationship. And I wasn't about to walk away from that, not until I'd made a lot more progress. Unsophisticated maybe, but a quitter I was not.

But if Grace and Dad had made me feel somewhat inadequate, they had nothing on this woman who had just arrived. Margot, whoever she was, made me feel like a complete retard.

"This is Margot Harris, one of my oldest friends," said Grace and then she went and introduced me as her cousin. I saw Mary's look of total astonishment and gripped her hand.

I knew what Grace was trying to do. This so-called oldest friend had no idea Grace had a sister. Explanations at this stage of the game would just get in the way. *Cousin* was the perfect compromise. Related—but distant.

"And this is her daughter, Mary," continued Grace.

Margot barely acknowledged us. I disliked her on sight. She was decidedly simian, small and lithe with olive skin and black hair. She had the beginnings of a moustache above her thin lips and she reminded me of a dissatisfied, edgy monkey.

"I've brought you a present. It's Kitty Kelley's new book, *The Royals*. An advance copy. One of my contacts in publishing got it for me." She thrust it at Grace. I noted the emphasis on the word *contacts*. I'm connected, Margot was shouting, and I'm going to make sure you know it.

"This'll be the third." Grace pointed to the bookshelf. "Everyone I know at Time Warner has sent me a copy but thanks anyway. You should have waited. I was going to come and pick you up."

"Is that brandy on your breath, Grace? Are you drinking in the morning? Poor sweetie, are things that bad?"

I saw Grace flinch as Margot embraced her.

"Who gave you a lift? You should have asked them in."

"You know who it was, don't you? Didn't you see?"

"Well, why didn't he come in?"

I was amazed at the sudden change in Grace. She was almost pleading.

"The truth is," said Margot slowly, "I didn't tell him it was you I was coming to stay with. I wasn't sure about how you'd feel about having him here. I only wanted what was best for you."

That was the sort of thing people said when they meant exactly the opposite. Like "trust me" or "believe me." When someone said that, you automatically didn't. It was obvious to me that this woman would only ever want what was best for herself.

"Who was it?" asked Mary.

"Harry Fox. An old friend of Grace's."

"Harry Fox!" squealed Mary. "And you let him get away."

"Bit old for you, isn't he?"

Mary gave Margot one of her "who asked you?" looks.

"He's working with someone out here."

"Yes, I know," said Grace.

"Oh, you do?" Margot was stopped in her tracks for a second. "Well, no doubt you also know he'll be out here for quite a while, right through to the film festival in October. I sat next to him on the Jitney. We really hit it off. He asked me to a Labor Day weekend party. I think Spielberg's going to be there. Donna Karan, maybe. Oh God, have nothing to wear. Have gained half a stone since arrival in New York. Must have cigarette and large multi-calorie alcoholic beverage to cheer self up and spend unnecessary fortune at nearest boutique. Prevail upon Grace to cough up for same."

"Why are you talking like a memo?" asked Grace.

"She thinks she's Bridget Jones," supplied Mary in a rather disgusted tone, "but she's at least ten years too old."

"Mary!" I was secretly pleased.

"Bridget Jones? Who she?" asked Grace.

"Oh, Grace, you always were hopeless. You just don't keep up, do you? It's only Britain's bestselling book all summer. Young. Funny. Very hip. Puts all those dreary old romance writers in their place."

What was wrong with Grace? Earlier in the day she'd been lacerating me with unpleasant revelations, and now here she was, letting this loathsome woman stamp her into the ground.

"Anyway, let me show you to your room. Mary's staying here, by the way, sleeping in the next room to you. You'll be sharing a bathroom."

"No, we won't," said Mary suddenly, "I'm going with Mum to stay with whatsername next door."

"Just as well," said Margot. "I'm hopeless at sharing bathrooms."

I was startled by Mary's announcement—and pleased. But I could see Grace was deeply upset.

"You don't have to go, Mary. You can share my bathroom."

"No, you two friends should have some time together," said Mary archly, "I'd only be in the way."

It occurred to me that if Margot was going to be here, she'd be a bit *de trop* if I came by for some more sisterly bonding. Margot's presence was going to hamper proceedings considerably.

"You staying out here long?" asked Margot as if she'd read my mind.

"As long as it takes," I said.

"As long as what takes? Why aren't you staying with Grace if you're her cousin?"

"Because you are," said Mary.

"Come along, Mary," I said sharply, "I think we'll go and take Linda out to lunch to thank her for her hospitality."

"Who's Linda?" asked Margot.

"Grace's best friend," said Mary quickly and with a certain amount of childish satisfaction.

"You were rather rude to Margot," I pointed out to Mary as we trudged back through the boundary shrubs between Linda's property and Grace's.

"I don't care." She was defiant and I was pleased. The old Mary was definitely back and her spirit would give her the strength she needed to face up to a decision about the baby. "She's trouble."

"I rather think I agree with you, but she is Grace's friend."

"But you're her sister. Why did she introduce you as her cousin? I wanted to jump up and down, say I was her niece."

"Grace must have had her reasons. We haven't really been close, Grace and I, and that's a little difficult to explain to people like Margot."

"Oh yeah, I see what you mean. She'd use it against Grace. Play you off against her. This way she, like, doesn't really have you all figured out yet."

I was amazed by her perception, her grasp of the situation, even if her phrasing was a little cockeyed. I was pretty sure Margot had me figured out perfectly well in two short words: no threat.

We approached Linda's house via the back porch. The kitchen door was open and we heard voices, Linda's and a man's. I was in front of Mary and it was what I heard that made me put out a hand behind me and stop her.

"Stanley, can I ask you something, something important?"

Mary and I stood behind the rhododendron, clasping each other so we wouldn't move. Mary had her hand over her mouth and I knew she was trying hard not to laugh.

"Sure, honey, go right ahead."

"This is kinda hard."

"Take your time. Is it about last night? Pretty hot stuff. You really got me going. I like it when you climb on top of me like that."

Of course I knew who it was. I'd heard the voice before. A nice voice, I realized. Gruff, growly, quite old but warm and humorous at the same time. Mary and I were trapped. I couldn't look at her. She'd laugh. I knew she would. And we couldn't move. A twig would snap and we'd give ourselves away. This was clearly a very intimate moment between Linda and Stanley, but who knew how long it would last?

"It's not really about sex," I heard Linda say.

"Oh, okay. Deeper than that maybe? About love? That what you want to talk about? Pass me the sugar, would you, honey. Because I do love you, you know that, don't you, Linda?"

"You do?"

"Well, sure."

"You never said."

"What's to say? I'm saying it now. I thought I'd been showing it, like how we were last night."

"I love you, Stanley."

"I love you too, Linda."

There was a silence. I could only imagine what was going on in the kitchen.

"So we have a relationship?" Linda's voice was shy, girly.

"We have more than that."

"How do you mean, Stanley?"

"I want to be with you. I'm fifty-three years old. I'm lonely. I'm asking you to... I'm asking you to be with me."

"To marry me?"

"To live together. I want to move in with you."

"Today?"

"Today. Tomorrow. Who cares?"

"Only I have these people from England staying. My neighbor's sister."

"So when they go back to England I'll move in. How long till they go?"

"I didn't ask."

"Linda," I heard Stanley say with some firmness, "ask."

Mary was on the point of collapse. Clasping her by the hand I dragged her quickly back the way we'd come and began to talk very loudly.

"I wonder if Linda would like to go out to lunch with us. What do you think, Mary?" I shouted.

"I don't know. Let's ask her," yelled back Mary.

By the time we reached the kitchen door, Linda and Stanley were miles apart.

"I'm so pleased you're here. Now you can meet Stanley," said Linda, propelling him towards us. He looked more like Jack Lemmon than Walter Matthau—with a beard and plenty of bushy hair.

I knew immediately that Stanley had obviously said nothing about walking in on me. He had stuck out his hand, but now he took it back and stood there, gauche, helpless, and really rather sweet.

"What's the matter, Stanley? This is Gracie's sister. I told you about her. Do you two know each other or something?"

"No. It's wonderful to meet you, Stanley." I held out my hand and smiled straight at him.

"Yeah." He looked relieved. I wasn't about to blow the whistle on him. "Look, I'm sorry…"

"What you sorry for? Stanley, this is Gracie's sister. You don't have to be sorry."

"We'll be going back to London soon," said Mary and dissolved into giggles.

"I hope to see you again before you go," Stanley managed to stutter. What would he do, I wondered, if he knew we'd heard everything he'd just said to Linda? He'd had real passion in his voice when he'd talked about their sex together. He might look like a bearded middle-aged bumbler but he was clearly a man with hidden depths. I felt rather proud of our secret previous meeting. "Honey, I have to get back now. I'll call later."

He pulled Linda towards him almost as if he wanted to show me what he was capable of. However clumsy I had thought he was, now I saw that these two had nothing to hide. She moved into his embrace and buried her face in his hairy beard without the slightest embarrassment. Stanley patted her on the back and planted kisses on the top of her head.

"I'll call later," he repeated at least three times as if it were some kind of mantra. "It was nice meeting you," he told us when he finally disengaged himself and turned to leave.

Linda stood at the kitchen door for several minutes.

"He loves me. I love him. It's going to work," she said. "I have a relationship after all this time. But how come you guys are back? I thought you'd spend the day with Gracie."

"Her best friend from England arrived," explained Mary.

"Oh, right. Her best friend from England," repeated Linda, nose clearly a bit out of joint. "What's she like?"

"Snotty," said Mary, "awful. Not at all like you."

Linda and I smiled at each other.

"Let's ring Dad in New York," suggested Mary. "Why isn't he here yet? Oh, you didn't reach him, did you? Well, let's try now."

It was nearly one o'clock. Six o'clock in London. If I rang now I'd probably get Gus just as he was finishing work. But I couldn't do it in front of Mary. I couldn't let her know Gus had gone back to England without telling us.

Linda saw me hesitate and I looked at her when Mary's back was turned, signalling with my eyes that I wanted Mary to leave.

"Linda, would it be okay if Mary comes to stay here tonight? Do you have room?"

"Oh, sure," said Linda without hesitation. "Mary, what I'm going to do is show you your room and the bathroom and then maybe you'd like to take a walk with me down the drive to see if the mailman's been. I've got a mail box in the shape of a pink poodle I'd like you to see."

"I already saw—" began Mary.

"Mary, it's very kind of Linda to have us stay."

She got the message and followed Linda out of the room.

"There's a phone in your room," hissed Linda as she passed me.

300

I could hear our telephone ringing and ringing in Shepherd's Bush. I couldn't remember how many times it rang before the answering machine picked up. What if Gus wasn't there? Would I leave a message? What would I say? Why hadn't I thought this through?

Just as I was about to hang up he answered. Out of breath. Curt.

"Hello?"

"Gus?"

"Yeah?"

"It's me."

"Yeah?"

"How are you?"

"Fine."

"You went home."

"Yeah."

"Without telling me."

"How was I supposed to tell you? I didn't know where the hell you were."

"I left the number of the Goose Neck Inn."

"I called. They said you were out."

"So why didn't you leave a message?"

"Why didn't you call me? Why do I always have to keep chasing you? You went off to find your long-lost sister. Fine. But don't expect me to come chasing after you."

I could hear the hurt in his voice.

"Gus, don't be angry."

"Who's angry? So did you find her? Is that why you're finally calling? To tell me how wonderful she is?"

"No. It's something pretty important. Not about Grace. About Mary."

"What's happened? She's freaked out because you've finally come clean about her having an auntie she never knew about and you can't handle it. Well, it's no use looking to me for support. You chose to do this. You're in this all on your own."

This was so unlike Gus. It sounded as if he'd steeled himself for my call and he was determined to punish me. He never spoke to me like this, harshly, confrontational. At least not until recently. I must have been fretting over the line he was taking with me longer than I thought because he spoke again and this time there was a hint of anxiety in his voice.

"What's up? Is Mary okay? What's going on out there?"

"She's pregnant." I blurted it out and at the same time a ludicrous thought crossed my mind. I'm calling long distance on Linda's phone. I must remember to pay her back. This is going to be a long call. This is going to take a while.

Gus's next words shocked me to the core.

"It was always a possibility."

"You knew she was pregnant? Did she tell you in New York?"

"No, no, no. I've been talking to Ned. You know? Your other child. We sat up one night. Sophie's away somewhere. You're in America. The house is a bit lonely. So we've been talking, man to man, and he told me you'd found Mary almost having sex on our living-room floor. I have to hear this from our son, you never considered sharing this with me?

Oh no, you're too busy seeking out your sister to—"

"Hold on, Gus."

"No, I won't hold on. I've been holding on all summer and now I've had enough. You've allowed Mary to get pregnant. How could you be so utterly stupid?"

I could feel myself starting to cry. Tears of frustration at being unjustly accused. Everyone thought I was stupid. Grace. Dad. Margot. And now Gus.

"I didn't let it happen. It had already happened back in England."

"That's exactly what I mean. She was here right under your nose and you didn't even catch on to what was going on."

"Well, she was under your nose too," I protested, "you live in the house. You're her father. Why do I always have to take the bloody blame?"

"Shouting at me isn't going to get us anywhere." Gus would choose this particular moment to revert to his old reasonable self. "What are we going to do about it? How far gone is she?"

"I don't know."

"You don't know? What on earth have you two been talking about since you've known about your little secret? Whether or not it's going to rain tomorrow and will you be able to go to the beach?"

"It's not our little secret. Mary only just told me. And now I'm telling you. What do you think we should do?"

"Well, there's only one thing to do. She'll have to get rid of it as soon as possible. What plane are you booked on?"

"I haven't..."

"You mean you haven't booked a flight? You're not coming home?"

"Well, yes, of course we are, eventually. But we've only just met Grace and Mary really likes her, she's been staying with her and..."

"So where is she going to have the abortion? How long do you intend to wait?"

"Gus, don't be so clinical. We can't rush this. We have to talk to her about it."

"We? What's this we? If you're not coming home where do I fit in?"

"I thought you'd come out here. Mary really wants you. She keeps asking for you."

"Where exactly am I going to find the cash to keep popping back and forth across the Atlantic? And what about the business? And doesn't Mary start school in about half an hour? What on earth is the matter with you?"

There was a noise behind me. Mary and Linda were standing there on Linda's purple shag rug.

"Is that Dad?" Mary asked. I didn't know how much they'd heard, but if Gus had been shouting then I probably had been, too. Mary took the receiver from my hand.

"Dad?"

Almost immediately she held it at arm's length.

"Mum, what's wrong with him? He sounds

so far away. He's shouting at me. He never shouts at me. Mum?"

I grabbed the receiver. Gus was in full flow.

"...and furthermore when you've got rid of it you're going to stay home after school every night and your mother and I will stand by you, but you're going to have to pay us back, Mary. You're going to have to behave. You're going to have to..."

"Gus!" I yelled down the line. "It's me. You've scared Mary off. Calm down."

"Well, are you coming home?"

"Yes," I said wearily, "we're coming home, I suppose. Call Dr. Green and make an appointment for Mary and me to see him next week after the Bank Holiday weekend. I'll call you with our flight arrival time. Will you come to the airport?"

Silence.

"Gus?"

"I don't know. I'll see."

I'll see. Not I'll see what my schedule's like, whether I have time, but I'll see if I'm still talking to you then. That's what he meant.

"He wants me to have an abortion," sobbed Mary, collapsing on my bed. Linda and I sat down on either side of her and put our arms around her. "Dad's always right and that's what he says. Will it hurt, Mum? Will I be okay?"

"You'll be fine," said Linda. "People have them all the time." She made it sound like a flu injection. "You can be in and out in less than a day and your mom's going to be with you and then it'll all be over. You'll see."

"I suppose so." Mary was wiping her eyes. "Then I'll go back to school. It'll be just like I was sick for a bit. And then I'll be better."

"There you go." Linda gave her a pat on the back.

"But Grace thinks I should have it."

"Grace thinks what?" I asked, astounded. I was beginning to feel decidedly miffed that nobody wanted my opinion on anything. Me. Mary's mother. Mary hadn't even asked.

"We were talking last night and as she kissed me good night she said, sort of in a whisper, "I think you should have your baby," and then she went to bed."

"Oh great, and what did she suggest you do with it after you've had it?"

"She didn't say. Oh, Mum, don't be angry. Maybe she meant you'd look after it. It'd be like you'd had another baby."

"At my age? Thanks a lot!"

But that set Mary off crying again. We were all sitting there in a row on Linda's shocking-pink bedspread in a complete emotional mess.

"Mary, darling," I said as gently as I could, "what would you like to do?"

The answer she gave me was far from anything I'd ever imagined hearing from her.

"I want to talk to Creepo," she said, blowing her nose.

Now she wanted to know if her brother had a view.

"Sweetheart, it's quite late over there." The truth was I didn't want to speak to Gus again that night, not in the state he was in.

"I want to speak to Creepo," said Mary distinctly and with a certain amount of menace, "and I know it's not late. It's only about seven o'clock. By the way, why didn't you tell me he'd gone home?"

"Linda, could you dial the number as you're closest to the phone and ask for Ned, Mary's brother?"

Ned answered. Linda handed the phone to Mary and then she and I got up and tiptoed from the room.

"I'll pay you back for these long-distance calls. Every cent."

"Oh, for pity's sake," said Linda, "you will not. Stanley loves me. I feel so rich and happy I'd buy you a house out here if you asked me."

"Don't tempt me. I might take you up on it."

"Hubby was a little cranky, I take it?"

"You could say that."

"I could and I do. You should stand up to him more. We heard you on the phone. You were like a lamb."

"I was shouting at him."

"No you weren't. You were pretending to shout."

"But he's never been like this before. He's never shouted at me."

"Maybe he's never had to."

"Oh God, what a mess."

"And it'll only get messier. These things always do," said Linda cheerfully.

How right she was.

Mary joined us in ten minutes, a changed person.

"I've made my decision. I'm going to have my baby."

"Ned thinks you ought to have it?"

"Ned doesn't even know I'm pregnant as far as I can tell. I've made my decision because of Frisky."

"Frisky's another of your kids?" asked Linda. "Creepo, Frisky and Mary. Cute names."

"Frisky's the cat," I explained.

"Oh, of course, you always take the cat's opinion on unwanted pregnancies."

"It's not an unwanted pregnancy," said Mary, "I do want this baby. It's because of what happened to Frisky that helped me decide."

"What happened?" I asked. "Is she all right?"

"I think so. Creepo took her to the vet to be spayed like we agreed and the vet called him on the morning of the operation or whatever it is and said we've opened her up and she's pregnant again. She had these little babies inside her."

"No!"

"And he said he had to ask Ned whether he could..." she was on the verge of tears again "...whether he could kill them. But at the same time he told Ned that it was so soon after she'd had kittens that if she had another litter she'd be exhausted and probably..."

At this point she did start crying and between the gulps we made out: "So of course Ned had to go ahead and okay it otherwise Frisky wouldn't be here any more. But it made me think. We made poor Frisky kill her babies. No one's going to make me kill mine. No one!"

Well, that's that, I thought. The first thing I was going to do was march over and ask Grace just exactly who she thought she was, advising Mary to keep the baby. And as an excuse I'd say I was there to collect Mary's stuff. Secretly I was just miserable that every decision about this baby was being made without me, whichever way it swung.

It was another Stanley–Linda situation. Only this time it was Margot I overheard as I let myself in the door on the front deck of Grace's house. She was on the phone in the kitchen and didn't hear me.

"I've really lucked into something good here with Grace, sweet," I heard her say. "Nice house, I think I'll stay a while. And I hooked up with a really nice crowd coming out on the bus. Going to see them this weekend. Grace'll be working on her stupid book, no doubt, so she won't be cramping my style. She's out now doing the shopping. What's the weather like in England? It's glorious here."

Running up long-distance bills on Grace's phone. Plotting to meet people behind her back. I was full of righteous indignation on behalf of my sister. Mary and I had been right.

Margot was trouble.

Grace

I told Margot I was going shopping, which was
nothing but a spur-of-the-moment lie. I
had to see Archie. I couldn't call him with
Margot listening in. She'd already asked
repeatedly when she was going to meet my mystery man. Who was he? Where was he? Why
all the secrecy? As if she couldn't guess.

I backed the car down the drive and nearly
ran over Lew who was walking up it, peering
over at Linda's, not looking where he was
going. He leaned on the roof of my car and
spoke to me through the window.

"You ask her about me?"

Oh shit. I hadn't gotten back to him. The
need to see Archie was urgent and made me
be blunt with Lew, which I regretted as soon
as I saw his dejected face. But he had to be told.

"I didn't say anything about you, Lew,
because she's met someone. She's seeing
someone. I didn't know. She met him while
I was away. I'm surprised you haven't seen him
coming and going."

"Only person I've seen around her place is
that old timer who reads the weather. Whiskery
fella. Seen him coming and going. Figured he
had to be a relative of hers or something."

"That's him."

"No!"

"Yes."

"Can't be. What she want with an old guy like him? It ain't decent."

For the first time I wondered how old Lew was. Forties maybe. It had never occurred to me that Linda would fancy an older man, but once I thought about it, it made sense. Fluffies always attracted protectors. Lew was just a younger variety.

"I'm sorry, Lew."

"So am I," he said, sounding angrier than I'd ever heard him, and stamped off through the woods.

I drove over to my house on the dunes and parked a little way down the road. It was pretty exposed, just the odd multimillion-dollar, ten-room "cottage," as they were known, dotted along the beach front, and a massive expanse of white sand. My modern shingle affair stood out a mile—literally. From where I was parked I could see if Archie came out of the back of the house on to the beach, or if he came out of the front and left by car.

After forty-five minutes I began to question my patience. Supposing he didn't come out all day? Supposing he wasn't even there? Supposing he was away in Manhattan? Supposing he came out with Harry Fox? How long was I prepared to wait?

He came out after I'd been there nearly two hours. Me, a woman in her forties, allegedly a successful novelist, reduced to behaving like a second-rate sleuth in a bad TV movie, sitting listening to the radio hearing

Linda's Stanley give me the weather report every half-hour. Quite a sexy voice, I had to admit.

Archie wasn't alone. There were two teenage boys in the Mercedes with him. Still, it was him and he was leaving the house.

I followed. Did he know my car? Did it matter if he saw me? No, of course not because the first chance I got I was going to grab him.

He drove along 27 for a while and then turned left on Egypt Lane, heading for Further Lane. He stopped outside a very grand house and the boys got out to be greeted by other kids yelling, "C'min, man, we been waiting." Before I could get his attention, Archie had driven away again. I followed him into East Hampton, saw him go to the hardware store on Newtown Lane and to the File Box to get some stationery.

Then he went into the Grill.

I found him in the back ordering himself a burger and fries. I slipped in beside him and put my hand between his legs under the table, rubbing my fingers up and down the denim of his jeans.

"Stop that, for Christ's sake." He really did sound quite angry.

"I had to see you. I needed to explain."

"Explain about what?"

"About meeting Sonia in East Hampton."

"I don't want to talk about Sonia. I wouldn't ever talk about you to her and I'm not going to discuss her with you."

"I'm not asking you to."

"Why didn't you tell me you'd met her?"

"It didn't come up. What do you expect me to do? Push you off when we're in the middle of fucking and say, 'Hey, by the way, I just met your wife, how about that?' And anyway, when I asked you if she'd arrived, you said not yet."

"That was pretty sneaky of you, given you already knew she was there."

"Has she mentioned she met me?"

"She did, as a matter of fact. She wants to have you over."

"Well, great, I'll come over for dinner one night. When would be a good time?"

"Very funny. And there's something else you've been sneaky about."

"I have? What's that?" I had pulled his shirt out of his jeans and was running my hand up his back. "Feed me some of your fries."

"You didn't tell me you knew Harry Fox."

"What makes you think I do?"

"He's out here. He came over to the house last night, said he'd sat beside an Englishwoman on the Jitney and he'd dropped her off at your house. You never told me you were the woman he based *Rapture* on. He feels like shit about that, by the way."

"Oh sure," I said. "So did you compare notes?"

"Don't start being ridiculous. I didn't even tell him I'd met you."

"Now who's being sneaky? So how did he know I'm here?"

"Your friend Margot. They talked about you

all the way from New York. She recognized him and told him she was coming to stay with you."

Suddenly I felt sick. What was Margot up to? She'd said she'd kept quiet about who she was visiting.

"Who is this Margot?" asked Archie, sensing me recoil.

"Just an old friend. Why don't you come back and meet her? That way you can come and visit and it won't look odd. I mean if she's mentioned me anyway and she's met Harry. Harry's probably mentioned me to Sonia by now..."

"And Sonia's met you. No. This is too incestuous. I couldn't handle it. But don't you want to see Harry?"

"I have you."

"Grace, I'm not a very nice person. I've deceived my wife. And I lied to you about her arrival here."

"I don't care. I know the score. It's not as if you're deceiving me."

"Even so."

"No, I want you whether she's here or not. I'm special. You told me so."

He didn't say anything.

"Archie?"

"Okay, all right." He turned in the banquette to look at me. He was gripping my hand fiercely. "But just remember you decided this. You said you knew the score. You came after me. You acknowledge that, okay?"

I was pretty taken aback by this intensity.

314

It seemed immaterial to me which of us made the running. We wanted each other, didn't we? Archie was the person who was there for me, the one I'd remember as helping me get over a particularly bad time in my life. The man who enabled me to trust someone again.

"So was that really your sister and your niece and was she really pregnant?"

I told him the whole story and I loved the way he listened, so interested in my situation.

"It's crazy. She arrives out of nowhere and expects me to play happy families just like that."

"What's she like?"

"Ordinary. She's okay but she's nothing special. She's just like a lot of women you meet."

"But you didn't dislike her?"

"No. Not at all. There's nothing to dislike. It's just she's so ordinary, as I said. In fact, the most interesting thing about her is the fact that her teenage daughter's pregnant, and that's a terrible thing to say. But the kid's great, by the way."

"She is?"

"Totally fucked up. Needs a firm hand. Someone to kick her around to show they've noticed her sort of thing."

"And you're just itching to do it."

I looked at him in total surprise. He was right.

"So how are Theo and Leo?"

"Oh, they need a firm hand, someone to kick them around to show them they care. Want to give it a whirl? They're in the back of the car."

We drove to Lantern Lane overlooking the

Accabonac Harbor. Archie let Leo out for a run and we climbed into the back seat of the Mercedes like a couple of teenagers. Theo, who of course would rather die than get out of a car and run around like a normal dog, was made to sit in the front seat where he curled up and shivered, placing his long nose in such a position that he could watch our activities with as much disapproval as he could muster in a canine expression.

It was only afterwards as we were driving back to my place in tandem that I realized Archie hadn't smiled once since I'd found him at the Grill; not during his lunch, not while we were fucking on the back seat. And he had hurt me while we were having sex. He hadn't waited to see if I was wet, he'd just come into me very fast and climaxed in a few short bursts. I'd glanced at his face close to mine and seen he was scowling, almost as if he were the one who was in pain.

"Hi," called Margot, running out onto the deck when we arrived. "Let me help you with the shopping."

Too late I remembered I was supposed to have been shopping.

"Oh, I ran into Archie here and we took his dogs for a walk on the beach instead. I thought I'd bring him by to meet you and then I'll go and do the shopping. Archie, this is Margot Harris, one of my oldest friends. Margot, this is Archie Berkeley. He's working with Harry Fox, doing the music on the film."

"Harry told me all about you. I'm a big

fan." Margot proceeded to rattle off Archie's credits. This was typical Margot. She was a regular walking *Who's Who* and never failed to impress. I could see Archie was lapping it up.

"Actually," she said, "I have to go to East Hampton myself to get something to wear for this party on Sunday."

"What party on Sunday?" I asked.

"Oh, you know, the one Harry Fox invited me to. I'm sure you could come."

I could sense Archie was getting uneasy. It was obvious why. He was probably going and he had to take Sonia. He didn't want the two of us bumping into each other again.

"Oh, spare me one of those Hamptons parties," I said with as much cool as I could muster.

"Archie," said Margot, "I was wondering, bit cheeky since I've only just met you, but maybe you could give me a ride and then I can take care of Grace's shopping at the same time. Grace, have you got a list ready?"

"I was only going to the Amagansett Farmer's Market right down the road," I lied, "but, Archie, if you could take Margot into East Hampton that'd be great. When do you have to pick up the boys?"

"In an hour or so. Fine. Come on, Margot."

He blew me a kiss behind her back. I wanted to ask him when I would see him again but I had to make do with a phony parting line from him: "We'll get together soon. 'Bye now."

Margot came back two hours later in a cab. She'd bought herself an elegantly casual silk jersey number from Henry Lehr on Newtown Lane and she put it on to show me. She looked all right but part of me was feeling hurt and angry as only a few hours in Margot's presence could make me feel. Why couldn't I go to this Labor Day weekend party? How dare Margot turn up and use my house as an hotel while she sashayed off to join in all the social action, social action I always claimed I wanted no part of. Who did I think I was kidding?

"Kim and Alec live down the road a piece. Did you know?" she said casually. "Wonder if they'll be at the party."

Kim Basinger and Alec Baldwin. Yes, their house was within walking distance of mine, but what was all this "Kim and Alec" shit? Surely Margot didn't know them. In any case, I wasn't going to give her the satisfaction of asking her.

"There's no reason to suppose they'll be at your party, Margot," I said rather acidly. "There are hundreds of parties this weekend, you know? You're just going to one of them."

She spent the entire weekend driving me mad, asking me why didn't I do this, why I didn't do that. Margot always knew best. How could I have forgotten?

"Why don't you have your caretaker build you a box to keep your garbage cans in so the raccoons don't empty them every night? You could keep logs in there instead of under the tarp on the back porch. It looks so messy back there."

She was right, of course, but she didn't have to point it out. Maybe I ought to put her on to Lew, see if she could get a few results out of him for a change.

"Why don't you get some nice plants, brighten up your deck?"

"Why don't you have air conditioning?"

"Why doesn't your dishwasher work properly? You need some of that water-softening stuff."

"Why don't you get a new outside light for the drive?"

"Why don't you get this screen mended?"

Why don't you? Why don't you? Why don't you? Why don't you shut up, Margot, I felt like screaming. I think I preferred "My therapist says..." And it wasn't as if she ever said anything nice about the house to offset her endless criticisms.

By Sunday evening I'd had enough.

"Take yourself off to your party, Margot, why don't you?" I snapped.

"I'm almost ready," she called from the bathroom in an annoyingly reasonable voice, "but, Gracie, I was wondering how I was going to get there. It's not far, it's just down the road..."

"I'll take you." I could take a hint as well as the next person.

"Think of all the hours you'll have to get some work done with me out of the house," she said. "I feel so awful taking up so much of your time."

I didn't tell her I had no more work to do for the time being. Let her feel guilty. It was as if my time and my emotions were stretched to the limit. I was driven mad by Margot on the one hand, but on the other I was the one beginning to feel a sense of guilt that I hadn't seen my sister and Mary. They'd called and I'd put them off, pleading Margot. But as the weekend passed I began to realize that facing up to my sister was the lesser of two evils and that I really did miss Mary. I wanted to see them and I was terrified that I might have put them off for good. That they might have already left.

But no. They were still there, as Linda's cheery voice confirmed.

"We've had a Labor Day picnic on the beach. Stanley's about to go to work. You want to get together?"

"Come over here," I found myself saying, "bring my sister and Mary and I'll make supper."

As I laid the table I found I was humming under my breath. Happy. Expectant. It was an odd feeling, one I hadn't had for quite a while, even with the excitement of Archie and the news about my book. For a second it struck me that this was a happiness that had nothing to do with Archie because it had nothing to do with men or romance or sex or any of that stuff. I was looking forward to something the way a child does, a child who does not yet know about the excitement of attraction. So I made pasta—what else? thanks to Villa—and a fruit salad and I was smiling and humming away to myself like a complete nitwit.

I was a little thrown when Linda showed up with a man on her arm.

I'd never seen her with a man before. I mean, I'd seen her in the presence of men and I'd seen her with Lew but he didn't count. A second after I thought that, I despised myself. Poor Lew. How could I ever say he didn't count? He was what David McIntyre used to call one of "nature's gentlemen." Someone who behaved immaculately to everyone and in return was treated like shit—mostly by people like me.

Thank God he wasn't around now to see Linda so obviously helplessly in love with this man. And he with her. I'd heard stories of this kind of rare occurrence but never actually witnessed it. People meeting and falling in love with each other almost immediately. I looked at Stanley—for it had to be he—and Linda and knew instantly that they had each found their soul mate, the one person in the world they were meant to find. But theirs was a kind of love that didn't exclude other people and make them feel lonely, like those dippy couples at Louse Point. You looked at Linda and Stanley and you were happy for them. You wanted it to work. It gave you hope to see them. If they were this happy together, it could happen to you.

"Gracie, this is Stanley," said Linda simply.

"I'm happy to meet you," he said, standing

321

there on my deck like Smoky the Bear, in jeans and a clean white shirt and sounding like he meant it. "You working on something good? Linda tells me you're a writer."

"Actually, I just finished and yes, I think it might be something good."

"Well, congratulations." Again he sounded like he meant it. "You better let me know when they bring it out over here and I'll alert the radio station, see if they can do something. Local author. They like stuff like that."

"Thank you," I said, "thank you very much. Will you come in and have a drink?"

"Some other time. That'd be great. Gotta run along now and go to work. I'm leaving Linda in your capable hands. Take care of her for me. Keep her out of mischief. Walk me to the end of the drive, honey."

"Be glad to," said Linda.

It was obvious she would have said the same if he'd asked her to walk with him to the edge of the crater of an erupting volcano and jump in. She hadn't let go of his hand the entire time he'd been talking to me.

"Don't be long now," I told Linda, "water's on for the pasta. Nice meeting you, Stanley. See you again."

"Sure," he said, "soon."

"Will they get married?" Mary asked when they were out of earshot.

"Without a doubt," I said. "What on earth could keep them apart?"

"Yuck, what are these?" Two hours later as Linda sat looking dreamy and distracted,

322

Mary was picking out the blueberries from her fruit salad in disgust. She and her mother had caught the sun. They looked healthy and relaxed. I kept having to remind myself that while they had become Linda's houseguests, they were in fact my family.

"Did you tell that horrible woman about my baby?" asked Mary.

"What horrible woman?" I feigned innocence.

"The woman who came to stay with you. The woman who's gone out to a fancy party and left you here like Cinderella."

"To cook supper for her ugly sister? You've got the story a bit wrong. Or do you think Margot's my ugly sister? You shouldn't call her horrible. She's an old friend of mine and you should respect that, whatever you think of her. But no, I didn't tell her. None of her business."

"Good," said Mary.

"Actually, I doubt she'd be interested."

"So will Harry Fox be at this party?" I nodded. "But why aren't you there?"

"I wasn't asked."

"Why?"

"Because I'm not part of the movie star crowd. It doesn't interest me."

"But it does interest your friend Margot. So why wouldn't she be interested in my baby?"

"Because you're not famous, if you really want to know. But I'm interested in your baby. What have you decided?"

"One second," said my sister. "Mary says you told her she ought to have the baby."

"I said no such thing. I think I might have implied that she might regret it if she didn't. But I said she had to discuss it with you and your husband."

"No, you did say you thought I ought to have it, when we said good night," said Mary.

She might be right. The truth was I did want her to have it. I didn't want this kid to go through an abortion.

"But excuse me, how do you think it's going to look back in London when she parades around with a huge stomach at her age?" asked my sister.

"It'll look as if she's pregnant. Which she is. Anyway what does it matter how it looks? You've decided you want the baby, have you, Mary? Isn't that what matters?"

"Yes, I do," confirmed Mary.

"And it'll look bad in London. I'm sorry, Grace, but it will. Appearances matter there. Maybe you don't appreciate that, living out here in the woods." My sister was getting quite het up and the nastier side of me was intrigued. She did have some fire in her belly after all. I couldn't help it—I decided to provoke her some more.

"No," I said, "that's just it. Appearances don't matter. They're superficial and they only matter to superficial people. Mary's real. Look at her. She speaks her mind. She feels. She hurts. She doesn't brush things under the carpet. So if appearances matter so much back in London, let her have the baby somewhere else."

Mary was looking at me rather thoughtfully.

"It's all very well for you to say that," said her mother. "You won't have to cope with the ramifications of the baby's birth, the adoption."

"Adoption? What adoption? I'm not giving up my baby to someone else. It's mine."

"Sweetheart," said Linda, who had been keeping a low profile up to now, "you want my take, I think you should go for the abortion. I'm pro-choice, by the way. Why I voted for Clinton. No other reason. But if you insist on having it, then you're going to have to have it adopted. They've got adoption agencies all over. There's no way a kid your age is going to want to be tied to a baby. You think you do right now before your little tummy has even begun to swell, but believe me, a year from now you'll remember my words if you hang on to this baby. Adoption, honey. Way to go."

But Mary was still looking at me.

"What do you think, Grace?"

"Why do you always ask Grace?"

I could see my sister was becoming really agitated now. She'd had a fair bit of local Sagaponack rosé—thank God I'd been able to offload it on to someone—and my guess was that she didn't often drink this much. It had loosened her tongue. Steamed her up a bit. Made her more interesting, at any rate.

"She asks me because she's like me and she knows it." I decided to take the proverbial bull by the horns. "She's a realist. She wants

325

the truth and she's prepared to face up to it, more than she probably even knows at her young age. That's why she gives you a hard time. She wants to provoke you into coming down hard on her, taking a firm line and saying what you really think. You're a bit scared of your daughter. Admit it, Favor."

"Don't call me Favor. And no, of course I'm not scared of Mary. That's ridiculous."

"But you care about appearances and that means you're scared."

"Well, so was our father," she protested. "He was always aware of who was coming to see us and how we must appear to them and how the place looked and why didn't I dress up more? It was such a relief when I met Gus and he didn't care about all of that."

"There you are," I said triumphantly, "I knew Lucas Cammell was a weak, insecure bully who was obsessed about appearances. That's why he subjected our mother to a miserable but oh-so-respectable life buried in the country so he could carry on like the deceitful hypocrite he was in London..."

"What in the world are you guys talking about?" asked Linda.

I explained quickly that our mother had lived alone in the country during the week while our father had lived in London pretending to be a faithful and loving husband. I neglected to point out that I didn't live with either of them.

"So that's where you got it from," said Linda.

"Got what from?"

"This burying yourself out here. I've been telling your sister you're never going to meet a man if you keep this up. You need to get out more. Look at me, how I met Stanley. Your life's too lonely."

"I'm not lonely," I protested. Why could people never understand that it was possible to enjoy one's own company? "Or even if I am occasionally, I can be just as lonely with people with whom I have nothing in common."

"How can we be so different? I couldn't bear to live on my own," said my sister. "I need people around me always, especially my family."

"That's where we differ," I told her, aware that I was being harsh. "Where is it written that just because you're my biological sister we have to be alike?"

"But we must be alike in some way," Favor protested. "We had the same parents, the same genes."

"But not necessarily distributed in equal parts to both of us. And anyway, our personalities are formed from the impression made on us by the people around us. If as children we have angry parents, we learn to be angry. We can't help it. We can try to fight it later on but it's going to be a struggle. We come out of the womb with potentially long legs and big heads or whatever—that's where you and I might be genetically alike, and even there I can't see much resemblance between us—but how you can believe that we must like the same things because we're sisters is beyond me."

"I just want us to be alike, I suppose," said Favor quietly, "because we're family. I want there to be some kind of tie between us."

"And I think it makes more sense to be realistic. We are sisters, I won't try to deny it, but we're meeting as two women. What if we had met and not known we were sisters? I bet you wouldn't have paid half so much attention to me. I'm not your type, admit it. I'm not the sort of person you'd normally be friends with and yet just because you know I'm your sister, you're obsessed with the idea that we can become close just like that. We can be civil to each other like we would be if we'd known each other all our lives and met once a year at Christmas with our respective families, and because we're adults, we'd bury our differences. And we would have had our differences if we'd known each other. No doubt about it. But to think that we can be instantly compatible just because we're blood relatives is idiotic. Get real. Please."

She didn't look very convinced, which rather proved my point that she saw our relationship through rose-tinted spectacles.

"You got on with our father," I said to cheer her up, "but I doubt I would have, even if he had bothered to claim me as his daughter."

"How do you know? You seem determined to put him down. You might have seen how wonderful he was if you'd met him."

"And if you were me you might have seen how awful he was."

"Well, I get on with both of you, so what does that prove?" asked Linda cheerfully. "Maybe I'm your long-lost cousin."

I looked at Favor, assuming she would instantly consider this a real possibility, so keen was she to gather family around her, but she wasn't listening.

"The big question is," she said thoughtfully, "how would we have each related to our mother had she lived? You had your foster mother. I had no one. I can't imagine what it must be like to have a mother. You at least had a foster father in place of Dad. If you really believe what you say about learning your personality from the people around you as a child then you must be like your foster father and not Lucas. Is that so?"

And of course I realized I was nothing like David McIntyre, but from what Biddy had said I might be like Lucas. Then again if I really faced up to it, I was probably rather like Biddy herself.

But I didn't want to think about that.

My phone rang.

"Probably Margot demanding a lift home."

I got up to answer. But it wasn't Margot. It was Stanley calling from the radio station for Linda.

"This is a first," said Linda, pleased, "calling me at night from work."

A few seconds later it was as if I had a sobbing baboon in my house. Linda was almost incoherent, her arms flailing about in front of her.

"Stanley says...they've just heard at the station...over the wire... Princess Diana's dead. Killed in a car crash in Paris."

Favor

No matter how firmly Grace urged Mary to respect Margot as her friend, Margot's attitude the night Diana died declared that she had well and truly been written off in Mary's eyes.

Once Linda had calmed down following Stanley's phone call the four of us sat in more or less stunned silence until we saw the headlights of a car venturing halfway up the drive. No one got out for quite some time and then a door opened and a somewhat dishevelled Margot appeared and stumbled up the steps of the deck. In our preoccupation with Diana no one thought to ask her who had brought her home. She'd heard the news, as was apparent the minute she walked in.

"Well, I guess she's going to be pretty pissed off at missing the millennium."

I felt Mary tense beside me. It was a funny thing about Mary. She was spiky and fancied herself as a tough little punk and terribly anti-Establishment, but here she was crying her eyes out and confessing to having been a big fan of the Princess of Wales.

"Just as well," continued Margot, apparently oblivious to the fact that we were devastated by the news. "Poor thing, it's not as if she'd have lasted very long anyway."

"What do you mean?" hissed Mary.

"Well, they wouldn't have put up with her and that Dodi Fayed for long, him being a Muslim and an Egyptian. Oh, I know everyone was going all gooey and saying wasn't it lovely she'd found true love and all that, but give them another month and it'd have been all over. They'd have been denouncing him as a bloody foreigner. There'll be conspiracy theories all over the shop. MI5, probably set the whole thing up so the little princes wouldn't have to have him for a stepfather."

"My lord, aren't you just a little bit sad?" Linda was looking at her, horrified.

"Why should I be sad? I didn't know the girl."

"She wasn't a girl," snapped Mary. "She was a woman. A mother. A wonderful mother."

"Yeah, yeah, I know. She was a bloody saint in lots of people's eyes. It's cold in here, Grace. Mind if I light the fire?"

She took a match from the stack of boxes beside the chimney and struck it, tossing it, before anyone could stop her, onto the fire that was already laid. Within seconds smoke billowed out into the room and a hideously loud wap-wap alarm sounded throughout the house.

Grace rushed to the chimney and seemed almost to plunge headlong into the fire. Then she retreated, sooty, and the smoke began to disappear up the eighteen-foot chimney.

"You didn't check to see if the flue was open, you idiot," she told Margot.

"I didn't know I had to," said Margot. "I don't know anything about flues."

"Well, that's a first," said Grace rather aggressively, "at least there's something you admit to knowing nothing about."

There was friction between these two hovering beneath the surface. Grace might claim Margot was her oldest friend but I had a funny feeling she didn't really like her all that much.

"Well, at least Diana's given us all something to talk about," said Grace. "This story's going to run and run. It'll be bigger than O.J."

"That's a horrible way to look at it," screamed Linda. "Diana wasn't on trial for murder."

"And O.J.'s still alive," said Margot. "Like Kennedy, then. Or Marilyn. We can all remember where we were when Kennedy was shot."

"I can't," I said. I was only about three and Grace couldn't have been more than eight.

"I think I remember something," said Grace, "but not much."

"Oh, come on," said Margot, exasperated, "I remember it perfectly. I'd met some boy at a bonfire party a few weeks earlier and we'd started going out. I remember we were necking behind the bicycle sheds at school and then he walked me home and we came into the kitchen and heard it on the radio."

"Necking?" Grace looked at her.

"Yes, you know. What do you call it now? Snogging?"

"So you must have been what? Fourteen? Fifteen?"

"Something like that..." said Margot, then stopped abruptly. Too late she realized she'd given away her age as nearly fifty, clearly much older than she'd ever let on to Grace, who was staring at her, amazed.

"Have you had a facelift?" asked Mary.

"No, sweet, couldn't afford it. Not the whole face but I have had my eyes done. You never bothered, did you, Grace?" Margot asked pointedly.

"Grace doesn't need to. She's still beautiful," said Mary.

"Yeah," said Margot doubtfully, "well, now we'll never know how Diana would have aged. Anyway, folks, it was a terrific party, by the way—thanks for asking—until Diana went and snuffed it, that is. Then it all got a bit depressing. But Harry was really excited about a project."

"Harry?" said Grace, looking very suspicious. "Harry was there?"

"Yes, of course he was there. I told you. He was the one who asked me in the first place. He was telling me about this book he's been reading. He's halfway through. It's being auctioned for the movies by some New York agent and Harry couldn't wait to get home to finish it. Says it has to be the picture he does after *Rapture.*"

I could see Grace wasn't happy with all this Harry talk.

"What's it about?" I asked. "Did he say?"

"He said it was a dark tale of the fight between good and evil."

"Sounds like a load of crap," said Grace quickly.

"Not at all, sweet," said Margot. "Great story. It's a sort of contemporary fantasy tale about this man who's a manipulator, a real operator. He fucks up everyone's lives just for the hell of it because he's so totally into power but he doesn't realize that one of those people is actually his own daughter and she's out to get him."

"What's it called?" I asked.

"*Luther,*" said Grace.

"That's right," said Margot, surprised, "how did you know?"

"Oh, I've heard about it somewhere."

"You and everyone else. This property's so hot, it's smoking. Anyway, I'm exhausted. I'm off to bed. Good night, everyone."

No one said good night back.

As we walked back in the moonlight to Linda's house, Mary said in a shaky voice, "I'll tell you something, Mum. I'm definitely going to have my baby now. For Diana. Diana would have wanted me to have this baby."

And I realized that until that moment she had probably still been of two minds about the whole thing. Now there was no going back. I found I desperately wanted to speak to Gus about Mary, about Diana, about us. But I didn't dare pick up the phone.

We spent the Sunday at Grace's glued to the television, fending off endless questions from Linda, who seemed to think just because we were English we would know every intimate detail about the Royal Family. Indeed it was eerily refreshing to watch American television, devoid of any particular reverence for the Royals, endlessly speculating as to how Charles must be feeling, whether he was on the phone to Camilla, how awful it was that he'd dragged the poor little princes to church in full view of the TV cameras only hours after their mother had been killed, whether this was curtains for the Queen.

Linda made comments that were at once perfectly reasonable but at the same time completely daft, like her assumption that Trevor Rees-Jones, the survivor in the crash, was probably related to Sophie Rhys-Jones, Prince Edward's girlfriend.

Lew came by at one stage and he acted rather oddly. I heard him talking to Grace downstairs in the kitchen.

"Watching it all on the TV, are you? Hell of a thing. She was so pretty. Too tall for me but she seemed like a real nice person. I thought you might be taking it bad, thought maybe I'd watch it on the TV with you, comfort you."

It struck me suddenly that he was a lonely person. I could hear it in his voice, that tentative hopeful request for company.

"Sure, Lew, come on up," said Grace and I was glad.

But then halfway up the stairs he looked up and saw Linda waving to him from the landing and for some reason he stopped, turned, and disappeared.

"Was that Lew? What was that all about? I need him, Gracie. He hasn't been near my place in a week," cried Linda. "Hey, Lew! Come back."

"Leave it, Linda," Grace told her.

"Why? What's going on?"

"Nothing. But just leave it."

Linda looked at me. She was as bewildered as I was, but Grace's voice had that aggressive tone I'd come to recognize and we didn't press it.

As we watched the stories of the massive outpouring of grief throughout England, and the pile upon pile of flowers being brought into the capital, I decided this was not the time to arrive back in London and deal with Mary's pregnancy. It wasn't as if I had to arrange an abortion.

Also, in a macabre way, Margot was right. The unfolding of the Diana story—"Death of a Princess" as one TV channel dubbed their non-stop broadcast throughout the week following the crash—was fascinating in the manner of a ghastly soap that we felt guilty watching with such relish but found compulsive nonetheless. I was amused by how the talking heads on NBC's new cable channel, MSNBC, had co-opted to spout their conflicting views every night and how they always called Jeffrey Archer "Lord Jeffrey" instead of Lord Archer. And, of course, it all helped to take Mary's mind off her more immediate problems.

However, I knew that I would probably always look back on the Diana week as the time when I had to face up to the fact that my little girl was a child no longer. I'd observed it in my friends whose daughters were a little older than Mary, a tearful relinquishing of a loved one that was almost akin to a lovers' separation. And often those girls were much younger than Mary.

As I watched the Diana saga unfold I realized there was one person who was conspicuous—at least to me—by her absence, and that was Frances Shand-Kydd, Diana's mother. And then I remembered that there had been some kind of rift. Hadn't she left the children in the custody of their father and run off with a lover, leaving Diana to grow up without her? But I had been there for Mary, right beside her. How could I have waited so long to face up to the fact that she was no longer a little girl, that she was so grown up?

Because I hadn't wanted to face up to it, that's why. I had been ostrich-like in my mothering. Passive. Uninvolved. Letting everything proceed as if nothing was ever wrong so as to avoid any kind of confrontation. I was guilty of everything Grace had accused me of. And now I was faced with a major event in Mary's life. Was I giving in to her decision to have the baby too easily? Was it really the right thing for her? Ought I to be insisting on an abortion even if it meant discord between me and my daughter?

I was making myself a cup of coffee in Grace's kitchen, thinking about all this, when I turned and nearly tripped over the telephone extension cord. In fact, I was almost trapped. Margot had taken the receiver into the nearby bathroom, and as I approached to ask her to untangle me I heard her muted voice.

"I'll try and get away this evening to meet you. They're all obsessed with Diana on TV. I could slip out after supper, say I'm going for a walk on the beach, meet you there."

Whoever she was speaking to obviously approved her plan because Margot concluded: "Fine. Get there about nine. Don't wait longer than half an hour. But hey, listen, you know what this would do to Grace if she found out, don't you? It'd destroy her. You still want to see me? Yes? Great. I want that, too. See you tonight."

Mercifully she then had a noisy pee and washed her hands, so I was able to pretend I'd just come into the kitchen and hadn't heard her.

"Oh, I'm sorry. Hang on, you're about to walk straight into the cord." And she stepped neatly around me.

I cornered Grace later that day. I couldn't let her be treated like this. But just as I had been questioning my standing as the good mother, I now began to wonder if I had any hope at all of playing the good sister.

"I heard her, Grace. On the phone. Fixing up to meet Harry Fox."

"What makes you think it was Harry Fox? Probably some guy she met at the party the other night."

I repeated what I'd heard Margot say: "You know what this'd do to Grace if she found out? It'd destroy her."

But Grace just brushed me aside. She completely and utterly pooh-poohed the notion of Margot and Harry Fox. And to make matters worse she accused me of being paranoid.

Yet I noticed she looked a little jumpy when she asked Margot if she wanted coffee at the end of supper and Margot said, "No, thanks, I think I'll skip coffee tonight and go for a walk on the beach to digest this delicious meal."

She wasn't back by the time Mary, Linda, and I left.

Linda's phone was ringing as we walked in. Mary ran ahead to answer it, yelling, "It might be Dad." I held my breath but her face fell.

"Hi, Creepo," she said in a flat tone, "what do you want? Yeah, hold on, she's right here. Mum?"

"Ned? How are you? Yes, yes, of course we've heard. We're watching it every day on the television. Is it a nightmare in London? Why are you up so late? It must be nearly one in the morning. How's Sophie? How's Dad?"

"Mum..." Hearing his voice, not quite a full-blown man's but deep and boyish at the same time, made me miss him suddenly. All my attention had been so focused on Mary that I had forgotten about my big hulk of a Ned. It was interesting how I could relinquish him so much more easily to someone like Sophie than I could Mary to womanhood.

"Mum," he repeated, "it's about Dad that I'm calling. When are you coming home?"

"I'm not sure. Mary needs me. You know about her situation?"

Did he know? For one horrible second I wondered if anyone had told him.

"Yeah. Dad told me. And I sort of got the picture when she started throwing a fit down the phone about Frisky. But I'm not calling about Mary. I know you and Dad will sort her out. Mum, Dad's done something really strange. Has he talked to you about Sheila?"

"Sheila? Who's Sheila?"

"She's this person he's hired to work for him. He keeps going on about how no one's interested in the business except him and how he needs help and now he's got Sheila and she's really keen and hangs on his every word—it's pathetic."

"When did this happen?"

"As soon as he got back from New York. Didn't you know about it? I thought you must have met her."

"How could I have met her? I've been here."

"Yeah, and so has she. Dad met her at the convention. She was working for one of the big guys like Yale or Chubb or something on one of their stands. He's lured her away. He's so pleased with himself, it makes me sick."

"Ned, are you trying to tell me there's something going on between your father and Sheila?"

"Well, I haven't actually caught them at it, no, but…"

"Just like you never actually saw him in bed with Amanda Bamber. For God's sake, Ned…"

Grace had already accused me of being paranoid once that day. I wasn't going to rise to Ned's bait.

"Anyway, how old is she, this Sheila? Does she know what she's doing?"

"That's exactly it, Mum. She's drop-dead gorgeous and she's only twenty-six!"

Grace

I discovered Lew was an insomniac quite by accident. I bumped into him coming out of the market in Amagansett and he announced, apropos of nothing, as far as I could see, that I should get a dog.

"I see you're still looking after those two mutts. Why don'tcha get one of your own?"

"Which two mutts?" As if I didn't know.

"The ones that come around with that guy in the Mercedes that you were looking after.

341

I'm an insomniac, see? Can't sleep nights for hours on end so I get up and walk. I saw the guy pulling away from your driveway with those dogs and I figured, hey, he's dropping them off to her again."

So Archie had been driving by my house and hanging around, presumably waiting to see me. My heart started beating again, literally. What with Margot there and my sister and Mary always around, how could he get to me? He probably hadn't wanted to call. I had to find a way to see him.

I looked in Lew's cart at the sad little collection of produce he'd purchased. A single beefsteak tomato, two apples, a half-pint of milk, a small jar of instant coffee, and three six-packs of beer.

"Raining again," he said glumly, "that granpa of Linda's, always gets it wrong."

Actually, I thought Stanley's forecasts were pretty accurate. Now I knew it was him, I'd taken to listening to them with rather more attention than I usually paid to the weather.

"Lew, I'm sorry about Linda. But he's a nice guy, really. Have you met him?"

"Nope. Don't want to," said Lew. "Well, gotta run. 'Bye."

"'Bye, Lew."

Lew and Linda. It might have worked. Why hadn't I thought of it before? Done something about it pre-Stanley. I looked in the shopping cart again and felt like shit. What Lew needed more than anything was a Mrs. Lew.

My sister and Mary were glued to the TV set watching round-the-clock Diana coverage on MSNBC. I think it had something to do with the fascination of watching the events happening in their country without actually being there. I had the feeling they felt slightly guilty that they were here, not there. They divided their time between my house and Linda's and I was curiously pleased to have them here. It was as if we could continue the pretense of a sisterly reunion without actually having to talk to one another. I felt rather grateful to Diana. Everything was sort of in limbo until her funeral. Watching the funeral together at five a.m. the following Saturday morning had become something we were all looking forward to, morbid though the idea was.

Margot, however, was not part of our plans. Margot, quite simply, was never there. I was furious with her for taking such advantage of me, but out of some kind of daft, misplaced loyalty for our somewhat mythical friendship, I refused to have a word said against her.

Also I was beginning to wonder about her and Harry Fox. It would be the height of betrayal if that was what she was up to and I couldn't really believe she would do such a thing to me. I don't know why I even cared. One thing I had come to realize in the last few weeks was that I was over Harry Fox. I didn't mind if I never saw him again. Now I had Archie in my life, Harry Fox was history. It had taken someone like Archie, who was the first man

I'd ever opened up to about my father, to show me how rotten Harry Fox really was.

So why did I just know that the thought of Margot and Harry together would kill me?

I finally solved the problem of getting to see Archie by driving down to the house on the dunes and leaving a note in the mail box asking him to meet me for some clams at the Lunch Place on Montauk Highway. It was a risk. Sonia might open his mail. I said I'd go there each day at noon until he showed up.

He showed up the very next day.

"Sorry I had to do that but I knew you'd been trying to get to me," I explained.

"You did?" He seemed surprised.

I told him how Lew had seen the dogs and he smiled.

"Ah, I was spotted. I didn't want to drive in unannounced in case I gave the game away."

"Oh, I think Margot's guessed."

"She has?" Now he looked alarmed.

"Yes, she's my friend. But don't worry. She won't say a word. Except maybe to Harry Fox. She seems to have become quite pally with him. Did you know?"

I was fishing. If Harry and Archie were working together and Margot really was seeing Harry, then Archie could well be on to it, but he probably hadn't said anything to me as he knew I would be hurt.

"Well, I've never seen them together," he said, and I only had to look at him to believe him.

I couldn't help it. Being with him again brought such a sense of relief that I found myself unburdening all my frustrations about Margot. It wasn't as if Archie and I had much time together, and I had to go and waste it like this.

"I have this crazy problem with her. I love her, she's my oldest friend, but I always feel bad when she's around. Everything she says, I feel it's some kind of putdown and yet it's probably all in my imagination."

"How do you mean?"

"Well, she'll say something like, 'Why don't you brighten up your guest bedrooms? Paint them a lighter color?' and I immediately think she's criticizing my taste, whereas she's probably just trying to make a helpful suggestion."

"People who criticize you like that are usually jealous of you. She probably envies you your success, your style."

I almost purred with delight. Archie was so supportive, I felt almost guilty complaining about Margot. But I thought I'd carry on a little longer, just to make sure I got rid of all my resentment.

"And the fact that she's never there, she goes out all the time, calls cabs and disappears. It makes me so mad and yet I asked her to come. I invited her. I remember saying to her, 'You must come and stay'. I wanted her to come, and then when she arrived I wanted her to leave. And it's always been like that, my friendship with her. I just don't know where I am."

"And now you think she's hooked up with Harry?"

"I'm probably imagining it."

"You probably are, but even if you're not, wouldn't it all be part of what I just said? She's jealous of your style, ergo she'd be envious of your relationship with someone like Harry. She's insecure, and if he took any notice of her on the Jitney, she'd leap at it when all he was probably trying to do was find out what he could about you."

"I suppose you might be right. With luck she'll be gone soon. She must have something to do in London. What about Sonia? When's she going back?"

"Why do you want to know?" He was immediately on his guard.

"So I can spend some time with you, of course."

"Listen, Grace, I don't want you to get hurt. This really isn't my style. It's demeaning for you, it's deceiving Sonia..."

"You don't want me any more. You're trying to end it."

"Don't be so prickly, Porcy." It was so long since he'd called me that. "I didn't say that, did I? I just want you to be aware of what you're doing. Be sure it's what you really want. I confess I'm not comfortable with this cloak and dagger stuff. I'm not the type, and if I wasn't so crazy about you, I wouldn't even consider it."

"Well, if you think I'm going to let you off the hook, you can think again," I told him.

"Thank God for that," he said. "I had to check, you know?"

"Of course I know, but I adore you." And I kissed him right there in the middle of the Lunch Place. I didn't care who was looking.

I was on a real high when I arrived home. So was everyone else, in anticipation of the funeral on TV the next morning. Even Margot was excited. It was all rather schoolgirlish. Linda, Favor, and Mary would come over at five to watch it with us. Alarms would be set for four-thirty a.m.

But of course Margot announced she was going out for a late drink with what she insisted on calling her "movie crowd."

"Why don't you ever bring Harry Fox here?" asked Mary.

"Why sure, why don't I?" quipped Margot, and before I could ask her if she really was meeting him, she cried, "Oh, here's my taxi. 'Bye, ladies."

"I'll set the alarm for us," I called from the deck, but I don't think she heard me.

I stumbled out of bed in a daze at four-thirty a.m. and crept downstairs to make a huge pot of coffee. I hit the "record" button on the VCR just in case the others didn't make it over. Then I went to wake Margot.

Her bed had not been slept in. She hadn't been home all night.

I freaked. I took a cup of coffee and collapsed in front of the TV set, weeping uncontrollably. Margot and Harry. Diana and Dodi. Diana was dead. The little princes had no mother. Margot and Harry. Everything was merging into a blur of misery in my mind, so that when the others arrived, they spent a good ten minutes mopping me up before they even looked at the screen. Of course, they thought I was upset about Diana.

And suddenly I noticed Margot was there, looking rumpled and glowing at the same time.

"Sorry I look so dishevelled. I just rushed out of bed and flung on my clothes," she said.

She didn't know I'd seen her undisturbed bed downstairs and that I knew it was another bed she'd just rushed out of.

Favor

What was wrong with Grace? When we arrived for the funeral she was sitting there, already a complete mess before the thing had even begun, although I had to admit if anything could set you off it was the sight of a procession with a gun carriage.

I suppose, stupidly, in my anxiety to track down my sister and bond with her I had overlooked such basics as her possible reluctance to have anything to do with me (despite Biddy McIntyre's oblique warning) and the fact that we might have absolutely nothing in common. But nothing could have prepared me for Grace's mercurial personality. I'd seen her signing books in Harrods, full of poise and confidence, yet even then I recalled I had noticed a sadness in the eyes, and sure enough, behind the cool façade lurked a much more complicated woman, an emotional mess bordering on breakdown. She contradicted herself from one day to the next. She was snobby about Linda but deep down she clearly acknowledged Linda's kindness and good nature and appreciated her for what she was. Yet she could be close to a bitch like Margot, although I was beginning to wonder just exactly what was going on between those two.

Throughout the funeral, which was punctuated by outbursts of hysterical weeping from Linda, the only non-Brit among us—maybe it's true about the British sangfroid, although I noticed Mary was joining Linda in her blubbing every now and then—Grace kept darting nasty looks in Margot's direction. The atmosphere, already charged by the lurid, overblown prose of the television commentary, was in any case tense, and I wondered why.

The night before, we had all been so chatty and cheerful, everyone getting along fine, even Margot. Given that Margot and I didn't like each other, Linda and Margot didn't like each other, Mary loathed Margot and, to be honest, I wasn't entirely sure how Grace felt about any of us, it was something of a miracle that we were all able to have such an enjoyable evening. I even forgot about Gus for as much as ten minutes at a time.

But now, the next day, the funeral was over, and my hangover was still throbbing. I felt awful. I was so confused. I didn't know which problem to address first: what to do about Mary's pregnancy (she'd been sick for the first time that morning in the middle of the funeral, emerging from Grace's bathroom white and scared), what to do about the fact that my husband might (if I were to believe Ned, who had been wrong before) be cavorting with a twenty-six-year-old, or what to do about the fact that it didn't look as if my sister and I were destined to be anything more than two women who had met by accident, were making the most of being thrown together and who, when they inevitably parted, would probably never see each other again.

I don't know what I had expected, but I know one thing I had been sure of, and that was when I finally found my sister, whatever happened we would then be sisters for life. But "life," if I had only bothered to stop and think for half a second, just wasn't like that, and what I did understand about Grace was that she had a better grasp of reality than I did.

Except, as it turned out, in one particular area: men. And yet even there, given my hopeless misunderstanding of Gus's inner feelings over the last year, maybe she was more experienced.

But as the television droned on throughout

the week, weren't these problems in my life a little petty when compared with the fact that Trevor Rees-Jones, Diana's bodyguard, lay in a coma, his life presumably shattered? And two young boys had lost their mother. At least we had no death in our midst.

But there again I was wrong.

By eleven o'clock I had pulled myself together and telephoned British Airways.

"I'd like two seats on any flight to London Heathrow, any time after four o'clock this afternoon. Economy," I added hastily. I reckoned I could pack in half an hour and it would take two hours to get to JFK.

"What are you doing?" yelled Mary above the television.

"We're going home," I hissed, "to see Dad and Ned and Frisky and sort you out."

"What do you mean? Sort me out? We've already agreed I'm not having an abortion."

"Shhh. Yes. Okay. Two seats. Seven-thirty. Check in two hours before. Thank you. No, aisle please, if possible. Yes, I'm holding a ticket. It'll need to be altered or whatever. It's one of those fixed-date things—yes, I know, a hundred-pound charge. Can I pay you at the airport? Thank you. Yes, I was booked on..."

As I concluded the booking Mary was literally pulling on my sleeve to get my attention. I resisted her and hung up.

"You can't drag me home. I won't leave. I want to stay with Grace."

"And what exactly do you think you're going to do about school?"

351

"I'm having a baby, Mum. I can't have it at school."

"You're not having a baby for at least another seven or eight months. You haven't even seen a doctor yet."

"Let her stay," said Grace, who had been listening in, "you've only just arrived. I'll put her on a plane next week."

I should have been thrilled but I was furious. Margot was Grace's official house guest and she was barely talking to her, yet here she was appropriating my own daughter from under my nose.

"Grace, I'm sorry, but I think I know what's best for Mary. She has to go home."

"Of course she does. Eventually. But what's the hurry?" said Grace. "Stay a few days longer, both of you. That's okay with you, isn't it, Linda?"

"Sure," said Linda.

"But you can't just decide my life for me like that," I protested, aware that I was beginning to sound childish, but I couldn't help it. I had suddenly worked out that the worry that was uppermost in my mind was my marriage to Gus and I wanted to get back and sort it out. Of course Grace knew nothing of my problems with Gus so I was being a little unfair to her. "I know you're my big sister but you don't have to act it out. We're grown up."

"Oh, cut the sister crap. It's not as if we grew up together. Matter of fact, this is a first for me, playing the big sister role, and I rather like it."

To my intense irritation I noticed Margot

had heard the last sentence and was grinning. It occurred to me that we'd let the cat out of the bag.

"As you've probably gathered, we're not cousins, we're sisters," I explained. "It's a long story. Grace will no doubt tell you one day."

"Oh, don't worry. I know all about it," Margot said mysteriously.

"How do you know all about it? You know nothing. What's Harry been saying? He knows nothing." Grace was suddenly very jumpy.

"He might have said something. I don't remember." Margot was being very provocative.

"We're all very tired. We've been up since four-thirty. Why doesn't everyone take a nap while I go and pack and—"

"Oh, for God's sake stop bossing everyone around and being so sensible. You're like a bloody nanny," said Grace rudely.

"Well, you're so pathetic, moping about here in this wretched house all alone, grieving for Harry whatshisname, you need a bloody nanny to take care of you. You're so lonely, you need some kind of relationship to give your life meaning, even if it's in the form of a nursemaid or whatever. It's unhealthy the way you live, it really is."

"Mary, come with me," said Linda firmly as my outburst suddenly came to an end, and Mary, surprisingly obedient for once, trotted out the door after her.

"I'm going for a walk on the beach," announced Margot.

"What a surprise," said Grace. "They say it's going to rain. Don't forget to call Harry and arrange for him to meet you there."

Margot looked at her, quite bewildered, before she too slipped out the door.

"What was all that about?" I asked. "Is she seeing Harry Fox? Was I right?"

"Mind your own bloody business. No. Of course she isn't. Why are you still here? I thought you had a plane to catch."

"I do and I will, but now I've started I want to knock some sense into you. I admit I hoped I'd find a sister who was like me, and the weird thing is, I have. Only it's not you. You might be what they call my biological sister, but Linda and I are sisters under the skin. We're very alike in many ways. I liked her Stanley. He'd get on well with my Gus, better than either of them would be able to relate to someone like Harry Fox."

"Sisters under the skin! You're nothing but an endless stream of clichés. You should wake up and see how most people live. Come out of your cozy little cocoon. Give poor Mary a break. That's the crazy thing about mothers and daughters. How often are they the same kind of woman when they grow up? If you and Mary met as friends you'd run a mile from each other. You're nice and suburban and into appearances and family life. What they call very apple pie over here. And Mary's seen beyond that. She knows she could stay safely inside that respectable middle-class safety net, but that if she did it would drive her crazy. There's something inside her that's pushing her beyond those boundaries, however dangerous it may be, and it's started already by her insisting she's going to have the baby. Abortion is wicked and sinful but it's the safe option, it's hiding it under the carpet so the neighbors won't see, rather than facing up to the reality. Mary's brave."

"Like you, I suppose."

"Yes, she's like me. I'm not necessarily saying it's brave to buck convention—it's probably just plain stupid. But I think Mary is brave."

I knew Grace was right. Mary had always stood up for what she believed, whereas I often compromised in favor of a quiet life, to avoid confrontation.

"You know, Grace, you may condemn my life as boring—oh, don't say anything, I know what you think, just as Linda knows you think she has appalling taste—you think you're oh-so-subtle but you don't bother to hide your snotty views half the time and it's hurtful, and rude. You didn't think of that, did you? So anyway, I know you think I'm boring but at least I'm consistent and I'm true to who I really am just as much as you are. The difference is I acknowledge my shortcomings—you don't."

"How do you know?"

"I can tell. You haven't taken a good, long look at yourself. You're still obsessed with this Harry Fox character and it's a waste of time."

"Well, hold on a minute because you happen to be quite wrong. You sit here in my house assuming you know everything about me after only knowing me barely two weeks and you try to play the amateur psychologist with me, and with Mary, and it makes me sick. If you really want to know, I'm completely over Harry Fox, and yes, I think he is sleeping with Margot and I think she's doing it just to get back at me because she's jealous of my talent and my style and she always has been and do you want to know how I know all this? It's because a man called Archie Berkeley told me. He's the new love in my life. See, I do have someone. He's the guy I was with when I came back from the beach that time with Mary and you were here with Linda. I saw him yesterday. We're in love."

So there! I could almost hear her say. It was as if we were small children. Little sisters fighting over whose doll to play with.

"So you can see how it bugs me to have you sit here in my house and preach to me about having a relationship in my life just because you're all happy and smug about your perfect marriage."

"Perfect marriage," I echoed, "what perfect marriage? There's no such thing. You see, you accuse me of knowing nothing about your love affair and here you are assuming you know everything about my marriage."

"Don't you have a good marriage?"

"I thought I did—until very recently. Now I discover that my husband left New York without telling me, and when I spoke to him in London he insisted Mary have an abortion and now my son Ned tells me Gus has hired a twenty-six-year-old glamor puss with whom he's working very closely. You're so brave, what would you do in my circumstances?"

"I'd fly straight back and sort Gus out," said Grace.

"Well, didn't you just hear me make a reservation on a plane to do just that and now you're trying to stop me."

"No, you have to go. I can see that now. But can't you leave Mary with me a bit longer? All right, I'll come clean. I feel I've made some sort of connection with Mary and it's important to me. You may be my sister but, as you say, we're not alike. We don't have much in common. Less, as you pointed out, than you and Linda. And I can honestly say I'm delighted you and Linda get on so well. But somehow I do feel Mary's family and it's strangely reassuring. Please leave her here with me."

This was what Linda meant about Grace being "real." Her defenses were down and she was showing her vulnerability in an appealing way. I sensed she had genuinely taken to Mary.

"What's hard for me to come to terms with," I said slowly, watching her face, "is that Mary so obviously relates to you better than she does to me, and what I keep asking myself is, if you and I are so different, Mary and I are so different and you and Mary are so alike, then which of us is like our mother? Was she a timid but sensible, passive—boring, if you will—family person like me? Or an independent, impatient fighter like you and Mary?"

"We'll never know for sure," said Grace, "you have to face up to that. We'll never know, but she must have had some force in her to commit an act so violent as suicide."

"I'll cancel Mary's flight," I said, getting up to go to the phone, but before I could get there it rang.

"Could I speak to Linda?" someone asked.

I handed the receiver to Grace. "Someone for Linda."

"She's not here, she went home. You tried there? Yes, she was here earlier. Well, they must have gone out. Yes, yes, I'm a good friend. Sure, I can give her a message."

As I listened, thinking about the conversation I had just had with Grace, impatient to be on the phone cancelling Mary's flight and then start packing, suddenly knowing that my "family dreams" would progress with this bonding between Mary and her aunt—not quite in the way I had imagined, but still—I saw Grace's face harden with concern. She was gripping the phone and I realized that she was going to collapse. I pushed a chair underneath her just in time.

"Oh, no, no, no," she said, several times.

"What is it?" I asked when she had hung up.

"It's Stanley. He was out over the water. All that meteorologist reporting stuff. He wasn't strapped in properly. He fell out of his chopper. He didn't have a lifejacket on."

"He didn't have a lifejacket on," I repeated dumbly.

"It was way out over the ocean beyond

Rhode Island or somewhere. I remember Linda saying he was on some reconnaissance trip, which was why she was free to spend so much time with us. And we joked about him talking with such authority about the sea and the marine coastal forecasts and the swells and the waves, because..."

"Because...?" I prompted, terrified of what I was going to hear.

"Because he can't even swim. He fell out of the chopper and he couldn't swim."

Grace

In the end I had to drive Favor to the airport myself to catch her plane, otherwise she would never have gone. She wanted to stay with her new friend Linda while she waited for news of Stanley, but I knew, having heard what she said about her husband and the twenty-six-year-old—did twenty-six make her more threatening than twenty-five or twenty-seven?—that she ought to get back to him and sort things out.

Yet I hung on to Mary. Of course, she couldn't stay with Linda, who was too distraught to deal with her. And in a way she really ought to have gone with her mother and confronted her father with her reasons for keeping the baby, but when it came down to it I found I couldn't let her go.

We deposited Favor at the BA terminal at JFK and I swung the car around to head straight back to the Long Island Expressway. As I drove away I realized I hadn't prolonged my goodbyes to my sister, not because I was glad to see the back of her but because somehow I knew I'd be seeing her again one day.

"Is Stanley dead?" asked Mary bluntly as we cruised along the highway.

"I expect so." I felt I had to be honest. "He can't swim and it's been hours since he was reported missing."

"Poor Linda. She's all alone."

"No she isn't. I called Lew before we left and he's gone around to be with her." For a fleeting moment I imagined Lew and Linda sitting listening to Bob Dylan's new album like a pair of old hippies. Linda played it over and over again because Stanley had bought it for her just before he left for his trip.

"Oh," she said. Then, "Your mother's dead, isn't she? And Mum's."

"Yes."

"How did she die?"

"I'm not sure."

"Mum said she died giving birth to her. Is that sort of thing hereditary?"

Oh God, I thought, nearly careering off the highway as I realized what she was getting at.

"No, of course it's not hereditary. I mean you do have slim hips, narrow hips, and that can make a birth a little hard inasmuch as I know about these things, but, Mary, your mother got it wrong. Your grandmother didn't die in childbirth, so you haven't any worries on that score. Look at your mother. Two healthy children. And the same with your grandmother: your mother and I were born without any problems as far as I know."

"So how did she die?"

"She committed suicide."

Mary's answer surprised me.

"I wondered if it was something like that."

"How come?"

"Well, she was never talked about. There was some kind of mystery hanging over her death. Okay, so Mum never knew her, but you sort of hear stuff about your grandparents along the way if they're normal people, and Ned and I never did. Mum talked about her father but she never mentioned her mother. It was as if her father had never talked to her about her mother, and I just didn't get it. But why didn't Mum at least tell us our grandmother killed herself? Why did she lie?"

"She didn't lie. She didn't know until I told her last week."

"So who told her her mother died giving birth to her?"

"I guess it must have been her father."

"But why?"

I almost told her the whole story about her grandfather and what a monster he was. But

I didn't. I remembered Favor's father wasn't a monster in her eyes. Only mine. And Mary was Favor's daughter, so wouldn't she be better off thinking her grandfather was the man Favor had known? Poor innocent Favor.

But as usual Mary surprised me.

"All right, don't tell me now. I know there's a story attached to all this. I don't know the truth, do I? Do you know why your mother killed herself?"

"I think so."

"And you told Mum?"

"Yes."

"Well, I'll ask her to tell me. I want to hear it from her. I want to make her talk to me about it. Mum hides everything, buries it. I want to get her to talk more to me."

I was envious of Favor. Whatever else happened to her, even if her marriage disintegrated, she had this daughter to go back to.

"We had this teacher at school," said Mary, "who used to go on about life and death and stuff and she always said that each time there's a death there ought to be a birth to make up for it, so if Stanley dies there'll be my baby to make up for it."

"I think that's a little simplistic," I said sharply.

"S'pose so," she said, not especially put out by my reproving comeback. "But you're pleased about my baby, aren't you, Grace?"

"You know I am." I wondered where this was leading. I was beginning to realize you never knew with Mary.

"Frisky knew just what to do with her kittens the second they were born. I wonder if I'll be the same."

"Mary," I said as gently as I could, "you probably won't see your baby."

"What do you mean?"

"If you have it..."

"I am having it. You know I am."

"All right, when you have it you're going to have to give it up for adoption. You must understand that, Mary. You're only sixteen years old. You can't give up school, university, youth, fun, and everything to bring up a child when you'll have plenty of opportunities to have babies later on. There are masses of people out there who can't have children and they rely on girls in your situation to provide them."

I was feeling rather puffed up and important and pleased with myself for having delivered what must have sounded like a very worthy and pompous lecture, so Mary's quiet reply hit me like a sledgehammer with its blunt and honest truth.

"What about orphans? Refugees? From Romania or China. They need homes."

"But there are loads of people who can't have children."

"People like you, you mean?"

"There's nothing to say I can't have children. I can conceive. I told you about my abortion."

"Yes, but you're a bit old now, aren't you, to have a first baby? And besides, you haven't got a man."

I glanced at her.

"Oh, sorry, I mean you haven't got a husband."

"I don't want a husband."

"Hmmm." I could see she didn't believe me. "Maybe you don't, but wouldn't you like a baby to look after and call your own? Haven't you thought about it just a little?"

"I've thought about it a lot."

This was true. I'd often thought I might be rather a good mother, and my observation of how Mary was crying out for the kind of affection she had obviously never received from Favor confirmed this. Yet I could also appreciate that probably every child wishes it had a different kind of parent, and it was all too easy to think you could be a good parent to another person's child.

"Supposing Mum died tomorrow and you could have me delivered to you on a plate, would you want me?"

"Mary!" I was shocked that she could talk this way with her mother currently being hurtled across the Atlantic at 35,000 feet.

"I'd rather have her alive and you visit. And in any case, if I were going to have a child I'd want a baby. I'd want to bring it up my way for better or for worse, but, as you so sweetly pointed out, I'm a bit old."

"But you talked about adoption."

"Yes, but I don't think they hand out babies that willingly to older women like me. It'd be hard."

"What if you didn't have to go through an adoption agency?"

The penny in my slow, dim-witted brain finally dropped. Oh, shit. Oh, shit shit shit. I'd really fallen into this one.

"It makes sense. Don't you see?"

Mary had sensed my realization and turned around in her seat. "I'd have the baby, turn it over to you, and it would still be in the family and I'd still see it."

"You've got it all worked out, haven't you?"

"It was when you and Mum were going on about appearances and you said appearances don't matter, but if they did matter in London, why not let me have the baby somewhere else, and I thought, of course, that's it, she wants me to have it here with her."

"You know I didn't mean that."

"Yeah, maybe not but I still think it's a cool idea and you should think about it."

I did think about it. For the next seventy miles I thought of nothing else. It made perfect sense. I had been thrown into one of those hypothetical magazine feature situations: what would you do if...? Well, I was being offered a baby, albeit by rather unconventional means, and it would clearly be my last chance to have one and at a time when I so desperately needed someone to love and had quite unexpectedly begun to realize what I had missed in never having been a mother.

When we arrived home the first thing I did was call Linda. I'd been calling her every couple of hours to see if she'd heard anything. My sister had been quite beside herself at the thought of leaving Linda at such a terrible time. They had become friends, those two, and it surprised me how pleased I was about that. Linda must have rare qualities in that she could develop relationships with two such very different sisters. Or two such very different women, for that matter. What difference did it make that we were sisters?

I knew part of the reason Favor was so upset was that there was nothing you could do to help. Linda was more or less oblivious to anything anyone said. She just sat by her little pink princess bedside telephone waiting to hear. She wouldn't eat, she wouldn't drink. She just nodded her head up and down every so often, pretending to take in the useless words of comfort being spoken to her. I felt bad, ringing her so often. I could imagine what a jolt she had each time the phone rang. But I had to find out what had happened, and as I had Mary with me I couldn't go around and sit with her.

But this time I did go around.

They'd found Stanley's body.

A woman from up the road answered the phone and begged me to come over. Linda was hysterical because Stanley's cousin had been asked to go to the morgue and identify him. No one had asked her to be the one. She was on the point of rushing over there and the woman couldn't restrain her.

"Are they sure it's him?"

"Oh, it's him, all right. The cousin's a formality. He's been in the water for some time. He don't look good. Linda shouldn't see him.

She should remember him, you know…like he was."

Remember him.

She had only just met him and now she was being asked to remember him.

I held her as tightly as I could. She was in such pain; her eyes were squeezed shut and she was tense, braced against the world. And then, every so often, she let out a howl of agony and shuddered violently in my arms. I had never really noticed how fragile she was. I did equate fluffy with small but I was shocked to feel how tiny her bones were. She felt like a bird. Her strawberry-blond hair was matted and filthy.

I ran a bath and then, very gently, with the help of the other woman I lifted her as if she were a baby and placed her in her tub. I washed her hair and her body and persuaded her to climb out of the bath and into her bed. I had called the doctor and when he came he gave her a sedative.

"She'll be all right. She'll sleep. But she'll need someone here when she wakes up. And then probably most of the time for a while."

I talked with the woman, someone I barely knew. I couldn't be with Linda all the time. I had Mary. We worked out a schedule. I would return in twenty-four hours for a spell and then again the next day.

As I walked back to my house I thought how amazingly lucky I was to have Archie. It wasn't what Linda had had with Stanley, but then I wasn't Linda. Whatever I had would always be complicated.

And I thought of the other growing relationship in my life and wondered where it would lead me.

I brought up the subject of the baby again as we were finishing supper that night—lobster bisque from the Fish Market followed by spinach-and-eggplant ravioli from the Farmer's Market, all very healthy in honor of Mary's baby.

"Okay, Mary, I'm going to make you a deal about this baby."

She didn't say anything, just looked at me. She was smart enough to know when to shut up and listen.

"You're still a child. The very fact that you came up with this simple little plan and imagined it would work just like that proves it. There's a hell of a lot more to having a child than just giving birth and I don't believe you've taken any of that into consideration. How it would alter my life, how I could continue to write with a squalling baby around. All those things. Yet, as with many simple ideas, there's something about it that appeals, so here's what I'm prepared to do."

Mary was beginning to look a bit uneasy by now.

"First you must go home and go back to school. The first thing I want you to take into account is that we have seven or eight months to consider all this before the baby is born. The deal I want to make is this: if we both feel the same way next spring when the baby's born, then we'll go ahead. I will make up my mind earlier than that so as to be prepared, but you can decide once the baby's born. Second: you have the baby here in America so it will have an American passport and can be brought up here with me. And third, most important, your mother and father approve of the whole thing."

"Can we call them now?" She was up from the table in a flash.

"No, we can't call them now. For a start, your mother won't even be there, and anyway we should give them a little time together before we start bothering them about this."

"Why?" asked Mary slyly. "Is there something wrong?"

"Why on earth should there be anything wrong? They're a husband and wife who've been separated. You're so smart, you work out why they need this time together."

"Oh, for God's sake, they're Mum and Dad. But you've made me think of something. If my baby stays with you who'll be its father figure?"

"I like the way you're asking that as if you're interviewing me for the role. I could just as easily ask you the same question if you were going to take care of your baby yourself. As it happens, I suppose if the baby lives with me it won't have a conventional father figure unless something very strange happens to me and I marry someone between now and then, but I do have a man I love in my life." I paused. "You met him, Mary. Remember that first time we met when you fainted on the beach and we brought you back. He'd be the man in my life."

"How would he feel about my baby?"

"Don't know. I'd have to ask him, wouldn't I? But what you have to understand is that the baby would be mine. I'd be a single parent just as you would be if you raised it yourself. At least in the beginning."

"But that man's married."

"That's true." I couldn't deny it. She'd heard Linda tell Archie she'd met his wife in East Hampton.

"And he's a bastard."

"He's not. Whatever makes you say that?"

"He deceives his wife with you and he two-times you with other women. You can't trust someone like that."

"Yes, he does deceive his wife but he's never done that sort of thing before. And he's only deceiving her now because he loves me so much. He's told me."

"Oh, yeah, and if he loves you so much what was he doing kissing Margot in his car the morning of Princess Diana's funeral?"

"What on earth are you talking about?"

"I saw them. Mum and Linda went through the woods to your house but I needed to wake up a bit so I walked down Linda's drive, along the road and up yours and that's when I saw them. His car was parked at the bottom of your drive. You couldn't see it from the house. Those two dogs were in the back and they started barking as I walked past and that's when I saw Margot. She was all over him. It was disgusting."

Strong disapproval from a pregnant teenager. I listened to her words but I refused to let them sink in.

"It was the man from the beach. I don't know if Margot saw me. I slipped past and up the drive. As I reached the house I heard her running up the drive after me. She looked a right mess, buttoning up her blouse as she ran."

And her bed in my house had not been slept in. What a complete fool I had been. Margot had been betraying me not with Harry Fox but, far worse, with Archie.

Favor

The first person I saw back in London was Ned. He came to the front door as my taxi drew up, and stood there at the top of the steps looking a bit shell-shocked. It had occurred to me only as I was riding in from the airport that I hadn't let anyone know I was coming home.

"Don't just stand there, Ned, help the driver with my bags."

And then he came to life and galumphed down the steps to give me a great big bear hug and I buried my face in his chest so he wouldn't see how close to tears I was. I had missed him so much.

He carried my bags into the kitchen, plunked it down, and put the kettle on.

"Have you had breakfast?" he asked.

"I had an airline scone and a cup of tea what seems like hours ago but I don't need anything. Just coffee."

"Where is she? Where's Mary?"

"She's stayed out there a bit longer."

"Why?"

"Oh, Ned, don't make me go through it all the minute I get home. She's okay. We'll get her home soon. Meanwhile, I need to see your dad. You'd better be right this time. I've come all the way back..."

"You want me to be right?"

"No, of course not. I'm hoping you're wrong as hell. Where is he, by the way?"

"Dunno. I've only just got up. He's not here, at any rate. So how was it in the US of A?"

"It was great. Oh no, it wasn't, it was bloody awful at first with Mary miserable in New York and we didn't know why. But once we got out to Long Island it was actually great fun, Diana or no Diana."

"No Diana anymore, Mum, although I don't quite see what she's got to do with it. So, Dad tells me I have an aunt."

"You have an aunt. Mary's with her right now. They've fallen in love with each other."

"I suppose it's pointless to ask why we never knew about this aunt before?"

"Absolutely pointless, but once I've got over this jet lag and sorted things out with your father, I'll sit down and tell you the whole story. And you'll meet her. Not quite sure when, but you will. You'll be very surprised. She's not a bit like me and the truth is we have absolutely nothing in common and I don't think we're ever going to become bosom buddies but I can't tell you how pleased I am to have found her. Imagine how you'd feel if you'd never met Mary."

"Simple. I wouldn't be Creepo. Mum, is she all right?"

"She wants to have it, thanks to you scaring her half to death with tales of Frisky's abortion. That's something else I've got to sort out."

"So I gain an aunt and become an uncle at the same time."

"Something like that. But she's going to have to have it adopted, of course—and I'm not quite sure she's taken that on board yet—so whether you actually meet your niece or nephew is not a hundred per cent guaranteed."

"You seem incredibly calm about the whole thing, Mum. I had anticipated you'd be climbing the walls, totally hysterical, and here you are bandying the word *abortion* about with no freak-out whatsoever."

"Well, I think you'll find I've changed just a little, Ned. I've had a crash course in discovering myself. Not entirely easy when you're my age but I think I'm a better person for it. So how are you and where's Sophie? Still in bed?"

"Here?"

"Well, I'm not stupid. I was sure as soon as

373

I was out of the house you'd import her into it."

"Nope."

"But all's well?"

"Well, I really don't know. I haven't actually seen her for a week."

"Why not? Is she away?"

"Dunno. It was all getting a bit intense, Mum. I couldn't handle it. The sex was good but I thought I needed a bit of space, you know, play the field a bit?"

"No. I don't know. What exactly couldn't you handle? I thought you were in love with Sophie?"

I couldn't believe it. Even my beloved innocent hulking Ned who only a few months ago had been a virgin was now acting like a jaded Lothario. What was it about men that they had to be unfaithful? No sooner had Ned entered the sexual arena than he was transformed overnight into a bastard like all the rest.

"Poor Sophie," I said with feeling.

"Oh, she's fine."

"How do you know? For sure?"

He had the grace to look a bit sheepish. My blood was up. I wanted to confront Gus as soon as possible. Like father, like son. I'd force him to have it out in the open with me and make him feel guilty for Mary's situation at the same time. Somehow.

"So where is your father? You don't know, I suppose?"

"He's probably gone to work."

"Right then. I'll go around to the shop."

I couldn't believe it. Sheila was sitting there bold as brass in the shop when I walked in, talking to a customer on the telephone about adding a digital communicator to his alarm system whereby the alarm bell didn't ring immediately, allowing the communicator to alert a central monitoring station via a computerized chip sent through the telephone line.

"The central station immediately alerts the closest police presence," she was explaining. "I'll be with you in a minute," she mouthed at me. "Oh yes," she returned to the caller, "Angus Hardy Security can do all of that. Let me send you a quotation and you can get back to us. We never pressure a customer."

We never pressure a customer. What kind of garbage was she spouting? Still, I had to admit she seemed to know her stuff. And she was pretty. Very pretty. Gus's type. Not a million miles removed from the way I'd looked at her age, only prettier. Sleek, fair hair, pink-and-white skin, little turned-up nose (which I didn't have), long lashes (didn't have those either), pretty hands with beautifully manicured nails. I can count on the fingers of one hand the number of times I'd had a manicure.

"How may I help you?" She smiled at me. Very friendly. Trying hard. Young. Ambitious, with a job that was important to her. She probably saw working for Gus as a promising career. I couldn't help wondering what Mary would make of her. Mary, who had been so keen on the idea of careers and who had possibly now ruined her chances of having one, although not if I could help it.

Suddenly I knew how Grace felt when she was being snotty and badly behaved. It must be when she felt ill at ease and insecure like I did now, infuriated by this bland, pretty creature who was unwittingly driving me mad.

"I don't think it's really a question of you helping me," I said, very Gracelike. Go on the attack, put the other party down before they can get the better of you. Oh, poor Grace, if she was like this so much of the time only God knew how unhappy she must be.

"Excuse me? I'm not with you."

"Sheila, isn't it?"

"Yes, that's right," she simpered again.

"My son's told me about you. You work for my husband. You met at the convention in New York."

Realization dawned. "Oh, you're..."

"Mrs. Hardy."

"Right. Well, welcome home."

"Where's my husband?"

"Gus is away. He had to go to...where was it? Wales?"

"Really?"

"Yes. He'll be back tomorrow. It's urgent. One of his clients up there...think there's been a break-in or something. Gus wanted to reassure them personally. He's so good like that. The personal touch. I've got to ring Ned and tell him his dad won't be home tonight. I don't think Gus was expecting you back, to be quite honest."

"Please don't bother. I'll ring Ned, or rather I'll tell him this evening."

"Would you like some coffee?"

"If I want coffee I'll make it myself, thank you. I know where everything is."

She gaped at me like a fish. "Why are you being so hostile?"

"Because...because I've just got off the plane from New York. I'm exhausted and because I didn't know anything about Gus hiring you, and I can only imagine the reason he didn't discuss it with me is because he's got something to hide."

I was being pretty blunt but I had reached the point where I felt I had nothing left to lose.

"I'm going to make that coffee anyway," she said in an infuriatingly soothing tone. I hate it when people say "that coffee," "that drink," "we must have that drink some day." You know for a fact that it'll never happen because they're always the people you'd rather die than have a drink with.

"All right, Sheila," I said, realizing there was no escape, "make me that coffee and let's have it out."

Strong stuff! I felt a flutter in my stomach. Were we about to have a confrontation? Lipsticks at dawn?

"There's nothing to have out. He's cute, your husband, and he's pretty vulnerable right now but no woman would touch him."

"Why ever not?" I was furious. Was I married to such an unattractive proposition?

"Because all he ever talks about is you,"

said Sheila to my utmost amazement. "I don't know what the problem is between you, and frankly I don't want to, but from the minute I met him in New York—and yes, I don't mind admitting now that a bit of extramarital hanky-panky did cross my mind those first few days when he bought me lunch at the convention—all he really talked about was you. How he'd brought you and your daughter out there for a great vacation but something had gone wrong and you were sitting in the hotel like two miserable old maids and he couldn't figure it out. Then lo and behold you up and disappear to—where was it? Long Island? And then I really did think I had a chance. Especially when he suddenly started talking to me about coming to work for him. But even then it was all related to you and how you weren't interested in the business like you were when you were first married. I wanted to hit him half the time, I was so bored.

"I don't know why I'm telling you all this. I really resent the way you've come trotting back from America expecting him to be there for you when you've treated him so badly. And you take it all out on me without even bothering to establish the facts. Frankly, Gus could really use some help around here but where have you been? Off looking for some long-lost sister you've never even met. Oh yes, I know all about that. Believe me, Mrs. Hardy, I know virtually everything about you that Gus knows, including that he loves you and adores you and can't understand why you are more interested in your sister than you are in him."

"He can't understand because he's a man. Surely you can see that?"

"Frankly," I hated the way she used the word 'frankly' all the time. "No, I can't."

"Well, that's because you're a man's woman," I spat at her.

"What other kind is there?"

"I'm afraid if you don't know that by now you're going to wind up a very lonely old woman," I said, considerably less confident of that fact than I sounded, and walked out of the shop.

Gus loved me. He'd told this young flake of a girl that he loved me. I was an innocent, as I had belatedly come to realize, but I knew that most men, when presented with a pretty, young twenty-six-year-old hanging on their every word, with a wife who was approaching forty and off pursuing other interests, would leap at the chance of a fling. Gus, apparently, had resisted. Better still, the idea didn't seem to have crossed his mind. He had merely used Sheila as a sounding board. I owed "poor Sheila" quite a lot. She had more or less single-handedly—if unwittingly—saved my marriage. If I hadn't learned from her in that short half-hour how much I meant to Gus, how sincere he was in his desire to have me back and to resume our relationship as we were when we first started out, I would probably have equally unwittingly pushed him even further away.

It was probably true, I reflected, that most

married couples, especially the husbands, change drastically, and a marriage only works if both parties adapt to the other's change. But Gus and I were different and I had been in danger of not understanding that Gus really did want us to continue as a family unit just as we had been in the beginning, the only change being the expansion of the business, which required more input from me, his wife, rather than less.

The mistake had been in trying to make Grace part of the family. She wasn't. She never could be. Then again, she might be part of Mary's family. That was something else. Just as Lucas Cammell had represented one kind of father to me and another kind to Grace. But Grace was never going to be part of my family here in Shepherd's Bush. She might meet Gus one day, they might have a few drinks together, imagine they had a lot in common for four or five hours, but at the proverbial end of the day, Grace was never going to be my best friend, and the sooner I wised up to that the better.

All of this was running through my mind as I drove to Wales the next day. Gus was out when I arrived at the farm, totally exhausted having driven flat out for three and a half hours while still under the influence of jet lag. The place was a complete mess. Gus was a walking disaster area if left to function on his own in any domestic environment. There were toast crumbs all over the kitchen counters—he always ate breakfast standing up—and the dishes were dumped in the sink. As far as I could make out, he'd brought all his dirty London laundry with him and dumped it in a heap in the middle of the bedroom floor. I was in the process of piling it into the washing machine when I heard the kitchen door slam.

"Hello!" I called out.

Gus came up the stairs two at a time.

"Before you say another word," I said, kicking the washing machine door shut behind me and propelling him out of the bathroom and onto the landing by placing my palm flat against his chest, "I want you to know I've come all the way back from America to offer my services to you. Professional and unprofessional."

We dealt with the unprofessional first and I found it hard to believe that Gus hadn't been practicing in my absence, it was such a glorious reunion. I found it equally difficult to recall that he'd had a "problem" in the past. I'd always hated that term New Man, but I had to admit, using it to describe Gus's newfound sexual prowess was certainly appropriate. There was also nothing quite like making love with sheep baaaahing away outside, echoing your every moan and groan.

Gus couldn't stop kissing me and yet there remained a tiny niggle of doubt in my mind. Was he really so pleased to see me or was it because I had told him while we were lying in each other's arms in the middle of the night, whispering to each other like a young honeymoon couple, that I would come back to work for him? Poor Gus. Even as he grew more and more excited about his plans for the business—as excited as he had been in sex? I wondered, and then mentally slapped myself on the wrist—I was scheming away beside him.

Sheila would be given her cards the minute we were back in London and if Gus thought I was just going to sit there minding the shop, then he'd have another think coming. I wanted more than I'd had working for Roger. I was damned if I was going to sit there propping up a man. If I was going to be part of the business again then I wanted something for myself, some area where I had total control. How many other conventions were there in America? How often could I find the excuse to get across there and see Grace? Even if we didn't have anything in common, she was still my sister....

"So," said Gus in my ear, "what are we going to do about Mary?"

"Whatever we do, it can wait until morning," I told him. "I need to get some sleep, otherwise I'll never turn around to London time."

"You just don't know how much I've missed you," he whispered. "I don't mean while you've been in the States. I mean, ever since I've been, you know...and you've...do you know what I'm getting at?"

"I know what you're getting at. You've got at it and you don't need to say another word."

"Promise?"

"Promise."

The phone by the bed rang just as we'd finally fallen asleep. Mary's voice sounded small and distant and terribly young, far away on the other side of the Atlantic.

"Mum? I know it's terribly late but I thought you'd ring when you got in. I'm sorry to wake you but Ned told me where you were. Listen, Grace and I have something to discuss with you...."

As I listened to Mary's excited chattering and Grace's more rational but equally optimistic endorsement of their plan, I couldn't help thinking that it was possibly the most sensible solution.

But what did it matter what I thought? I turned to the slumbering Gus and roused him gently with the words: "Sorry, darling, I don't think Mary can wait till morning after all."

Grace

After she'd dropped her bombshell, Mary and I sat around at the supper table in absolute silence for several minutes. Then I proceeded, with extraordinary clarity given the shock I had just received, to lecture Mary on men. I suspect it was rather like the way some people behave when someone close to them dies. They go on some kind of automatic pilot, become fearfully practical, start organizing everything and laying down the law in order to have something to do and keep control of their emotions.

"I seem to remember telling you, Mary, that men are cruel and that they never stop being cruel. Some women, more charitable than I, suggest they don't ever realize how cruel they are but personally, I don't buy that. They can be incredibly kind to us, but it's rather like a mood swing with them. They feel kind that day and the woman closest to them benefits. And then they become cruel again. It's up to us to brace ourselves for that cruelty, to work at building up some kind of armor so that we are protected from them."

"But if the armor's really good and we are properly protected from them so we can't be hurt any more, how's the kindness going to get in?" asked Mary in a solemn little voice. "Surely we'd be protected from that, too?"

"Oh, fuck it!" I yelled. "I don't know. It's one or the other. At least that's the way it seems to be as far as I'm concerned. The truth is, Mary, the only way to deal with it is to get mad. Fill yourself up with flat-out rage...."

I had to calm myself down for Stanley's funeral the next day. Many of the shops and businesses had displayed black ribbons and wreaths for Diana. Now they had made subtle changes to show that they were in mourning for Stanley. He had clearly been a much loved local figure. Everywhere you went, people commented on the tragedy of his death, and the turnout at the funeral was impressive.

I was touched that Linda should turn to me and seem to expect me to be beside her throughout the service. Stanley's family from New York, whom she had not met, were nice to her but understandably preoccupied with their own grief. She needed me and I was only too pleased to be able to support her in some way. She did not, of course, wear black, but cut a dramatic figure in a deep purple cape and large picture hat. Personally I thought she looked as if she'd been raiding a child's costume box, but for once I didn't care, and to show solidarity, at the last minute I dashed home and grabbed a large purple shawl and flung it across my shoulders.

"Beautiful!" said Linda gratefully.

"I found it while I was out antiquing one day last fall," I lied.

"Really?" said Linda. "I could have sworn I gave it to you for Christmas and you went home and pushed it to the back of your closet never to be seen again. Until now. But you know what? That's okay."

We hugged each other and I held her arm throughout the service.

And as we left the church I saw a figure I didn't recognize nod his head to me. And then I realized I hadn't recognized him because I'd never seen him in a suit before. Indeed, I hadn't even known he'd possessed a suit. It was Lew, come to pay his respects.

That night Mary and I cooked Linda a light supper and walked her home and put her to bed. Mary hadn't come to the funeral. She hadn't wanted to and I hadn't made her. Now, on the walk back home, she turned to me in excitement.

"I've thought of a way for you to get your revenge."

"How?" I was curious.

"We'll get rid of Margot. She's out. We can guess where but let's make sure she never returns."

We jumped up from the table and rushed into Margot's room. I found I was even grinning. Together we flung her belongings into her suitcases and carried them out to my car. We took them as far as the end of the drive and left them in a row in the middle of the entrance from the road with a large notice on which Mary had scrawled: SORRY, MARGOT. YOUR TIME'S UP.

Then we double-locked all the doors with a key I knew Margot did not have, pulled the telephones out of their sockets and climbed into my bed together, giggling.

"I suppose you have to be just as careful about protection against your female friends," said Mary in the darkness. "I'm never, ever going to speak to Shannon again."

Around two-thirty we were awakened by banging. Since the entire house was made out of cypress wood, a mere tap on an exterior reverberated everywhere, and Margot was hitting the walls for all she was worth.

I went downstairs, taking my time. From the

kitchen I turned on the big globular bulb that flooded the side porch with light, illuminating Margot and a couple of startled deer in the woods behind her.

"My key doesn't work," she whined. "Let me in, sweet. Sorry to wake you."

"Didn't you see your bags at the end of the drive?"

"Those were my bags? We nearly drove right into them. Thought it was the garbage." I knew she was lying.

"They are garbage and so are you. Now piss off, Margot, run back down the drive. If you hurry, Archie might still be waiting."

"No he won't, we had a row and..." Too late she realized she'd confirmed she'd been out with Archie.

"And...?"

"Okay, so I've been seeing him and you've found out and you're angry but we're well rid of him, sweet. He spent the whole evening talking to a woman who just arrived out here. His wife has gone back to London with the kids and suddenly I'm history."

"Well, there's always Harry. Haven't you tried him yet?"

By the look on her face I could see that no, she hadn't, but give her time.

"So will you come down and help me with my bags?"

"*No!*"

"Well, will you at least let me come in so I can get some sleep and we'll sort this out in the morning."

"No."

"Grace!"

"I want you and Archie Berkeley and Harry Fox and everyone like you out of my life, starting now," I yelled and slammed shut the window I'd opened to talk to her. Two seconds later I opened it again.

"And, Margot, if I see lights going on at Linda's I'll know you've gone around there and you really will be in trouble. Big time."

And then I really did close Margot out of my life forever.

"What will she do?" asked Mary nervously. "You really were terrific."

As it turned out, Margot sat huddled on the back porch, which was relatively secluded, for most of the night and at around six I took pity on her and called a cab to come and get her.

"Where are we taking the passenger?" they asked.

"She'll tell you," I said, and sent Mary out to let Margot know what was happening.

"She says she never wants to see you again either," I heard Mary tell her in a rather school-playground tone of voice, but then my line out the window the night before hadn't been much better.

Reality hit me the next day. I could feel the misery rising all morning and told Mary I was going out for a walk on the beach. Alone. Once there, I burst into uncontrollable weeping and slumped down in the sand. The sandpipers scuttled away from me in fright and for once it didn't make me smile to watch them scurrying along the water's edge. The seagulls waddled down to the sea in outrage at being disturbed and flew off, skimming over the waves breaking on the beach to land on calmer sea, where they swam away, their bodies gliding smoothly along, belying their furious paddling beneath the water.

Mary didn't know the half of it. It wasn't as if Archie and I had just been lovers. I'd trusted him with my most intimate secrets about my family and myself. How could someone who claimed to have written a love song especially for me as the theme song for his movie behave like this? How could a man who said he hated deceiving his wife, that adultery wasn't his style, move so callously from one woman to another? Why did Sonia stay with him? Surely she must know what he was up to when she wasn't with him? All that stuff I'd poured out to him about Harry Fox? I cringed when I thought about that. Archie was far, far worse than Harry Fox. Archie knew more about me than my own sister and it obviously meant nothing to him.

In fleeting rational moments I could appreciate that he might possibly have developed an affection for me beyond sex that had allowed him to seem interested in my background, but it had been nothing more than a passing fondness, one of many. He was, after all, an affectionate man. That was what had attracted me to him. But ultimately, like all the others, he had proved himself to be cruel. He had thought nothing of betraying me with

Margot. He had known I had been humiliated by Harry Fox and that he was about to subject me to more of the same. The thought of them sitting in my house on the dunes, laughing at me, set me off on another bout of crying.

And then I felt a hand on my shoulder and I thought, oh no, everything's going to be all right. It was only Margot trying to undermine me—Archie would never do a thing like that to me, Mary was wrong, she didn't see them together, it was someone else. Of course Archie loves me, he's come to find me and tell me what a fool I've been to imagine he could be so cruel. I looked up and saw Lew.

"There, there, there." He was patting me on the back.

"Sorry," I blubbed, "sorry, Lew. Can't help it. Sorry."

"Go on. Spit it out. What's the problem? Is it a fella?"

"No, of course not."

"You mean yes."

"Yes."

"Usually is."

"How would you know?"

"Well, with me it's usually a woman. You women can be pretty mean creatures when you want to be."

"No we're not."

"Are too."

"How so?" I peeked at him.

"Well, you know I'm always going on about how I take my girlfriend here, there, and everywhere? To Maine, to New York?"

"Yes."

"Well, she don't exist."

"What do you mean?"

"I don't have a girlfriend. I just tell everyone about her to make me feel like I have one. Makes me feel better, more one of the crowd. I live with my mother. See, my wife ran off and left me twelve years ago and I saw a few women off and on after that but they always let me down. Act real nice, take me to bed, cook me fancy meals, make like they wanted to settle down, and that was the truth except they always seemed to settle down with someone else. Got so I couldn't face being disappointed no more, so I got myself a pretend girlfriend. Things suddenly got a whole lot more reliable, I'm telling you. She was always where I wanted her to be and she stuck by me."

As I walked slowly back to the house with Lew I imagined that I might have to revise my line on men to Mary to include softies like Lew. And until Favor had got wind of the twenty-six-year-old, Gus had sounded like he was one of the rare breed of trustworthy men. They did exist. I just had to go on believing it.

"I was just on my way to see Linda," said Lew. "What do you think? Good idea?"

"Great idea, Lew. She was asking after you. Said she really appreciated it that you came to the funeral."

"She said that?"

"Sure." She'd said nothing of the sort, but the sweetness I'd sensed in Lew just now, the sympathy for my problem with a "fella," made me think he'd be wonderful with Linda in her present state. And who knew where it might lead him?

"Well, maybe when I've stopped by for a visit with Linda I'll come on over and fix your shower door for you."

This was a first. Lew actually offering to do something himself. Of course, he never made it over and in a way I was glad. It meant that his visit with Linda might be going better than I had dared to hope.

"Some guy from California's been calling every twenty minutes," Mary told me when I got back. I looked at the name on the piece of paper by the phone. My movie agent.

The movie auction for the sale of *Luther* had progressed at a very healthy pace and had now escalated to an obscene amount of money and a bidding war between two major studios. I wasn't really concentrating as my agent became more and more excited and started spouting a lot of movie jargon that always irritated me, but suddenly he said something that made me grip the receiver with horror.

"They're both going crazy to get major players on board. TriStar has Harry Fox in the bag and Warner says..."

"Harry Fox? To direct?"

"Yeah. He's read it. He's absolutely insisting he wants to do it. His agent's negotiating the deal now and—"

"Do I have any say in who directs this picture?"

"No. Not really."

"But Harry Fox is attached to TriStar?"

"Yes. It's a hair away from a done deal."

"Then go with Warner."

"But Harry Fox is so hot, he's—"

"Smoking." All these movie people came out with the same old clichés. "I know he is. But I want whoever Warner wants. In other words, not Harry Fox."

"But TriStar..."

"If you don't go with Warner then I'm removing my book from the auction. I have the right to do that, don't I? It's not sold yet."

"Harry Fox isn't going to like this at all."

"Tough."

"What am I going to say to TriStar?"

"You'll think of something. Good luck."

"Writers," I heard him mutter before I hung up.

First Margot, now Harry. And I wasn't above a cliché of my own. Revenge was sweet and something told me I wasn't finished yet.

That night, before I realized what she was doing, Mary picked up the phone and called Wales to speak to her mother. She confessed she had already called London while I was out and been told by her brother that Favor had gone to join Gus in Wales.

I don't know what bothered me the most: the fact that she was calling long distance as if it were Linda's house, no "Please, Grace, may I..." etc., etc., that she was calling at eight-thirty our time which meant it was way after midnight over there, or the fact that she wanted to tell Favor about our tentative plans for me to adopt her baby.

In any event I did nothing to stop her once she had reached her mother and was in the process of outlining the entire plan with child-like simplicity, making it all sound like arranging a a visit to a summer camp.

"...so then I'll come out here in the Easter hols and have the baby and hand it over to Grace and then I'll be back for my exams in the summer term. What? Well, then I'll just have to resit them. You and Dad'll have to clear it with Miss Flowerdew."

Miss Flowerdew, she explained to me afterwards, was her headteacher. I had tried my best to explain to my sister exactly how this plan had come about, and to give her her due she didn't sound too dismissive. Maybe she just wanted to get back to sleep.

The next morning the phone rang and a very attractive English male voice asked, "Is this Grace?"

I told him it was.

"Oh, hi, this is Gus Hardy. Mary's father. Your, eh, brother-in-law."

He was so unlike what I'd expected I was momentarily taken aback. I'd imagined, somewhat unfairly, that Favor would be married to a wimp, and this man sounded anything but. He had a firm, warm, really quite sexy voice and, as I learned from our brief conversation, he was extremely charming and diplomatic. He was calling, he said, to ascertain that I was in agreement with the rather extraordinary plan that Mary had outlined to her mother. I told him that indeed I agreed with it in principle but that surely we ought to see how he and my sister, and indeed Mary, felt nearer the time. At which point he thanked me very politely for my understanding during what must have been a difficult time (very difficult, if only he knew, but nothing to do with Mary) and said he looked forward to meeting me at some point in the future. He then asked, again with the same measured courtesy, if I could put Mary on a plane back home as soon as possible and I promised to call him with the flight details.

It was a rather ludicrous situation given the circumstances and I was somewhat relieved when he asked to speak to Mary.

"Hi, Dad, isn't it cool about the baby?" I heard her say, and wondered if her father's restraint would extend any further.

"Dad says I have to go home," she reported glumly.

"I know," I responded, "but before you go let's have some fun. We've had our revenge on Margot. Now what about Archie?"

If I were a nice, understanding, mature person I would rise above my betrayal and forgive Archie, remember the good times, be thankful that I had found him at all. But I wasn't an especially nice person: I was normal, thank God, and I wanted revenge.

Archie's official rental had in fact run out on Labor Day at the beginning of September but I had received a call from my lawyer, who had heard from the studio that he was behind schedule and needed to stay on and extend the rental for another two months in order to complete the film's score. I had foolishly imagined that this was a white lie dreamed up by Archie so he could continue his romance with me after Sonia returned to London. Now I knew better.

My lawyer had drawn up draft contracts for the extended rental and they were currently with the studio's legal department pending Archie's signature. It could take weeks. I called my lawyer and told him, to his amazement, that I wanted to put my house on the dunes on the market and could he please tell the studio that the extended rental was cancelled forthwith. I had changed my mind. The tenant would have to leave.

The word came back that "my tenant" would be more than happy to let the house be shown to prospective buyers while he was still there and that he would guarantee to be out of the house before a closing. In the meantime he'd like to stay on.

Okay, so Plan A hadn't worked. Time for Plan B.

The house had been rented on an everything included basis, which meant that for the exorbitant amount of money the studio was paying, Archie had free electricity, phone, and cable television.

I started with LILCO (the Long Island Lighting Company) and spent an extremely enjoyable afternoon cancelling my electricity at the house on the dunes, before moving on to Bell Atlantic to cut off the phone, and Cablevision to discontinue that service. It was coming up to October and while we had been enjoying exceptionally mild weather, the hurricane season was imminent. At best we could expect a few nor'easters, severe rainstorms coming up the East Coast from Florida. My house on the dunes had electric heat, and I had just cut off the power.

For the *pièce de résistance* I enlisted Mary's help. We were nothing if not compassionate, so before we dealt Archie the final blow we filled his mail box with candles. Then I parked the car a little way down the beach and Mary and I crept through the dunes. It was just after eleven o'clock at night and I could see Archie moving about the house. There was someone with him. His latest victim, I assumed.

Archie was a creature of routine. Unless he had changed his habits, he would let Theo and Leo out for their last pee at eleven o'clock. Sure enough, the sliders onto the deck eased open and the dogs ran out, or rather Leo pranced out and bounded down to the ocean and Theo turned around and immediately tried to go back in only to be booted out again. He inched across the deck, shivering.

"Theo," I hissed, "here, boy."

Theo's ears pricked up and his spindly legs carried him across to the dunes where we were hiding.

"Grab his collar, Mary, don't let go. I'll go after Leo."

I had to run along the beach after Leo for several minutes. He bounded up to me, licked me, and ran off again before I could put him on the leash I'd brought with me.

Eventually we persuaded both dogs to climb into my car with promises of "walkies" and "din-dins." As we drove home I wondered how long it would be before Archie realized they were missing. Better still, how would he explain to their owner that he had lost them?

His power was cut off the following day, and when my lawyer reported that the studio had been on to him, I instructed him to tell them that I wanted my tenant out and that they should reveal my identity.

"I know what I said," I told him when he protested, "but if I'm selling the house what does it matter? In fact, I insist that my tenant be told who the house belongs to. And one other thing..."

"Yes?" said my bewildered attorney.

"Please find out from the studio who the costume designer is on the film. I believe it's a woman who lives in New York City. I'd like her address and phone number."

One day, of course, I would have to return Theo and Leo to their rightful owner, but in the meantime I would enjoy their company.

And of course there was someone else who had to be returned to their rightful owner.

I sat in the parking lot at Kennedy and let Theo and Leo lick the salty tears from my face. I had put on a brave smile as I waved Mary through the gate to board the plane back to

London but inside I was already beginning to crumble.

Who knew what would happen as her pregnancy progressed? For while I was now a hundred per cent certain that I wanted to adopt her baby and give it all the love fate seemed to prevent me giving to anyone else, who knew how Mary would feel when the time came to hand the baby over?

Favor

I didn't have a problem with Gus about Mary's baby, for one very simple reason.

Mary had a son.

It was like some kind of bizarre version of primogeniture. To begin with, Gus more or less acted as if Mary wasn't expecting a baby at all. He was affectionate towards his daughter, sparred with her as usual, inquired after her progress at school, but made virtually no mention of the forthcoming child.

The person he did talk to, quite regularly I noticed, was Grace. They became real telephone pals. And he reported back to me on their conversations in a rather annoyingly patronizing way, as if he was responsible for everything to do with Grace.

"She's sold some property. House she had on the beach. Two point five million. Dollars. Pretty successful, she is. She's going to invest it for the baby. My grandchild's going to get a good start in life."

Snippets like this tossed out to me just as I was going off to sleep. But not a word to Mary.

And it was always his grandchild. Not mine. Or Mary's child. And he'd taken it as a given that Grace would bring up the baby, although I'd told him over and over again that we'd agreed to wait and see how Mary felt nearer the time. I didn't want Mary to feel pressured in any way, but if she had decided she wanted to keep the baby I don't know what we would have done.

Which is why when Grace came over to London once during Mary's pregnancy, we decided not to tell Mary. Grace agreed, although I could tell it was a big sacrifice on her part. However, she came over for a sad reason which took up most of her time anyway.

Biddy McIntyre had a stroke. The lawyers contacted Grace and she called me and asked if we could put her up, which was when we decided we shouldn't have her in the house disrupting Mary's routine.

"It's not as if she can't afford to go to a hotel," said Gus.

"Gus..." I warned, but I knew it was just that he was apprehensive at the thought of meeting her.

I sent him off to meet her on his own. My intuition told me it would be better that way and it was. He came back from a drink at her hotel saying how extraordinary she was, how impressive. It was only after quizzing him relentlessly for half the evening that I deduced that what Grace must have done was to sit back and let Gus talk, to draw him out and listen to him, make him feel important.

From then on, virtually all of his sentences began with the words: "Grace thinks I should..." and I spent most of my time shutting him up if Mary was within earshot.

Grace asked me to go down and see Biddy and help her choose a nursing home. That was one of the great things about Grace having money. She didn't have to worry about who was going to take care of Biddy. She could just pick a home and pay for it. If I thought she was being just a little clinical about the whole thing, I kept my thoughts to myself. But when they told her that Biddy was never going to recover and that she should sort out Biddy's affairs I could see she was shocked.

It was while we were going through Biddy's things that I found the letter. It was on Biddy's desk, the desk where she had suffered the stroke—several pages written in large spidery scrawl. Beside it lay an envelope already addressed: TO BE GIVEN TO GRACE CAMMELL AFTER MY DEATH. Maybe she knew something was going to happen to her. She had clearly been in the midst of writing the letter when she had the stroke.

I was about to put it in the envelope when I began reading. I couldn't help myself. It was

401

there. I glanced at the first line as I was folding it up and then I couldn't stop.

My dear Grace,

There is something you should know. It has been haunting me ever since your eighteenth birthday when we had that misunderstanding about Lucas's present of Vanity Fair and you wanted to meet him. You telephoned him and left that silly message and of course he called me to talk about it. What I have to tell you—and please forgive me for being such a coward that I cannot let you know until after I have died—is that I lied to you. Not just at that moment but all the time.

I told you that he didn't want to meet you when you were eighteen. It wasn't true. He desperately wanted to meet you but I told him he couldn't. Just like I told him he couldn't all the time you were growing up. But he saw you, Grace. He came to your school events, carol services, he even came and watched from afar when you had that birthday picnic in the woods. I often never saw him myself, he was so careful to keep his distance. I'm surprised he wasn't arrested for being a potential child molester.

You will no doubt wonder why he never made himself known to you and this is the hardest thing I have to confess to you. I lied to him, too. I told him you didn't want to see him. I spoke to him about you regularly on the telephone. We had never been married, Lucas and I, but it was as if we were divorced, discussing our mutual child. David knew nothing of our conversations. Because, of course, he would have told Lucas that you began to ask about him as you grew older. I pretended that you barely knew he existed and when you did understand, you were so angry with him that you didn't want to see him. We agreed to wait until you were eighteen and then let you decide for yourself. That's why he sent you that first edition of *Vanity Fair* and it was then that you came closest to meeting him.

I suppose I am most ashamed of what happened then. From our talk this year at Stowe you will know of my attraction to your father. When he telephoned me I agreed to meet him to discuss the best way for you to be introduced to him. I wanted to have control of the proceedings. But—and I don't know how to break this to you gently—I ended up going to bed with him. We had the affair I had wanted to have all my life. And then he began to tire of me. Indecently soon. And I knew that if I allowed you to see him he would transfer his attention to you and I would be left out in the cold. And I knew what he would give you was what I would never receive from him. Love. Pure, unconditional love.

He was fascinated by you. And so proud of your achievements. If you did well at school I never heard the end of it. He was so impressed by your notes on the books he sent you. He had big plans for you. He was going *to give you a job at his publishing house, turn the family business over to you. That was before he sold out to Mason House. He would have died if he'd seen the trash you wound up writing for a living. Just as well he never read any of it.*

So I lied to him, to you, to David—to protect myself. To keep him interested in me, to hold on to you. And it was all for nothing. He dumped me. And I lost you when you left home so young.

Your father loved you, Grace, and you must never confuse your disenchantment with men with your father's

It was the last line of the unfinished letter that made me show it to Grace. She had to know that our father had loved her. What I was not prepared for was her reaction concerning Biddy. I had expected her to condemn Biddy as a cruel and heartless bitch, but all she said—and she was shaking as she said it—was, "Poor Biddy."

"What do you mean, poor Biddy? It's monstrous what she did, keeping you away from your father for all that time."

"And away from you." Grace was actually smiling now. "That's what you're really angry about, isn't it? She deprived you of your sister."

"But why poor Biddy?"

"Because he was a monster to her just like he was to our mother. That's what she was trying to tell me. The love that a man has for his child is different from the love he has for a woman, and she knew she couldn't compete. Nor could our mother. He was probably the world's worst misogynist, by the sound of things."

"You're still maintaining he's a monster even though he clearly loved you inasmuch as he was allowed to, and he was wonderful with me. And what does she mean 'your disenchantment with men'?"

"She was cleverer than I thought. She knew I was hopeless with men. Probably a case of 'it takes one to know one'."

And then Grace told me all about her love life. I had never asked. I had never dared. And as I listened, I was horrified by how badly she had been betrayed by both Margot and Biddy, not to mention Harry Fox and Archie Berkeley and what seemed like a thousand men before them.

"Well, at least *Rapture* was panned by the critics," I said cheerfully. "Were you pleased it was dedicated to you?"

"I never knew. I never went to see it," said Grace. "At least I know Harry will never get his hands on *Luther*. In a way that's the real tragedy, that Lucas never knew I was capable of writing something like *Luther*. What makes me truly happy is the knowledge that the movie sale has resulted in my work being taken seriously by publishers in New York, and I've found myself working with a wonderful editor, someone who will take me seriously as a writer, someone, ironically, for whom Lucas was a publishing hero. And I have Lucas to thank for that. *Luther* is inspired by him, of course, for all the wrong reasons as it turns out. It's about an arch manipulator who is brought down by his own daughter, and in the end Lucas seems to have been the one who was manipulated all along by Biddy."

"Biddy was very fucked up, wasn't she?" I said tentatively, not knowing quite how Grace would react.

"I was raised by a very unhappy woman. You remember when I was expounding my theory that we learn anger, happiness, sorrow, or whatever from the people around us as we grow up, and you pointed out that with David McIntyre as a father figure I should have been fine? Well, it wasn't David who influenced me, it was Biddy. I wonder if at the end of the day she felt her passion for our father was worth it. We can't ask her now. We can't even ask her what she was trying to say at the end of her letter, but in fact I think I know."

"What?" I asked, intrigued.

"Well, she meant that even if I had been unlucky in love with men, I should remember that my father's love for me had been love for a child, very different from the kind of love he wasn't capable of giving to women, and I should cherish that. Of course, she had no way of knowing that I might have a child one day."

And once I heard that, I knew I would just have to hope and pray that Mary would decide to let Grace adopt her baby.

To be honest, I think if it had been a girl there would have been a problem. She was so utterly convinced that she would have a daughter. She talked endlessly about her "little girl," so when she gave birth to a boy weighing nearly nine pounds in Southampton Hospital, Long Island (we had gone to join Grace at the start of the Easter school holidays, a full month before the birth, just to be on the safe side), I think she was completely thrown. Despite the existence of Creepo, in her mind she had broken some kind of important female line— my mother, me, Grace, her—that she had assumed would continue *ad infinitum*.

As for Gus, I could tell he was immediately planning ways to bring his grandson into the business, and Ned pronounced himself "pleased as punch" at having a nephew.

Mary had a relatively easy time of it—only four hours' labor—and now she had to go back to school. It was touch and go whether she would get her finals. I thought she had a chance.

I was secretly rather horrified by how little scandal her pregnancy had attracted at school, almost as if it were an everyday occurrence. We had decided to be as open about the whole thing as possible, and in the end it was for the best. There was no stigma attached to her being pregnant. It didn't get in the way of her studying. She didn't start showing till fairly late on. In fact, I think some of the girls were really quite envious of her.

The father, Jason, had left school and moved

away. I never met him. He never knew unless the dreaded Shannon guessed it was him and told him. Mary said she had refused to tell Shannon who the father was and she didn't speak to Shannon any more, but I'm not sure I entirely believe that.

So Grace became an overnight mother and our arguments began. I sent Mary straight back to London as soon as she was able to travel, and stayed on a week to get Grace settled and show her the ropes. She resented my every move.

"He's my son and I've got to learn," she said stubbornly. And she was right. It was just that I found it so painful to watch her struggling to persuade him to take the bottle in the middle of the night when Mary could have been breastfeeding him. But those kinds of regrets, as I knew only too well, would get us nowhere.

Then we argued about the name. Grace wanted to call him David after David McIntyre. I wanted to call him Lucas after our father. In the end we compromised and called him David Lucas McIntyre but agreed he would be known as Luke.

The next argument was over who would be godparents. The only two we could agree on were Ned and Linda, but when Linda started knitting endless pink and purple baby clothes we began to have second thoughts. And then we thought of Lew, who had become something of an item in Linda's life following Stanley's tragic death. So it was Ned, Linda, and Lew and the christening would be some time in the summer.

But where?

And then we were off on another argument. Mary got her "A"s, and the minute she had her results she demanded that we all celebrate by going off to Long Island and having Luke's christening there.

"But how on earth am I going to fit you all in?" moaned Grace down the phone. "I suppose I could ask Linda. She's a godsend when it comes to babysitting, by the way."

"I've already asked her," I said, "it's fine."

"What do you mean, you've already asked her? Why didn't you consult me first?" Grace was furious. "I've just begun writing a new book and I've at long last managed to get Luke used to some kind of routine. Now you'll all come out here and mess everything up."

"Well, how long do you want us to wait before we have this christening...hang on, there's someone at the door."

"I'll get it," said Gus.

I heard him go into the hall and open the front door. As he came back in he shouted something over his shoulder to the person following him, something I didn't think I'd ever hear him say: "She won't be a minute. She's just on the phone arguing with her sister. You know how it is with sisters."

Grace

It came to me much later.

Luke was about two. I took him down to the beach every afternoon for a walk. I wanted him to grow up sharing my love of the sea, to have no fear of the Atlantic breakers crashing on the shore.

We could walk for a while and then we came to an inlet, a tiny channel of water running inland between the dunes into a large pond surrounded by wetlands. At high tide the current was strong. It was dangerous to wade across the inlet. We had to turn around and come back later when the tide was out and there was just a trickle of water to paddle across.

But Luke didn't like waiting. He screamed when I picked him up and took him away. I suppose, given his age, it was stupid the way I tried to explain to him why he had to wait.

"Don't be so impatient, Luke," I told him. "Patience is a virtue..."

And that's when I remembered.

I am perched on a footstool at my mother's knee while she sits at her dressing table and brushes her hair. Maybe I'm romanticizing the image a little but I think my hands and face are grubby from playing outside on the farm and she is trying to persuade me to do something about it. But I am impatient to go back outside.

"Don't be in such a hurry," she tells me, "be patient. Patience is a virtue, and virtue is a grace and Grace is a little girl who wouldn't wash her face. Patience. There! That's what we'll call your sister. Patience Cammell."

I don't know who else she told before she died but they obviously shortened it to Pat.

But what I realize now, as I restrain Luke from hurling himself into the current, is that those were the last words my mother ever spoke to me. And I realize something else. She never knew Patience. She never knew my sister. Favor never existed.

I was her only one. I was her favorite.

I am Grace *and* Favor.